I0590658

PRAISE FOR MALCOLM WOOD

In this fast-paced, lively, and enjoyable finale, Wood offers a wide array of intrigues, battles, and retreats.

—Kirkus Reviews

A satisfying wrap-up to a multispecies sci-fi saga that delivers plenty of aliens and clashes.

—Kirkus Reviews

DAWN

Clash of the Aliens

M. B. WOOD

WFP
WORDFIRE PRESS

Dawn

Copyright © 2018 Faucett Publishing LLC

EBook ISBN: 978-1-68057-058-8
Trade Paperback ISBN: 978-1-68057-057-1

Cover artwork by Michael J. Canales
Kevin J. Anderson, Art Director
Published by
WordFire Press, LLC
PO Box 1840
Monument CO 80132

Kevin J. Anderson & Rebecca Moesta, Publishers

WordFire Press eBook Edition 2019
WordFire Press Trade Paperback Edition 2019

Printed in the USA
Join our WordFire Press Readers Group for
sneak previews, updates, new projects, and giveaways.
Sign up at wordfirepress.com

❋ Created with Vellum

THE STORY SO FAR

In Book 1, Middle Eastern fanatics paralyze Western Civilization with massive EMPs, creating a post-apocalyptic world that is a sea of chaos and near-anarchy. Refugees create a society under a primitive rule of law. Proud, fierce, and free, Taylor MacPherson and a tight-knit group of survivors known as the Clan take their first steps to restoring law and justice ... as a race of hermaphroditic aliens, the Qu'uda, arrives to find a post-apocalyptic Earth.

In Book 2, Taylor MacPherson witnesses a strange light in the night sky, which is a leftover missile-defense weapon that blasts the giant Qu'uda spaceship, stranding it in an unstable orbit. The Qu'uda send one of their own, "Billy," down to Earth to fashion parts necessary for repairs. A war among surviving human factions comes at a terrible cost to each, and Billy is abandoned by his race; he throws in his lot with Taylor and his refugees. The aliens leave the surface and plan to return and bomb the Earth into a new Stone Age.

Book 3 tells the back story of the clash of the alien races, the Qu'uda with the Hoo-Lii, a rigid society ruled by Hive-Mothers, with a warrior class of mating males and a great under-class of unripened, non-mating males and females. Under their new

Hive-Mother, the Hoo-Lii send an exploratory ship to Earth where they encounter the gigantic Qu'uda asteroid-ship, with disastrous results.

In Book 4, Taylor MacPherson's Clan—now allied with the alien Billy—mobilizes and conquers Ohio to get C-17 planes so they can rescue the Qu'uda survivors stranded on Andros Island in the Bahamas. Using alien fusion drives as engines of C-17 aircraft, a Clan delegation flies to the West Coast and meets up with the remnant US Navy submarine forces. They form a defense alliance, and as part of the deal, install alien fusion drives on submarines and launch them to orbit to construct an orbital defense station.

A Hoo-Lii craft emerges from a warp in space-time and heads toward Earth. Later, a massive Qu'uda vessel approaches Earth and attacks the Hoo-Lii ship already there. The Qu'uda bombard the human space station and in response, the humans respond with nuclear missiles and overwhelm the Qu'uda ship. The humans try to communicate with the Hoo-Lii aliens and in the process, send them water. The aliens accept the water, which is a symbol of submission to them. They depart and promise to return....

CHAPTER ONE

A desk chair crashed through a window in the brick three-story building and arced down to the sidewalk below amid a shower of glass and paper. Two men in white lab coats sprawled in the laboratory building's entrance. Fresh blood stained their clothing.

In the tree-lined street of suburban Berea, a large crowd of men dressed in shabby work clothes faced a row of brown-clad soldiers lined up in front of the laboratory. The soldiers inched forward, their quarterstaffs held erect, a thin brown line holding back the crowd. Someone in the crowd hurled a rock, which struck a soldier on the head. The soldier staggered and fell. The mob made a sound like that of an angry beast.

"Forward." Chris Kucinski made a chopping motion with her hand. She was a tall, thin woman, her auburn hair streaked with gray, who wore the brown uniform of a soldier.

"On the double," she said.

The line of soldiers smashed into the crowd.

Quarterstaffs rose and fell with flail-like intensity to a rising chorus of screams. As the soldiers advanced, bodies fell, twitching and bleeding. The crowd sagged and broke under the soldiers' remorseless advance.

"Hold up," Chris shouted.

1

The soldiers halted, a solid line across the street.

The mob retreated, scattering amongst the houses and side streets. Moans and cries echoed up and down the road. The metallic smell of blood filled the warm, spring air. Splashes of bright red blood splattered across the fresh, green grass.

Chris turned to her aide. "Get the medics, then find out who organized this." She paused as the corners of her mouth turned down. "Is Doctor Encirlik okay?"

"Yes, ma'am. We got here just as the first rioters broke through the laboratory's front door." The aide pointed at the two men in white lab coats in the main entrance. "They went down as we arrived. Two rioters got in and they locked themselves in one of the labs." As he pointed to a second story window, a piece of lab equipment came sailing out. "Which they're still trashing. It's only a matter of time before we get them out."

"Break the door down if necessary. We must stop the damage as quickly as possible. This is our only source of pharmaceuticals. We must protect it. Move it."

"Yes, ma'am." The aide ran off, shouting orders.

~

Chris stepped into a room and sniffed. It smelled faintly of ether and other chemicals.

A boarded-up window was the only evidence of the recent attack. An exhaust fan droned steadily. In the background, a peristaltic pump clicked while timers ticked. Pale beige walls, cracked and crazed, were barely visible behind the mass of equipment. Black, chipped counters lined the lab's walls, which were covered with glassware and vials.

"Doctor Encirlik?" Chris said.

"Oh? Er, yes," Meltem Encirlik said.

The small, dark haired woman's eyes flashed. She had few lines on her thin face, which made it hard to tell her age, and her slender body was encased within a voluminous white lab coat.

"I'm sorry. My nerves are still shot." She buried her face in her hands.

"Are you hurt?"

"No," she said. "You arrived just in time. Thank you."

"We received a tip."

"Praise be to Allah," Meltem said. "Those rioters seemed well organized. I had no idea there was so much resentment about me getting paid for my drugs," she said. "They called me a thief, an exploiter."

Meltem had began selling pharmaceuticals to cover the cost of research and made possible an increase in the output of medicines. The small machine shops and specialty fabrication businesses found the university would pay anything to have the right equipment made. As a result, costs had skyrocketed.

She was always over budget until she began selling the laboratory's antibiotics and drugs, which had grown by leaps and bounds. It was almost by accident she became one of the wealthiest persons in the Confederation, for she seemed to have the knack for making smart business decisions. The money made it possible for her to continue research, which included growing stem cells from skin samples for the life-extending stem cell-grafted DNA (SCG-DNA) technique.

However, she kept this work secret.

"Did you recognize any of the rioters?" Chris asked.

"One of the faces looked familiar. I think he might be a delivery person from one of the shops that makes our equipment."

"Sources say our old friend Monahan may have had his fingers in this," Chris said.

Meltem paused. "It wasn't spontaneous?"

"Far from it." Chris stopped at the door. "It was aimed at you and your husband. You have enemies."

"I haven't thought about that. Thanks for coming so quickly.

In another fifteen minutes, everything would have been destroyed. I thought I was going to die."

ॐ

Billy Potato burst through the door of the laboratory and altered direction with an agility most humans would find difficult. He came to an abrupt halt before Meltem's desk. "I found out how to make a biocomputer for humans," Billy said without any preamble in his typically clipped speech pattern.

Billy was five feet tall, which was large for an alien Qu'uda. He always wore a wide-brimmed hat, which covered the sparse bristles that passed for hair on his head. His body was pear-shaped and his shoulders blended into his neck and head. His ground-sweeping cloak hid his peculiar gait, which came from having an extra joint in his lower limbs.

Meltem put down her pencil. She had been working on restoring pharmaceutical production. Dry but necessary work. She welcomed his interruption. "Are you sure?"

"Yes," said Billy. "I went through the files from the Egg-that-Flies and found there is a way to adapt our neural growth technology to mammalian cellular tissue, which you humans possess—"

"Yes, yes, I know that," Meltem said. "Tell me, how do you grow a biocomputer for a human?" She had been astounded when she'd discovered Billy's genetic makeup included a DNA vaguely resembling that found in amphibians.

But how could that be? She wondered. *He came from a different star system.*

Billy wobbled his upper torso that was the Qu'uda gesture equivalent to a shrug. "Not easy to do."

"How long does it take? What kind of equipment is needed?"

"The information is still in Qu'uda-speak." Billy waved his hand at the computer. "I will put it in there. You have everything you need to make biocomputer in this laboratory. You will have to start with a piece of neural tissue from person who is to receive biocomputer—"

Meltem raised a hand. "First, we'll do it on a dog. Then I'll practice on a cadaver." Hand on chin, she stared without seeing into the distance. "A biocomputer would be like having an assistant that knows everything...." She shook her head and focused her eyes on Billy.

"I will bring data files when translated. I must go now," he said. "I must contact the Hendersons."

"Ah, yes, the deep-space telescope. How's it going?"

"I find out soon. The equipment for the automated observatory has now arrived on back side of the Moon." Billy was referring to the optical and radio telescopes that would peer into space from a location free from the Earth's electromagnetic noise and atmosphere.

ॐ

"Now, what's this for?" Malachi "Ki" Mapes pointed at a control surface.

Ki let go of a handhold and drifted in the zero-gee A trace of perspiration gleamed on his mahogany brown, almost bald head. The only indication he was the commander-in-chief was the four stars on the nametag attached to his dun-colored one-piece work suit.

Floodlights augmented the normally dim, yellow light of the control room of the Little-Egg-that-Flies. It was hot, which made it comfortable for the Qu'uda. Sweating human technicians were paired with their Qu'uda counterparts to label the controls in English and take inventory of the damage. Readout panels and control surfaces covered every wall of the small room. Handles protruded at convenient locations for zero-gee operation.

The room was at the front and center of the nose of the ship. The control room had not been designed to hold more than a few persons at any one time. Even though the asteroid-based battleship was in stable orbit around the Moon, Ki wanted to move it to the L1 Lagrange point on the sunward side of Earth where it would become the future defense station to guard Earth against any attack coming from that direction.

"The battle technician says it was for beam weapons," Cha KinLaat DoMar said. "No longer usable." The beam weapons which deflected debris in transit were located at the front of the Little-Egg and had been used against the humans. The nose of the ship had taken the brunt of the nuclear blasts prior to its capture.

"It seems like things are under control." Ki turned to Colonel Bud Inez. "After you get the controls labeled, start making an operational manual. I'll also need a listing of what you require for repairs."

"Yes, sir," Bud said. "We also need to go over the internal bearings of the habitation module." The living quarters rotated within the ship to provide artificial gravity for its crew. "We tried to spin it up but an overload warning kicked out the command. It may be jammed. I hope there's nothing wrong with the bearing itself."

"Let me know when you have it fixed." Ki eased his way out of the control center. He never really felt comfortable in zero gravity. He always felt he was about to vomit.

We've got a helluva job ahead of us, converting the Little-Egg into a permanent space station, he thought. *Since we no longer need its fuel tanks, we can convert them into internal docks and workshops for our spaceships. Then we'll have real defense capability, a second defense station with permanent living facilities.*

The trip through the asteroid spacecraft seemed to take forever to Ki. Since the front part of the ship had been fused smooth, the only access was through the drive service hatch at the rear.

We've got to get a new hatch, and soon, thought Ki. *This takes too damn long.* He wanted to get back to the comfort of his own ship and its gravity. His ship was familiar from long use; first as a submarine and now as an orbital space station. *We need more shuttles, something like the Qu'uda have on their mother ship, the Egg-that-Flies.*

It still astonished him the shuttlecraft's compact fusion drives could lift several hundred tons at a time into orbit. That aroused in him twinges of both envy and admiration.

Even so, he thought. *It's going to take the other Qu'uda a while to get the supplies and provisions on board for their trip home. And those Qu'uda sure do want to take a lot of souvenirs with them. The young Qu'uda, the "wrigglers," and the older Qu'uda are fascinated with our stuff.*

The Home Seekers faction, led by DalChik DaJuga, archivist for the Keepers-of-the-Egg, had not sought confrontation with the humans. They opposed the Defender faction who had come to bombard the Earth into a Stone Age condition. When DalChik learned the eggs sent down to Earth had hatched and most of their "wrigglers" were alive and well due to the efforts of Bilik and the humans, she was more than grateful. The wrigglers had learned English from human children and wanted to take familiar play items home with them.

They were Qu'uda and something more, Ki thought. *What would be their reception when they reached their home planet? Too bad the Qu'uda can't take the library of Congress with them on their twenty-year trip home,* he thought. *That'd give them something to chew on.*

Several libraries had survived and were being translated into Qu'uda. *That young man, Tim Van Minh, the one badly injured by a Qu'uda weapon in the battle for Defiance, had developed a system for transferring data files between our computers and the Qu'uda biocomputers. How long did he say this would take? Three months?*

Through a window at the rear dock of the Little-Egg, Ki watched the space shuttle approach. Its once-white body and wings had long black streaks from multiple re-entries. Its payload bay doors slowly folded open like a butterfly's wings. It was ancient—one of the original space shuttles from the late twentieth century. They'd dug it out of a museum and fitted it with an aneutronic fusion drive to make it into a true space truck, one that flew constantly.

Still, he thought. *It's small compared to a Qu'uda shuttle.*

The shuttle drifted slowly toward the long, corrugated tube fitted to the dock. As they merged, the tube shook and quivered as it inflated with air.

"Sir?" a voice called. "We're ready for you to board."

"Okay," Ki said. "I'm coming." *Only a couple more hours and I'll be back in gravity. God*, he thought. *I'll never get used to this zero-gee shit. Until we get this station moved and operational, we're still blind on the sunward side of Earth.*

CHAPTER TWO

CHOICES

"So, the Others bore no hostility toward you?" Suh-Joh shifted the rear four of her six limbs on the polished red granite resting mound.

Orange light glittered off the metal walls in the cave-like chamber she used as her command center. Brown curtains covered the doors and gave an illusion of privacy. Clusters of quills plucked from defeated enemies adorned the walls commemorating her hive's many victories. The hum of the power generators and the sigh of the ventilation system were familiar sounds. The smell of machinery mingled with aromas of densely packed multitudes. The Mother's Servant, an immense transport ship, was Suh-Joh's home during her exile.

"Perhaps, gracious Hive-Mother, the Others were defending themselves from the asteroid-ship aliens. We may have misunderstood them." Son-Nih flexed his head close to the floor in a motion that showed his uncertainty.

The old Chosen-Male warrior bore many scars of hard service to his Hive-Mother. He wore a garland of prayer beads that were the insignia of the warrior-priest caste; a disguise he had yet to shed from his last mission.

"They used fusion weapons only after the asteroid-aliens attacked their orbital station." He paused and his spines erected. "Still, it was obscene." He rose with suppleness unusual for one of his age, which came from his use of the illegal life-extending juvenile hormones.

Suh-Joh rose onto her two hind limbs and turned toward Nok-Joh, the pilot-navigator. "They refrained from attacking you and then tried to communicate with you?"

"Yes." Nok-Joh was a small, unripened female who had piloted the exploratory ship, the Good Child. She quivered with excitement, for she had just learned that Suh-Joh had not rejected her petition to be ripened. Her desire to become a Mother was apparent to all.

"We sent them a learning algorithm for our language. They sent us water, water so pure it was safe for consumption without any treatment. That made possible our safe return." She crouched lower on a crossed quill emblem in the floor covering that was the symbol of Suh-Joh's hive.

"Did they follow?"

"They made no attempt to pursue us."

"I cannot return to Hool." Suh-Joh squirmed as though uncomfortable. "If I do, the priests at the Shrine of the Mother will demand I ripen my successor, which means I die." She raised herself, her belly plates clattering off the resting mound. "So, I must leave." She turned to Son-Nih. "Which is it?" she said. "Invade Kamah and carve out a domain or accept the invitation of the Others on the distant world of water?"

The colony world of Kamah teemed with daughters of the Hive-Mothers and their hordes of Chosen-Male warriors.

Son-Nih lowered himself. "I cannot make that decision for you. I can only advise you on the facts as I see them. Should you choose Kamah, it will be bloody, very bloody."

ॐ

Six shuttlecraft—small stubby vessels originally used to haul material from the surface to orbit and now armed with weapons created with technology taken from the archives beneath the Shrine of the Mother—headed away from Hool on long tongues of fusion flame. Young Chosen-Male warriors from many hives crewed the craft. They were the select of the select; fierce, brave and totally loyal. They were on their way to the system's asteroid belt, seeking to find the renegade Suh-Joh in her mining and manufacturing complex.

An old warrior-priest from the Shrine of the Mother led the expedition. None of the Chosen-Male warriors would let anyone from another hive lead them. The old priest had to be firm with the crew who openly showed they believed they were better qualified. The atmosphere in the cramped command module, boxed in by the austere, bare metal walls, was redolent with marker fragrances from many hives.

"Something is wrong." It was the pilot-navigator on the lead ship who pointed at the holographic display. "Look."

Within the scattering of pale yellow points that indicated asteroids, a red tetrahedron glowed brightly. "I do not see the cause of your concern," the old priest said. "Explain it."

The pilot-navigator extended a limb as the image in the display expanded. The tetrahedron shape changed into multiple components: A round object changed to yellow, it was the asteroid from which metals were mined. Several tiny cubes orbited it. The image shimmered and briefly became fuzzy. "That is the limit of magnification," he said. "See?"

The old priest noisily exhaled through his breathing orifices. "What is it?" he said.

"Where is the Mother's Servant?" The pilot-navigator referred to Suh-Joh's immense transport ship.

"It is your role to answer my questions," the old priest said. "Not to quiz me."

The pilot-navigator flexed slightly, showing barely a trace of submission. "Yes, honorable one. Little radiation comes from the mining and manufacturing complex; no one is there. The Mother's Servant is gone. It means the heretic has fled."

"Then find her."

"Where?" asked the pilot-navigator. "Space is large and she left no scent to follow."

The old priest sighed heavily through his breathing orifices and emanated an aroma of frustration. "Send the ships out in a hemispherical search pattern, away from the system's core. Set scanners at maximum to probe the greatest distance. Once we get a signal return, we concentrate our forces and pursue." Though he may not have seen combat in space, battle experience made the course of action seem obvious.

The pilot-navigator flexed low, almost to the command module's textured metal floor. "Yes, of course, honorable one. Immediately." He moved quickly, the spines and plates of his hide scraping and rattling against the communications console. He gave the orders. The shuttle surged with acceleration.

In less than one day, a faint echo from a scanning beam revealed the location of the Mother's Servant. The shuttlecraft changed their courses to converge on Suh-Joh's ship.

Soon the pilot-navigator detected they, too, were being scanned, the Mother's Servant drive flickered into life. The giant ship began to accelerate. However, the smaller shuttles had higher velocity.

It was apparent they would soon catch Suh-Joh's ship.

"Mother's Servant," the old priest spoke into the communicator system. "Prepare to receive emissaries from the Council of Hive-Mothers." He repeated his demand several times.

There was no answer. "Submit, or we attack."

Still no response.

The six shuttlecraft moved into a hexagonal formation onto a course to encircle the Mother's Servant. "With our new weapons," the pilot-navigator said. "We shall soon disable it. After all, it is slower and far less maneuverable."

The old priest said nothing.

"Adjust velocity," the pilot-navigator said. "Do not overshoot the Mother's Servant. That would expose us to its debris-clearing beam on the forward part of the Mother's Servant. That will be its only weapon."

The shuttlecraft drew closer.

The Mother's Servant was a ring connected to the central stem with three spokes. At the head of the drive stem was a globular fuel tank almost the same diameter as the ring.

"Commence deceleration," said the pilot-navigator.

The Mother's Servant's main drive faded at the same time. Its maneuvering drives winked into life and the ship's course shifted slightly. The main drive flared brighter than the sun. A violet beam of energy flashed into existence. The holographic display now showed only fragments where one of the shuttle-craft had been.

"It is a transport ship." The pilot-navigator's spines slowly rose. "It should not be armed."

"Obviously it is," said the old priest. "That is the just the kind of unethical thing Suh-Joh would do."

"Now what is the Mother's Servant up to?" The old priest stared intently at the holographic display.

The pilot-navigator adjusted the long-range scanners. The Mother's Servant was again changing course.

"Take evasive action," the old priest said.

"They shouldn't be able to hit us at this range—"

"They have and can and will. If you value the spines on your hide, you'll avoid that ship's weapon. Increase velocity and get closer. That'll make it more difficult for them to aim their weapon." As the old priest finished speaking, the Mother's Servant again flared brightly.

The violet beam moved in an arc to touch a shuttle. A stubby wing disappeared amid a cloud of sparkling metal. The shuttle lurched and began to spin. The beam winked out of existence.

"All craft accelerate at maximum velocity toward the Mother's Servant," the old priest said. "Get within range so we can grapple with them." His spines rose in a combat posture.

"We should use our missiles." The pilot-navigator referred to the two missiles each shuttle carried. "They can reach the heretic's ship."

"All craft, target missiles on the outer part of the Mother's Servant," said the old priest. The ring-shaped outer structure of Suh-Joh's craft held the living quarters and other occupied areas. A strike there would cause the most casualties. "Launch when ready."

The holographic display showed a ragged formation of tiny slivers converging in a circular pattern on the large transport craft. The missiles closed rapidly.

The rear of the Mother's Servant flared brightly. The violet beam cut through the eight tiny slivers. Two missiles disappeared with bright flashes. Another shuttlecraft flowered into fragments.

The missiles knifed into the Mother's Servant. Six incandescent splotches appeared on the slowly rotating outer ring. A curved section of metal floated away amid a storm of flotsam. A cloud of vapor blossomed, briefly illuminated by electrical flashes dancing along jagged openings, and then faded.

"Ah, our spines have slashed her," said the old priest. "Now, closer and we shall finish her." As he spoke, the main drive on the stern of the Mother's Servant flared anew. The last thing the old priest saw was the world around him disintegrating into incandescent fragments.

꒰

Alarms bleated. Orange lights flickered as the Mother's Servant shuddered under six successive blows. Air howled and the pressure dropped. Distantly, a chorus of screams began.

"All internal doors closing." The warning echoed as a cavalcade of clanks rattled through the ship. Vibration from the ship's engines rose and faded. "Another enemy destroyed," a voice announced. One by one, the alarms fell silent.

"Enemy reversing course," said another.

"Orthogonal course change. Target acquisition not possible," a high-pitched voice said.

"Enemy out of range."

Suh-Joh glanced at Son-Nih. "Well?"

His eyes blinked open. "The attack is over. They have hurt us. How much, I do not know." He rose and headed for the curtain-covered door opening. "I shall find out."

ર

Suh-Joh's command center was quiet. Though its thick curtains muffled the sounds from outside, the Cycle of Life prayer could still be heard, chanted many times for those who had died, filling the ship with its mournful sound.

"Almost one-quarter of our warriors and crew are dead. And more will die," said Son-Nih. "There is much damage to the ship's structure. Should we jump through the space-time transfer point, our structure will fail. We must make repairs."

"So many of my brave warriors slaughtered." Suh-Joh slumped lower. "How long to make these repairs?"

"The engineers do not wish to say. When pressed, they showed me the many steps they must go through to restore the ship to deep space operating condition," said Son-Nih. "They are concerned about the damage to its structure." He flexed submissively. "They must fabricate many parts, some large. We need to set up our manufacturing facility on an asteroid. Without that, any repair effort is doomed to failure. If we survive." He hesitated. "I fear they do not tell me the worst."

"There are many asteroids out here. What else?"

"Water," he said. "We lost almost all our water and air. We need volatiles, also." His concern reflected the rarity of asteroids containing those precious substances. "Until we rebuild the Mother's Servant and replenish our stores, we are very vulnerable. Some say we should ask the Hive-Mothers for mercy."

"No," Suh-Joh said. "That way is certain death."

Suh-Joh lowered her head to the floor, the position of complete submission. "Oh, Spirit of the Mother," she said. "I beg of you, have mercy on this humble child and all those around me." It was the opening of the prayer of the Chosen-Male warriors going into battle, those prepared to die.

CHAPTER THREE

THE NEW FRONTIER

"Commander Mapes." Carver Washington's voice echoed through the assembly room for the Human Confederation.

They were in a hall with its elegant marble floor of black and white marble, with pink granite columns supporting the overhead dome. On the open floor before the circular rows of seats in the center of the Rotunda was a worn bronze emblem—the seal of the former State of Ohio.

Over a hundred delegates, a spectrum of ethnic faces serious and intent, leaned forward to watch the newly elected Speaker of the Confederation announce Ki Mapes's promotion. Carver towered over him, his bulk contrasting with Ki's slight build. "It is my pleasure to confirm your appointment as commander-in-chief of the Space Force. The defense of Earth, is now in your hands."

Commander Ki Mapes stood straight and erect. Light gleamed off his nearly bald, mahogany brown head. His cheekbones were prominent in a thin, almost aquiline face. His tan uniform, crisply pressed, bore the four-star insignia of commander-in-chief.

As Carver's words droned on, Ki's mind wandered. *The world's defense has been my game for some time now*, he thought. *They've just got around to acknowledging it. I guess the newer members of the Confederation want to have a say in who'll be over their heads with all that firepower.*

Once the former Qu'uda battleship—the Little-Egg-that-Flies—had been moved to the L-1 Lagrangian position on the sunward side of Earth, it was named Defense Station Number 2, or DS-2.

Ki's crew worked on converting it into a space station, making its huge fuel tanks into docks for future spacecraft. *We'll launch more converted submarines, changed from ocean-going to space-going craft*, he thought. *That'll keep the Tacoma boatworks busy for years.*

The demands for materials on DS-2 just kept growing and hauling everything up from Earth was time consuming. That forced Ki to look elsewhere. Billy's data download from the Qu'uda ship revealed a large number of asteroids in near-Earth orbits, some of which posed a potential collision danger in the distant future.

Removing that danger, Ki realized, *will be another project. I want to move two small asteroids to the Earth-Moon L-5 Lagrangian position to get metals, minerals, water, and organics for an orbital manufacturing center. And then*, he thought, *we'll get a metallic asteroid to make the next space station, DS-3.*

"Congratulations." Carver Washington enveloped Ki's hand with a huge brown, callused one of his own, followed by a bear-hug.

"Thank you," Ki said. "I am deeply honored by this appointment. I will keep the trust you have shown." He spoke sincere words of comfort to those who were uncertain about promoting a former US submarine commander to control the space-based military. The needed words flowed freely from his heart; he truly believed he had been given a position of trust and intended to fulfill it to the best of his ability.

૨

"You think you can build these weapons?" Ki asked.

"Yes, sir," said Tim Van Minh.

The slightly built Vietnamese man smiled a crooked smile from a ruined face. One-half of his body had been seared by a glancing blow from a Qu'uda beam weapon. After he had recovered, he'd met and married Sally Butterworth, which had restored peace to his soul, for she'd convinced him he was a complete man.

"You see," Tim said. "The info in the Qu'uda download solved the difficult theoretical problems. Now the rest is just engineering." A half of a mouth smiled.

The laboratory was crowded with electronic equipment to the point of being almost impassable. Somehow, Tim navigated his way through a warren of stacked data acquisition and processing modules. The room was warm, almost stuffy, with the steady drone of cooling fans and faint electronic beeps. Diode lights flickered on and off in random patterns of red, green, and white. At the far side of the laboratory was Sally, tall, red-haired, and freckled. Only Tim could match her math and engineering skills. Their love for each other burned brightly and openly.

"Sally and I think we can build a prototype. Yeah, we'll need more technicians and fabrication capacity, but we don't see any major problems—"

"Look," Ki said. "This is important and top secret. Fusion pumped X-ray lasers are big time weapons—"

"Yeah, I know. Like I said, it's just engineering from now on. The hard part is behind us. Fact."

Ki sighed. "I hope you're right."

"Personally." Tim plucked at his lower lip. "I think the Hendersons had a tougher job. Y'see, building charge-coupled optical scanning equipment required setting up a whole new level of manufacturing. Clean rooms, electron etchers, God knows what else. Whereas, you've got lots of nukes ready for use. Yeah, yeah, I know they need to have their tritium refreshed, whatever." He held up his hand to forestall Ki's impending objection. "The lasers, well, we think we know a way to make the special glass they use. As for the chemicals, we'll scrounge around until we find them. They're not that exotic."

Ki wriggled his nose. He'd heard Tim Van Minh was bright and resourceful; now he'd got a glimpse of his confidence. "When d'you think you'll have a unit ready for testing?"

Tim frowned. It was a formidable frown because the scar tissue on one side of his face creased into a ferocious pattern. "Hmm. I'm not sure. I just don't know how long it will take to get the chemicals. I can fab most of the other stuff in, er, oh, perhaps six to nine months. That is, unless someone else comes along with another rush-rush project that sounds like fun." He grinned crookedly as though it were a joke.

"This is a defense item to protect our planet. There is nothing more important." Ki's voice had a steely ring.

Tim's face went blank and his body stiffened upright as though preparing to salute. "Yes, sir."

"Good. Carry on."

ॐ

Brilliant sunlight starkly etched the Moon's gray, rocky land-scape. Sooty black shadows blotted out the details of the shaded areas. A silvery dome reflected light with a savage intensity. A metal-wheeled vehicle slowly drew closer, leaving sharp, defined tracks, indelible prints in the Moon dust as it unreeled a shiny metallic cable. Behind came another vehicle pushing Moon dirt over the cable and hiding it from view.

"Mr. Henderson," a voice called. "The cable laying robots have arrived."

Butch Henderson paused from sending details on how to use asteroids as observatories to technicians on DS-2. "Finally," he said. "The link from the farside station. Now we'll be able to use the interferometer." He referred to a remote station almost halfway around the Moon. Its data, along with those gathered at the main Moon observatory, would greatly increase their viewing range and ability to spot small objects.

It had been a difficult project, for the Moon had proven to be unforgiving. The robotic cable installation equipment had run into several impassable obstacles requiring human intervention.

It was one of those occasions when Sonya Peters, a repair technician, slipped and fell into a crevasse. The fall had knocked her unconscious. The locating beacon only showed she was in a shadowed area. It wasn't until she recovered consciousness Butch learned that she was several hundred meters down a crevasse, completely out of reach.

Butch shivered at the memory of having to listen to Sonya suffocate, or was it freeze to death? He wasn't really sure what had finally ended her life. She had become quietly delirious until she faded into silence. News of her death had made many cry; Sonya had a lot of friends among the male-dominated staff on the Moon, some of whom had been very close.

God, what a price we've paid. Thank you, Lord, for bringing this to an end.

"Sobinsky," Butch called. "Are your people ready to receive the link?" He saw no sign of movement outside except for the two robotic cable layers.

"Yes, Mr. Henderson, we'll go Moonside once the cable laying operation terminates."

Yes, thought Butch. *No sense in going out until they can do something. How close are they supposed to come to the dome? Ten meters? Something like that.*

He'd been so busy working on a secure link to DS-2 he hadn't paid much attention to the details of the cable laying operation. Even with the tremendous range of the interferometer, the defense stations still could not see certain sectors of space, especially those washed out by the sun's brightness.

Madeline Henderson got the idea to put remotely operated

deep space monitoring equipment on Aten-type asteroids with high-inclination orbits, such as 2102 Tantalus and similar bodies. All they really needed were a couple of large photovoltaic panels and they'd last just about forever. Butch sent the details of this setup to Ki Mapes on DS-2.

The existing databases and information gathered during the Qu'uda's approach revealed over a thousand objects in near-Earth orbits, some of which were potential impact threats to Earth.

Butch and Madeline used the Moon observatory to survey those closest to the Earth. What they learned made them uneasy; there were a lot of asteroids of all sizes in near-Earth orbits, some of which came close to Earth, very close.

Butch remembered his discussion with Ki Mapes about the near-Earth asteroids and his ideas on how to deal with the problem. Ki pointed out he needed to get his Space Force up to strength to effectively protect Earth from threats from space. He also remembered Ki saying, "It is our responsibility. We need ships to handle this."

ᘔ

"Look," said Patrick Monahan. "We keep the pressure on Encirlik. Keep raising the issue of workers dying 'cause they can't afford her high-priced drugs, and workers being beaten during a peaceful protest about high prices—"

"Ain't that kind of a stretch?" Charlie Ramsey leaned back in an over-stuffed leather armchair and grinned.

His office was a large room with hand-crafted walnut furniture and walls covered with hunting trophies. He was enjoying the situation, with Patrick's report on his activities. Through the window, below was the Rocky River, which flowed slowly at low water during the heat of the summer. Cicadas sang their chorus, a cascade of sound covering the daily sound of life on the Hill.

"Well, mebbe." Monahan frowned. "Look, we keep repeating this story, especially to those who aren't well informed, and after a while, it becomes an accepted fact."

Ramsey leaned forward and placed both hands, palms down, on the desk. "So you make her unpopular. How do we benefit?"

Patrick smiled slowly. "Money is power. I want to strip that away from MacPherson and his crowd. Ever since he married Encirlik, they've become richer and more powerful. I want to get a law passed to control the price of the drugs she sells. My people will keep raising the price of her supplies. We bleed her to economic death. If we get a chance to grab the pharmaceutical operation, so much the better."

"Be careful you don't get Kucinski pissed off at you. She's close to MacPherson. She can be real trouble if she gets you in her sights."

The smile faded from Patrick's face. "That's why we use fronts to cover what we're doing. Never let the victim see whose hand wields the knife, so to speak. I have a score to settle with Kucinski, too. The key is crippling MacPherson, then we can ease him, and her, out of any position of real power—"

"In the meantime, be damn careful to keep me out of it." Ramsey's voice rose as he wagged his finger at Patrick.

꒜

The first automated launch of a submarine hull into space motivated Ki Mapes to watch on a monitor.

The Strait of Juan de Fuca was chosen due to its proximity to Tacoma's boatworks, the closest deepwater location for launching a submarine into orbit. The submarine, now about forty percent of its original weight, had a large aneutronic fusion drive temporarily attached to its former stern. All non-essential items within had been replaced by equipment to make the sturdy hull into a space-faring vessel. Even the conning tower had been cut down to a stub prior to launch. A ballast tank was temporarily attached for upending the submarine hull prior to launch.

It was time to make the Space Force a reality. Ki ordered the submarine hulls be sent to DS-2 where docks and equipment were ready to convert the former Los Angeles class vessels into spaceships.

"... five—four—three—two—one—launch!"

A black fish-shaped object rose from the water on a huge ball of brilliant white fire and a giant column of steam. A white ring expanded across the surface of the water at tremendous velocity as the black object accelerated straight up.

The sound from the speakers became a roar as the noise of the fusion drive at maximum thrust reached the remote observation station. The sound faded as the black object rose until it disappeared, leaving only a tiny point of light trailing behind.

"Passing one hundred kilometers altitude," a voice said. "Velocity is nine point eight kilometers per second and increasing." A monitor showed the vessel's climb to orbit. Three sets of figures at the bottom of the screen represented the percentage of available thrust deployed, relative velocity, and altitude. All parameters were within spec.

Ki let out his breath; the launch was successful.

Kip Ryan's design for the deep space craft was similar to that of the first submarine-based space station: Two hulls would be "paired-up" and take on spin to generate internal gravity. The two hulls connected at their former conning tower locations would share a single fusion drive. When viewed from the front, this new ship, officially called an Eagle class ship, would have a dumbbell outline. Hence its nickname of Dumbbell.

Ki felt a wave of relief.

Good, he thought. *It's becoming routine. And no crew required anymore if anything goes wrong. I hope to God it doesn't.* He glanced at the schedule. The fusion drive would be removed from the submarine hull and sent back to Tacoma for use with another hull that was due in ..., what was it? Ten days. *We'll mate them together for our first true deep space craft.* He found it ironic the deep diving submarines would be the first human-operated spacecraft to explore the depths of space.

CHAPTER FOUR

THE GATEWAY

Pip Ryan watched his Eagle grow. He was proud of his idea to use submarine hulls to make a space station and his design would also be used to build an interplanetary spaceship.

Pip was short and stocky with a face that looked as though it might have seen a fight or two. Smokey brown eyes peered out from beneath bushy eyebrows matching his dark curly hair. He wasn't handsome, but something about the way he spoke—with a trace of New England—made him attractive to women. His sense of humor accounted for his nickname, which he'd picked up when he was young and told by all that he was a "Pip."

Welding torches flickered on and off as workers joined the two Angeles class submarine hulls together at their former conning towers with a fifteen-foot diameter tube. Haze and smoke hung heavily in the bay of the "Little-Egg-that-Flies."

Soon, it'll be time for another pump-down, Pip thought.

Air contamination from welding was a constant problem. As a result, the air in the construction dock had to be pumped down to about one percent Earth-normal and the balance vented into space to get rid of the fumes.

Such a waste, he thought. *But we need an atmosphere to get the work done quickly.*

Ergonomics controlled the design of the Eagle. Since there was no satisfactory solution to the loss of bone density and strength in zero-gee, the ship had to have gravity, either from acceleration or rotation. It needed mobility, as well. To achieve this, the Eagle was built with two submarine hulls aligned on a parallel longitudinal axis and rotated about a common point. One hull was primarily for fuel and supply storage, the other used for living quarters. Centered on the former keel of the inhabited hull was the drive unit, which pushed at right angles to the long axis. When the craft was about to get underway, the crew took its spin off. Once the drive unit fired up, its thrust made its passengers feel as though they were standing upright. When on station, the spin-up provided gravity with the same orientation.

Pip thought it was a sound solution. *Sure, it wasn't going to look sleek, but who cared?*

"Mr. Ryan," said a junior officer. "I just heard there will be a delay in getting the drive unit."

"Why?" Pip looked up quickly.

"Something to do with the needs of the Chinese." The junior officer shrugged. "Rumor has it they were kicking up a fuss again and threatening to leave the Confederation unless they got more fusion reactors."

"That's what comes from dealing with an alliance of warlords," Pip said. "I could ease up on the construction schedule and give the workers some time off, but I'd also have to listen to Commander Mapes bitch about priorities and project deadlines."

The junior officer's face brightened. The long hours had worn them all down. A break would be welcomed.

"We'll stay on schedule," Pip said. "I'll send down the revised construction flow schedule. We'll just have to find a way to work around the delay."

~

"So that's why we're behind," Pip Ryan said.

Commander Ki Mapes's frown eased. He turned in his chair and tapped on a computer keyboard. "Lemme see." He scrolled through some pages. He highlighted something and then typed quickly. "Maybe I can get an idea how soon we can get the components," he said.

"Sir?" Pip wondered why the commander's quarters were as austere as the rest of the officers' quarters in the former Little-Egg-that-Flies, or LETF as most of the crew called it.

Hell, he was the commander-in-chief. Sure, it was larger and had more monitors, but there was no paneling or leather; just painted metal and plastic upholstery—in gray, no less.

"O'Neil, who runs the fusion drive manufacturing facility, and I have worked together. I can count on his giving me an honest answer." Ki selected another address and typed another message. "Might as well get an answer from the top."

"And who is that, may I ask?" Pip said.

"Oh, it's just a distant relative." Ki smiled.

Pip nodded. He knew of Ki's relationship to Carver Washington, who was the Speaker of the Confederation's Assembly.

"Y'see, it's a policy call," Ki said. "If our leaders have decided things on Earth are more important than protecting the planet, there's nothing we can do about it." Since moving to DS-2, he'd made living quarters available for spouses of the permanent crew. Having his wife, LaTasha, nearby had given him a new perspective and tranquility.

The LETF originally had quarters for over one hundred Qu'uda. That had proved to be sufficient for fifty crew and spouses. In addition, a section of the fuel tank would soon become another rotating living section, primarily for the workers who had shifts on the DS-2 during the construction phases. When they completed the twelve spacecraft based upon submarine hulls, the new section would become the living quarters for the ships' maintenance personnel as well as transient spacecraft crew. The new section was twice the size of the existing living quarters and more comfortable. Eventually, DS-2 would be home to more than three hundred.

"Shall we continue to send personnel over to DS-1 for training?" Pip referred to the original space station constructed from two Ohio class submarine hulls, which had become the training center for the new spacecraft crews. The layout and controls on board were similar to those of the Los Angeles class submarine hulls being converted into Eagles.

"Of course. We'll never have too many trained spacecraft crews." Ki remembered the problems in the past when personnel shortages had hampered operations. Besides, it was better to have a roster from which to select the best personnel.

The computer pinged, announcing an incoming message. Ki tapped in his access code and squinted at the monitor. "Hmm. Looks like the delay in getting drive units will hold us up for two manufacturing cycles—unless someone else jumps ahead of us again. I'll be glad when we can make our own units."

Ki and Pip had discussed the possibility of making their own drive units and had started to assemble the manufacturing machinery to do so. First, they had to find out if there were economic amounts of helium-3 on Pluto or another outer system planet.

Gawd, he thought. *We're going all the way to Pluto to get fuel—amazing. If so, we could make drive units based on Qu'uda technology exploiting that resource as well as using the boron-hydrogen aneutronic fusion drive currently employed.*

"What did he say?" DuKlaat YataBu, the former principal analyst for the Keepers-of-the-Egg said. He had decided to remain on Earth to investigate the strange anomaly in the vicinity of Pluto, which appeared to be a violation of space-time.

He had also found the scientists from the former Ohio State University and other Earth academic institutions had a good grasp of physics. The chance to be among those who understood his calling had been too much for DuKlaat. He missed the intellectual stimulation of being among equals. Since there were significant language barriers, he needed Billy as a translator.

"He said it is time for you to learn English," Billy said.

"Why does he not learn Qu'uda-speak?" DuKlaat asked.

"English is the language of science on Earth. Few, if any, will learn our tongue." Billy wobbled his upper torso in the Qu'uda equivalent of a shrug. "It is time you had the language-teaching algorithm installed in your biocomputer. It may not be easy, but it is very worthwhile."

DuKlaat started to protest, but he saw the group of human scientists had gathered around and were waiting, silent.

The room, a former classroom, had one wall of blackboards covered with equations and diagrams. White dust from repeated erasures stained the once-black surfaces as well as a light dusting on the creaking floorboards. A long folding table held four small computers, each with a monitor that displayed a different set of equations. It had been an exciting afternoon of scientific ideas and information exchange.

Already, DuKlaat had picked up several ideas for solving previously intractable theoretical issues from these humans. *Why did we ever think they were primitives? Their theoretical basis is as extensive as ours, except that their focus is on the more basic nature of matter.*

"You may be right," DuKlaat said. "Perhaps it is time. But I will need an Earth person to practice what I learn—"

"These scientists have all volunteered to teach you their language. They believe what they have learned from you is reward enough." Billy turned to the humans and spoke rapidly.

The humans began their high-pitched chatter with many nodding their heads in a fashion DuKlaat had already learned was agreement.

Why, they're not so bad after all, even if they're not Qu'uda.

The first of the Eagle-class spaceships hung motionless next to the DS-2's dock, with bright sunlight glittering off its aluminum foil cover. Crinkled aluminum foil covered most of the hull and the connecting tube. After completion, it had been taken for a series of test runs to verify its systems, with the final trip lasting seven days. The two hulls, each about three hundred feet long, were connected at the middle. A large, high-gain radio and microwave dish antenna hung off what had been the stern of the living quarters' hull. On the other end was a triangular array of optical receptors for the laser communications.

On the keel of the fuel and supplies' hull was a small geodesic dome centered in a large dish receiver. This was the flight path radar. It would detect objects in the path of the Eagle to provide warning against collision with anything that could cause damage. It would send a very powerful radar pulse once every thirty seconds and listen for echoes. Slaved to the radar system were two Qu'uda technology particle beam weapons to destroy smaller objects in the Eagle's flight path.

Attached to the deck side of the supply hull was a fifty-foot-long tube-shaped craft only slightly smaller in diameter than the main hull of the Eagle. It was a small fusion powered shuttle designed to investigate the gas resources of Pluto and observe the space-time anomaly that seemed to follow the planet Pluto.

"It really looks weird," Ki said. "It looks a dumbbell going sideways." The Eagle traveled at right angles to the long axis of the hulls. "It's got so much crap hanging off it, it looks like a damn junkyard."

Pip Ryan said nothing. He knew Commander Ki Mapes understood all the reasons for building the craft that way. Both understood the configuration had no impact upon its velocity in space. The fuel and supply hull was crammed full so the Eagle could use a high acceleration-deceleration flight plan to get to Pluto. It was the only quick way.

"Three months there, six months on station and three months back," said Ki. "That schedule would drive me crazy." The plan was to have an Eagle on station continuously to watch the strange space-time anomaly. The first spaceship, Eagle-One, would get there in about three months, using a constant acceleration and deceleration flight plan. There it would deploy sensors around the anomaly and then spin-up to watch and wait. The shuttle would take a closer look and see if it was feasible to mine Pluto's atmosphere. Nine months later, Eagle-Two would relieve Eagle-One.

If the atmosphere of Pluto didn't have any helium-three, Ki planned to find some way to get enough to use it as fuel. *In the meantime, I need more ships,* Ki thought. There are a bunch of near-Earth asteroids that need investigating. Some must have metal, and maybe even water and volatiles. We've got to reduce our dependency on shuttles bringing everything up from Earth.

CHAPTER FIVE

WHAT TO DO?

Shortly after Suh-Joh fled the Hool system, I, Kot-Nih, had the opportunity to be like a naat-jii in the corner and observe a special meeting of the Council of Hive-Mothers. They convened, even including the ambassadors of the Hive-Mothers from the Kamah system, to decide a course of action against Suh-Joh. I believe you humans call Kamah the Zeta Reticuli-A system, but I digress. The priests of the Shrine of the Mother called the meeting for they had made some disturbing discoveries.

Bok-Tah stood at the front of the bowl-shaped opening surrounded by high rock walls. Bok-Tah, old and stooped, carried many scars from his former life as a Chosen-Male warrior. He was now the chief priest of the brotherhood serving the Shrine of the Mother.

Within the rocky vale deep red vines draped down much of its steep sides and underfoot lay short springy vegetation. Water, precious water tinkled in rivulets down its walls. Smoothly rounded stones made a regular pattern across the floor of the vale. They were resting mounds, separated by enough distance to prevent fights between adjacent Hive-Mothers.

"Recently, when acolytes checked the seals of the prohibited areas in the archives," Bok-Tah said. "Their helpers, young never-ripened males, detected a faint trace of an unfamiliar scent." As Bok-Tah spoke, Hive-Mothers listened carefully for his words carried the authority of the Spirit of the Mother. "That prohibited area of the archives holds forbidden weapons."

At his utterance of the word forbidden, a collective hiss swept the assembled Hive-Mothers. That word was often associated with the pejorative of obscene and perverse, which could lead to death. It was as though the Council collectively felt the cold spine of fear. Breathing orifices rippled nervously in unison.

"When investigated, we found the scent to be that of Suh-Joh's hive. We believe she penetrated the prohibited areas." Bok-Tah rose on his hind limbs and raised his fore limbs. "Designs of energy weapons were disturbed. With the scent of Suh-Joh's hive upon them, my conclusion is she has them."

The Hive-Mothers exhaled sharply through their breathing flaps, displaying their agitation. The aromas of anger and fear filled the vale. A babble of voices rose.

"Silence." The old priest's steely voice rang out. "I am not finished." He lowered himself onto his resting mound and pivoted his head from side to side to look at every Hive-Mother present. "Using technology from the past, we also found trace amounts of the synthetic life-extending hormone on the seals."

Though no Hive-Mother was free to use ancient technology, the priests could use what they believed necessary to preserve the Way of the Mother.

"Suh-Joh continues to defy the edict of the Council and the Spirit of the Mother by extending her life and her unworthy subjects by unnatural means."

For several moments, the assemblage hissed and voices rose

in loud complaint. The word unnatural was only a degree lower in danger than the word "forbidden."

Bok-Tah waited until the Hive-Mothers grew quiet. He waved his forelimb at Nah-Kih, a young Hive-Mother whose political skills had won his favor and was the de facto spokesperson for the Council. "What does this Council wish to do?"

Even though the old priest asked the guidance of the Council, all knew the final course of action would be the one receiving the blessing of the priests of the Shrine of the Mother.

This was a dark tunnel to traverse.

"Most honored Bok-Tah, we Hive-Mothers need the guidance of the Spirit of the Mother before we can reach a collective decision." Nah-Kih flexed in submission toward the old priest and his advisors. She turned toward the assembled Hive-Mothers. "Many of us gathered here have much experience and knowledge. So, my esteemed Hive-Mothers must be heard so we may choose a wise course of action. Perhaps it would be best to review the visual record of the pilot-navigators who returned from the treacherous ambush by Suh-Joh."

Nah-Kih referred to a pilot-navigators' report of the grave damage inflicted on Suh-Joh's ship, the Mother's Servant. Images from the shuttlecraft, one of the two returning from the encounter, flashed onto a blank space on the wall of the vale. The images did not show a dying craft, but rather one fleeing into the depths of space.

"Were I hunting dak-li, I would not count on eating it if it fled as this," said an older, more conservative Hive-Mother. She used the analogy of the Mother's Servant to the flying crustacean much prized and hunted as a gourmet food item.

"It is like any wounded prey," another Hive-Mother said. "Suh-Joh will surely perish in the barrens of outer space—"

"You forget the riches Suh-Joh garnered from barren space," another voice called out. "She took much of her manufacturing capability with her. I fear she may build powerful weapons and visit destruction upon us."

For a moment the vale was silent. Even the soft sound of water tinkling in the rivulets seemed loud. The unspoken fear had been uttered. They remembered Suh-Joh's hive had been found empty; all of its many Chosen-Male warriors were gone. They knew the Mother's Servant was large enough to hold most, if not all of them, and Suh-Joh had enough warriors, which if armed with energy weapons, would be a threat to all their hives.

"Then you must act." Bok-Tah's voice, though not loud, was clear to every Hive-Mother. "You must take the battle to her."

"How? We have but few spacecraft," a voice said.

"We can build them, if it is permitted." The ever-careful Nah-Kih flexed in the direction of the head priest.

"You may access the archives to get technology equal to or better than that used by Suh-Joh in her craft," Bok-Tah's breathing flaps rose and fell, emitting aromas of anger. "She is a danger to the Spirit of the Mother."

"What weapons shall we use?" asked the Hive-Mother whose pilot-navigator had failed to return from the encounter with Suh-Joh's ship. "Ours were no match for hers." At once, many voices rose, each proposing a solution to the problem.

I, Kot-Nih, believe much of what was proposed was impractical. Many of the Hive-Mothers had no experience with space travel, nor what warfare there was like.

The old priest closed his eyes and settled comfortably onto his resting rock. His breathing flaps took on the regular rhythm of one at rest. The debate continued, circling around the question of how to track down and destroy Suh-Joh. Some Hive-Mothers sent for their scholars to advise them. Gradually, the debate focused upon what was practical.

After several hours, hunger and weariness drove the Hive-Mothers from the vale.

ॐ

In the morning, Bok-Tah, erect and wide awake, waited patiently as the Hive-Mothers assembled. Hool's orange sun rose above the lip of the vale to illuminate the red vines lining its walls and the old priest raised his forelimbs and began to pray.

"Oh, Spirit of the Mother, guide us, your children ..." He continued with the prayer as the Hive-Mothers assumed the position of symbolic submission, heads touching the ground.... "Let us never forget our savior, the Spirit of the Mother, who has kept us on the path of righteousness, who leads us away from our foolish impulses, as only a true Mother can."

The old priest lowered himself onto his resting rock, closed his eyes, and breathed deeply. Even praying seemed to leave him weary these days. His eyes opened and glittered brightly. "Have you decided on a course of action?" His breathing flaps flared as though sniffing out a trail to follow.

"Most honored Bok-Tah," Nah-Kih said. "We do indeed wish to pursue and destroy the abomination, Suh-Joh. We have settled on the type of craft to construct so we may pursue her. However, with the weapons she possesses, we may not succeed, especially if she creates more energy weapons similar to those that destroyed the noble warriors of my fellow Hive-Mothers."

At this time, I, Kot-Nih, as a priest, was shocked by what my master, Bok-Tah, the head priest of the Shrine, next said:

"I authorize this Council to use energy weapons against Suh-Joh," Bok-Tah said. "These weapons, whose design I will provide, must never be used on Hool. So, they cannot be made here, only in outer space. It is better to violate the prohibition than let the holy soil of Hool be again laid to waste. The Way of the Mother has been threatened by a heretic, which calls for the extreme sanction," Bok-Tah said. "Suh-Joh must be destroyed. This calls for a holy war."

At his words, all the Hive-Mothers flexed into submission and for an instant, the vale was silent. A murmur of voices began, increasing until it seemed that everyone was speaking.

The old priest raised his forelimb.

Quiet descended.

"Select a Chosen-Male warrior and a scholar from five hives and send them to me. They will be the guardians of the technology from the archives. Once they have learned it, they must leave the surface of Hool and never return."

Bok-Tah turned as though to go and then hesitated. "Remember," he said. "Suh-Joh needs a home and she knows of the water planet with primitives who are willing to be servants. That, I believe, is where you will find her. Do not delay, for if she digs a deep hive on that world, she will be difficult to grub out."

The old priest turned to leave, moving slowly and stiffly. Two younger priests hurried to his side to support him by his mid-limbs as he shambled out.

"Show again the report on the Water-Gem," a voice called.

"Yes, do that," said another.

Even though all had seen the report, it soon became obvious some of the Hive-Mothers were more interested in the potential of the Water-Gem and its compliant natives than the threat of Suh-Joh, especially those with many daughters who approached their time of ripening. Many stated they believed Suh-Joh had tried to conceal the existence of a planet rich in water. That planet, they reasoned, is ours.

I, Kot-Nih, noticed some of the more thoughtful Hive-Mothers were disturbed by the ferocity of the Water-Gem people when they fought off the asteroid-aliens.

After much argument, the Council agreed to establish a levy on every hive, including those on Kamah, to pay for the construction of spaceships with powerful weapons to pursue Suh-Joh and occupy the Water-Gem.

I, as archivist, recorded much of what was said and found the self-serving approach of some to be troubling. It seemed to me an infection of greed had swept through the Council. Some of the Hive-Mothers bickered incessantly they should be the ones to provide crews for the ships. If it were not for the distance between each resting rock and the tradition no blood would be shed while in the vale at the Shrine of the Mother, I believe some might have attacked others. It was the realization that many riches and rewards would come to those who colonized the water planet with its indigenous serving class that tempted and tormented them.

That, I perceived, portended trouble.

CHAPTER SIX

BUSINESS AS USUAL

Brown leaves scurried across the square, driven by a cold wind out of the north whistling through the city's canyons. People hurried along gray streets, hunched over, coats pulled tight.

Charlie Ramsey turned away from the window of his office that looked down on the center of Columbus and glanced at the visitor sitting on his sofa in front of a wall displaying a collection of ancient weapons.

"At the next Assembly meeting," Ramsey said. "I'm submitting your name for assistant deputy minister of defense with responsibilities for improving state security of the Human Confederation. That position won't attract a lot of attention. After confirmation, you'll report directly to me."

Patrick Monahan smiled. "Kucinski will have nothing to do with my activities, right?" He referred to Chris Kucinski's role as head of US Public Security, or police.

Ramsey pursed his lips, choosing his words carefully. "No. Your role, on the surface, is to improve the coordination of information flow between the national defense forces under control of the Human Confederation. What I really need is an intelligence service in several areas. Those damn Chinese are giving us fits with their constant shifts in power and demands to change our deal with them. Their government of warlords isn't stable. You'll have to recruit agents over there so we can have our own source of information."

Patrick nodded. He'd heard this before. Already he had started to seek out agents on the West Coast where there was a sizable Chinese community. He planned to delegate much of this activity to a Chinese-American associate, Shao-Li Peng. It was the other responsibilities of the job that interested him.

"You'll also need to develop internal sources of information," Ramsey said. "To keep your fingers on the, er, mood of our country and its political establishment. To take necessary steps to, er, control anti-government elements."

Yes, thought Patrick. *I already know who they are*. "Well," he said. "I'll put together an outline of what I believe needs to be done and review it with you prior to taking any action."

Well, Patrick thought. *Not everything. I've got my own score to settle with those who've brought shame to my family*. He felt a touch of warmth in his cheeks. *Kucinski and her clique will get theirs, eventually*. "I'm honored that you've chosen me out of so many well-qualified people—"

"Nothing in writing on that," said Ramsey. "You know quite well I chose you because we share a common set of goals. I want complete and total loyalty, do you understand? Any sign of freelancing and you'll be out. Is that clear?"

Patrick lowered his head. "Yes, sir. Absolutely." *One day*, he thought, *I'll have your position, too*.

Crockery clattered as voices rose and fell. Aromas of kuchen and coffee filled the air. Condensation on the windows of the Overlook Teahouse blurred the view of the park below.

"Tell me, Ms. Vargas, what's the real reason you wanted to

have coffee with me?" Patrick Monahan asked. He'd enjoyed talking to her but sensed there was more to it than a chat about politics.

Joyce Vargas, the former wife of Taylor MacPherson smiled over the rim of a chipped coffee mug and took a sip. "Well, I did want to congratulate you on your promotion. You're right, Patrick, there is something else. I don't quite know how to say this without being direct." She smiled. "So, I won't use words."

Patrick felt her foot—minus its shoe—rise along his leg.

"You see, I find you appealing ... Intellectually as well." She smiled and blinked at him. Her toe slid along his thigh. "There are ways to communicate without words, don't you agree?"

Patrick felt the beginning of a flush. "Yes, I think so." *Why do I get red so damn easy?* he thought. Though Joyce was older, he thought her sexy.

Her overall physique and generous breasts gave her a voluptuous quality he found riveting. Her long, mahogany-colored hair framed strong features and when she smiled, full lips revealed even white teeth. The touch of her leg inspired long-suppressed erotic wishes and he felt the beginning of arousal. She wasn't at all like the women he usually met at church suppers or at political meetings.

"Perhaps we should continue this discussion, er, elsewhere?" Joyce faltered a moment, yet her meaning was obvious.

"Er, yes, I'd like that." Patrick almost staggered as he rose to his feet. The urge was strong, insistent, and compelling.

Joyce rose and led the way outside. She paused at the edge of the sidewalk and leaned close to Patrick. "My apartment is two streets over," she said quietly.

ꝶ

The dull gray, potato-shaped asteroid hung motionless against a blackness of space and an extravagant carpet of multi-colored stars. Starlight glinted off flat, angular slashes that were scars of the mining operations.

Ki Mapes watched it on the monitor in the command center of Defense Station 2 and shook his head. "You're nothing but trouble."

It wasn't so long ago he'd found an M-class asteroid—eighty thousand tons of iron-nickel, a natural stainless steel—was good material to build the space station. The Space Force ship Eagle-I had captured the tiny asteroid on the end of its return trip from Pluto and had towed it to the DS-2, which hung above Earth in a Lagrangian orbit.

Eagle-I's two-man, fusion powered shuttle had made several fast trips through Pluto's atmosphere and returned with almost two tons of liquefied gas. The initial analysis showed it contained about one hundred parts per million helium-three. It was the richest source of fuel discovered so far. They brought back enough liquefied gas to develop a purification train for extracting helium-three. With that, they would be able to test it in a small-scale Qu'uda fusion drive engine.

So, the Eagle-I had returned with two treasures. Ki felt a surge of excitement at the thought of getting a helium-three fusion drive.

However, there was another analysis causing Ki heartburn. When Connie Nagy, a reporter with The Trusted News, had called him on the radio and asked, "Can you confirm you've struck it rich?"

"I don't know what you mean, Ms. Nagy." Ki frowned, puzzled. "What're you talking about?"

"I just heard about the metal analysis of the asteroid Eagle-I brought back," said Ms. Nagy. "D'you know what it is?"

"Sure, it's iron-nickel, a natural stainless steel."

"It has almost one-tenth of a percent platinum," Ms. Nagy said. It was as though she had discovered a whole new world. "A very valuable metal." She continued talking.

Ki ignored her words as he ran the numbers in his head.

Eighty thousand tons at one-tenth percent was over two million ounces of platinum, which at one hundred New Dollars per ounce, was many times the entire budget of the new US government.

"So, what do you plan to do with it?" she asked.

Ki thought about the capabilities of the extraction units that distilled water and other volatiles out of carbonaceous asteroids: they couldn't melt metals. The metal casting unit used to make flat stock and beams had no refining or centrifuging capabilities. "Ms. Nagy, we intend to use the asteroid metal to expand our orbital defense station—"

"You don't plan to do anything with the platinum?"

"No, I can't extract the platinum. It has no value to me."

The asteroid metal drew the attention of other news medium on Earth. It was the fact the metal—a stainless steel mixture containing almost one-tenth percent platinum, a metal used in high value currency coins, would be used by the Space Force as a basic building material. Critics of the administration and those who felt more should be spent on social programs jumped at the chance to accuse the Space Force of gold plating its projects.

"I wish we'd never got that damn chunk of metal," Ki said. "But we're stuck with it."

"I think it's a case of being too honest," Pip said. "Sure there's a lot of platinum in the asteroid, in fact, there're platinum group metals in every metallic asteroid. They're inaccessible to us because we can't refine it out here. As it stands, it's just a cheap source of metal." He had already started on his next project to create another defense station. Only this time he would use a metallic asteroid as the starting point.

To do so, Pip had designed single-person ships, or soloships. They were miniature one-person spacecraft analogous to work boats or miniature submarines, except they were for hard vacuum and zero gravity. To accommodate the fleet of soloships, he had started building a structure that would become their docking port. Already, workers using fusion torches had cut slabs of metal from the asteroid fragment and welded them into a long, box-like structure that was two hundred meters long. At one end, a framework made a spider web-like hoop, which would contain the crew's living quarters. Once they moved it into position, the module would be attached to a near-Earth M-class asteroid. Excavating cavities within the asteroid would produce more metal, thus providing the materials for the new defense station to become a manufacturing center.

ॐ

"Yeah, well, you may be right about that, man, but it ain't me you gotta convince," Carver Washington said.

He was the chief US representative to the Human Confederation Assembly, housed in the former State Capitol Building in Columbus, Ohio. The Human Confederation was the loose alliance pulled together in the aftermath of the alien Hoo-Lii attack. The Assembly had become a means to transfer wealth and technology from the re-established US to the undeveloped areas of the world. Carver's office was lined with shelves loaded with books, below which a worn leather couch sagged. He heaved his bulk back in a heavy oak armchair.

Ki stared at Carver over a desk with papers stacked over a foot high. He was finding the pull of gravity unrelenting. Even though he had done his exercises, it took a week or so to readjust from the one-half gravity of the station. He resented being called to Earth to answer questions that had nothing to do with defense. He was more worried about the return of the Hoo-Lii and fighting another battle with them. "You know this issue over the asteroid's platinum is bull-crap."

Wind and rain rattled the windows. The room smelled of wet wool. Carver ran his hand over a dark brown forehead. "Word's out in the Assembly your Space Force boys don't care they're using a fortune in platinum to build their toys—"

"Well, what am I supposed to do about that?" Ki said.

"You gotta be politically sensitive, man." Carver sighed and put his hands behind his head. "Share the wealth. Yeah, I know you can't refine the platinum, but there's gotta be some way you can make the people feel they benefit from paying taxes."

"Benefit?"

"Supporting the Space Force is a tough job. You've had cost overruns in every budget. We've had to cut back in other areas," Carver said. "I understand why, but it ain't easy when there're those who just want an easy life with us funding it. There're all kinds of demands on the budget, 'specially from China."

Ki rose and pulled back the curtain. A veil of rain swept across the square below and through the trees lining the walks around its grassy center. No one was about. He felt alone, as empty as the square. He turned to Carver. "What," he said, "if the Space Force sent down some of the asteroid metal?"

"Depends on how much and who gets it." Carver stroked his chin and pursed his lips. "Gotta be to someone who isn't aligned with you, or anyone who supports you."

"Like who?"

"Mebbe the Chinese." Carver's eyebrows rose. "They're nobody's friend. An' they're far enough away from the newsies who're raising the fuss." He chuckled. "If your space boys sent down half of the metal, they'd be happy."

"That's a lot." Ki stared at Carver. "I don't know how we'd get it down. We don't have the shuttle capacity."

"You can't give 'em just a drop in the bucket. That'd piss 'em off even more. You gotta send them a big chunk of it."

"How?"

"Dunno. Don't care. Bet your Space Force boys can figure out how."

Ki sat down and played with a pencil. He nodded slowly.

Carver raised his hand and wagged his finger. "Don't do anything in a hurry. Let your critics vent for a while, just say you agree you gotta do something about sharing the wealth of the universe, or whatever hogwash you want to use. Y'know, eat a little humble pie. Oh, yeah, call in the Chinese privately and see if you can squeeze them in exchange for the right to extract the platinum from the asteroid metal."

"Like what?"

"Oh, support for your program, whatever." Carver shrugged. "I'll send a staffer over with an outline of what we want from them. They've been such a pain in the ass I want to give them something they'll regret."

"Regret?" Ki's eyebrows rose.

"Sure." Carver's smile revealed a mouthful of even teeth. "Enough platinum'll stick to their fingers to make their leaders very rich. Now, if the Chinese masses don't share in the wealth, they'll finally realize their leaders are corrupt. Mebbe that'll bring about some changes, hopefully for the better." He rose stiffly and extended his hand. "You take care, Ki. I'd hate to see your hide tacked up as a trophy."

"Thanks, Carver. Sometimes you just amaze me," Ki said.

∿

"Patrick." Joyce ran her finger over the reddish blond hair on his chest. "D'you know how much money Doctor Encirlik's pharmaceutical operation earned last year?"

They were in a large bed whose coverings draped onto the floor. The candle on the dresser provided just enough light to see softened details. The room had thick curtains covering the windows and the dresser mirror had been adjusted so the bed's occupants could view themselves. Clothing lay scattered on the floor.

Patrick Monahan opened his eyes. He felt splendid, sated. He'd never experienced anything like this before. He'd thought he knew what great sex was; now he realized that he'd always been with beginners or amateurs. Joyce on the other hand, had taken him to places he'd never imagined existed.

"Money?" He struggled to focus his thoughts. Encirlik was the wife of MacPherson and an ally of Kucinski; therefore she was their common enemy. "No, I don't. I do know that it was a lot, but I can find out. That is, if she paid her taxes—"

"Exactly." Joyce sat up to put a band in her hair. Her breasts rose. She smiled at Patrick. "Rumor has it she earns more money than any other individual in the Human Confederation. The word is she's got a multi-million-dollar income. All from Qu'uda technology that should belong to everyone."

Patrick eyed Joyce's breasts. A quick swelling of lust surprised him. "So?" he said. His tongue felt thick.

"Obviously, I know a lot about the MacPhersons, especially him," she said. "But I don't know anything about their current finances or activities. If I did, I might be able to point out their weaknesses." She held her pose and smiled.

"Yes, I should be able to get those numbers—"

"Maybe we should share them with the news media? Especially if she didn't pay her full share of taxes."

"Yes, I like that. It could make them both look bad. It could be the thing to trigger the legislation to control her profits. Yes, I'll check into it." Patrick sat up, revealing his desire for her.

"Hmm, that looks too good to waste." Joyce's eyebrows rose and she reached for him. "Patrick, you're wonderful. I think we make a great team, and we sure do have a lot of fun together."

CHAPTER SEVEN

THE EAGLES RISE

Whitecaps marched steadily across gray-green water. In the distance, snow covered mountains outlined the Olympic peninsula. A long, dark rounded hull rolled uneasily in the waves as a rusty yellow tugboat retrieved its lines. Slowly, the bow of the submarine hull tilted and rose out of the water as it became upright.

Wick Wilson, the tugboat skipper, always enjoyed being on this part of the Strait. Several months ago, he'd argued a submarine was a poor towing vessel, that a tug was better. As a result, he and his tugboat had the responsibility to take a much-modified Los Angeles class submarine hull out into the Strait of Juan de Fuca for its launch. "Not much different than towing a string of barges full of fuel," he said.

The naval officer in charge of the launch raised his eyebrows but said nothing.

"So, when does this thing get airborne?" Wick asked.

"In ten minutes, that's how long you have to clear the launch zone. I'd suggest you increase speed." The naval officer pointed to the circle drawn on the map. "We need to be outside of this area when the boat is launched." He put on a set of headphones.

Wick pushed the dual throttles forward and the tugboat plowed through the waves toward Puget Sound. Behind, the nose of the submarine hull was a barely visible black mound with waves breaking over it. As the distance increased, only a patch of barely visible shoal-like water defined its location.

"... five—four—three—two—one—ignition," came the voice over the speaker.

The submarine hull, distant and tiny, emerged from the water almost reluctantly. As it rose to full erect length, a huge ball of steam, glowing brilliantly from the contained fireball, billowed from its base. A visible shock wave radiated out from the ball of steam. The black hull rose faster into the air, trailed by a column of brilliant white steam.

The roar of the launch swept over the tugboat almost like a blow from a giant hammer. The sound faded as the black shape disappeared through the cloud deck.

"Holy mackerel," Wick said. "I had no idea it'd be like this. My ears are ringing."

The naval officer removed his headphones. "Looks like we have a good launch," he said. "Well, let's head back. We've got more boats to get ready to launch."

ᘒ

"Look," said Pip Ryan. "We need more time to build the H3D." He used the term H3D to mean helium-3 deuterium fusion drive that would be used in the new Eagle class ships being assembled at DS-2. "They're different from the old-style fusion drive. Before I send any of them up, I want to make sure I've done enough testing to be sure they'll be reliable."

His office, overlooking the Tacoma shipyard, had walls of cracked and peeling bile-green paint. An ancient drawing board and a rack holding voluminous tattered and faded blueprint drawings dominated one end of the room. Stacks of file folders and a computer monitor covered a dented metal desk whose faded gray paint was chipped and scratched.

"Yes, I understand," Ki Mapes's voice said from a speaker. "We've got to keep working on other Eagle components, otherwise we'll have work crews sitting on their hands."

"Look, the H3D is different. It requires new motor mounts, and you've changed the mission definition. That means the entire interior has to be changed. It needs larger fuel tanks to run on a constant gee acceleration-deceleration flight plan."

Pip pointed to the drawing on the board. A camera on top of the monitor stared diligently at the board. "We'll have to reduce the crew by half just to get enough fuel capacity. Maybe we can put tanks in the crew hull."

"No, I don't agree," Ki said. "Why not put another tank on the fuel and supply hull where the shuttle was previously parked?"

Pip stared at the drawing for a moment and nodded. "That might work. Lemme do some figuring and I'll get back to you." He reached toward the monitor.

"Not so fast," came Ki's voice, "I've got a couple of other things for you. We need something to protect the front end of the Fast Eagle class ships from collision with small debris. At the velocities they'll reach on the Pluto run, they'll need a shield to protect them from impacts with small space debris."

Pip scribbled rapidly on a notepad. "I've got some stuff on high-velocity impacts," he said. "I'll look it up."

"Next, I want you to complete your design of the tanker ship needed to bring helium-3 from Pluto, Uranus, or wherever, including a purification train."

Pip nodded. "I'm nearly done on that. The way I figure it, we'll need to build a fleet of tankers to serve as a supply pipeline." He nodded. "Everyone will want H3D power once they find out about it."

"Right," Ki said. "Design it so it can be built out of something that already exists and quickly. I figure the first of the Fast Eagles will be ready in six months or so. Those tankers will need to be ready soon after that. My ships will be going to a lot of places and some have no source of fuel. So, we'll need a steady supply of fuel at home base."

"Yeah, sounds like I'm back on the sixteen-hour seven-day routine," Pip said, but he didn't sound unhappy. These assignments were in addition to designing an unpowered re-entry body to bring down asteroid metal, which was destined to land in China. And the heavy-lift shuttle still wasn't finished.

ᘓ

A quiet murmur of voices filled the circular hall. Representatives and their staff drifted in and out past the tall pink granite columns that lined the room that was the Assembly meeting place for the Human Confederation.

The Speaker, Carver Washington, rapped his gavel, its sound echoing off the high ceiling. "Order," he called. "The representative from China, the honorable Mr. Guang Xhi, will speak on the introduced legislation, number 2052-116, the Right to Medicines act."

The level of conversation declined. Chairs scraped as representatives sat. Paper rustled as staffers distributed copies of the speech.

"We too, believe the fruits of the Qu'uda technology should be shared by all mankind. That is the basis for the existence of the Human Confederation," Guang Xhi said. "Yet capitalist exploitation of the masses of the Human Confederation still exists, festering like an open sore on our society."

A murmur of voices grew. The Chinese used archaic communist vocabulary for their political speeches even though the Chinese political system was a collection of warlords. His words had a way of grating on the many representatives who were fiercely dedicated to a Libertarian philosophy.

"In particular," said Guang Xhi. "The profiteering in the pharmaceutical industry, especially by Ataturk Industries, which is owned by the wife of the leader of the American side, is despicable. That woman exploits the masses of the Human Confederation by using technology belonging to all of us. She extracts unseemly profits to become the richest person in the world.

"That is the reason for the introduction of the legislation, 2052-116, the Right to Medicines act, which the Chinese democratic peoples support. This piece of legislation will redress the grievous burden grinding the poor and down-trodden masses who must choose between health or starvation."

"Man," Carver Washington said quietly. "Better brace yourself. He's just warming up."

Taylor MacPherson, face stony, stared back at Carver. "He's making Meltem seem like a heartless beast. Yes, she's making a profit, but she puts most of it back into research, and that's after paying taxes on the income. I hope someone will speak to that issue later."

Carver sniffed delicately. "Well, as Speaker, I ain't supposed to put my two cents in on pending legislation, but I just may say a few words to set the record straight. I may even mention China did get the asteroid metal concession, along with the platinum. Problem is Ramsey supports this legislation. Y'see, there's a lot of pressure to get cheap medicine." He raised his hand as Taylor opened his mouth. "Yeah, I know. They're gonna kill the golden goose if Meltem don't have the money to continue the medical research."

"It isn't the money," Taylor said. "I think I can push a medical research funding bill through Council. It's her reputation and my political power that's under attack."

Carver's eyes squinted tightly as he stared at Taylor. "Go on," he said.

"My sources think the Monahans are behind this."

"Y'mean Ms. Kucinski's ferrets have picked something up?"

"Ever since Patrick Monahan went to work for Ramsey, he's

requested all kinds of information and special audits from the tax department on Meltem. This legislation was going nowhere until the news media somehow found out about Meltem's income."

Taylor pointed at Guang Xhi who was pounding his fist into his palm and expounding upon the cost of drugs to the people in his poor country. "Where d'you think he got his information?"

"You're probably right," Carver said. "D'you have any proof it's an illegal activity?"

Taylor sighed. "No," he said.

"Y'see, this's legal." Carver gestured toward the podium. "Now, don't tell me what your police department is up to. Just be damn sure it looks legal. Y'understand?"

"Carver," Taylor said. "You know me better than that." He put his hand on Carver's back. "I'm leaving. I'll get back to you if I find out anything. If something is illegal, you'll hear about it in the news."

Carver nodded. "Take care, my man. I'll do what I can for you here, but I think it's a lost cause."

ॐ

Pip Ryan looked out of the window at the stark, dun-colored salt flat of Groom Lake. Behind him a half-dozen technicians stared intently at monitor screens. In the distance were the Sheep Range Mountains, pink in the late afternoon sun, with just a faint dusting of snow on their peaks. Almost a mile away stood a silvery column. It was the first of the tanker ships. Pip was dead tired, for it had been hectic the past few months. He was pleased how the tanker ship had come together so quickly.

A chemical engineer, Linda Masciani, had pointed out there were a lot of tanks around the country that had stored cryogenic liquids; nitrogen, oxygen, even hydrogen and helium. Some of them held upwards of ten thousand cubic feet of liquids. Getting them to Tacoma required rail transport, which required several new links to be restored. Building the tanker ships was easy: Assemble a purification train into a package matching the diameter of the storage tanks and put it between the two tanks. Then add a standard aneutronic fusion drive. With the low mass of the tank, there was more than enough power to launch the tanker ship. For good measure, he added a second external layer of insulation, well wrapped in an aluminum sheet.

"... five—four—three—two—one—ignition," came the voice from the speaker.

The silvery column rose quickly from the desert floor, leaving a huge blossom of dust. The tanker ship accelerated. Something sailed off the ship in a wobbling arc. Moments later, the ship split into two pieces with a cloud of fragments.

"Aw, no." Pip beat his fist on the wall. He turned toward the bank of monitors. "What the hell happened?"

"Ah, not sure yet," said a technician. "It looks like the drive system was functioning properly. It may have been a structural failure."

At these words, Pip began to review the design in his mind. *Oh, crap*, he thought. *I never checked the strength of the cryogenic tanks. I just assumed they were strong enough to take the thrust. They don't weigh very much, which means their walls are not very thick. How could I have been so stupid?*

"Sir, Commander Mapes would like to speak to you."

Pip picked up the phone. "Yes, sir?" He listened for a while. "Right," he said. "I got some ideas on what happened. They're out recovering the pieces as we speak. Once I get a chance to look at them, I'll let you know." He listened a while longer. "Look, this is what I think happened. I made a mistake, which can be corrected easily. Thank God that no one was on board...." He spoke a while longer, explaining his theory and what he proposed to do to solve the problem.

Two days later, Pip was back in Tacoma, modifying the design of the tanker ships. The fragments of the tanker ship pointed to the collapse of the tank at the bottom where the fusion drive was mounted. He'd also found the new series of drive units had ten percent greater output, of which he'd been unaware.

What a screw-up, he thought.

The solution was to distribute the thrust over the entire structure of the tank using compression trusses. This delayed the schedule for getting the tanker ship in service to provide fuel for the Fast Eagles now coming online. In addition, he had to postpone work on the heavy-lift shuttle.

"Yes," Pip said into the phone. The dark patches under his eyes were enormous. His clothing was rumpled and stained. He needed a shower and shave. "The tanker will not be ready for another twenty-four days.... Yes, we're working seven twenty-fours. I don't see any way to speed up the schedule ... Yes, I do want to build a safe craft ... Yes, I understand the service conditions clearly ... The only thing I can suggest is to send up the development purification train, along with a tank that'll fit into a shuttle's cargo bay ... Yes, that would provide a means of refueling a Fast Eagle and bringing some fuel back." He ran his hand through his hair and closed his eyes as he listened.

"All right," Pip said. "I'll make the arrangements and let you know the schedule. 'Bye." He hung up the phone carefully and sat down heavily. "Ah, shit," he said. "Another project."

The shuttle eased up to the DS-2. Above it floated a docking collar that looked like a piece of large diameter corrugated tubing. The payload bay doors of the shuttle were already open revealing a tubular framework tightly stuffed with equipment. The purification train had arrived. Nearby, several workers attached lines to the shuttle's cargo and the boom arm that would transfer the purification train to the adjacent Fast Eagle.

At right angles to the Fast Eagle's living quarters' hull was a stubby tube that was the H3D drive system.

Even though the Fast Eagle and Eagle-I shared the same basic hulls from Los Angeles class subs, their appearances were quite different. The Fast Eagle looked even more unbalanced; its fuel supply section had two hulls that were capped with a slabby tent-like structure. Attached to the crew hull was a squat tube-like shuttle and a small tank that soon would be mated with the purification train. The Fast Eagle lacked the protruding antennae seen on the Eagle-I ships. Anything that might suffer from impact with space debris at high velocities lay behind a canopy of high-carbon stainless steel.

The Fast Eagle had two powerful beam weapons based on Qu'uda technology controlled by a lidar system—the laser equivalent of a radar detector, which sent a narrow cone of high energy radiation down the ship's flight path to detect anything in its way. With a constant one-gee acceleration-deceleration flight plan, the Fast Eagle would reach tremendous velocities.

It was the only way to reach the outer solar system in a short period of time.

That, Ki knew, was exactly the flight characteristics used by the Hooley-aliens. "How long will this take?" he asked.

A distorted voice replied from the speaker. "So far, we're on schedule. It should be another eighteen hours before everything is tightened down and checked."

"Very well," Ki said.

꒰

It took almost thirty hours to complete the installation to the satisfaction of the engineering staff. Everything just seemed to take longer when done in hard vacuum and zero gravity.

"Eagle-II reporting all systems go," Colonel Bud Inez said. He had requested the command of this ship even though he could have had a much higher position in the construction side of the Space Force. Somehow, the jet-jockeys always want to try out the hot machines, and the Fast Eagle would be the fastest of the fast.

"Commencing drive ignition," Bud Inez said.

A small tongue of violet light sprouted from its drive. The ship began to move. Maneuvering jets flared at the end of the ship's fuel and supply hull. As the Fast Eagle accelerated away from the long, dumbbell shape of DS-2, it curved away from the sun.

"Increasing drive to nominal ten percent output."

The violet light momentarily became brighter then faded as the Fast Eagle accelerated out of sight.

"Final course correction underway," Bud Inez said. "Will commence one-gee acceleration in thirty minutes. See you guys later."

ॐ

Pluto lay below. The monitors showed it was a pale green color, an artifact of the infrared vision system used in the darkness of the outer system. Eagle-II seemed almost stationary as it orbited the planet. The monitors, built to compensate for the rotation providing the crew with gravity, showed Pluto as hanging motionless in the velvet blackness of space.

The anomaly, invisible to the naked eye, followed Pluto like a puppy; sometimes close, sometimes distant in its elliptical orbit. Even with sensors closely orbiting the anomaly gathering data, the scientist still did not know how it functioned. After four months, interest in the anomaly had waned—nothing seemed to happen.

Pluto lacks excitement, Bud Inez thought.

The purification train and fuel tank proved to be problematic.

The biggest problem, Bud realized, *was Pluto's minimal atmosphere. That made gas gathering slow. Sure, the original shuttle had been able to collect gas fairly quickly, but it was traveling at orbital speeds through the atmosphere, ramming gas into its collection system. I guess,* thought Bud. *We're gonna hafta go elsewhere to get our fuel. Probably Uranus.*

A klaxon sounded. Shouts erupted from the control deck.

"What's going on?" Bud asked.

"Omigod," a radar technician said. "Look at it."

Bud looked at the screens. "That can't be right," he said. The anomaly had become visible. Glowing energy outlined its form: It looked like a giant transparent box-like grid work of orange neon tubes. Within, a gigantic ring-shaped craft slowly changed from transparency to solid and emerged from the glowing frame-like structure. "It looks like a goddamn doughnut."

"But, but, its size," the technician said. "It's almost a mile in diameter. There's more craft with it, too."

CHAPTER EIGHT

WEATHER CHANGE

Patrick Monahan glanced out the office window. "Sure do have a nice view of Columbus from up here." He turned back toward Charlie Ramsey.

"You've done what?" Ramsey said. His normally florid face was redder than usual and creased in an angry frown.

Patrick's smile was one of practiced innocence. "I've taken, er, steps, to see that Ms. Kucinski doesn't stick her big nose in our affairs again." His smile became a smirk.

"How's that?" Ramsey asked.

"She's gonna get real sick." Patrick paused. "It happens all the time to old people."

"What kind of illness?"

"Er, it'll look like cancer."

"Oh, my God." Ramsey took a deep breath and covered his face with his hands. "Can any of this be traced back to us?"

"I don't think so. My buddy, Shao-Li, got an obscure chemical from some of our Chinese friends. Some kind of polycyclic amine that's highly toxic." Patrick smiled proudly. "It's supposed to take about ten, fifteen days before the cancer symptoms become apparent. Then it's very quick. She's already ingested it in a special meal at the Vietnamese restaurant where she goes regularly."

"How did you manage, no don't tell me," Ramsey said. "I find this very disturbing. That's assassination."

"Dammit. She's one of the enemy," Patrick said. "A very dangerous enemy who's been sniffing around our operations. She probably already suspects our Chinese connection. However, I've shut down all contacts for the present time. So she shouldn't come up with anything before ..." He hesitated to get just the right words. "She retires." He laughed, high-pitched and almost hysterical.

"You really hate her, don't you?"

"What she did to my father was worse than death. She trumped up evidence banning him from politics." Patrick's eyes flashed. "As far as I'm concerned, nothing's too bad for that woman."

ॱ

The line of brown-clad militia on the sidewalk completely encircled the two-story building, facing outward, their quarterstaffs neat and erect like exclamation points. A river of people in the street flowed slowly around the building. They carried signs denouncing Ataturk Industries and labeling MacPherson as an exploiter of the working class.

The tree-lined street, normally quiet and empty, was turbulent as voices rumbled with an angry edge. Trash blew through the street. So far, there had been no trouble.

"Taylor," Meltem Encirlik said as she turned away from the window. "What am I going to do? Even though the Confederation passed that stupid law forcing me to sell at my cost plus fifteen percent, the demonstrations haven't ended."

Taylor sighed and nodded.

"After paying taxes, there's nothing left for research." Meltem looked at Taylor. "I'll have to get a grant from the Council to continue work, or else let my staff go."

Taylor put his arms around Meltem. "The demonstrations are to block funding in Council for your pharmaceutical research," he said. "This isn't spontaneous." He gestured toward the demonstration. "It's organized, well organized."

"Why?" A frown creased her forehead.

"I'm not sure. It may be aimed as much at me as you." Taylor released his wife and sat on the edge of the desk in the cluttered office. "Yesterday, there was also a demonstration against tax money earmarked for the Space Force."

"So, what's the link to you?"

"The Restored United States holds the Qu'uda technology and shares it with the rest of the Confederation. Much of the technology comes from the university, which is my baby." Taylor looked out the window.

"What I don't understand is the link to young Patrick Monahan and Charlie Ramsey. I had always thought they were patriots and above petty politics. Chris tells me it's Chinese money that's paying for these demonstrations. She thinks it's because they want less spent on the Space Force and more on them. They weren't satisfied with getting the platinum. They want more power generators, too." He referred to the intelligence work done by Chris Kucinski's police department. "Chris thinks they want to get control of the Qu'uda technology." He frowned. "We're losing on the political front."

"That reminds me," said Meltem. "Chris is coming in for a checkup. Something seems to be bothering her. She said she hasn't been feeling well lately."

 ~

The tall double doors closed with a soft click. Across the room, heavy curtains covered the two windows overlooking downtown Columbus. A thick Persian rug lay on the floor, pictures filled the walls, and fresh flowers graced the sideboard. A wide, highly polished cherry wood desk sat before the windows, its top bare and gleaming.

Seated behind, in a high-backed leather chair, was a smiling Guang Xhi, representative of China.

Charlie Ramsey, now US Minister of State Security and delegate of the Human Confederation Assembly, stepped forward and extended his hand.

"As usual, the pleasure is mine." He didn't know why he'd been summoned. He glanced to the side. There was an Asian man, a black woman, and dark-complexioned man of uncertain ancestry sitting around a coffee table.

"Ah, yes, my, er, colleagues," Guang Xhi said. He made the introductions. "So nice to see you," he said. His round face gleamed and rolls of fat spilled over an ornately embroidered silk collar. "Ah, please be seated." Guang Xhi gestured toward the couch, and then sent for tea.

They spent ten minutes in small talk and sipping tea before Guang Xhi said, "I want to make sure the benefits of the alien technology do not get wasted on foolish projects in outer space. The needs of my country and those of our allies." He nodded and smiled at his colleagues. "Are significant and pressing. It is imperative we work together to meet our mutual needs. It is important the supply of power plants be resumed and increased."

Ramsey nodded. *Nothing new here*, he thought. "I'm sure we can work to achieve mutually agreeable objectives."

"Yes," said Guang Xhi. "It is now time for you to work toward increasing the budget for the Chinese side and our allies." He smiled and nodded again, as though expecting agreement.

"Now wait a minute, you just got the platinum concession—"

"It was nothing. That was only thirty thousand tons of asteroid metal. At one-tenth percent platinum, it was almost an insult." Guang Xhi referred to asteroid metal dropped from orbit by unpowered re-entry bodies and delivered to Chinese refiners.

"That's over a hundred million New Dollars—"

"You forget processing costs, administrative overhead, taxes, etceteras. The net was far less than that. With the population of China and our allies." He waved as though dismissing a lowly servant. "It was a pittance, barely a New Dollar per capita."

Ramsey said nothing. He'd heard China's population was now twenty million, plus an unknown number in those countries allied with China. *The luxury of Guang Xhi's residence*, he thought. *Is this an etcetera?* "What d'you have in mind?"

"To allocate a more equitable share of the budget to the developing countries based upon population."

"No, we can't do that," said Ramsey. "A lot of folk believe you got a windfall. Tough to gin up support." He knew the demands of the Chinese had begun to grate upon many in the Restored United States, which supplied much of the resources and technology going to the "needy" countries.

"If the delegates do not believe in social justice, then we must seek other ways to, er, persuade them," Guang Xhi said. "You must gather personal information on the delegates, facts they do not want made public. Your operatives are very good at that, even in my country." His smile was thin and mechanical.

"My operatives?" *Uh-oh, what does he know?* Ramsey allowed a puzzled expression to creep onto his face.

"Do not act so surprised, my friend. I know all about your servant, Monahan, and his information gathering operatives, especially Shao-Li Peng, who will be our 'guest' for some time to come." Guang Xhi slid a sheet of paper across the desk. "You wish I should bring this before the Human Confederation Assembly?"

Ramsey glanced at the list of names on the sheet. It was an incomplete list of Monahan's agents in China. *Damn*, he thought. *How did he sniff them out?* "Well, these names sound like they might be American ..."

"You will get to know them better. They are on their way back to this country," Guang Xhi said. "You have no need to spy on the Chinese Democratic Peoples Republic. If you wish to know something, ask me. I will tell you all you need to know." He smiled thinly. "You will gather information for me on the HC delegates so we may persuade them to see the wisdom of allocating additional resources to those nations which have the greatest needs."

"Why would I do that?"

"Must I spell it out, my friend? I discovered a major spy network and will say nothing about it. If I keep quiet, you keep your job and help me pass legislation my country desires." Guang Xhi steepled his fingers. "We can fund our needs by reducing the amount of resources sent into outer space."

"Reduce it?" Ramsey felt sweat trickle down his back. "I don't think so. You, you've got to give the Space Force its fair share of the budget—"

"No. It is a waste, and a blatant example of warmongering. It also puts dangerous weapons over our heads—"

"Can't," Ramsey said. "Some slow down, maybe. But a major reduction, no, we need space defenses against the aliens."

"A return of the aliens, such a fantasy." Guang Xhi sighed. "We shall see. In the meantime, put your operatives to work here. It is known many delegates enjoy the pleasures of the flesh, and drugs, perhaps to excess. Get that evidence, unless you wish to answer questions in the Assembly about your spying."

His smile was without warmth. "In addition, continue to gather information on MacPherson. He is a dangerous reactionary and must be removed." He glanced at his jeweled wristwatch. "Now, if you will excuse me...."

こ

Ed Kerr watched the shuttle carefully inch closer to the DS-2's docking collar.

The gigantic, tubular station had three partially completed Fast Eagles, awkward and ungainly, hanging onto its midsection like puppies feeding. Near the drive end of the defense station was a long, rectangular structure that had a round section at the far end. It resembled a two by four stuck into a tire, except the long box-like section had shadowy openings at regular intervals.

So, that's what I'll use to build DS-3? He thought. It was the docking port that was capable of holding two hundred soloships —the one-person work ships that would be used in DS-3's construction.

Ed felt a tinge of nausea; it was his first time in zero gravity. He still didn't completely understand why Taylor MacPherson wanted him to become the commander of the next defense station, DS-3. He carried a letter for Ki Mapes from Taylor, something too confidential to be trusted to radio transmission.

It felt strange to step out of the elevator onto the rotating section of DS-2's living quarters and experience gravity. "Thanks," Ed said when the technician caught his elbow.

"You'll get used to it," said the technician, a young woman clad in a shapeless tan jump suit. "We all go through it. Ah, we're here. This is Commander Mapes's office."

~

"So, let me get this right," Ed said. "Defense Station Three will be much more than just a defense station?"

Ki Mapes leaned back in his chair and smiled.

His windowless office was cramped, with photos of family and fellow officers on the walls. His desk, gray and battered, was covered with file folders. The air smelled like machinery and too many people.

"It is becoming increasingly clear we must become more self-reliant. The political atmosphere in the Human Confederation is deteriorating. It's focused on providing for the masses and the idea of using Qu'uda technology solely as means to a better life, even if it means short-changing defense. That may well be. However, Earth's security is my responsibility, even if I've got to take matters into my own hands." He smiled. "Fortunately, I have the support of some very important people."

"Like Taylor MacPherson?"

"And others. However, it will be your job to build DS-3, not only as a carrier for Eagles, but also as a manufacturing center." Ki rose and uncovered an easel with a large pad of paper. "This is a preliminary outline of the DS-3."

Ed whistled. "It's more like a city in space. I had no idea it would be so large." He stepped closer to the drawing that showed layer after layer of living space. Some was for crews' quarters, but much was dedicated to manufacturing. DS-3 would be based on an M-type or metallic asteroid about one-quarter kilometer in diameter. A footnote on the drawing stated the excavated metal would be used to construct external facilities.

"So," Ed asked. "When d'we move this into position?"

Ki nodded. "We started the operation about six months ago. We installed three thrusters to remove its rotation and get it oriented properly. Three months ago, we anchored a large fusion drive on the end of the asteroid and it has been running since then to move it into the right orbit."

"How long will that take?"

"Not sure exactly," said Ki. "Depends upon what you do to it in the meantime." He smiled. "May take another nine months."

"Er, what will I be doing?" Ed's eyebrows rose.

"There's a lot of excavation needed plus installation of external facilities." Ki touched the controls of the computer on his desk and pointed to the monitor. "That'll be your living quarters until the internal areas are completed." Pictured was the long boxy structure with the tire-like section he'd seen upon his arrival at DS-2. "It still needs more soloships before it's taken to DS-3."

"What're soloships?" Ed frowned.

"Well," Ki waved toward a seat. "A soloship is sort of a cross between a spaceship and a space suit. Basically, it's a miniature one-person spacecraft analogous to a workboat that functions in hard vacuum and zero gravity.

"Think of a box about three meters tall, both sides measure one and one-half meters, that's made from asteroid metal (iron-nickel) about ten centimeters thick, with micro-foamed rock insulation layer. The thick walls provide protection from solar flares and cosmic radiation. It also has an airtight inner metal lining that holds ten pounds pressure.

"The soloship's upper section has observation ports on three sides so the pilot or operator can see out. Naturally, the soloship has computers, instruments, power generation equipment, internal life support, etc. The bottom of the soloship fits to the ports or airlocks on the docking facility." Ki pointed to the long box-like structure. "The soloship's door cannot open unless it's mated to a pressurized airlock."

"We have completed about thirty soloships," Ki said. "During your training period, we should finish up another ten soloships, plus other equipment you need to get started."

Ed glanced down the inventory of equipment. "Where did all this stuff come from?" he asked.

Ki sighed. "When we sent the asteroid metal to the Chinese, we had to make unpowered re-entry bodies so the metal could land safely in China's western desert. Then we found the Chinese were still trying to cut off our funding." He smiled thinly and took a deep breath. "Well, as payback, we divert re-entry bodies every now and then to Nevada, to friends of ours. They use the platinum to buy equipment for us." A trace of a smile crept onto his face. "Off the books, so to speak."

"What else do I need to know?" Ed asked. "Or should I say, what else will I need to do?"

"We've started to move a CI class asteroid close to DS-3."

Ed had a blank look on his face. "A what?"

"Sorry," said Ki. "Ivuna class carbonaceous asteroid." He paused. "That's an asteroid which is a mix of rock, metal, ice, and organic compounds. It'll be your source of water, atmosphere and organics, which is a very important part of making DS-3 a stand-alone manufacturing center."

$$\mathrm{\wr}$$

The room was filled with equipment that blinked, clicked, and had lots of dangling leads. It smelled faintly of antiseptic and bleach. Overhead, an excess of fluorescent lights glared brightly off the white sheet on the examination table.

"Chris," said Meltem. "There's no easy way to say this. You've got tumors in both breasts, in your lymph nodes, and elsewhere. You've got extensive cancers in advanced stages of development."

Chris Kucinski, pale and thin, closed her eyes. "This all happened in the last two weeks. I've been checking for lumps regularly. I first noticed them about ten days ago...."

Meltem ran her hand over Chris's brow. "I know how you feel. I've had cancer." She paused and looked at the wall with a distant stare. She raised her hand to her chin. "Maybe," she said. "Just maybe." She hurried to the door. "I'll be back in a minute."

Meltem returned with a stack of petri dishes and handful of scalpels. "I've got to gather skin samples from you," she said. "I must see if I can cultivate some stem cells."

"Why?" Chris asked.

"If I can get a stem cell culture started, there's a chance I can arrest your cancer. But time is of the essence. Your cancer is advanced, and growing stem cells takes time. Time is one thing you don't have."

CHAPTER NINE

A TIME OF STRESS

"I've got you on cancer growth suppresser chemo," Meltem Encirlik said. "It's to buy you time. I've started cultivating your stem cells, which I have to modify. That'll take time, too. I've got to keep you going until I get the stem cell DNA derivative prepared." Meltem had dark shadows under her eyes and her hair hung limply. "I'm going to do everything I can for you," she said. "I know how Taylor feels about you."

Chris Kucinski's eyes turned slowly toward Meltem. "You do?" she said in a voice that was both soft and faint, difficult to hear. "I don't even know how he feels about me."

Meltem reached out and caressed Chris's forehead. "It's like." She hesitated. "You're like a daughter to him, but the feeling goes even deeper. He told me how you hunted down the man who killed his wife, your mother, and how much he loved her, still loves her. And, he loves you in a way that's hard to describe. Yes, you're like a daughter, but you've done things that would make any father proud if done by his first-born son. You mean a lot to him, and because of what I've heard from Taylor, I love you also." Tears filled Meltem's eyes. "I wish I'd been closer to you when you were younger. You're such a good person."

Chris sighed and closed her eyes. "Yes," she said in a whisper. "I do love Taylor, too." She reached out and clasped Meltem's hand and pulled it to her lips. "I love you for making him happy and giving him a son. He's always wanted children. I'm glad you chose him to be the father of your child. It's such a wonderful gift." As her breathing deepened, her hand went limp.

Meltem looked at the monitors. Chris's basic body functions were weak but still acceptable. *It's going to be close*, she thought. She rose quietly and returned to the laboratory.

Ed Kerr reviewed the progress of the construction of DS-3 from over the past year and looking at the record, which took him back, there, again. When he'd arrived on DS-3, he'd seen a shuttle pilot maneuver the soloship dock into position at the tip of the type-M asteroid that was in the process of becoming DS-3. It was a delicate maneuver since the giant drive on the far end of the asteroid was still running at full thrust. He felt a gentle bump as the short, stubby section of the dock contacted the asteroid.

"Deploy drills," a voice called.

Ed remained silent. *They know what they're doing*, he thought. *No sense in saying anything*. He noticed a faint vibration and wondered if it were due to the oxy-hydrogen drills or from the asteroid's drive. The vibration ceased then started again. Must be the drills.

He scrolled through the images available on the monitor. The long rectangular docking section had dozens of tiny solo-ships protruding from it like boxy warts. Nearby, a shuttle hung motionless in the bright sun. It would retrieve the fusion drive motor attached to the soloship dock once it was anchored.

Two tiny wart-like objects detached from the soloship dock

and drifted toward the long end of the dock where the fusion drive was attached. More soloships floated away from the dock, toward the foil-wrapped bubbles attached around the ring-shaped living quarters, which held the mining machinery that would excavate solid metal from inside the asteroid to make their living and working space.

Once the technicians set up the mining machinery, it would run automatically, discharging lumps of metal cut from the asteroid according to a carefully laid out plan.

Ed scrolled through to the schedule. *It's amazing*, he thought, *how we can take asteroid metal, melt it using fusion power, send it to the centrifugal caster to extrude standard-sized flat stock and structural beams*. He liked how the automated equipment took the hot flat stock and sent it through the mini-rolling line to make sheet metal.

We even use the metal, an iron-nickel alloy that resembles stainless steel to make machinery so we can further exploit the asteroid's resources. Even though the equipment is small, he thought, *its continuous operation adds up over time to significant production.*

He remembered how the tiny, box-like soloships looked like ants trying to move an impossibly large object. A flash of sunlight glinting off the foil of a bundle caught his attention. It was being moved by a group of soloships toward the waist section of the asteroid. Two soloships moved from one end of the bundle to the other as they descended toward the surface, out of sight from the camera on the dock.

Ed switched to the camera in one of the soloships.

"Increase thrust," said a voice over the speaker. "Increase to plus three percent gee, match the asteroid's acceleration before set-down." The surface of the asteroid, dark and lumpy with many small boulders, grew larger in the screen.

"Applying vertical vector at one percent gee."

The surface of the asteroid came closer and then went black.

Ed switched to another camera. The bundle lay on the

surface of the asteroid, a small cloud of dust drifting out of view. "What's the status of the set-down?" he asked.

"Er, I think it's okay," said a voice. "We had a small difference in horizontal vectors at touchdown. It splashed into the regolith. We'll find out its condition when we unwrap it."

"Keep me posted," Ed said. *Nothing I can do about it*, he thought. *I hope that mining machine isn't damaged.*

It wasn't.

ᘯ

Ed Kerr was sick of his quarters in the soloship dock. Twelve months of being stuck behind a desk in front of a monitor sixteen hours a day, then eight hours in a bunk previously occupied by who-knows-who on the earlier shifts in a noisy metal coffin. And odors—unwashed bodies, stale food, bad breath and smelly toilets—he never got used to it. No, he wasn't just sick of the assignment; he was desperate to leave it.

It was too many people in too little space with marginal bathing facilities. It was worse than being a soldier in the field. At least on the ground, there was always a stream or a pond for a quick bath. Here, it was non-stop work, grouchy workers, smelly conditions, and monotonous food. The only solution was to work hard and finish the project.

Thankfully, he thought, *the first section of the asteroid living quarters will open soon.*

The mining machines had made two parallel circular galleries within the waist section of the asteroid. One of the mining machines completed excavating rooms at right angles to the two circular galleries. Soon, it would make more on the other side. Meanwhile, the other mining machine excavated another parallel, circular gallery.

Ed glanced at the monitor where a dark shape hung motionless above the surface of the asteroid. Tiny flashes of light showed where soloships were maneuvering around the CI asteroid that was rich in organics. They were cutting blocks of material for the extraction facility.

Whoever planned this operation, Ed thought, *knew what they were doing.* Originally he'd wondered why getting the extraction facility going was such a high priority.

The extraction facility was located on the surface near the main entrance to the interior of DS-3 and had accumulated piles of leftover material. The metallic fraction of the debris went to the melt facility to make construction metal. The rock fraction went to a smaller melt facility that produced foamed insulation panels.

Surveying and testing had confirmed the asteroid was solid and would withstand the rotational forces. Two months ago the maneuvering drive motors had been installed at the waist of the asteroid to impart spin to the station. Already, there was some internal gravity within the asteroid. Rotation also evened out the thermal stresses from the sun's radiation.

"Pete, come in, Pete," he spoke into his communicator, calling for the foreman in charge of internal facilities.

"Yes, Commander Kerr?" Pete spoke with the nasal twang of a native Australian. "Another problem?"

"Just an update on the living quarters' commissioning."

"Ah, let's see," Pete said, relief palpable in his voice. "We've just opened sections A through G. We've got the main entrance airlock and a temporary airlock in the main gallery at section M working. We've started to pressure up and check for leaks. There was a seal problem on the airlock at section M, but we've fixed that. So far, we've seen a three percent loss over four hours. We think that's mainly due to absorption."

"How's the plumbing in the extraction facility?" Ed referred to the water supply. Everyone wanted the bathhouse brought online; there'd even been a lottery for first dibs.

"We've, ah, got a small blockage. I think something's frozen," Pete said. "I've got a couple of blokes outside taking a look-see. As for the decontamination facility, it's ready to go." It was

Pete's private joke to refer to the bathhouse as a decontamination facility. "We've got heaters on full blast to get things warmed up. There was frost every bloody place when we let air in." The interior of the asteroid was still frigid. "We've got to get the main storage tanks warmed up before we dare introduce water."

"All right," Ed said. "Thanks for the report."

ᘔ

It had taken eleven months after starting work on DS-3 for the mining machines to complete the corridor through the core of the asteroid along its axis of rotation. It was through this corridor materials would be moved from the spaceships docked at the end of the space station. Axial shafts rose in a curving fashion from the central corridor to the galleries. Shafts left the central corridor at right angles, and by the time they reached gallery level, they were parallel to the surface. Not elevator shafts but true roadways.

Ed marveled at the engineering of the landing station on the "up" end of the central corridor. It was a tower about one hundred meters high, a spider web of welded iron-nickel structural members. At the top was a hundred-meter-wide flat platform with an elevator to lower ships after their arrival. The tower's attachment to the surface was a huge maglev bearing allowing it to remain stationary as DS-3 rotated. An air lock within the tower admitted people and material to the interior of DS-3.

The airlock had an angular momentum transfer turntable that passengers and cargo used to spin-up to match DS-3's rotation. Once up to speed, they were at the same rotational velocity as the interior of DS-3.

On the base of the landing station were three launching arms extending at right angles to DS-3's axis of rotation. Each arm was attached to DS-3's body and rotated with it. They were two hundred meters long and could be oriented in different directions to launch traffic to all points.

Each launching arm was brightly lit with strobe lights. They had radar, lidar, and radio detection systems feeding data to DS-3's traffic control computer. The hard vacuum side of the landing and launching operations was completely automated.

To launch a ship, it was placed on one of the three arms and the low-friction maglev cradle. Each arm's angle could be adjusted to point to almost any place in the solar system as DS-3 rotated. A computer controlled the launch sequence and the brake release on the maglev cradle, including the time of travel down the launch system arm. Thus the angular momentum of DS-3 gave the ship its initial (though low) velocity. The launch system, sometimes called the Flicker, got the ships far from the DS-3 so they could safely use their fusion drives at full power.

We still have much to do on the interior, Ed thought. *However, we've got a launch and retrieval system, plus we can manufacture about eighty percent of our needs. Still, I do miss the food of Earth,* he thought. *Especially steak.* His mouth watered at the thought of a tender piece of beef.

Panels of giant mirrors focused sunlight onto lenses that became the artificial suns in the station's hydroponics centers that raised crops. They were the first of many structures on the surface of the station that would grow food. Until there was enough capacity to support chickens and fish, the only food grown made the crew unwilling vegetarians.

Yes, he thought. *I've lost a lot of weight during the time I've been here.*

He touched a control on the monitor. The Fast "Eagles" appeared on the screen tethered to the base of the launch system. *Soon we'll have them ready, too,* he thought.

At the end of a long tether was the soloship dock, warty with docked soloships. Another partially completed soloship dock lay just beyond, larger and gleaming brightly in contrast with the rough-cut appearance of the original dock.

Soon, he thought. *We'll send that out on a mission to Mars's Moon, Deimos.*

ʔ

Meltem watched the instruments above Chris Kucinski's head. It had been twenty-four hours since she had given Chris the first dose of the SCG-DNA derived from her own cells. "Shouldn't be any immune rejection," she said.

However, the instruments indicated no change in condition: Chris was on the edge of death. Only oxygen and an occasional trickle of adrenaline kept her alive. "Please," she said. "Please hang on until it begins to defeat the cancer."

Meltem had already discovered something odd about the cancer. When she'd done a biopsy on a piece of tissue removed from a tumor, she'd found a strange chemical marker, something she'd never seen before. She wasn't sure what it was; however, it wasn't normal or natural.

I need to look into this further, she thought. *First, I've got to do more for Chris.*

Meltem measured out another dose of SCG-DNA and added it to a bottle of saline solution. Carefully, she hung the bottle above Chris and hooked up the transfer line to the needle taped into Chris's arm. She slowed the flow so it would take an hour to complete the transfer.

"Dear Chris," she said in a whisper. "This is the last of your stem cells. I pray to Allah this works."

She knelt on the floor by the bed and prayed every prayer she could remember. She closed her eyes and waited. And waited.

"Meltem," a hoarse voice whispered.

Meltem opened her eyes. Several hours had passed.

Chris licked her lips slowly. "I'm thirsty, so thirsty."

Meltem bit her lip to suppress her tears, but they came anyway. "Oh, Chris, I'm so glad you're ... I'll get you something to drink." She hurried to get water.

ↄ

"Yes, Taylor, she's awakened ... Yes, it's a good sign ... No, she was in a coma. I'm sure it's working. I have to get back to her. She asked for a drink and she managed to get it down and keep it down ... Yes, bye, I love you, too."

ↄ

"What?" Patrick Monahan said. "Kucinski recovered? Thanks for the info." He put down the phone. A deep frown creased his forehead. "That doesn't make any sense." He turned toward Ramsey. "I don't understand this at all. Everything I heard said she was on her way to meet her maker. Something isn't right."

Ramsey said nothing. The corners of his mouth turned down further and his frown deepened.

"I need to contact some people," Patrick said. "Maybe something was wrong with the, er, medicine."

"Just be damn careful about who knows what," Ramsey said.

The phone rang. Patrick picked it up. "What? Who're they? What're they doing...? Well, damn-well find out." He slammed the phone down.

"Aliens, goddamn fucking aliens. The Space Force just reported an alien ship came through that stupid anomaly out by Pluto." His face was pale.

"What're they doing?" Ramsey half rose from his chair.

"They don't know. The aliens just appeared. That's all the message contained."

CHAPTER TEN

THE SERVANTS

Son-Nih pushed aside the heavy curtain and entered Suh-Joh's command center.

The room resembled a cave in her hive on Hool and was the largest open space in the Mother's Servant. The floor coverings, replete with the crossed quill emblems of her hive, were soft underfoot.

"Gracious Hive-Mother," Son-Nih said and flexed low in submission.

"Come, my brave counselor, come sit next to me." Suh-Joh waved a forelimb to the thick floor covering adjacent to her resting mound, which was the place of honor in the room and was richly decorated with crossed quills with a border of the miniature entwined emblems. "You have news for me?"

Son-Nih settled into a comfortable but respectful position next to Suh-Joh and raised his head. "Only two of the scouts returned." He referred to the three stealth-class ships made from a carbon polymer that were sent to gather information on the activities of the Conclave of Hive-Mothers on Hool.

"One failed to make the rendezvous. We do not know what

happened to it." He hesitated. "The others bring news the manufacturing complex in the asteroid belt is constructing a fleet of ships, large ones. Many seem close to completion."

"For what purpose? Is it because they have discovered another world suitable for colonization?"

"No, gracious Hive-Mother, I think not," Son-Nih said. "A scout ship confirms the only ship capable of traveling through space-time is still on the Kamah run. They observed it make the jump as it left the system."

"How many ships are under construction?"

"The scouts report eight large ships along with many smaller craft." Son-Nih raised his mid-limb in a defensive posture. "Prudence prevented the scouts from getting close. It was after the other scout ship was sent to approach from the other side, it failed to return."

"How large are these ships?"

"At least as long as the Mother's Servant, however, they do not have the profile of heavy cargo carriers. If not for cargo, then I must conclude their only other purpose is for war." Son-Nih moved uneasily. "The transmissions intercepted from Hool indicate no serious discord among the hive."

"That worries me. I fear I've angered the priests at the Shrine of the Mother and they've mobilized the Hive-Mothers."

"That is my thinking, also."

"Can we shorten the schedule for our departure?" Suh-Joh asked. She referred to the repairs underway on the Mother's Servant for the past year. "Do we have enough fuel?"

Son-Nih flexed slightly; he'd expected this question. "Our engineers believe we can complete the critical elements of the structural repair in eight squared work-periods. Fuel is not a problem. There is a gas planet within range we can mine. We need more volatiles, which depends upon our scouts' ability to find those asteroids which contain water."

"Review the report of the Good Child. Perhaps the system containing the Water-Gem planet has the resources we need. In the meantime, send out the scouts. I pray to the Spirit of the Mother we may depart in time."

Bok-Tah rose off a resting mound. The cave, just off the vale of the Shrine of the Mother, had austere, bare rock walls and a dirt floor. "So you captured one of Suh-Joh's spies?"

Nah-Kih, Speaker for the Conclave of Hive-Mothers, flexed submissively, showing respect to the old priest. "Yes, honorable one. Our brave Chosen-Male warriors were testing a new craft, a small combat craft, when they detected drive emissions where none should have been. They continued on course, without power, and closed on a small vessel. It was unlike any they had seen before. Since their approach was from behind, they were able to get very close before their presence became known." She twittered with pleasure. "They used one of the new weapons to great effect and disabled the vessel's propulsion system. After that, they boarded the craft and found two warriors and several unripened ones from Suh-Joh's hive."

"Are they still alive?"

"The warriors fought to death, however, two of the unripened ones are still alive, just barely." Nah-Kih dropped her mid-limb in a gesture of surrender. "Our Chosen-Male warriors did the best they could under the circumstances."

"What did you learn?"

"After some ..." Nah-Kih hesitated. "Persuasion, we learned where Suh-Joh hides. Her ship is in the outer cometary belt, close to the place for a jump to the system of the Water-Gem world." She flexed slightly. "Undergoing major repairs."

"When will your ships be ready for action?"

"Ah, the hulls are complete and we have started on installation of the drives and armaments. The schedule calls for completion in about one year—"

"Did you find out Suh-Joh's travel plans?" demanded Bok-

Tah. The old priest's spines rose and his breathing flaps flared with the odor of anger.

"We got conflicting answers from the prisoners. One stated that it would take a half-year to complete the repairs and gather supplies for the ship. The other claimed the ship was about to depart momentarily. Unfortunately, this one resisted us and has since expired." Nah-Kih waved her mid-limbs as though swatting an immature dak-lih that swarmed harmlessly at the peak of the growing season.

"Which do you believe?"

"When we pressed the other for details of the repairs to the Mother's Servant, she said that there was structural damage that weakened the outer habitation ring. It sounds as though it is not fit to make the jump through space-time." Nah-Kih exhaled vigorously and her spines rose momentarily. "I wish our ships were ready, for now is the time to strike."

"What about the smaller craft? Are they up to the task?"

"Unfortunately, no. They do not carry weapons of sufficient range to grapple with the Mother's Servant. We have analyzed the weapon she used on our craft and learned that its range depends upon the power of the fusion drive used. With a large craft—"

"Yes, yes, I've heard this before." The old priest's breathing orifices flared. "If," he said, "if more resources became available, could you finish your ships sooner?"

"Of course." Nah-Kih raised his forelimbs in supplication. "Where would we get more resources? The Conclave has established a levy, and we're using every bit of it—"

"I will issue a writ in the name of the Spirit of the Mother to increase the levy by one-half. It is necessary. This is a holy war. Mobilize workers, finish the ships, and destroy the heretic Suh-Joh."

"All systems operational," came a voice from the pilot-navigator center. "Increasing power." The Mother's Servant with a fleet of smaller craft trailing behind, headed directly into the space-time anomaly at the outer edge of the Hool system.

Distantly, a faint sun glowed as the brightest star in the sky, dimly lighting the outer ring of the Mother's Servant as it touched the edge of the anomaly. The cubical framework of pale orange strings of the anomaly glowed and expanded to accept the Mother's Servant. The cube of energy stretched and flexed to accept the ship within its strange fabric of space-time. The energy framework grew larger and the strings of energy shimmered brightly, slowly resuming its perfect cubical shape.

Smaller craft followed closely behind the Mother's Servant like naat-jii scurrying after something good to eat, to enter within the cube.

"We are within the portal," came the pilot-navigator's voice. "Expecting the jump momentarily."

The glowing cubical structure collapsed with a kaleidoscopic flash of colors. All objects within shrank to tiny points of light and vanished from the Hool system.

Inside the Mother's Servant, it was a time of no time, a place of no space. All things material became immaterial and flowed as superluminal energy through the gravity string to the next node. Within, time was meaningless. It was as though all had taken a deep breath but could not breathe, as though time had come to a standstill. Computers stopped, power systems went offline and the ship became silent, seemingly lifeless.

Son-Nih hated the jump. It was like the ultimate surrender to forces unknown. It was like being born, without senses, physically weak, helpless, and out of control.

The Mother's Servant vibrated like a stringed musical instrument. From a single point of light, stars streaked toward them and became still. The cubical constraints of the energy strings glowed around them once more. For an instant, just an instant, as the Mother's Servant emerged from the boundaries of the anomaly, the cubical construct celebrated with one last kaleido-scopic flash of light.

The Mother's Servant basked dimly in the light of a distant star. For long moments the craft drifted aimlessly without power, seemingly dead. Within, mechanical systems, immune to the strange effects of the anomaly, began to reactivate the electronics and power systems of the ship. Alarms hooted and ventilation systems whooshed up to full flow. The air was filled with aromas of fear and voided bowels.

Son-Nih activated the scanner. *Good*, he thought. *It worked.* Nearby was a tiny, icy planet. *As it should be.*

In the distance, a bright star glowed with fierce brightness, far brighter and whiter than Hool's star. He recognized it from his previous visit.

We have arrived, he thought. A proximity alarm brayed and an object flared in the holographic display. There was a power source nearby. "What is it?" he asked.

"Aah," came the voice of the pilot-navigator. She was still in the throes of disorientation from the jump. "I don't know."

Son-Nih activated the controls and expanded the image. Within the display was an image of a strange two-hulled craft that slowly rotated. Icons in the holographic display indicated they were being painted with electromagnetic energy from the craft at levels too low to do any harm, he noted.

"Battle stations," he said and activated the ship-wide alarm. "Alien craft within one light second distance." It was far less than that; it was practically on top of them.

The Mother's Servant's status indicator flashed orange, showing power systems and defensive weapons were operational. Several showed signs of powering up for use.

"Do not, I repeat, do not fire upon the alien craft." Son-Nih's voice echoed through the ship. "Orient the Mother's Servant to face the alien craft." The front of the ship had powerful beam weapons and a thicker skin. "Wait for further orders." He felt his spines erect.

Son-Nih opened a private link to Suh-Joh. "I think this ship belongs to the natives of the Water-Gem world. It has the same configuration as the satellite we saw above that planet."

"Then greet them and tell them to lead us to our new home."

"It will be done, most gracious Hive-Mother." Son-Nih made the ritual flex of submission even though he was not in her presence.

This, he knew, was a job for the scholar, Lil-Tih, and Not-Joh, the pilot-navigator from the Good Child who had previously visited this system. They had already prepared for just such a set of circumstances.

Son-Nih activated the communications link. "Not-Joh and Lil-Tih, contact me immediately." He waited impatiently.

"This is Lil-Tih."

"There is an alien ship close by. It is similar to the satellite we saw above the Water-Gem world. Establish communications with them and report back what you learn."

"Yes, honorable counselor," two voices chorused.

Monitors and holographic displays crowded the ersatz cave that Suh-Joh used as her command center. The heavy brown curtains were drawn back from the entranceways to accommodate the heavier than usual traffic. It was a period of uncertainty.

Suh-Joh stared at the alien ship in the holographic display. It had ceased to rotate after the scholar and pilot-navigator found a common communication channel and hailed the ship. It wasn't long before it responded. It did not take long to realize the aliens could not speak their language and only sent meaningless phrases. Efforts to communicate bogged down.

"You see," said Son-Nih. "There is a device on the ship, here." He indicated the end of one of the cylinders. "It is oriented toward the Water-Gem world. I think it is some kind of optical transmission device."

"You think they are communicating our arrival?"

"That is the most reasonable explanation, gracious Hive-Mother." Son-Nih adjusted the image. "These objects," he pointed, "I believe are weapons." Two tubular devices pointed in their direction. He had seen them on the craft that had attacked the Good Child on the previous visit to the system.

"Are we in any danger?" Suh-Joh asked.

"I do not believe so. If they had wished us harm, they would have attacked when we first arrived, while we were recovering from the effects of the jump."

The scholar twittered to the pilot-navigator and bent closer to the communications module. "Yes," she said. "I understand." She turned toward the center of the room. "Most gracious Hive-Mother, the aliens responded to our request."

"What did they say?"

"I think it was 'your return is welcome, water.' Then some other words that sound familiar, but badly mispronounced—"

"Tell them to lead us to our new home," Suh-Joh said. "Surely that is not a complicated message."

"I will do my best, most gracious Hive-Mother." Lil-Tih abased deeply, almost to the floor, flexed to expose every piece of connective tissue between the bony plates of her back.

"Leave us," Suh-Joh said. "Return to the communications center. Provide them with food and drink and see they are not to be disturbed in their efforts." She made a lifting gesture toward Lil-Tih with a mid-limb. "Please," she said. "I know you'll do your best."

ᘓ

Within one work period, Lil-Tih and Not-Joh returned. "Most gracious Hive-Mother," they said.

"What have you learned?" said Suh-Joh.

"We have a message," Lil-Tih said. "They wish us to follow them to their home." She paused. "They do not know the word

'Water-Gem.' They have sent us many of their words, which we do not understand. However, we did establish a visual link." Lil-Tih flexed low. "They are not like us. They are different."

"How are they different?" Suh-Joh asked.

"They are ... deficient...." Lil-Tih flexed low.

"Show me," Suh-Joh said.

Wordlessly, Lil-Tih touched a control. In the holographic display grew a small rectangular image. Inside was a round-headed creature, without any plates or spines on its skin, all naked connective tissue and lacking mid-limbs. It had a loose covering over much of its body that looked like the skin of a sea creature. It had no breathing openings on its body.

"Hoo-lii," it said. "Welcome to ..." It was an unknown word. "Come to our home. Follow us ..." Its remaining words were like an ancient dialect that sounded like words but made no sense.

"We have recorded and reworked their other words," said Lil-Tih. "Their pronunciation is barbaric. So, we used a word synthesizer to create what we believe they are saying." She touched another control.

"Welcome to our world. Please follow us to our planet to your new home. We will depart soon."

"Are you sure this is what they said?" Son-Nih asked.

"We have listened to their message many times in many different forms. We believe this is what they said."

Son-Nih turned to Suh-Joh. "If this is true, then we have a new home."

"Perhaps," Suh-Joh said. "We cannot remain here, at the outer edge of this system forever by the portal. To do this, is to waste away. We need to get onto the surface of a planet to grow and multiply." She beckoned to Lil-Tih. "Tell them we will follow them, to the Water-Gem, to our new home. Tell them we have returned."

"Yes, oh most gracious Hive-Mother."

The alien craft slowly rotated away from the Mother's Servant, tiny low-temperature jets of gas providing thrust. The warriors on the Mother's Servant watched carefully, never far from the ship's heavy weapons. A flame flickered into life on the alien ship they quickly identified as a fusion drive.

"They, too, use controlled fusion for propulsion," Not-Joh said. As pilot-navigator, he understood such things.

The alien craft swung onto a course toward the center of the system. On the Mother's Servant, Son-Nih gave the orders and the ship's drive came to life. The huge ship turned in the same direction as the alien craft until it reached the alien ship's course. The alien craft's fusion flame grew brighter and increased acceleration. It soon became apparent the alien craft had greater acceleration than the Mother's Servant and steadily drew further and further away. Its drive winked out and it coasted.

The Mother's Servant caught up with the alien craft, which again began to accelerate. Except this time, it matched the rate of acceleration of the Mother's Servant.

"At this rate of change in velocity, assuming the same rate for deceleration, we should reach the Water-Gem world in about ninety sleep periods," Not-Joh said, looking up from the navigation console. "Please advise Son-Nih and our most gracious Hive-Mother of this fact."

༞

The Water-Gem world was big, and blue. *Truly a dazzling planet*, thought Son-Nih. *It is even more beautiful now than the first time I saw it.* He watched the alien craft that led them to this planet veer off and head toward a tiny asteroid. "Navigation, scan the asteroid where the alien ship went."

"Son-Nih," a voice called. "The asteroid shows significant amounts of radiation, both in electromagnetic and fusion power generation. I believe the asteroid body is a space station."

Is it possible? Son-Nih thought. *This space station is the asteroid-*

ship, the one that had belonged to the other Others? It was closer to the planet. "Give me visuals on that body."

The holographic display glowed into life to show a cylindrical body whose ends looked like it was an asteroid.

Yes, he thought. *It is the asteroid-ship. But it's different somehow.* He expanded the display. *Ah, it has openings along its body, and more ships, just like those that met us at the portal.* "Most gracious Hive-Mother," Son-Nih called.

"Yes, my brave counselor?"

"The aliens of the Water-Gem have much greater space capability than before," Son-Nih said. "They have the ship of the asteroid people, a truly large craft, and other ships like the one that greeted us."

"Are you sure?"

"Most gracious Hive-Mother, it is my business to be sure about such things."

"Ah, yes," Suh-Joh said. "Why do you think they have more capabilities?"

"Perhaps it is the result of the attack by the asteroid people." He hesitated as a message symbol appeared on the holographic display. He waved his forelimb to accept the message and simultaneously cut off his voice to Suh-Joh.

"There is another space station to the sunward side of the planet, even larger than the nearby space station. That makes a total of three space stations around this world," a voice said.

"On display."

A lumpy, elongated irregularly shaped object appeared. Angular structures hung off the object and the radiation spectrum readout showed significant power generation and emissions.

Son-Nih activated his communications. "Most gracious Hive-Mother, we must be very careful. This planet is ringed with space stations, whose capabilities we do not yet understand."

CHAPTER ELEVEN

NEGOTIATIONS

"Sweet Jesus," Ki Mapes whispered as the image of the Hoo-Lii ship grew on the large monitor on the wall of the command center.

It was the first time they'd received visual images at Defense Station 2, the former Little-Egg-that-Flies or LETF. The grainy images transmitted from the Fast Eagle escorting the Hoo-Lii ship to Earth did not have the detail the charge-coupled optical telescope provided.

"It almost looks like a tire on an axle, 'cept it's got a basketball on the other end of the stalk," Ki said. The command center was a long, metal-walled room crowded with electronic equipment, with rows of monitors above the counters that ringed the room. He sat down at his desk, which had three monitors and two phone-style handsets.

"Er, Commander Mapes." It was the tinny-sounding voice of Bud Inez from the speaker. He was on the Fast Eagle heading toward DS-2. "It's damn big."

Ki looked at the scale indicator on the bottom of the image and whistled. "I see what you mean." The long central axis of the ship was about one kilometer in length, while the structure looking like a tire was almost a half kilometer in diameter; except everything was metal, not rubber. He noted the ship slowly rotated. "It's a big one, all right."

"Is Ulrich patched in?" Bud asked. "We need a translator."

"We can patch him through anytime." Ki turned to a communication's officer. "Are we ready to go with the link to Ulrich?" Ulrich was a linguist at the University of Nevada who'd worked on translating the Hoo-Lii language during their previous visit.

The communication's officer nodded. "Yes, sir."

Ki picked up a handset and spoke, "Ulrich, it's time to do your thing. Just make sure to keep us posted." He put down the handset and turned to watch the large screen monitor.

ॐ

In a matter of hours, the huge alien ship took up a high orbit around Earth. Several smaller ships separated from it and took up positions fore and aft.

For several hours, Ulrich had nothing to report. Then he said, "I believe the aliens are peaceful and want to establish some kind of direct contact."

His words touched off a storm of communications between the defense stations and Earth.

ॐ

It was almost a day later when Ki received a coded message. "So, we're to send representatives?" Ki spoke into the handset and then listened attentively. "To visit the aliens? Okay, when will these two people arrive?" He listened for a while. "Got it. I'll make sure our communications people set up a secure link to stay in touch with folks in Columbus." Ki frowned.

That meant the politicians would control this contact.

Somehow that didn't make him comfortable. He hoped they'd include a military officer. Maybe he could arrange that.

꒱

The ancient space shuttle, now fitted with fusion drive, its white sides streaked with re-entry burns, hung motionless relative to the end of the long central column of the gray metallic alien craft. The smaller alien craft guarding the mother ship were still much larger than the shuttle. Two of the alien craft followed the shuttle closely, shining lights on a portal at the end of the large ship's central axis. A small device pulled a line from the portal toward the shuttle, while the giant ship continued to slowly rotate before them.

Two humans, bulbous in their starkly white space suits against the velvet black of outer space drifted from the shuttle toward the large alien craft. They clung to the line that extended stiffly from the opening. The arrangements to make their transfer to the ship had been done through the use of diagrams and drawings held up for inspection. It had taken two days to finalize the details. During this time the mathematicians and scientists established a common ground. From this they were able to determine the aliens were oxygen breathers.

Ulrich felt dizzy. His heart pounded and he was short of breath. He'd never been in space before. He desperately wanted to get his feet on solid ground. Outer space was like being over a bottomless canyon and falling forever.

Why, he wondered, *did I ever agree to do this?* He was accompanied by an electronics technician who maintained the voice synthesis equipment and carried a miniature TV camera.

"Mr. Ulrich," came a voice in his ear. "You're doing fine. Take a deep breath and concentrate on pulling yourself along that line." It was the electronics technician.

Gawd, Ulrich thought. *It was so easy to say and so difficult to do.*

He pulled and the line rippled slightly. He pulled again to no resistance. He felt another surge of panic until he realized the line was sliding through the safety ring without effort as they approached the hexagonal column that formed the central axis of the Hoo-Lii ship.

Ulrich could see along the central column to where three spokes radiated out to a gigantic ring structure. From his vantage point, the ring appeared to be at least fifty feet thick and three hundred feet wide. As he got closer, its true size became apparent.

"My word," he said, gasping. "It's mammoth." The opening at the end of hexagonal column drew closer and closer.

The aperture, which looked like a bare metal box, glowed orange. Inside, a yellow light began to flash steadily on the center of what looked like a side door.

"Mr. Ulrich," came the voice of the tech behind him who was carrying the electronics and other supplies. "Heads up."

"What d'you mean?" Ulrich had passed the point of politeness; he was on the ragged edge.

"Get your feet out in front of you. We're about to land."

Land? Ulrich realized the opening was very close, but he was heading into it on sideways. "I dunno if I can turn—"

"Grab the line and swing your feet toward it," the technician said quickly.

Ulrich followed the directions blindly without understanding what he was doing. The opening appeared to move back to beneath his feet. The opening swallowed him and he was surprised by the gentleness of the landing. Seconds later, the tech landed on top of him and sent him sprawling.

"Sorry about that," came the tech's voice. "Y'all right, Mr. Ulrich?" There was a touch of the South in his accent.

Shortness of breath slowed Ulrich's answer. He had no sharp pains, no feeling of shock, just the nausea of zero gravity. He felt a vibration. He rolled and looked up.

The door to the outside had closed. A red light came on. Nothing seemed to happen for several moments.

Ulrich had never felt claustrophobic before, but he did now. He bit his lip to maintain control. If it hadn't been for the voice in his ear counseling patience, he might have screamed. He became aware of other sounds and his space suit no longer bulged. He felt too miserable to figure it out.

"Hey, Mr. Ulrich," came the tech's voice. "We've got air." It was the tech's responsibility to monitor the instruments that would tell them whether it was safe to remove their helmets. He didn't know who the tech was or what he did. He just knew the tech was one of the most physically fit people he'd ever met. And the tech treated him with kid gloves. Probably military.

Another light flashed amber and the inside door shuddered and moved slightly. There was a momentary hiss and the door swung open.

"Oh, my gawd," Ulrich said.

Framed in the doorway was an apparition: It was a four-foot tall creature with some resemblance to both an armadillo and a porcupine—except it was neither. It had six limbs, a head much larger in proportion to that of an armadillo, and it had no nostrils. Large spines protruded in a sparse pattern over a body covered with a brown plate-like hide separated by yellowish skin. It stood erect and stared at him with tiny, beady eyes.

The creature beckoned and stepped back. Its movements were quick, like that of an insect, only it wasn't an insect.

Ulrich noticed it had a row of some kind of flaps along its body that moved continually; another difference from an armadillo.

"Well," Ulrich said. "Moment of truth." Before his heart had been pounding, now it raced. He wasn't sure if he could walk on his trembling knees.

The creature skittered away and came to an abrupt stop. Again, it made the beckoning gesture.

Gawd, he thought. *Not only do they sound like birds, but they also move quickly like small birds.*

"What's going on?" came the voice in his ear.

"We're inside and we've been greeted by a six-limbed crea-ture," Ulrich said, then he remembered that they already knew that, no, they could see it, too. "What do I do next?"

"The plan is you'll talk to them, right?"

The voice in his ear was almost like a nag. The carefully made plans came back in a rush. They seemed so stupid now he was here. He was inside an alien ship with a..., a Hooley-alien, a brown, prickly armadillo with yellow trim who wanted him to follow it.

Well, he thought. *I guess I don't have much choice. Dear God, I wish I did.* "Okay. I'm going to follow the alien."

Ulrich eased forward and found that it was difficult to move in zero gravity. He made slow progress, for the space suit made it difficult to walk.

They followed the bare metal-walled corridor for about one hundred yards until they reached an opening that contained a small room. The Hooley-alien quick-stepped inside and beckoned.

"Well," said Ulrich. "What's this?"

"So far, so good," said the tech. "Nothing hostile so far."

Ulrich stepped inside, followed by the tech. Up close to the alien, he saw that its spines were decorated; all had the same pattern of colored rings. *I wonder why.*

The door slid shut.

For a moment, nothing happened. Something clicked and Ulrich felt weight for the first time since arriving. *I'm falling,* he thought for an instant, then he realized it must be an elevator. "Er, I think we must be going to the outer ring."

The elevator clanked to a halt and there was solid ground underfoot. It was real gravity. Silently, he gave thanks. The door opened into a large room with orange lighting with brown curtains lining shiny metallic walls. In front of the opening were four Hooley-aliens about a dozen paces away. Two were smaller than their escort and they had almost no spines. There was another, very much like their escort except its hide was covered with marks that looked like scars. Behind him, stood the fourth alien who was bulky and almost six feet tall. Along the walls, at regular intervals, stood more aliens resembling the escort.

Okay, Ulrich thought. *They're escort-type aliens, maybe guards.*

"Tie me into the speech synthesizer," Ulrich said.

He had been the one to realize the Hooley-aliens speech was several octaves above what humans could easily achieve.

"Check," said the tech.

"Hoo-Lii," Ulrich said. The box twittered.

"Hoo-Lii," came a twittering chorus that sounded like a group of sparrows. The aliens bowed slightly.

Ulrich noticed the big alien did not bow. He also noticed something scurried across the floor, and another.

Gawd, he thought. *They've got cockroaches, too. And the Hooley don't seem to be bothered by them, either.*

A smaller alien in front inched forward and waved a limb.

So far, so good, nothing hostile in that, thought Ulrich. *Now comes the difficult part.* He gestured toward his helmet and put both hands up and made the motion of turning and lifting.

The two smaller Hooley-aliens twittered among themselves.

Ulrich removed his helmet. He silently prayed the tech was right about the air.

He took a breath. The air was filled with incredible animal, no, pungent aromas. He gasped. The room had a mixture of smells; animal, fermenting vegetation, and something sweet, almost rotten, and yes, fart. He gasped again.

"What's wrong?" demanded a voice in his ear.

"The smells," he said. "It smells like a zoo."

The Hooley-aliens made more bird-like twitters.

Ulrich spoke the phrase into his microphone he believed was the equivalent of giving his name. He pointed at himself.

The two smaller Hooley-aliens twittered again.

In his ear, Ulrich heard something that sounded familiar. The tech said in his ear, "What did they say?"

"They don't understand. I was afraid of that. Okay, back to

basics." He turned toward the tech and gestured he was going to open the box. When he heard a clicking, almost clattering sound, he glanced up.

A dozen of the escort Hooley-aliens had moved between them and the four in front of him, were crouching, spines erect.

Ulrich raised his hands slowly and stood still.

The large Hooley-alien twittered.

The escort Hooley-aliens skittered back a dozen feet.

Ulrich lowered his hands and turned toward the large Hooley-alien and bowed slightly. He heard several quiet twitters. From the box, he removed a bottle of water and a small cup. He poured some water into the cup and drank it. He held out the bottle of water toward the group before him, offering it to them.

"Water," he said slowly and distinctly.

One of the small Hooley-aliens came forward and took the bottle and with a twitter, handed it to an escort alien who hurried from the room.

After reporting what had happened, Ulrich said, "I'm beginning to overheat. The room's warm and the spacesuit isn't cooling me any longer. I've got to take off the suit."

The voice in his ear said, "I can't see how that'd cause a problem. We've got to start from the position they're not going to harm you or us."

Easy for you to say, Ulrich thought. *You ain't here*. He gestured the removal of his suit and waited a moment before starting.

There were more twitters, but no motion. It was silent for the ten minutes it took for him and the tech to remove their suits. He remembered it had taken an hour to put it on with help. It probably would take even more here.

He returned to the box and removed a pad of paper and a marking pen. *Now*, he thought. *Here's where it gets interesting*. He sketched a stick figure of a human; two arms and two legs, pointed and said, "Human." His box twittered.

One of the smaller Hooley-aliens came closer to examine the sketch. It twittered something.

"I got it," said the tech.

A sound played in Ulrich's ear. He repeated the sound and the box twittered. It was the same sound.

"I've assigned it to you saying the word 'human,'" said the tech, following earlier agreed upon instructions.

"Okay," Ulrich said. "We've got a lot more to do yet." He began sketching and collecting words.

After about a half an hour, the large Hooley-alien left, along with most of the escort-type Hooley-aliens. He found it was both tedious and exciting at the same time as he built a vocabulary for the voice translation system.

After several hours he stopped and took out a package of sandwiches and began to eat. He offered one to the small Hooley-alien who was working with him.

The alien took it and departed. It soon returned with a rectangular flat metal sheet with pale clumps of what looked like shrimp or fish flesh. The Hooley-alien ate from the platter and offered a portion to Ulrich with a twitter.

The voice translation system buzzed. "Food human yes."

He picked up a small piece and tasted. It was pungently spicy with a rich almost fatty texture and a trace of bitterness; it reminded him of Indian food from long ago.

"Good," he said.

The small Hooley-alien twittered and tore a piece from the sandwich and put it into the opening at the end of its muzzle and sucked it in. It twittered the same sound again.

"I think that's either food or good," Ulrich said. He was beginning to become more confident he would be able to communicate with the Hooley-alien. He realized he'd grown very tired.

It must be the strain, he thought. *I need to rest.*

Even after five days, Ulrich still noticed the smells. *By now, I*

probably smell as bad to them as they smell to me. He also had learned the name of the small Hoo-Lii; it was Lil-Tih and she was a scholar. Between the use of the voice translation system and his knowledge of languages, Ulrich had a start on basic communication with the Hoo-Lii.

He invited Lil-Tih to accompany him to Earth. When he made the offer, he found she could not make this decision. It was the large Hoo-Lii, whose name he learned was Suh-Joh, who had to listen carefully to the invitation. Her response was to point to Lil-Tih and several escort Hoo-Lii as those who would accompany him. That was also when he first learned a new Hoo-Lii word that was applied to all humans and most of the Hoo-Lii. It puzzled Ulrich; it had something to do with the Hoo-Lii social structure.

The shuttle returned, bearing items Ulrich had requested, among which were clean clothes. Other items were television monitors that received images from various locations on Earth. Scientists on Earth believed they would give the Hoo-Lii insight into human life and build trust.

They had no idea of its impact.

$$\sim$$

"I do not understand the new servants," Suh-Joh said. She moved slowly over her favorite red granite resting mound as though seeking a more comfortable position.

She gestured toward the box that conveyed images of human activities taking place between several large structures that appeared to be on the surface.

"They do not worship the Spirit of the Mother, nor, it seems, does any other religion guide their lives." She shifted her paat-kli to another location. The tiny crustacean clicked contentedly and resumed rasping dead flakes from the connective skin in an area Suh-Joh had an itch. "We will understand more about them when the scholar, Lil-Tih, visits the surface to learn more about our new servants. Then, perhaps, we will know how to best use them."

Her counselor, Son-Nih exhaled an aroma of frustration. "They do not appear to have discipline. I cannot see a distinction between their classes, nor respect for those who appear to be warriors."

"If we can trust these images, it appears ripened females mix freely, without the respect that is their due." Suh-Joh exhaled noisily. "They are like our Disobedient."

She referred to the great social rebellion led by Wod-Jur who had preached for the universal ripening of all females that would have displaced the Hive-Mothers from their role. That led to civil war and the exile of the Disobedient to the penal planet of Chud-Loo. It was the impact from the crash of the Others' spacecraft on the Disobedient's penal colony that had destroyed it. That had caused the Hoo-Lii to seek out the Others.

"You may be right. Perhaps we will learn different once on the surface," Son-Nih said. "I fear the new servants' heretical behavior may have infected the unripened ones—"

"How could that happen?"

"The images sent by the new servants have been viewed by all on the Mother's Servant," Son-Nih began.

"What? Did you not stop it?"

"By the time I realized the nature of the new servants' society, many had seen the images. News of a world of Disobedient spread like dust before a storm." Son-Nih flexed submissively. "It was impossible to keep it from the unripened ones. It may be the new servants are heretics."

"If that is so, then they may prove to be unworthy to serve us," Suh-Joh said. "Perhaps we have to live separately from them." She exhaled noisily.

"Yes, but we need a home on the surface," Son-Nih said. "Forgive me for speaking up, but we must find a home soon, a new hive. Food grows short, supplies are depleted, and there is a vast world below, ripe and ready for us."

"Are there places suitable for us?"

"Yes," Son-Nih said. "There are many areas like Hool. Areas where the land is dry and bare of excessive vegetation, yet still with enough water to cultivate surface crops. Yes, and many of these suitable areas are where none of the new servants live."

"Then we should act quickly to secure a new home on this planet," Suh-Joh said, rising. "Remember, the Coven of Hive-Mothers will eventually send a ship, and we must be ready for them. That means we need more Chosen-Male warriors and more weapons."

Son-Nih flexed low in submission. "Yes, most gracious Hive-Mother, at once."

CHAPTER TWELVE

A NEW HOME

Ki Mapes listened carefully as he stared at the radar display that glowed green with five white flecks. Five Hoo-Lii ships, one after another, departed from the Hoo-Lii mother ship and began a descent toward Earth.

The command center was warm and filled with people wearing the tan jumpsuits that were the uniform of the Space Force. Its air was filled with aromas of sweat and fear. Only a week had passed since the Hoo-Lii had sent a ship with an emissary to Columbus for three days of discussions.

"No, they're definitely not missiles," a voice said. "They're a part of the Hoo-Lii fleet."

"Where are they headed?" Ki said.

A tracking monitor flashed as its image changed. "Ah, it looks like they're on a re-entry course for, ah, about thirty-two or three degrees latitude north," the same voice said.

An image of the Earth appeared on the screen with five triangles moving slowly from west to east over the Pacific Ocean. "I'll project probable set-down areas based upon current rates of descent."

A dotted line extended from the leading triangle toward the United States and stopped over New Mexico. A dotted outline of a box appeared that ranged from Phoenix to Fort Worth. "That's their collective descent path."

"Are you sure?" Ki asked.

"As they get closer, our prediction will get better."

Ki rubbed his almost-bald head. "And when they land, you'll know for sure, right?" He picked up a phone handset. "Contact Columbus," he said. "Let them know that five of the fifteen ships that came with the Hoo-Lii mother ship are heading in. Transmit the data we've collected and hook them up for real-time data."

Ki felt frustrated.

Two Eagle class ships were preparing to depart from DS-3 to follow but they were at least an hour behind. And none of them could descend into the atmosphere to follow the Hoo-Lii craft. He also knew there were no bases or military aircraft within close range of the area projected for the Hoo-Lii touchdown zone. Even though the landing path did not suggest hostile intent, he felt very uneasy about this unannounced course of action by the Hoo-Lii.

What are they up to? he wondered. *Why that particular area?*

"The Hoo-Lii craft have tightened up their descent course," came a voice. "Projected touch down area will be in south-eastern New Mexico."

"Damn," somebody said. "They're heading for Roswell. It's a replay." The voice held a brief chuckle of nervous laughter.

"Er, your geography's a little off," came another voice. "They'll be south of that by about one hundred miles."

"What kind of assets do we have in that area?" Ki asked.

"We don't have anything in that area. It's empty country, kind of dry—"

A voice interrupted. "Yeah, it's a part of the Llano Estacado, high-country limestone plateau. I was stationed at Alamogordo for a while. While I was in that area I visited the Carlsbad Caverns, not many towns, just rangeland—"

"All right," Ki said. "That's enough. Deploy an Eagle into a geostationary above their touchdown location to observe." He paused a moment. "And put the other into a low Earth orbit that'll pass over the location on a regular basis to get high resolution imagery. Keep a sharp eye out for any other Hoo-Lii craft movements."

∂

Son-Nih flexed submissively before Suh-Joh. Her command center was quiet, the brown curtains once again covering the entrances. He settled on the floor covering, almost on top of the crossed quill emblem of the hive. "Most gracious Hive-Mother," he said. "The data interpretation proved correct. There is a large natural cave, quite suitable for a hive."

Suh-Joh's breathing orifices flared and emitted aromas of sweet satisfaction. "Large, you say? How large? Is there water nearby?"

"So large that its limits have not been found, and it has water. There is also a river, so we can raise surface crops."

Suh-Joh rose off her resting mound. "Good. Now, we must move equipment and material to build our new home." She paused. "Is there anything else?"

"Yes, most gracious Hive-Mother, the new servants." Son-Nih hesitated. "Lil-Tih reports they are demanding an explanation. They have sent urgent messages directly to the Mother's Servant. They want to know what we are doing—"

"The new servants question us?" Suh-Joh's breathing flaps flared and her spines rose.

"Yes, and they have positioned two of their craft above the planet to observe our new home—"

"They dare to threaten us?" Suh-Joh rose to her full height and emitted the bitter aroma of anger.

Son-Nih flexed low into the position of complete submission. "No, most gracious Hive-Mother, it does not appear so. Their craft have not taken up attack positions. I believe they want to know what we are doing—"

"Then tell them. It is time they learned this is our new home."

"As you wish," Son-Nih said. "I will instruct the scholar Lil-Tih to do that."

~

The Assembly chamber of the Human Confederation was packed. Voices echoed off its marble walls with a sustained rumble that had an angry edge. Carver Washington stood behind the Speaker's podium and pounded the gavel. "Order, please, order. Honorable delegates, please be seated." He rapped the gavel once more. Its crack amplified loud and clear above the hubbub. Slowly the voices quieted, replaced by the scraping sound of chairs moving on the polished stone floor.

"This emergency session has been called to deal with the latest actions of the Hoo-Lii," Carver said. "To bring you up to date, I have arranged a direct link with the Space Force defense stations. The Commander-in-Chief of the Space Force, Commander Ki Mapes will address this body to provide you with the latest information." He pointed to the large projection screen set up against the front wall. Around the chamber were other monitors linked to the same system.

Carver had chosen to go public with the briefing to build common support for whatever course of action the Human Confederation chose.

"Commander Mapes," Carver said. "Will you please provide the delegates to the Human Confederation with an update on what the Hoo-Lii are up to."

Ki Mapes's face swam into focus on the large screen. Bags

hung under his eyes and his uniform was no longer crisp. A sheen of sweat gleamed on his dark brown forehead.

"Honorable delegates," he said. "Seventy-two hours ago, five Hoo-Lii ships landed at Carlsbad, New Mexico. It appears they have taken possession of the caverns at that location. Forty-eight hours ago, three more ships landed and discharged a large number of aliens who disappeared into the cavern. Seven of the Hoo-Lii ships returned to the mother ship, apparently picked up equipment or supplies and returned to Carlsbad about six hours ago."

A murmur of voices swept through the hall.

"Order," Carver called, rapping the gavel.

"They carried many containers into the cavern." Ki paused. "You've already learned from the Hoo-Lii, Lil-Tih, they plan to establish a new home in the caverns. If our translator understands correctly, their normal dwelling is underground."

A rumble of voices erupted, with delegates rising to their feet, gesturing for the right to ask questions.

Carver hammered the gavel on the podium. "Order, please. There'll be time for questions later, when Commander Mapes has finished his presentation. As you have already learned, Lil-Tih is not empowered to negotiate on behalf of the Hoo-Lii—"

"This is an invasion," a voice called from the front row.

"Order," Carver bellowed and pounded his gavel again. "Let Commander Mapes finish."

The noise subsided, prodded by repeated raps of the gavel.

"Honorable delegates, it appears the Hoo-Lii decided to occupy land they observed was not in use. At least, that is what our translator believes the Hoo-Lii, Lil-Tih, said. Remember, it is very hard to understand an alien. Not only is their language unlike any on Earth, but their culture is totally different.

"I've forwarded a complete record of the communication to the Assembly and it is available for your review." Ki paused and ran a hand over his forehead. "In the translator's opinion, the Hoo-Lii have a desperate need to set up some kind of facility on a planetary surface. He believes they may be either starving or running out of critical materials. The Hoo-Lii state in clear terms they expect us to understand their need—"

A wave of voices swept the chamber.

Carver repeatedly rapped the gavel until quiet returned.

"I have been informed," Ki said. "The H-C ground forces are now in the Carlsbad area. They observed the Hoo-Lii plowing and tilling land around the clock alongside a small creek that drains into the Pecos River. They have seen our forces. Neither the Hoo-Lii nor H-C Forces have taken any hostile action. The Hoo-Lii activity does not appear to be a military one—"

A vista of distant mountains swept onto the screen. The focus changed to rolling hills covered with gray-green sagebrush. "This is the Carlsbad area," a voice said. The image moved to a line of low, beige-colored jumbled cliffs, which appeared to move rapidly closer. "This is a part of the Guadalupe Mountains where the Carlsbad Caverns are located."

The focus moved to a shallow valley of sagebrush that wandered out of a canyon in a rocky cliff. In the flat section of the valley bottom, three red boxes slowly moved over a dark brown strip of freshly turned earth.

"These machines, manned by Hoo-Lii, have been plowing, tilling, and grading this ground. Since there are no compaction activities, we do not believe this is for construction purposes. Since this activity is confined to the area along the side of the creek—and does not form a perimeter around the entrance to the caverns—we have to eliminate it being a construction or defensive activity. That leaves agriculture."

The presentation continued for another hour, repeating much of what had previously been shown. Little by little, delegates began to slip out of the assembly hall.

Carver sensed it was time to stop. "If there are no objections, this emergency session will adjourn for lunch. When we return from this break, the Assembly will entertain comments from delegates in the normal order of business." Carver intended to use his parliamentary rules to maintain control of what was said.

ᘐ

Lil-Tih stared at the group of humans. They smelled odd; a chaotic mixture of emotions mixed with plant and animal odors. Their ability to communicate with words was quite good; however, the emotional content of their communication aromas was missing. It was difficult.

"Lil-Tih," the communications box squawked. "Why Hoo-Lii to Water-Gem world come?" It was the same question that had been asked many times.

The room was severely rectangular and illuminated to a level that almost hurt her eyes. The humans sat on strange rectangular constructs and leaned onto a flat erect platform. They all wore body coverings of different kinds. And, most disturbing, there were both male and female humans present. The females' aromas clearly indicated they were fertile. Without question, these new servants were Disobedient.

"We came because you invited us, you offered water and we accepted you as our new servants." *Why*, Lil-Tih thought. *Do they not understand?* She felt uncomfortable standing continually on her hind limbs; she longed to stretch over a resting mound. "We came to establish a new hive, here on this world where you offered to serve us." She felt even more uncomfortable speaking the only answer that Suh-Joh would approve. It was obvious to her that the humans would never be servants; they were Disobedient.

The humans crowded around the box that spoke both their languages. The human with the small growth of spines below his eating mouth, the one who had come to the Mother's Servant and had first communicated with them had the name Ul-Rik. He was at the center of the group and spoke into the box. "Lil-Tih," came from the box. "What are servants?"

"I am servant to Suh-Joh," she said. "You are servant to Suh-Joh, all of you." She hesitated. "A servant is one who does what Suh-Joh wishes."

She was acutely aware of the Chosen-Male warrior who listened carefully to her replies. She knew if she said anything that even hinted of disloyalty to Suh-Joh, she would die quickly, no matter where she was or who was present. From the little she had seen of the humans on this planet, she knew there were no Hive-Mothers and all humans could breed. She felt a raging jealousy. She wanted to become a Mother.

The humans communicated in their deep, slow tones, continually interrupting each other.

Lil-Tih watched carefully. She knew the Chosen-Male warriors were uneasy in the presence of such undisciplined behavior; she could smell their anxiety. But they were disciplined; they had their orders, she knew that. She noticed the humans had grown quiet.

"Lil-Tih, it is food time," Ul-Rik said. "Come." He beckoned toward the opening in the room. It would be the last meeting with the humans before returning to the Mother's Servant.

Their eating practices no longer surprised Lil-Tih. They ate with the ceremony of a Hive-Mother, something she had never observed until she came to the surface of this planet. She liked the way they ate; in fact, there were a lot of things that she liked about the human culture.

ৎ

"Most gracious Hive-Mother." Son-Nih slid to a halt before Suh-Joh and flexed into a position of absolute submission. "A group of the unripened ones have become Disobedient." The ersatz cave Suh-Joh used as the command center was empty except for a half-dozen Chosen-Male warriors.

"Then kill them," Suh-Joh said without hesitation.

"Most gracious Hive-Mother," Son-Nih said, flexing again.

"They took a ship, the Good Child, and fled. Among them are two scholar-apprentices of Lil-Tih."

Suh-Joh rose to her full height off her resting mound. "Those of Lil-Tih?" A mid-limb rose in a defensive position. "She and her scholars know the most about translating the human language."

"Forgive me, most gracious Hive-Mother, but there are also several engineers who left, too."

"Which means?"

"They have complete knowledge of the Mother's Servant. Its weapons, its structure, all our strengths and weaknesses."

"What about the Chosen-Male warriors guarding Lil-Tih?"

Son-Nih flexed low again. "They became unstable when they returned. They advocated killing all the humans because their species is Disobedient. Fellow Chosen-Male warriors questioned them about their experience and when their veracity was questioned, they went berserk. Naturally, they were killed—"

"And Lil-Tih's apprentices?"

"Apparently, in the confusion, they joined a group of unripened ones who went Disobedient and took the Good Child and departed—"

"Which can jump through space-time." Suh-Joh slowly slid back onto her resting mound. "Is there more?" she asked.

"Yes, most gracious Hive-Mother. Another group of Disobedient, engineers and technicians, fled shortly after in one of the shuttlecraft."

૨

The two Fast Eagles hung motionless one kilometer from DS-2. Both craft faced the two Hoo-Lii craft floating in front of a dock that was open to space. Their Qu'uda technology beam weapons were aimed at the Hoo-Lii craft. Both craft had made powered approaches, using their engines to bring them to a halt. The defenses of DS-2 were also focused upon the two craft.

One of the craft was large, a stubby cylinder about three hundred feet in diameter and about one hundred feet long with a dome-shaped end. At the other end of the cylinder were a half-dozen large spheres. Extending from between the spheres was a stalk about three hundred feet long with a cluster of pods at the far end, glittering like a jewel in the sunlight. Clinging to the side of the stubby cylinder were two bug-like structures, each about fifty feet long. The other was very much like the stubby shuttle-craft that had made previous descents to Earth.

Ulrich had been wakened from a sound sleep and now waited to be patched through to the two alien craft. He had mixed feelings, for he had been informed there were Hoo-Lii scholars in one of the two craft. They had asked for him, which had been no small task considering their vocal equipment was ill-suited to human speech. He'd also been informed the Hoo-Lii on the mother ship were very agitated about the arrival of the two ships at DS-2.

"Ulrich?" said a voice that he belatedly recognized as that belonging to Ki Mapes. "You ready to talk to these guys?"

"Yes. What's going on?" Even with coffee, there were still cobwebs in his head.

"These two Hoo-Lii ships made a hot transit to us," Ki said. "They almost got shot down. Fortunately, they broadcast your name almost continuously, which bought them some time."

"Why?"

"Dunno. We've heard a lot of Hoo-Lii broadcasts over the last hour or so." Ki paused. "One of these ships is the spitting image of the Hoo-Lii ship that first visited us a while back. In fact, I'm almost positive it's the same one. Anyway, are you ready? I'll hook you up to your Hoo-Lii buddy."

"Thanks," Ulrich said dryly and activated the translation equipment. *I've got to get more of these made,* he thought. "Hoo-Lii," he said.

Something twittered. "Greetings, Ul-Rik," the translation equipment said. "We seek to join you."

"Who speaks to me?" Ulrich asked, speaking into a microphone. The box twittered loudly.

"Yes, I am Buk-Kih, scholar-apprentice of Lil-Tih."

Yes, Ulrich thought. *I think I've heard her name before.* "Why are you here?" He'd learned from Ki Mapes that Suh-Joh wanted the occupants of these ships returned and had stated ships would come to retrieve them.

Ki had sent the message from the Human Confederation that no Hoo-Lii ships were to approach any orbital defense station. If they did, the humans would strike them.

"We have become like you," the box spoke. "We have become those who do not follow the Mother." The box made an unintelligible sound that signified a sound or word not in its vocabulary. "We go out from mother ship."

"Did Suh-Joh send you?" Ulrich said through the translation system. He knew she did nothing without Suh-Joh's approval. The Hoo-Lii twittered briefly, paused, and twittered again. "No." After a pause she said, "We want to live here. Like humans. No want to live with Suh-Joh."

Ulrich lifted up the phone that gave direct communication with Ki Mapes. "I think there's been a split in the Hoo-Lii ranks," he said. "I think we've got a defection." He paused. "This ship is one that can jump through space-time."

For a moment, he thought of history and Trojan horses. *No*, he thought. *These two ships aren't enough to make up an invasion fleet.* "It was the first vessel to visit."

Ki's voice squawked. "Have them enter the dock so we can inspect their ship."

Ulrich lifted the microphone of the translation system. "Buk-Kih," he said. "Come, come in here, into the ship." Unconsciously, he beckoned. "You can live with humans."

CHAPTER THIRTEEN

THE ARRIVAL

Ki Mapes felt queasy. He always felt this way in zero gravity, but that was the price he had to pay to get a direct look at the Hoo-Lii craft nestled in the Number One Dock of Defense Station Two. He stared at the craft that completely filled the width of the dock, gleaming under bright floodlights. It would take another fifteen minutes to bring the dock up to atmospheric pressure. The ship left little space within a dock that Ki previously thought of as spacious.

Ki's portable handset buzzed; it was tied into the ship's communication system. "Yeah?" he said. "Hey, Taylor, we've got a, er, situation here."

He explained the arrival of the Hoo-Lii who had apparently defected from the mother ship. "And we believe this ship is the one that made the jump through space-time." He paused, listening carefully.

"Right. 'Cept I don't have any real scientists on board ... right. You have someone?" Ki reached into the pocket of his tan jumpsuit and pulled out a small, blue covered notepad and a pencil. "Van Minh?" he said. "Okay, and who? Yata-what? You'd better spell that out for me." He copied down the name. "Why him? Oh, that's the one who stayed behind because he wanted to learn more about our sciences, right?"

Ki glanced up through the thick quartz viewing port into dock number one. "It looks like they're coming out." He paused. "The, er, Good Child, that's what they call it."

Four tan-clad Space Force officers clustered around an opening in the middle of the cylindrical section of the Hoo-Lii craft. One officer carried a video camera. Two Hoo-Lii emerged from the door and floated to the center of the group of officers.

The handset squawked, "Hoo-Lii." It was the audio portion from the video camera. "Quiet, let Ulrich be heard." The jumble of voices went silent.

Ki heard twittering sounds over the handset.

The Hoo-Lii twittered back.

"I've told them to go with you," came Ulrich's voice. "So they can see my image on a monitor inside."

Ki watched the humans and Hoo-Lii drift in zero-gee along a line toward him. They headed for the main axial corridor, which would take them to the rotating section of the defense station that provided gravity for its crew.

Well, he thought, *it's time to do the diplomat thing.*

The door opened and the group entered.

"Commander Mapes," an officer said. "This is Buk-Kih. She used to assist the scholar, Lil-Tih."

"How d'you do?" Ki nodded toward the yellow trimmed, brown creature that reminded him of an armadillo.

The creature bent, almost bowed, in his direction and twittered something that sounded like "Hoo-Lii."

"This way." Ki pointed along the cable and conduit lined corridor. He grasped a pipe on the side of the corridor and launched himself forward. He really hated the feeling. His body knew it was falling to its death even though his mind knew otherwise.

It seemed to take forever to reach the slowly rotating

momentum transfer table leading to the elevators that would take him back to the world of gravity. A world where he wasn't nauseous.

The huge elevator, designed for both freight and people, easily accommodated the dozen bodies of the now-silent party. The doors closed and as the elevator descended to the outer rim of the rotating section, the gravity steadily increased. It stopped and the doors opened. Ki led the way toward the command center, which also held the communications center.

Along the way, Ki noted the crew with sidearms were at most of the corridor junctions.

Good, he thought. *Even if this Hoo-Lii is a defector, we can't afford to be stupid.* He didn't look back.

The command center was crowded. Every crewmember that could think of an excuse to be on duty in the command center was there.

Ki surveyed the scene quickly. "Basic crew on the deck," he said. "All non-essential personnel are excused."

Silently, the rest filed out.

Ki turned toward the officer in charge of communications. "Get the link to Ulrich transferred onto the main monitor."

"Yes, sir."

Ulrich's face appeared on the large flat screen monitor at the bulkhead in front of the commander's station. "Ah," Ulrich said. "We're back in touch." The speaker began to twitter.

The Hoo-Lii defector twittered on for a long time.

"What's going on?" Lines between Ki's eyes deepened.

"Buk-Kih is explaining why she left the Mother's Servant."

"Mother's Servant? What's that?" Ki asked.

"It's the name of the large Hoo-Lii ship, the one we've been calling the mother ship," Ulrich said. He reached for his pipe and leaned back as though preparing for a lecture.

"Ask her if their ship can jump through space-time."

Ulrich's eyebrows rose. "Er, I'm not sure I know the words to say exactly that—"

"Find a way," Ki said. "This's important."

The speaker began to twitter, paused, and then twittered more. Buk-Kih made the bowing movement toward the monitor then repeated the motion toward Ki.

"Er, I'm not sure I got it right." Ulrich had beads of sweat on his forehead. "She said something about the Good Child and, er, a door, maybe, through space—"

"Ask her if we can inspect the Good Child's engines."

"Er, I'm not sure of those words—"

"Then tell her we're going into their ship to take a look for ourselves—"

"I don't think you want to do that."

"Why not?" Ki said. His lips tightened.

"Er, it might be construed as an unfriendly thing to do—"

"She came to us. Does she want us to be friendly?"

"Let me see what I can do." Ulrich mopped his forehead, which gleamed wetly.

The speaker twittered at length, back and forth between them. After a particularly long burst of bird-like sounds from the small alien, there was silence.

"Well?" Ki asked.

Ulrich took a deep breath. "I'm not exactly sure I've got this right, but I believe she has people, that is Hoo-Lii, who know how the door through space works, and they will show us how it works—"

A rumble of conversation rippled through the command center.

The handset at Ki's command station buzzed. He picked it up. "Yes?" He listened for a few moments, his frown easing.... "Right. I can do that. Sure, no problem." He put the handset down and turned toward the Hoo-Lii and bowed slightly. "Buk-Kih," he said. "Welcome to Earth."

In less than twenty-four hours, a team of engineers and scientists comprised of three alien species had removed the mechanism that let the Good Child jump through the anomaly in space-time. The Hoo-Lii engineers showed the mechanism to the team led by Tim Van Minh and DuKlaat YataBu who quickly determined its power requirement. Its operation was more difficult to understand.

However, with Ulrich's help, the Hoo-Lii engineers explained its function. Now, it was a matter of duplicating it. Many of the parts would be easy; however, several solid-state electronics were beyond human technology. Tim and DuKlaat built a number of hard-wired devices, slowly closing in on an assembly that replicated the function of a tiny chip.

ↄ

"This is Eagle-Two C," a voice crackled from the receiver. "Twenty, no, make that twenty-three craft have just emerged from the anomaly." The voice faded amid the hissing noise of excess signal amplification.

The communication's operator reached for the control that would slave all laser receptors onto the incoming signal.

The communication's officer grabbed the handset. "Commander Mapes, Eagle-Two C reporting a large fleet of craft exiting the anomaly." The officer paused. "Yes, sir, we're doing that."

The command center, a metal-walled compartment in DS-2, the former Qu'uda LETF, was packed with monitors and electronic equipment. The only two people present wore the tan jump suits that were the uniform of the Space Force—the operator and officer on duty. It was the normal sleep cycle of the ship.

"The alien ships are heading in our direction," came the voice from the receiver. "About eight of them."

A series of strumming noises burst from the receiver. "Omigod, they fired at us."

Distantly, a general alarm signal warbled into life amid a background babble of voices. "We've lost our external video." The receiver went silent. The hiss of the amplifiers grew loud. The operator punched in codes and the hiss faded. He shook his head. "Their laser communication is gone—"

"Switch to emergency radio band," the duty officer said.

"Yes, sir."

A roar of static erupted from a speaker and faded. "A breach in fuel storage hull ..." The static rose and fell in a rhythmic fashion. The communication operator typed in a set of commands on the control panel. The static eased. "It'll take a while to optimize the signal," the operator said, his eyebrows raised hopefully.

Ki Mapes hurried into the command center and sat at his desk, which had three monitors and two phone-style handsets.

"Gimme an update," he said. He was breathing heavily.

The communication operator played a recording of the transmissions, leaving out the periods containing solely noise. An hour had gone by since the new arrivals had come through the anomaly.

Ki picked up a handset and nodded toward the communication's operator. "Connect me with ..." He paused, "MacPherson." As he waited, the receiver came to life.

"We've been boarded by six-limbed demons. They're killing us." The receiver fell silent.

Ki's lips tightened and his jaw muscles worked. "Yeah, Taylor, bad news, Eagle-Two C at the anomaly has been attacked by aliens that came through ... Yeah, last message confirmed hostile action, boarded and attacked crew ... Yeah, six-limbed demons, sounds like Hoo-Lii ... Yeah, highest level. The Human Confederation authorization? Hell, no. I don't need it for an attack on my ships ... right. Yeah, I'll send another Eagle to see if they can rescue what remains of the crew ... A maximum constant acceleration will take ..." He hesitated a moment. "About three weeks to arrive ... Yeah, that's right ... We'll keep a close eye on the Hoo-Lii."

Ki picked up the other handset. "Attention." His voice echoed through DS-2. "All officers report to the command center. All Eagle crews report to duty and prepare for immediate departure."

ਨੂੰ

Patrick Monahan sat hunched over, watching the monitor in Ramsey's office. It was a news program reporting the arrival of new aliens through the space-time anomaly. "Goddamn aliens," he muttered. "They've fucked-up our legislative agenda—"

"Look." Ramsey leaned back in his armchair and put his hands behind his head. "Think of this as an opportunity. Anytime there's a threat, it unites the people behind the government. What better threat than aliens? Aliens in orbit who send hostile messages about us accepting their defectors. Aliens coming through the space-time whatchmacalit, attacking our ship. We should be able to cram all kinds of legislation through as an emergency response to the situation." He sniffed.

"Besides, we've cut off MacPherson's cash cow and we're going to do more when we impose new taxes." He referred to the cost and profit controls enacted by the Assembly on the pharmaceutical plant operated by Taylor's wife, Meltem. "We'll just have to seize opportunities as they arise."

"Yeah, but what about Kucinski?" Patrick took a deep breath. "She's supposed to return to work this week. This week." He let out his breath in an explosive burst.

"We'll find out sooner or later. Meantime, get rid of anything that can link you to what happened, including the Shao-Li Peng character," said Ramsey.

ਨੂੰ

Carver Washington repeatedly pounded the gavel on the podium while he bellowed, "Order. Order."

The Assembly room of the Human Confederation, elegant in white marble with pink granite columns, teemed with delegates and staffers. On the floor, in the center of the semi-circular rows of seats, a cluster of delegates surrounded the rotund figure of Guang Xhi, the Chinese representative, waving their hands in the air and talking loudly.

"Order, Goddammit, order." Carver gestured to the sergeant-at-arms who deployed a team of uniformed aides to the floor to quiet the legislators angered over the discovery the Space Force had only three Eagles ready for duty.

The anger had coalesced upon the Chinese-led faction, which had successfully reduced funding for the Space Force's construction projects in prior years. Slowly, the sergeant-at-arms separated the arguing factions, steering them to their respective seats.

"Honored members of the Assembly," Carver said. "A moment of silence for the brave members of our Space Force who lost their lives in space and gave us warning of the approach of a hostile force." He continued to read an accolade into the record.

He yielded the floor to representatives from the countries that had crewmembers on the ill-fated craft.

"Y'know," Carver said quietly to Taylor MacPherson. "It's a damn good thing Ki and you figured how to smuggle platinum to fund the Space Force. We're a helluva lot stronger in space than the official record shows—"

"Don't say a word about it," Taylor said. "Ki's already sent a new solosuit docking module to Mars's Moon, Deimos, to start another space station—"

"No shit." Carver's eyebrows rose. "When?"

"It's been there about three months—"

"Anything else I don't know?"

A trace of a smile briefly touched Taylor's lips. "We just got our first tanker back from Uranus with almost a hundred tons of helium-three and deuterium."

"Which means?" Carver said.

Before he got an answer, a uniformed aide of the sergeant-at-arms said, almost out of breath. "Mr. MacPherson. There's an urgent message for you. Commander Mapes wishes to speak to you immediately."

Taylor followed the aide to a nearby office and picked up the phone. "Taylor here."

"Listen," Ki's voice cracked. "I've just got confirmation from the Hendersons there's a bunch of ships heading toward Earth from the anomaly."

The Hendersons had installed the interferometer on the Moon and had put remotely operated deep space monitoring equipment on 2102 Tantalus, an Aten-type asteroid in a high-inclination orbit. "They believe they'll arrive in about thirty-five or forty days. I've called off the Fast Eagle that was heading toward them—"

"Good," Taylor said. "What're you doing to get mobilized?"

"I've got the manufacturing sector cranked up to produce munitions, and I've got requests in for supplies—"

"What kind of supplies?"

"Everything that we can't make. I'm expecting trouble."

CHAPTER FOURTEEN

FIRST ENCOUNTER

Bok-Tah, the old priest, stared at the dead aliens.

Dark fluids pooled about their pink and brown bodies. He found their large size and softness repulsive. His spines rose. His breathing orifices flared and emitted an odor of anger.

He turned to the pilot-navigator and the Chosen-Male warrior who served as his tactician in the fleet of the Mother's Vengeance.

"So, these are the servant species from the Water-Gem world?"

"Yes, most honored Bok-Tah, these are the ones on the odd-shaped craft." Tik-Tah, a Chosen-Male warrior, lean and scarred, was a candidate for the priesthood and had a reputation as a cunning leader and brave fighter. "We caught them by surprise. Even with the weapons their ship possessed, they were no match for us. And in personal combat, they were like food creatures, slow, soft, and easy to kill." He emitted an odor of disdain.

"Dissect them, find out as much as you can about them, and give their remains to the insects to see if they are edible."

Bok-Tah rose off the metal hemisphere that was his resting

mound. The small room served as his command station. It had bare metal walls decorated with the stylized symbols of devotion to the Spirit of the Mother: A body flexed in submission; a representation of a young one suckling its mother's teat; an image of the bloated body of a Hive-Mother bulging with an unborn litter.

"Shall we prevail when we meet them again?" Bok-Tah had earned his way into the priesthood by winning many bloody battles while a Chosen-Male warrior. His experience made him cautious. "When do we take possession of the Water-Gem?"

"We should attack in two waves," Tik-Tah said. "First, we make a fast pass while on the course to round the star. That way, we can learn their capabilities before we commit our whole fleet to battle. The second attack will be with the combined forces after we round the star."

Bok-Tah's breathing orifices flared in agreement. "Yes, Tik-Tah, excellent thinking. Deploy two-eighths of the fleet, the scout ships, to closely approach the Water-Gem and destroy any craft encountered. Watch and learn from them." He nodded to the priest who served as his deputy. "The balance of the fleet will round the star before approaching the Water-Gem."

$$\sim$$

Madeline Henderson pursed her lips and frowned. She stared at the screen and cocked her head.

A half-dozen glowing monitors displayed electronically gathered data. Racks of electronic equipment with tiny diode lights blinked and glowed on the wall. Readout displays flickered with changing numbers; something beeped softly in the background.

"Butch, there's something strange going on." She had been a lecturer in the university before being posted to the astronomical observatory.

A chair squeaked and rattled as Butch propelled himself

toward Madeline. "What is it, m'dear?" As he leaned toward her, light glinted off his bald head.

She pointed to two tiny clusters of dots on the monitor and then tapped a command on the keyboard. Two bright lines extended on a diverging path from the two clusters. "The aliens have broken into two groups. One appears headed toward Earth. I'm not sure about the second group."

"You've checked this, right?" Butch nodded.

"Yes."

"The source of these data?"

"It's from the interferometer and the remote on 2102 Tantalus," she said.

"I suppose we'd better let Commander Mapes know what's going on." Butch rubbed his head and added, "What's the course of the remote vis-a-vis the alien ships?"

Madeline tapped the keyboard for a few moments. Three columns of figures scrolled down the screen. She traced down the middle column with her index finger. "Er, if they continue on this course, 2102 Tantalus will have the larger cluster in sight for, maybe, another twenty days. At that time, they'll be sunward of it, which means that glare becomes a major issue."

"And the other?"

"All the way in." Madeline swiveled in the chair to face Butch. "We'll get a good visual on them with the interferometer on the Moon in less than a month."

੨

Six dark, slender scout ships held the course that took them between the Water-Gem world and its orbiting Moon.

Tik-Tah maintained a triangular formation divided into two echelons. Already, they had detected three stations orbiting the planet. He had already decided the first echelon would attack all three simultaneously, following up with a similar attack from his second echelon. Their distance separation was sufficient enough there was little chance their own fire could damage their craft.

"Warriors," Tik-Tah called. "Commence firing when pilot-navigator confirms range and coordinates."

It was silent inside the ship except for the continual sigh of the ventilation system and the hum of the power generators topping off the weapons' storage cells.

The pilot-navigator compiled data from all three ships, triangulating the position of the orbiting craft about the Water-Gem world. A solitary electromagnetic pulse confirmed the range.

"Orbiting craft showing fusion drive activity."

Two of the craft above the Water-Gem world had begun to maneuver, changing their orientation.

"They're turning their narrow sections toward us."

Yes, thought the pilot-navigator. *That makes good defensive sense. Smaller cross-sectional area as a target.*

"Warriors," The pilot-navigator spoke in the high-pitched tone of an unripened female. "Coordinates entered into weapons systems for main targets. Entering into firing range." The pilot-navigator hesitated. "Now. Commence firing."

Invisible beams of radiant energy touched the orbiting craft. Sparkles of light indicated places where incandescent metal erupted from the orbiting craft under their beams.

The hum of the power generators at maximum output rose to a loud thrumming sound as they re-filled the now-empty storage cells.

"Attention," the pilot-navigator called.

She detected something moving in the vicinity of an orbiting object. She stared at the column of data overlaid on the symbols of the items that moved.

Odd, she thought. *Chemical propulsion?* However, their velocity increased rapidly, putting them on collision courses with the leading ships. "Secondary targets present danger. Switch aiming to secondary targets."

The familiar shuddering sensation of an energy weapon

discharging shook the ship. The pilot-navigator noted with satisfaction that one of the oncoming items had flared and disappeared from the displays. More flares, and more of them disappeared. Two more missiles approached trailing chemical residue.

Two flashes emptied the display of threatening missiles. "Continue attack on orbiting craft," came the voice of Tik-Tah. "Launch close range missiles, now."

Four missiles streaked away from each of the three Hoo-Lii craft, silent silver slivers that quickly disappeared. Moments later the pilot-navigator saw two missiles strike with bright flashes on the orbiting craft closest to the planet. Two missiles disappeared into the planet's gravity well—they must have missed. The other missiles struck the two more distant orbiting craft.

The window of attack closed as the first wave of Hoo-Lii ships passed between the planet and its Moon. The pilot-navigator adjusted the ship's sensor in time to catch a brief image of a large craft moving into the shadow of the planet's Moon.

Odd, she thought. *There's another craft*. She stared at the fragmentary image. *It almost looks like the Mother's Servant*, she thought. She quickly switched the sensors back to the craft orbiting the planet.

Yes, she thought. *The one closest to the planet appears to have sustained significant damage. The others, well, maybe.*

"Second echelon," Tik-Tah said. "Commence attack."

The second echelon of ships, on an identical course, pumped tightly focused beams of energy at the craft orbiting the planet.

The pilot-navigator tapped into the display from the second echelon ships. Something bright flared from the front of them.

"This is second echelon, number two, we have been hit by a beam from an energy weapon," came a familiar voice high-pitched with excitement. "We have damage to external sensors and targeting system. Cannot continue to use weapons."

The orbiting craft flashed brightly again. The pilot-navigator waited expectantly for a report. Nothing.

"Launch close range missiles," came the voice of Tik-Tah.

Two sets of four missiles tracked across the display, diverging toward the two outer orbiting craft. Something flared on the front of the closer of the two craft. Simultaneously, one set of missiles disappeared from the display.

The second set of missiles closed on the second outer orbiting craft. Four flashes in the display confirmed they hit their target.

The three ships of the second echelon passed beyond the orbit of both the Water-Gem world and its Moon. They headed toward the star at the center of the system. The rest of the Hoo-Lii fleet was on a far different course. The pilot-navigator reset the display to navigation data. She ordered a small course correction.

Now, she thought. *We have to join with Tik-Tah and the fleet of the Coven of Hive-Mothers.*

Thin streams of smoke streaked through the corridor as Josie Armstrong clambered through the hatch. Once through, she dogged it down and adjusted her breathing gear. She struggled to move forward, fighting the variations in gravity.

Something, she thought absently. *Has knocked the station off its rotation.* Ahead lay the command center. A green light above the door indicated that it still held pressure. *Not like the aft section,* she thought. *Nothing but a hole out to space. Thank God I had my pressure suit on.* She shuddered at the memory of her fellow crewmembers hemorrhaging to death in the vacuum—blood seeping from their mouths and noses. *What a horrible way to die.*

She plugged her microphone link into the comm box next to the closed door. "Hello?" she said. "This is Josie, I'm at the aft door to the command center." She waited.

"This is Meholic," a voice crackled. "The air lock is damaged. I can't seal it off. I can't open the door."

Oh, shit, thought Josie. She looked back at the hatch she'd just dogged shut. *Maybe*, she thought. *Just maybe it'll hold pressure.*

"Meholic, listen, I've got the hatch to the rear section shut tight. Lemme see, it's pressure tight—"

"Look, I can't open this hatch and take the chance I'll lose pressure." There was a note of panic in Meholic's voice. "I've been trying to raise DS-2 and get help—"

"Didja get hold of them?"

"No, but—"

"Look," Josie said. "I know how to work the communications system better than anyone. Let me in, please." *Oh, God, please don't let me die.* "Listen, I'm gonna crack an air line to repressurize this corridor. If it holds air, then you can let me in."

If not, she thought. *I'm dead.* Her emergency breathing equipment held less than twenty minutes supply of air and she'd already spent ten minutes getting here. *I pray there's air left in the line.*

Josie retreated to the center of the corridor where a cluster of piping and conduit formed a right angle before descending through the floor. *Aha*, she thought. *There is a valve.* She tried to turn it but it refused to budge.

She looked up and down the corridor. At the end was a fire control station. She hurried to it and found a bag of tools and dragged it back to the air pipe junction.

What? she thought. *None of these friggin wrenches fit?* She dumped the bag on the ground. The variable gravity made the tool bag lurch to one side, scattering the tools out. *Aha! A hacksaw*, she thought and grabbed it.

It took Josie five minutes of frenzied effort to cut the pipe, which released its air with a brief howl; there was atmosphere, but not much. She had to beg and plead with Meholic for three minutes before he agreed to open the airlock. Two minutes dragged by until he opened the door. Her air indicator was at zero.

Meholic, a thin, red-haired young man with a blood-covered

face, was the only one alive in the command center. He owed his life to his propensity to strap himself in tightly whenever on duty. The remaining personnel had died from the impact of the two explosions that tore off the front section the crew area of DS-1. That had changed the center of gravity of the rotating mass and given it an erratic motion.

"Okay, Meholic, I'll take care of your injuries as soon as I get a message out." Josie pushed past Meholic to the communications module. Quickly checking the panel revealed most of the equipment still functioned.

Okay, she thought. *Let's see if the spare antennae system is still there.* It had been installed in preparation for the arrival of the first alien encounter when she'd manned the communications system under Captain Mapes. She remembered the command sequence and typed it in. Seconds ticked by slowly until the monitor flashed with the message the reserve system had been activated.

She typed in a series of commands to activate an emergency frequency broadcast. "Mayday, mayday, mayday. This is Josie Armstrong on DS-1. We have sustained severe damage and need assistance as soon as possible. Air supply limited, many casualties. Mayday, mayday, mayday."

Josie waited. The receiver's speaker remained silent.

After two minutes, Josie repeated the message.

"Ah, DS-1, this is DS-2, we're having difficulty understanding your message, can you come back again?"

"Mayday, this is DS-1, many casualties, limited air supply, we need help. We need help NOW," Josie's voice steadily rose in volume through the message.

"Copy, DS-1, we got your message. Will relay your request to our command. Ah, we sustained some damage, too. DS-2 out."

ح

Ki Mapes rubbed his eyes and leaned back in his chair. *Damn*, he thought. The command center was full of officers, many clustered around the communications module. The metal-walled compartment was warm, stuffy, and the electronic equipment lining the walls glowed brightly with a myriad of diode lights.

"So, your Hoo-Lii buddy recognized our visitors, eh?" He spoke to Ulrich, the linguist who was on the flat screen monitor above his station.

"Not exactly, sir." Ulrich's voice was distorted by the radio transmission. "Buk-Kih said these Hoo-Lii were sent by some other faction, whoever they may be. The important thing is they're looking for Suh-Joh, the Hoo-Lii commander of the Mother's Servant. Buk-Kih asks if she may contact Suh-Joh to warn her about these Hoo-Lii—"

"D'you really think that's necessary?" Ki said, with more than a touch of sarcasm in his voice. "Y'think she missed the fireworks display?"

Ulrich swallowed hard. "No, sir, but I think what she means is we should ally ourselves with Suh-Joh—"

"Oh, I get it. Now your little buddy's homesick...."

"No, sir, absolutely not," Ulrich's voice rose. "Her life is still forfeit for deserting her Hive-Mother. She believes these new Hoo-Lii are a bigger threat to both of us. She's certain there are more of them and they'll return to attack again."

Ki took a deep breath. He already knew the Hoo-Lii force had split in two and the larger of the two forces was heading somewhere in-system. "Ulrich, gimme a moment. I need to check on something." He cut Ulrich out of the communications loop. "Henderson. What d'you have on the course of the incoming aliens?" He'd already talked to Butch earlier.

"Commander Mapes," a female voice came from the receiver. "This is Madeline Henderson—"

Ki's voice softened. "What d'you have for me, Madeline?"

"We've refined our data on both groups of ships. Their courses will take both of them close to the sun. It's my guess they're going to use the sun's gravity to change course and slow down. What their course will be after that, I don't know. However, I did compute a possible course that would bring both of them back in the vicinity of the Earth at the same time. It would take about sixty days, assuming they'll shed velocity during their swing-by." Her voice trailed off.

"Thanks, Madeline," Ki said. "I was afraid something like that might be coming. I'll get back to you later." He broke the connection and brought Ulrich back up on the monitor.

"Okay, Ulrich, set up a conference with Suh-Joh. Lemme know when you're ready to dicker with them."

Ulrich smiled and reached for his pipe. "Certainly."

Ki broke connection. "What's the status of DS-1?"

"Er, we've got an Eagle on site and personnel on board. So far, they've only found a half-dozen survivors. DS-1 is a mess. One whole hull is breached from end to end, plus the front section of the crew section is smashed open."

Ki listened carefully to the report.

Bastards, he thought. *They've killed over seventy of my people. Those incoming missiles had a lot of kinetic energy. Fortunately, we'd managed to get DS-2 and DS-3 turned so we had the thick metal fronts toward them.* He realized his defenses didn't work so well against these aliens. *Maybe it's time to take the gloves off and deploy the nukes. I wonder what a fusion bomb pumped X-ray laser would do to them?*

DS-3 lost a dozen people when an energy beam ripped open a food-raising chamber and a missile hit a solosuit dock damaging fifteen solosuits.

Fortunately, Ki thought. *They hit none of our Eagles. I don't think the Eagles have what it takes to go up against those Hoo-Lii ships. I wonder if Suh-Joh does?*

ॡ

Bok-Tah reviewed the holo-images of the encounter with the aliens from the Water-Gem planet. He was particularly interested in the weapons the aliens used against their six scout ships. It seemed almost too easy. That made him nervous. He had fought too many battles to become over-confident; caution was a shield against defeat. He was also a believer in firepower; half measures would not do. He rose from the metal resting mound in his austere cell; it was time to plan the attack. He went to the pilot-navigator's station and summoned the cohort leaders.

The room, dominated by the holo-display tank in the center, was crowded with Chosen-Male warriors who shifted uneasily in such close presence with each other.

"We shall commit the entire fleet to the invasion," Bok-Tah said. "We shall arrive in one wave and open fire simultaneously."

"Most honored Bok-Tah," said the pilot-navigator who had been with the scout ships' initial attack. "I recorded an image which may be that of the ship Mother's Servant—"

"Show me," Bok-Tah said, breathing orifices flaring.

The pilot-navigator summoned the image in the holo-display. The Moon glowed brightly, almost overwhelming a faint shadow slipping behind its mass. Even with enhancement, there was no clear resolution to reveal the distinctive radial living quarter ring of the Mother's Servant, or its cluster of engines containing the deadly laser.

"Perhaps it is another of the servant species vessels—"

Bok-Tah raised himself and flared an odor of anger through his breathing orifices. "It is that heretic, Suh-Joh; she is here. This is our chance to get her."

"Then we should surround both the planet and its Moon."

Bok-Tah remained silent as the Chosen-Male warrior cohort leaders argued different strategies. He beckoned to the pilot-navigator. "What is the best way to approach this planet and trap the heretic?"

The pilot-navigator touched a control and an image of the Water-Gem planet and its Moon appeared. A yellow line advanced toward the planet and began to curve into an orbit. Before the yellow line completed a half-circle around the planet, a line split off to encircle the planet's Moon, catching up with the slower moving line that formed a circle about the planet.

"I believe this may be a way to catch the ship that hides behind the planet's Moon."

The cohort leaders crowded around the holo-display to offer variations on the suggested plan while the pilot-navigator patiently explained the limitations of orbital mechanics.

"Enough," Bok-Tah said loudly.

The room fell silent. "Think about this plan. If you and your scholars can devise a better one, show me." He lowered his head as though preparing to leap into combat. "We have eight squared sleep periods before we return to the Water-Gem world. We have enough time to select the best plan of attack."

The undercurrent of conversation in the Assembly hall of the Human Confederation bristled with tension as the Chinese delegate, Guang Xhi, leaned forward over the Speaker's podium, stabbing his finger viciously at the ground before him.

"The Space Force has not delivered on its promise. One-third of its facilities destroyed in one attack. And those culpable go unpunished, those who claimed to be building a space defense, those who want to tax us into poverty to build a platinum-plated Space Force, for they did not do what they said they would do."

Guang Xhi glared in the direction of the US delegation. "Especially those who put national interest before the internationalist Human Confederation, profiteers extracting unseemly profit from the sick and injured."

"Taylor," Carver Washington said from behind a massive hand. "I think he's got you in his sights."

"It's going to get worse," Taylor said. "Especially when they learn these aliens are the same as the ones who took up housekeeping in Carlsbad Caverns."

Carver raised his eyebrows. "That a fact?"

Taylor sighed. "Yeah. These new aliens came after Suh-Joh's bunch, which are the aliens who arrived first. It's some kind of holy war. And we're involved, whether we like it or not."

"Damn," Carver said.

"Ki is busting his ass getting ready for their return. He figures we've got less than two months."

"Y'know there's a petition goin' around to hold a recall election on you?" Carver's eyebrows rose.

Taylor shrugged. "No, I didn't know that."

"Monahan is doin' it," Carver said. "Problem is, you're the best person for the job under these conditions."

"Yeah, right." Taylor chuckled without mirth. "But there's plenty of volunteers who want to take my place."

と

Son-Nih flexed low, almost touching the brown floor covering. "Most Gracious Hive-Mother," he said.

"Come." Suh-Joh gestured to the favored spot next to her resting mound. "Tell me what you think of these ..." she hesitated, "humans and what they believe will happen." They had just finished a conference call with the traitorous Buk-Kih and the human, Ul-Rik, who had opened communications with them.

"The pilot-navigator has already confirmed the Coven of Hive-Mothers' ships are likely to return after rounding the star as the humans stated." Son-Nih waved his mid-limbs as though swatting a daa-lii fly. "So, what do we do?"

Suh-Joh's breathing flaps flared. "Do we stay and fight?" She moved as though uncomfortable. "Or, do we flee? What do you think, my esteemed counselor?"

"If we flee, whence to?"

Suh-Joh crouched lower on her resting mound as though seeking to hide. "So, we fight?"

"The new servants have no choice but to fight. Perhaps they

will defeat the Coven of Hive-Mothers." Son-Nih sagged as though he did not believe his own words. "We must take that chance."

Suh-Joh's breathing orifices rippled in disbelief. "They did not fare so well on their initial encounter—"

Son-Nih rose. "The initial encounter? What about when they fought with the asteroid-ship?" He stared at his Hive-Mother. "However, previously, when seemingly defeated, they used those obscenities to destroy their enemy—"

"Ah, I meant their most recent encounter."

"If cornered, they might ..." Son-Nih absent-mindedly moved his paat-kli to his neck so the small crustacean could groom an area needing attention. "Those weapons ..." he said, almost as if thinking aloud. "Those weapons could make a difference, if they can get them close to the Coven's fleet."

"Will they have a problem doing that?"

"Perhaps," Son-Nih said. "They did not succeed in their most recent encounter. Perhaps the Coven has obtained more advanced technology from beneath the Shrine of the Mother." He referred to the archives that contained information from the distant past, information hidden away due to its destructive nature.

"So, esteemed counselor, do we fight or flee?"

"We need a little less than eight squared days for the harvest to ripen, to get food to provision our ships. So, we cannot leave just yet," Son-Nih said. "Fortunately, water is no longer a problem. We do need to get more fuel whether we flee or stay. Sooner or later, we have to go to an outer planet of this system." He settled close to the ground as though getting comfortable. "The problem is the size of the Coven of Hive-Mothers' fleet."

"You have an idea?"

"Yes, most gracious Hive-Mother," Son-Nih said. He flared his breathing flaps as though amused. "Maybe this will work...."

CHAPTER FIFTEEN

SUNDAY, BLOODY SUNDAY

"Gentlemen," Ki Mapes spoke quietly.

Officers from both DS-2 and DS-3 filled the command center as well as officers from the three functional Eagles. Too many people in the small, metal-walled compartment had over-taxed its ventilation system for the past hour. Odors of partially digested food and unwashed bodies wafted among the milling ranks of humanity pressed against the banks of electronic equipment and monitors that lined the walls.

"We face twenty-four ships of two different types. We saw the smaller class when it passed fifty-seven days ago. We don't know the capabilities of the larger class of ship. We can only assume they are more heavily armed and more dangerous. The enemy fleet is slowing which suggests they plan to orbit Earth. That can only mean one thing, they plan to invade our home.

"We face our greatest challenge. The approaching fleet is hostile and possesses beam weapons that can cut an unprotected Eagle in two. Their kinetic missiles can wreak severe damage on all of our installations. Yet we must confront this enemy. We are the only barrier between them and our home, Earth. I expect every man and woman to do their duty. You have your orders. Dismissed."

The officers with long and serious faces silently filed out of the command center. The only ones who remained were the staff of the command center. They had been briefed on the strategic plans to ward off the coming attack.

It isn't going to be easy, Ki thought. *We just have to execute well and pray everything works just right.* He knew the odds were against that happening. He wondered how many of his officers and men would die. Already he knew it would be too many.

Ki picked up the handset. "Get me the Hendersons." He needed to talk to them and get an update on the progress of the alien fleet from the deep-space observatory on the Moon. "Yes ... right. I understand. About seventy-two hours? Got it." He replaced the handset and rubbed his head for a moment before picking up the handset again.

"Kerr?" Ki asked. "Did your engineers get the Eagles armored?"

Kerr, the commander of DS-3 and his engineer, Pete Baldwin, had developed a composite of foamed rock and nickel-steel to protect the Eagles and the defense stations.

"He did? Good. Tell him I appreciate his efforts. Now, the other project ... Right. Did he get them launched? Good. What was the final count? Only nineteen? Damn, I was hoping for more. How about the decoys? Good. Well, tell the team I appreciate their efforts. When this is over, I'll speak to them personally ... Yeah, you take care of yourself, too."

Ki replaced the handset and swore silently. *No matter how well we aim the fusion pumped X-ray lasers, we still don't have enough. As for the rest of our weapons, we'll just have to see if they work on these alien ships.*

༊

For the next forty-eight hours, Ki directed the deployment of his forces. *Too little*, he thought. *And too much volume to cover.* Even though he'd communicated with the alien Suh-Joh, she wouldn't commit to joining the defense of the planet. *Damn her*, he thought. *She's the reason that fleet's heading this way.*

"Sir," a voice called. "We've got a clear image of the enemy." The large flat screen monitor above Ki's station flickered and changed to show a cluster of bright dots in a star field. Each dot had a number attached to it, which changed from time to time. "We're showing their relative velocity."

"Does targeting have these data?" Ki asked.

"Yes, sir."

The enemy's velocity was about thirty kilometers per second and continued to decelerate.

"ETA?" Ki asked.

"Within range in about twenty-three hours, assuming current delta-vee maintained. Terminal velocity estimate of twelve kilometers per second."

A fast-moving target, carrying kinetic missiles with high initial launch velocity, thought Ki. *It's gonna be rough*. He picked up a phone handset.

"Pete," he called. "Yeah, you got anything else we can use as decoys...? I don't care what it is, something to confuse the enemy. Sure. Yeah, we can always make more. How'll you get them into position? I see ... Do they have a chance of surviving? Y'sure? Okay, do it." He replaced the handset and rubbed his head.

The command center had a full crew manning the equipment. The backups would soon take over, so the most experienced operators could get some rest before the action started.

Well, he thought. *I really oughta try to catch some shuteye, too.* He felt too wired for sleep.

༄

Bok-Tah stared at the holo-display that showed two large

orbiting bodies surrounded by numerous smaller objects. Some emitted radiation; most were as cold as space. "So," he said. "You're sure you can tell craft from the space debris?" He turned toward the pilot-navigator.

"Yes, honored Bok-Tah," the pilot-navigator twittered. "Once cohort leader Tik-Tah explained the tactic of decoys, it was easy to devise a means to detect those powered craft from the decoys. The ones emitting radiation will be identified and their location transmitted to the weapon stations."

"Tik-Tah," Bok-Tah called.

An image of Tik-Tah appeared in the holo-display. "Yes, honored Bok-Tah?"

Tik-Tah commanded the group of ships that would split off the main fleet to orbit the planet's moon before rejoining the main fleet. His group of ships consisted of the larger attack vessels, more powerful and better armored than the scout craft. Reports of the damage inflicted by the Mother's Servant deemed this a prudent course of action.

"Proceed with the plan. If you find the Mother's Servant, destroy it." Bok-Tah's breathing orifices flared and emitted an odor of anger. "Then join us to sweep this impudent species of servants out of space. They need to learn we are their masters and they must submit to the Way of the Mother."

"As you wish, honored Bok-Tah." Tik-Tah flexed, showing respect. "Course change will be initiated on schedule."

"When will we be in range?" Bok-Tah asked.

"We are almost there," the pilot-navigator said. "I've transmitted the range data to the weapon stations. When the symbols next to the identified craft change from yellow to red, they are within range of the main energy weapons."

Bok-Tah remained silent, watching the holo-display. The symbols of those items identified as craft began to wink from yellow to red. The largest object remained out of range, being closer to the planet. The other large object, on the opposite side of the planet would not be in range until the fleet orbited the planet. "Commence firing."

The ship shuddered from the discharge of multiple energy weapons. Objects in the holo-display sparkled as cascades of energy sliced into them. The hum of the power generators at maximum output rose to a loud thrumming sound as they refilled the empty storage cells.

The pilot-navigator rose and moved closer to the holo-display. She tapped a command onto a small console at one side. The holo-display flashed briefly and one object began to flash.

"Something is wrong," she said. "Only one of these objects has ceased to emit energy. Only one has been put out of action."

Bok-Tah's spines rose and his breathing flaps flared. "Is it a trap?" he asked.

"I do not know." The pilot-navigator flexed toward the ground. "I do not know military strategy, I only know what my instruments say."

"Can you gather more data on the objects before us?"

"Yes, by active scanning." The pilot-navigator touched other controls. The holo-display flashed and dozens of objects began to twinkle. "The tagged items contain electronic equipment, probably craft of some kind. I'm sending these data to the weapons stations."

"Why didn't we detect these sooner?" Bok-Tah asked.

"Because they are as cold as space—"

"Warriors, fire on the new targets," Bok-Tah spoke into the communicator.

The ship again shuddered from the discharge of the energy weapons. More objects flashed in the holo-display. Several began to flash.

"We are in range to use the missiles," said the pilot-navigator. "I've advised the weapons stations."

The holo-display flashed brightly before fading to black.

"What happened?" demanded Bok-Tah.

The pilot-navigator scrambled to the opposite side of the

room and opened a compartment. She worked feverishly for several moments. "Ah," she said. "Got it."

The holo-display brightened and again showed the space ahead. It looked peaceful as though nothing had changed. An icon appeared on the edge of the display and began to flash. The icon moved to the center of the screen and grew large.

"Something burned out the main optical sensor," the pilot-navigator said. "I've activated a spare." She looked back at the holo-display. "No, oh no," she said. "It can't be."

"What is it?" Bok-Tah asked.

"It is them. They who use obscenities."

"Obscenities?" Bok-Tah's spines rose. A strong waft of fear and anger emitted from his breathing orifices. "Fusion bomb obscenities? The Others?"

The pilot-navigator flexed to the floor. "Spirit of the Mother, save us, please, from those whose obscene means—"

"Answer me." Bok-Tah kicked the pilot-navigator.

The pilot-navigator shuddered. "Yes," she said in a tiny voice. "It was the discharge of multiple fusion bombs—"

"Where? What did they use? Is there any damage?"

Bok-Tah stood over the pilot-navigator and kicked her again.

The pilot-navigator scrambled to the navigation console. She tapped its controls for a few moments. The holo-display flashed and replaced the previous view with one encompassing a spherical volume that included all of the ships of the fleet of the Coven of Hive-Mothers. Every ship continued on course, coasting in to take up orbit around the Water-Gem planet.

"Nothing seems to have happened," the pilot-navigator began. She touched the controls. The holo-display flashed and six craft carried a yellow flashing symbol. "Oh, Spirit of the Mother, save us," she said. "Those ships are dead."

"Dead?" asked Bok-Tah. "What do you mean, dead?"

"Their systems, all of their systems have been destroyed. And that means their crews." The pilot-navigator resumed working with her controls, touching and tapping rapidly. "Radiation," she said. "Massive, short wavelength radiation, from the fusion bombs."

A large object emerged onto the holo-display from behind the planet's Moon. Something flashed from the object, something very bright. The craft was under power, heading away from the star.

"What is that?" Bok-Tah asked.

"That," the pilot-navigator said. "Is the Mother's Servant. It was her that I saw earlier."

"Set a course to follow the heretic. She is the reason we are here. We can return later to deal with these ..." Bok-Tah hesitated. "Disobedient alien servants." He paused again. "Launch the missiles on the large orbiting objects and anything identified as the servants' ships."

The ship hummed from the acceleration. Several times the ship vibrated as missiles surged away. Bright flashes appeared on the large orbiting object from the impact of the kinetic missiles. As they closed on the large orbiting object, beams of energy flashed out. The holo-display showed three ships sparkling where touched by the beams from the servants' object.

From a cloud of space debris, cold and passive, multiple small, boxy objects came to life and headed directly into the paths of the oncoming vessels. They converged on a collision course with the fleet with a velocity difference so high impact would be soon and potentially disastrous.

"Evasive action," Bok-Tah said.

The small, boxy objects quickly grew large in the holo-display and vanished as the fleet passed them by.

"Damage assessment?"

The pilot-navigator bent to the console. A column of figures appeared on one side of the holo-display. "Two of our ships have been breached, casualties unknown. One has reduced engine power from damage by collision." She glanced up. "Beam weapons from large object have inflicted minor surface damage on six more."

The holo-display flashed again and another column of figures appeared. Icons changed to warning yellow.

"Three of our ships closing on the Mother's Servant have sustained severe damage—"

"Break off active pursuit." Bok-Tah sagged as though tired. "It's that Mother-cursed weapon powered by the ship's main engines. Follow out of range. We will get her, sooner or later."

"Bok-Tah, honorable Bok-Tah," called a voice from the communicator. "We have been hurt. The Others used obscenities that killed two of my ships ... And the Mother's Servant has damaged three others—"

"Who is this?"

"It is Tik-Tah, honorable one, I beg your permission to withdraw before I lose the rest of my ships." His voice was faint and his breathing ragged as though injured.

"Tik-Tah is a brave warrior," Bok-Tah said. "The situation grows more difficult." His breathing flaps slowly collapsed. "Break off engagement," he said. "It is time to regroup."

He directed the pilot-navigator to gather the fleet on a common course. As the fleet vectored toward the outer reaches of the system, eleven ships continued drifting toward the Water-Gem planet without power, dark and out of control. He stared at the data flowing onto the holo-display.

It was worse than he had believed: Eleven ships dead, lifeless; four ships with major damage and unlikely to survive. More than half the fleet out of commission and neither the heretic punished nor the servants of the Water-Gem world submitting as they should.

"Navigator," Bok-Tah said. "Set the course toward the opening in space-time." It was time to return home.

ᘒ

The gabble of voices grew steadily louder. The main part of the enemy fleet had passed between the Earth and the Moon; a smaller contingent had broken off to orbit the Moon.

Ki watched the monitor above his station carefully. Thirty solosuits towed bundles of flat sheet metal directly into the path of the enemy's main fleet, scattering the metal. It was, he realized, a variation on chaff with radar. Except the solosuits had hidden among the chaff. So far, twelve solosuits had taken direct hits from the enemy beam weapons—they had not stood a chance. Twelve more had powered up to become impact objects in the alien fleet's path. Three made contact, inflicting visible damage. Only two from the suicide mission survived the energy beams from the alien craft. Out of the original thirty, sixteen returned to the defense station.

Ki glanced at the report which said the enemy's missiles launched at DS-3 had ripped away much of its food production facilities on the outer surface, along with portions of the launch facilities. Missiles had hit two Eagles; however, their composite armor seemed to have absorbed much of the shock of the high-velocity impact.

Still, plumes of molten metal had penetrated both hulls. Sure, Ki thought. *It's easy to think the Eagles weren't hurt badly, but forty-three crewmembers would go home in body bags and others would not survive. And there'll be more than a few empty coffin funerals—some vaporized, some lost in space. What a price to pay.* He sighed. *And two of the Eagles will need months of repair before they can go out again.*

The only bright note, he realized, *was the performance of the Mother's Servant. Mercy,* he thought. *The power of its laser was unbelievable. And we had the nerve to threaten Suh-Joh with our puny weapons.*

"Sir," a technician said quietly. "Here's the report on the fusion lasers, sir." He handed Ki a single sheet of paper.

Ki glanced at the report. *So, it appears that only eight of the nineteen fusion bomb pumped X-ray lasers hit their targets. I wonder why.* He reached for his handset. "Yeah, Pete ... you've seen the report? Right. Now, is there a problem with the targeting system?" He listened carefully for several minutes and held the phone away from his ear. He frowned.

"... The bloody bastards would have to pick this day. Fair ruined my Saturday night. Missed me regular pint, I did. But my ace technician had a skinful last night, off his game today. Of all days, why did they have to choose Sunday, bloody Sunday?"

"That's enough," Ki said. "I'm sending the Eagles to check out the eleven Hoo-Lii ships that're on course that's taking them close to Earth. We've got to make sure they're in stable orbits with no chance of crashing."

"Y'sure you want to do that right away?" Pete's voice carried a rich Australian brogue. "There may be some of our chaps still out there, injured and needing help."

"Use the shuttle to tow a string of solosuits out there for search and rescue. Look, if we need to nudge a dead Hoo-Lii ship to a higher orbit, that'll require the power of an Eagle."

"Ah, yes. I understand." Pete's voice carried heavy doubt.

CHAPTER SIXTEEN

LOOKING INWARD

"Look." Suh-Joh pointed to the yellow lines in the holo-display. It showed the course of the Coven of Hive-Mothers' fleet had changed. The display had a column of figures tied to each individual ship connected by a yellow line. "They retreat."

The navigation station of the Mother's Servant—a small compartment intended solely for the pilot-navigator—was crowded with the Chosen-Male warriors guarding Suh-Joh.

Son-Nih flexed slightly toward his Hive-Mother. "About half their ships survive." He gestured toward the eleven ships that continued on course toward the Water-Gem planet. "These are dead. It was the obscenities the new servants used that killed them."

"Navigator, whence head those ships?" Suh-Joh gestured toward the now rapidly accelerating ships of the Coven of Hive-Mothers. It was away from them.

The holo-display flickered and changed scale as the pilot-navigator operated the astrogation controls. The display showed the Water-Gem world and its Moon as two tiny objects about which two tiny clusters sparkled. A green line extended from one group on a slightly curved course to the limit of the display. Again it flickered to show a complete projection of the planetary system. The green line extended almost to its outer limit.

"Ah," the pilot-navigator said. "They've set course for the transfer point. They are leaving."

"Are you sure?" Suh-Joh asked.

The pilot-navigator hesitated and then flexed low before her Hive-Mother. "Gracious Hive-Mother, they can always change course. However, as time goes by, the energy cost to reverse direction becomes very high. Therefore, most unlikely."

"Return to orbit above the Water-Gem." Suh-Joh moved to the exit. "Advise me immediately of any change in the fleet's course. Come, Son-Nih, we must talk."

Once back in the ersatz cave Suh-Joh used as her command center, she slipped onto the polished red granite resting mound. Dim orange light glittered off metal walls that looked like quartzite. She signaled the servants to draw the heavy brown curtains across the entrances to increase the level of privacy.

"We must talk to the new servants; I think we have much to learn." She hesitated. "I fear they will not be good servants. We must find out why they used those obscenities, and why they are Disobedient. It seems we have greatly misunderstood these ...," She paused. "These Others."

$$\sim$$

"Ul-Rik," a synthesized voice came from the communication module. It was a refined version of the device Ulrich had painstakingly used to pair English words with the sounds made by the Hoo-Lii. After many corrections, he had transferred them onto a memory chip and into a small computer driven system.

Those who dealt with the aliens used these communication modules. However, the Hoo-Lii continued to contact Ulrich.

"This is Lil-Tih, Suh-Joh need to speak to your bzzz-mother."

The module obviously did not recognize the Hoo-Lii word she used.

Ulrich adjusted a second device and replayed the unknown word. "What person is this bzzz-mother?" Ulrich asked. "What does this bzzz-mother do?" Sweat gleamed on his forehead as he chewed on an empty pipe. The desk in the book-lined office was piled high with papers and electronic modules.

"Your bzzz-mother make humans, bzzz-mother speak for humans. I not speak to warrior, speak only to bzzz-mother."

Ulrich mopped his brow. "I get bzzz-mother to speak to you. Bzzz-mother not here now. Wait. I call back." Ulrich found a simplified speech pattern worked better with the translation system. As time went by, he added more words but simple speech patterns still prevailed.

He reached for the phone. "Taylor?" Ulrich said. "I just received a call ... yes. Suh-Joh wants to speak to some kind of mother. She did not mention any name ... No, she also said no warriors ... right. Yes, I can patch a call through. When? Sure, that'll be fine."

～

Taylor leaned back in his armchair and glanced at Carver Washington across the room. Books and filing cabinets crowded the walls of his office. Meltem sat at the desk normally occupied by Taylor. Chris Kucinski and Billy Potato filled the remaining chairs.

"Getting back to the original question, why did Suh-Joh attack the other Hoo-Lii?" Recovery operations had revealed the inactive ships held only Hoo-Lii corpses.

"I gather they came here to kill them, there was some kind of ..." Meltem hesitated. "Schism? Or perhaps they've done something, committed a crime that has a death penalty." She frowned and glanced at her notes. The desk faced the window overlooking the campus of Baldwin-Wallace University. "They were pursued. Suh-Joh was emphatic about that." She wrung her hands.

"Taylor?" Ulrich's voice came over the speaker. "Suh-Joh responded very well to Meltem and said things I haven't heard before. It seems she prefers to talk to a female."

Meltem shrugged.

"Er, what was this thing about long life?" Taylor asked.

"I don't know," Ulrich said. "Suh-Joh never mentioned that before. She brought up the bad servant thing, for the second time, in connection with our relations. I don't understand it."

Carver cleared his throat. "Y'know, I get the feeling this Suh-Joh guy—"

"Lady," Ulrich's voice cut in. "She's female."

"This boss lady." Carver's voice dripped sarcasm. "Would like to give us orders. What d'you think, Meltem?"

Meltem sighed. "I'm not sure. There's such a cultural difference. Suh-Joh is female and is also their absolute leader. I feel she wants to deal with her equal who is also a female. She doesn't understand why we haven't welcomed them to settle on our planet. She really doesn't like the weapons we used against the other fleet."

"The weapon Suh-Joh used against the Johnny-come-lately Hoo-Lii scares me." Ki Mapes voice came from the speaker accompanied by a faint crackle of static. "It's got both power and range. Way more than our stuff." He hesitated for a moment. "Kinda glad they jumped in when they did. If the fleet had orbited Earth, I'm not sure the final outcome would have been to our liking. We'd used up most of our ammo...."

Silence hung over the meeting until Carver cleared his throat again, signaling his intention to speak. "Well, there's a bunch in the HC Assembly that're mighty upset. They're complaining about all the money they spent on the Space Force an' then it took an alien to chase off another buncha aliens. Like they didn't get their money's worth. An' they're still pissed—'scuse my language—about having an alien ship in orbit. They're lookin' for a way to hang this on you, Taylor, an' they're working on it like true believers."

"If they hadn't short-changed us, we might have been ready." Ki's voice held an angry edge. "If we hadn't taken things into our own hands, we'd have been in much worse shape."

Those present knew about the smuggled platinum and black-market supplies that kept the space construction project moving forward.

Carver sighed heavily. "Yeah, well, you ain't heard the rest of their fantasy. Somehow, they got this thing in their heads you're soft on aliens. There's gonna be some nasty politics in the near term. I hope they get over it."

"Well," Ki said. "I've submitted a budget request for rebuilding the Space Force. It'll require a fifty percent increase over last year's amount for at least the next three years. That is, if we want a credible space defense."

"Oh, man," Carver said. "You're asking a lot."

"Suh-Joh sounded like she had no intention of abandoning those caverns near Carlsbad, either," Taylor said. "In fact, they're now sending more ships back and forth."

"I think they need the caves for food and breeding purposes," Ulrich said. "Suh-Joh said something about needing to get beneath the ground, that their needs were great—"

"That'll stir up the anti-alien faction," Carver said.

"Do we want Suh-Joh as an ally or enemy?" Taylor said.

The ticking of the clock grew loud as eyes flicked back and forth. The static on the speaker seemed to increase.

"Ally," Ki said. "I'd prefer not to fight that ship."

Billy rose and swiveled his head to look around. "There are many things we can learn from these Hoo-Lii. They held the secret to the path between the stars. What else do they know that may be of great value? Perhaps we have something they need, also. We should continue to talk, to find out more. It seems that Doctor Encirlik ..." He wobbled his head in Meltem's direction. "Has success in talking to the alien, Suh-Joh. Perhaps she should talk more." He sat down abruptly.

Taylor looked at Chris Kucinski. The lines had disappeared from her face and her complexion was clear, and her eyes sparkled brightly. She was the picture of health. "Commander Kucinski, do you have any comments?"

"With my illness and all, I've been a little out of touch," she said. "However, my main concern is the Hoo-Lii settlement at Carlsbad. They've cut a lot of vegetation and taken it below ground. We've got a count on how many have gone in—about one hundred and twenty—along with the dozen or so containers the size of semi-trailers they use to transport stuff back and forth. They've got something significant going on down there."

She took a deep breath. "Yet, they haven't made any aggressive moves. Currently, we have three full battalions of militia, with artillery in reserve, stationed at a five-mile perimeter. Other than that, I'm not sure what we should do."

"I heard a couple of comments Ramsey's people thought they should be in charge," Carver said. "In fact, he wants Human Confederation soldiers to take over the quarantine—"

"This is still the United States of America, and until there's a clear and present danger, it's a police issue," Chris said. "Until that changes, or we need assistance, I see no need to involve the H-C military."

Taylor nodded. "You have my full support on that."

The phone rang. Taylor frowned and picked up the handset. He'd given orders that they were not to be disturbed. "Yes ... What? Two of the derelict Hoo-Lii craft entered our atmosphere? Omigod. Where...? Ah, shit." His face became drawn and pale as he set down the handset.

"Two of the derelict Hoo-Lii craft have crashed on Earth. One landed in the Indian Ocean, the other hit a small town in southern China. The impact was equivalent to a two-kiloton nuke."

༅

"The Yankee imperialists of the Space Force care only about extending the hegemonist ambitions of the United States. They take money sweated from the proletariat to build platinum-plated palaces in the sky, and, when asked if they can do their duty, they confess failure." Spittle sprayed from Guang Xhi's mouth. The hall of the Human Confederation Assembly was silent. Heads in the Sino-Asian bloc nodded in agreement.

"After all the money they spend, they claim they need even more to build other defenses." Guang Xhi turned slowly in a circle. Whispers rustled the air. "This is a confession they cannot do what they said they would do. They build platinum palaces in the sky to frighten off the aliens who will never return. They are paper tiger." His words dripped scorn.

"They cannot even defend us from a spacecraft crashing onto the defenseless workers of Ning-Hsiang."

Guang Xhi referred to the small town in the Kwangsi province of South China where the derelict Hoo-Lii craft had crashed. "Therefore, they are not fit to command the forces that are supposed to protect us from the dangers in space. I must note they were able to stop the one that would have struck the United States of America. Instead, they let it hit China—"

"I object." Carver Washington's stentorian voice echoed through the hall. "That's completely untrue. You have no basis to say that. Stick to the facts."

Guang Xhi turned toward Carver. "Untrue, you say? Did the Space Force defeat the aliens? No. Was not the town of Ning-Hsiang destroyed by the crash of an alien craft? Did the United States suffer any damage from objects from space? No. My sources tell me the Space Force moved to save the United States from such fate on the orders of their capitalist leader, Taylor MacPherson.

"In addition, the Chinese Democratic Peoples Republic has uncovered a major spy ring, which tries to overthrow our socialist workers' paradise. Spies, on order of another United States reactionary, now standing before us, Carver Washington—"

Carver pounded the gavel loudly. *You double-crossing slime ball*, he thought. *I ain't gonna put up with your crap.* "Point of order, argumentum ad hominem. Personal attacks ain't allowed. Delegate Guang Xhi, you've violated the rules of order; be seated—"

"You cannot do this." Guang Xhi's voice rose to a shriek.

"The hell I can't." Carver's finger jabbed toward the Chinese delegate. "Sit down and be quiet or I'll have the sergeant-at-arms eject you."

First one voice yelled, then another. Soon, the roar of voices overwhelmed the repeated raps of Carver's gavel. "Order, order," he bellowed.

A chant started in the Sino-Asian bloc. "Capitalist Yankee pig. Capitalist Yankee pig. Capitalist Yankee pig."

"Meeting adjourned." Carver cracked the gavel loudly.

More than half the North American delegation rose and exited from the hall. Remaining seated were those who'd expressed opposition to Carver's policies.

◌

Charlie Ramsey leaned back in the over-stuffed leather armchair and put his hands behind his head. "Y'know, I think we've got MacPherson just where we want him." His office, high above downtown Columbus, was warm and stuffy. "Y'see, we now have an issue we can use against him in an election."

"Who's going to run against him?" Patrick Monahan asked. He sat on the sofa opposite from the desk behind which Ramsey sat. Joyce sat next to Monahan. A frown creased her face.

A shadow of a smile crossed Ramsey's face. "Why, you are," he said. "You'll go after him for not getting the Space Force ready for the alien invasion." His smile increased fractionally. "Then letting aliens occupy sacred American soil, and Kucinski has done nothing about it. We're going to paint him and his gang of cronies as ineffective do-nothings."

Joyce lifted her hand from Monahan's knee and coughed quietly. "I learned something the other day I just can't make heads or tails of," she said. "A source overheard Encirlik talking to Kucinski, about some treatment for an illness that would add to her longevity." She glanced around. "Does this mean anything to you?"

Patrick stirred and turned toward Joyce. "Treatment for her illness? Does your source have any way to find out more about the treatment? My people have heard rumors, but not this."

Joyce shrugged. "Possibly. She works in the hospital. I'll have to pay her for the information. That's what I've been doing all along." She sighed as though it were a burden.

"Er, that won't be a problem," Ramsey said. "We need to find out about this treatment. I've also noticed both MacPherson and Encirlik seem pretty damn healthy. Others have noted the same thing over the last year or so." He nodded his head. "Maybe she really has found something."

Patrick took a deep breath. "If she's come up with a longevity treatment and is holding out, we could use that as an issue—"

"Don't be too hasty about sharing that information with the hoi-polloi," Ramsey said. "Think about the implications before you raise a hue and cry." A frown crept onto his face.

Patrick stared blankly at the opposite wall. The room grew quiet and faint sounds of the street below became audible. Motes of dust moved slowly in the sunlight beaming through the window.

"Well," Monahan said slowly. "I think a treatment such as this—if it exists—should be regulated by the government, and those receiving the treatment should be chosen by the government, only those who are truly deserving ..."

Ramsey's face relaxed into a smile. "Yes, those who support the government, top level people—"

"Before you get ahead of yourselves," Joyce said, "I have to confirm the treatment did take place. Then find out if longevity is the main benefit of the treatment—"

"Wait," Patrick said. "Kucinski was sick, on her death bed, dying, right?" He looked at Ramsey. "This treatment cured her from a fatal condition, right?"

"Wait a minute," Joyce said. "How d'you know she was dying? That she had a 'fatal' condition?"

Ramsey's lips took a thin, grim line. "Don't repeat anything you hear in this office, understand?"

Joyce stared at Ramsey for several moments. Her eyebrows rose and she nodded slowly. "I'm not stupid," she said. "I just didn't realize you played by those rules. Now I do."

"The point I was about to make," Patrick said. "Is this treatment does more than add longevity. It cured her from a cancer, which I'm told, was widespread, or should have been, throughout her body. That's a powerful treatment. We've got to get control of that technology, for us, if nothing else."

"To do that, we must have control of the government, which means winning the next election, by whatever means it takes."

ॱ

Suh-Joh eased down on her resting rock and turned her head to one side. Her paat-kli chirped and began grooming the stretched skin between two chitinous plates in her neck. "So, the Hive-Mother, Meltem." She hesitated. "Not Hive-Mother, mother of only one offspring, has a long life. The others live for about seventy of their years."

She had been surprised at the normal life span of the humans, which was several times that of Hoo-Lii. "It is only a special treatment that makes her long life, which, she said came from the other aliens." Her breathing flaps waffled, showing her puzzlement.

Son-Nih stirred from his position on the brown floor covering, his breathing flaps flaring as though scenting a faint aroma.

"This must be their way, too, of rewarding their leaders for their efforts." He flexed slightly toward Suh-Joh. "Her breeding partner, Tay-Lor, must be her counselor, much as I am to you." He flexed again.

Suh-Joh emitted a sweet aroma of satisfaction. "Yes, my good and faithful counselor, much like you. May you live long." She raised her body off the resting mound. "Yet, she said there are others who object to our new hive on the planet below."

Son-Nih unconsciously scratched a belly plate with his mid-limb. "This species is more fractious than ours. They squabble among themselves until faced with an external threat and only then they unite. So, if we can make them believe we are an ally, then they will continue their fractious ways—"

"Yes," Suh-Joh said. "We must reassure Meltem we will help them, that we need their protection for our hive below, that it will only contain young and food producers." She slumped onto her resting rock and closed her eyes.

"We really have no other choice," Son-Nih said. "Meltem and Ul-Rik are the only ones who have learned how to speak to us. Others, who do not speak our tongue, are the ones who oppose us. Therefore, we are forced to take Meltem as our ally."

Suh-Joh rose. "Come, let us contact Meltem and propose an alliance."

౬

The chanting shouts increased in volume and a stone arched through the air and crashed through a first story window of Meltem's Ataturk Pharmaceutical laboratory. It was almost like a signal. A wave of brown-clad Clan soldiers trotted forward, staves raised, into the multi-hued mob. The black painted staves rose and fell with mechanical rhythm, slowly turning crimson. The voice of the mob changed pitch, ever higher as screams sang out a counterpoint to the hoarsely chanted slogans.

Even though the soldiers were outnumbered at least ten to

one, their size and discipline combined with the ruthless use of the staves, battered the mob and forced them to retreat from the building, leaving the street littered with battered bodies, abandoned placards and dark stains.

"Your soldiers are giving my crowd a beating," Patrick Monahan said as he lowered the binoculars. He moved back from the edge of the parapet of the building at the end of the street that overlooked the laboratory.

"My soldiers?" Ramsey shrugged. "Don't you mean Kucinski's?" He smiled as he raised his eyebrows.

Monahan smiled thinly. "Yeah, right."

He knew full well that a mid-level officer loyal to Ramsey had prepped the unit to deal severely with the protesters. The protest was a direct result of the speech Monahan had just given about the inequity of medical treatment given to Taylor MacPherson and his close allies, combined with a rousing criticism of the Space Force's performance. Political operatives did the rest.

"We need some cracked heads and blood on the pavement to get out the vote." Ramsey smiled without warmth.

"Jeffries isn't going to like what you're going to do to him afterwards, for this," Monahan said. He referred to the captain of the squad sent to put down the demonstration. "The cost of doing business." He shrugged.

"You're right. I really liked the part where you tagged Taylor for proposing a tax increase for lousy performance," Ramsey said. "Now we can accuse him of using soldiers to put down a peaceful demonstration."

"We've got to sustain the level of violence until next week. Until the election." In the six months since the space battle it had taken to get the recall election underway, they had used increasingly violent tactics to mobilize opposition to Taylor.

"Just keep the demonstrators from doing any real damage to the laboratory," Ramsey said. "That's where Kucinski was treated. That's where they've got the secret to longevity."

Monahan glanced at his watch. "Got another meeting. Got to go stir up some more people."

ᘔ

Meltem knew they were in trouble. Ever since Taylor lost the election to Monahan a week ago, her problems with the pharmaceutical business had multiplied.

Now, someone had just torched their home and they'd barely escaped. "Taylor, I'm really afraid. Every day there's another demonstration, each bigger than the last. Now, they're trying to kill us."

She shivered in the pre-dawn darkness as she huddled against Taylor, holding their son, Kemal, tightly. Behind, flames flickered in the shell of their home. Fire fighters worked diligently to prevent the fire from spreading to adjacent homes.

"Taylor," a voice called from the darkness.

"Yes?" Taylor answered cautiously.

"Taylor, it's me, Billy." The short, cloak-clad alien emerged from the darkness. "Several people came to my home and set it on fire. Then they tried to attack Cha KinLaat and me. We defend ourselves—"

"Billy, are you hurt?" Taylor asked.

"They not hurt me," Billy said. "They too slow." His Qu'uda muscles, developed on a higher gravity planet, gave him a strength and quickness that made him a formidable adversary in the lower gravity of Earth. "Now I have no home."

"We have the same problem." Taylor glanced down the street. He heard the thud of feet trotting in formation. It was a contingent of militia led by Chris Kucinski.

A voice rang out and the militia came to a halt. Chris stepped close to Taylor. "I came as soon as I got word. I'm sorry I'm late." She stared at the house and shook her head. She lowered her voice, "I think Monahan's crowd is behind this."

"Can you prove it?" Taylor asked.

Chris sighed. "No, and he may not even know it's his people. It may be people just carried away by his rhetoric. Did you save anything?"

"No, but we got away unharmed." Taylor pointed. "Billy got burned out, too."

"This is getting out of hand," Chris said. "We've got to find a way to put an end to this type of violence. If we don't, people are going to get killed."

"Yes," said Meltem softly. "We must go somewhere that is safe, really safe." She whispered into Taylor's ear.

"Yes, it would be," Taylor said. "Okay, let's do it."

Meltem looked at Chris and beckoned her close. "Can you get us to Hopkins?" He referred to the former airport of Cleveland.

"Yes, what's this all about?"

"Suh-Joh asked we visit her," Taylor said. "She'll send a shuttle for us."

"Why do you need a Hoo-Lii shuttle?" Chris asked.

"When I tried to arrange a visit to the defense stations," Taylor said. "I found I'd been denied access to our shuttles. I don't know how that happened, but I suspect some of Ramsey's operatives may be responsible. So, we need to get to a communicator and then the landing site."

Chris turned and snapped her fingers. "Stanek," she called. "Send a runner to get some horses." She turned back to Taylor. "Who else is going?"

"The Qu'uda," Taylor said.

"Stanek, get a dozen horses and a mounted contingent. Not a word to anyone, okay? On the double."

"Yes, Commander." Stanek saluted and trotted away.

"Chris," Meltem called. "Can we make a detour on the way to the airport? I need to stop at the lab before we leave."

"They what?" Monahan's face turned bright red. "They left this morning on a Hoo-Lii shuttle?" His knuckles turned white as he gripped the phone handset tightly and stared at the window. Outside the twentieth story window, a rainstorm swept a gray veil over downtown Columbus. "To where? Well, tell the Hoo-Lii to send them back." He slammed the handset down.

Ramsey's frown deepened. "You'd better get Ulrich to send that message. We better get it right."

Monahan exhaled strongly and picked up the phone. "Yeah, get me Ulrich, ASAP." He put the phone down.

The phone rang. It sounded loud. Monahan grabbed the handset. "Yes? ... Yes. Send a message to the head Hoo-Lii to send MacPherson and Encirlik back to Earth ... Why? Because there're warrants out for their arrest; they're enemies of the state. And do it now." He put the phone down quickly. "Get some arrest warrants prepared and back-date them. I've already got people working on the charges. Now, we'd better send a team over to the laboratory to secure the medical technology."

"Make sure it's one of our better operatives," Ramsey said. "We don't want any screw-ups over there."

CHAPTER SEVENTEEN

PREPARATIONS

I, Kot-Nih, remember it well. The Grand Coven of Hive-Mothers assembled at the Shrine of the Mother. It was in the bowl-shaped valley and filled with Hive-Mothers from Hool, and even two from Kamah. The Hive-Mothers perched on every smoothly rounded stone set in a regular pattern across the floor of the vale. Neatly shorn springy vegetation carpeted the ground, and water, precious water, ran in rivulets down the walls. It is the image of Hool when it was a paradise.

Nah-Kih, the young Hive-Mother whose political skills had won her the position of spokesperson for the Coven stood before the Hive-Mothers. She bowed to the scarred warrior-priest. "We seek your guidance, so we may humbly follow the Way of the Mother."

An old warrior-priest had recently come to the position of head priest after the expedition led by Bok-Tah returned, having been defeated by Suh-Joh's new servants. You see, Bok-Tah had disappeared. Rumor has it the priests of the Shrine of the Mother, in their anger at his failure, fed him to the insects.

"The heretic remains," the head priest said. "You must destroy her."

Even if the new head priest had wished to change their course, he could not, for holy war had been declared. "It is the will of the Spirit of the Mother." He flexed submissively and shuffled away.

Nah-Kih moved in front of the assembled Hive-Mothers. She raised her mid-limbs and spread them wide in a gesture of welcome. "What does this Coven wish to do?"

A rumble of words flowed through the Coven. Heads bobbed. The delegate for the Hive-Mothers from Kamah rose. "We have seen the images of the Water-Gem world and its riches. We have also seen how these new servants of Suh-Joh fight." From the envy in her voice, it was obvious even the riches of Kamah did not equal the abundance of water on this new world. "So, we must prepare a force sufficient to overcome them."

"Well-spoken." Nah-Kih rippled her breathing flaps to indicate approval. "There is the matter of constructing a new fleet of ships." She explained even with the restoration of the asteroid manufacturing facility, the effort to build a fleet of the needed size would be costly. "I propose each hive contribute one worker in eight to the effort."

Chittering voices filled the vale with sounds of complaint. Many felt the cost was too high to fulfill the edict of the priests of the Spirit of the Mother.

"There is much wealth to share from this enterprise," Nah-Kih said loudly. "This world has vast areas suited to our way of life, and much water." A holo-image of the Water-Gem world appeared, rotating slowly before them, highlighting its various landforms and terrain in colors. "See, there are large parts most suitable for hive creation." She pointed to the extensive desert areas of the planet's mid and central latitudes.

The vale reverberated with the basso-profundo sounds that came from the intake of air through constricted breathing orifices they used to indicate their desire. Or was it greed?

One after another, Hive-Mothers rose to speak on how the holy war should be undertaken. A few openly discussed their desire to move their hives to the new world. As light faded and the cliffs surrounding the vale grew murky, all factions had spoken their piece. Only a few cautioned against pursuing the war.

"*To undertake this holy war, we must commit our Chosen-Male warriors and unripened ones so the burden is born fairly by every hive.*"

Nah-Kih spoke briefly as to the requirements to build the new fleet and the number of Chosen-Male warriors needed as crew. "*Do we undertake this holy war with a levy at this level of commitment?*"

A rumble of approval swept over the assembled Hive-Mothers.

At that moment, the head priest of the Shrine of the Mother stepped forward in front of the Hive-Mothers. He raised a forelimb. The vale became silent. "*May the Spirit of the Mother bless you and your fecundity, for you have chosen to follow the Way of the Mother. Go forth and destroy the heretic.*"

Even though Nah-Kih strived mightily to forge a consensus, the Hive-Mothers soon reverted to their quarrelsome ways. A few tried to shortchange their contribution to the effort and some tried to profit excessively from their construction activities.

I, Kot-Nih, saw much of this first forelimb. Indeed, the burden of feeding the workforce at the asteroid manufacturing center soon became onerous. Levy-workers had to be diverted to food production. As a result, the size of the planned fleet was reduced, not once, but twice.

It was about then Nah-Kih got plans for new weapons from the archives beneath the Shrine of the Mother, weapons from the dark ages of destruction, weapons of fearsome design. She persuaded the head priest this was acceptable since it was only for the holy war effort. The conservative Hive-Mothers believed this was nigh on heresy, and by comparison, the crimes of Suh-Joh appeared less vile.

Even with levy-workers assigned to food production, hunger stalked Hool. The ancient curse of raiding—the practice of taking food and servants by force reemerged. At first, the Coven of Hive-Mothers took action against the offenders, but as hunger increased, the raiders soon learned to destroy their victims' hives, thus leaving no witnesses to their crimes.

With fear of destruction uppermost in thought, a smaller hive moved *from the surface of Hool out to the manufacturing asteroid and took over a partially completed ship. They moved into the one of the larger battleships, and once ensconced, they activated its weapons and defied any to remove them. Of course, no one could. Yet, an odd thing happened as a result. You see, with the discipline of a hive, the battleship's completion moved forward at a faster pace. There were more workers available than needed to complete the ship they'd taken over, so, the ship-hive earned supplies by supplying its excess workers to other craft under construction.*

The unexpected success of the first ship-hive takeover prompted others to do the same. Some of the hives that followed this example were not so small and were not fleeing to escape certain destruction. Ambitious Hive-Mothers who had spoken of their desire to start a hive on the Water-Gem world led those who took over other ships. Their action, it was clear, was to ensure they would get the first pick of the best locations on the new world where they planned to set up their new hive.

Since I did not travel with the fleet, I view images from the records in the archives. Even those poor holo-images conveyed the size of the holy fleet. There were those who spoke in awe of the assembled might of Hool, and likened it to the restoration of the greatness of Hool to the levels seen in its glory days. It must have been a sight to be seen....

Welding torches flickered violet-white flashes within the ranks of the assembled ships. The fleet was almost ready. One-quarter of the eight squared vessels built were large battleships of similar design to that used by the heretic, Suh-Joh.

They had living quarters in a ring connected to a central hub by three spokes. A huge globular fuel tank, of almost the same diameter as the living quarter ring, was at the head of the hub. At the rear of the stem-like hub was a cluster of engines. Many of the battleships had grown larger living quarter rings than first planned due to their conversion into hives.

The fleet orbited about the manufacturing center in the

asteroids. Multiple shells of small asteroids hung like diseased fruit from the trunk of the long, box-like structure of the central metal processing line, stripped of their metals. Seemingly tiny shuttles hovered like insects around the ships, waiting their turn to deliver supplies, like daa-lii seeking nectar.

Indeed, the image of success brought about by the fleet was in sharp contrast to the discord foisted on those left on the surface of the planet. Constructing this fleet had sorely tried the resources of our civilization, and for what purpose? To destroy the one Hive-Mother who had made possible Hool's return to the technological prowess once known in the past, whose only crime was to extend the life of her servants....

CHAPTER EIGHTEEN

THE DARKEST HOUR

A phone rang. Monahan turned from the window over-looking downtown Columbus from the twentieth floor in the former BankOne building on Broad Street. He stepped to the wide cherry wood desk and picked up the handset. "Yes? What? They refuse to send MacPherson and Encirlik back to us? Why? What d'you mean, they don't give a reason?"

"Patrick," Joyce Vargas said softly. "Put us on the speaker, please." She sat on the sofa against the wall.

"You see, it's not as though they're refusing to send them down, it's more like they're ignoring our request." Ulrich's voice sounded tinny.

Ramsey frowned and cleared his throat. "Y'mean they're ignoring our authority?"

"Who's that?" Ulrich asked, surprise evident.

"This is Charles Ramsey, Human Confederation Minister of Defense. Now, why are they ignoring our authority?"

"Ah-um." Ulrich paused. "Er, I think it has to do with their cultural bias. Y'see, I believe they're an autocratic matriarchy.

Their view is a request should come from an absolute leader of similar status. That is, er, a mother—"

"Look, I don't need any long-winded explanation, just tell them we do things differently here, and since they're on our turf, they do 'em according to our rules."

The phone's hum grew louder in the following silence.

"Ulrich, did y'hear what I said?" Ramsey tapped his fingers impatiently on the side of the chair.

"Ah, yes, I certainly did. I just don't quite know how to say that without provoking an incident—"

"Incident? They've got one already," Monahan said.

Ulrich's pause was not as long this time, but long enough for Monahan and Ramsey to exchange glances.

"I don't think the Hoo-Lii believe they're subject to our jurisdiction. In fact, I've finally translated the word they use for us. Do you want to know what it is?"

"What's this got do with getting MacPherson and Encirlik back into our custody?" Ramsey's voice rose in volume.

"Oh, everything." Ulrich chuckled nervously. "They refer to us as their servants. Obviously, they consider any request from us as being something to which they might or might not wish to respond, but only if it suits them."

࿐

Ki Mapes looked up from his desk. "Yes?" His office was painted in the standard gray paint and had a battered metal desk, cluttered with files, two phones and a computer. A pair of two-drawer filing cabinets supported a tabletop that held a photo of his wife LaTasha and his two sons, along with a coffee maker.

Ed Kerr stepped into the office. "Got a minute?"

"Sure." Ki gestured to the seat in front of the desk. "Like a cup of coffee?" Ever since real coffee had again become available, Ki used every excuse he could find to enjoy it.

"No, thanks." Ed frowned. "They've cut our budget, again."

Ki leaned back in his chair and nodded slowly, pursing his lips. "Yeah. No real surprise. Carver's been warning me about it for weeks. Seems Monahan and his crowd believe since peace has broken out, it's time to enjoy a peace dividend. I just received this." He handed Ed a flimsy sheet of paper.

Ed frowned as he read. "This orders us to start shipping a hundred tons of helium-three per month to Earth." He stared blankly at the wall. "Can we do that?"

"Oh, it's theoretically possible if we cannibalize the Eagles into tankers." Ki's hand curled into a fist and he dropped it to the desk. "I have no intention of doing that."

"So, what do we do?"

"It's time for plan B." Ki smiled thinly. "We still have friends down below, out west."

He referred to the military located in Nevada and Puget Sound that received the smuggled platinum-rich asteroid metal.

"If they don't appropriate sufficient funds so we can rebuild the Space Force, well, I guess we'll just have to get the money from elsewhere."

Ed nodded slowly. He had submitted a long requisition list to restore DS-2 and DS-3 to their previous capabilities and had been rebuffed by Monahan's new administration. "We're going to need a lot of equipment to build the new L-4 station." He referred to the new defense station to be located at the L-4 Lagrangian orbit. "Never mind developing Deimos."

"Fortunately Taylor set things in motion before the election, and with Pip Ryan's heavy lifters up and running, we no longer have a transportation bottle neck." He referred to the three spacecraft made from ferryboat hulls.

Each heavy lifter had a pair of huge doors at the rear to provide easy access and short turnaround time. Each held one hundred thousand cubic feet, or about one thousand tons. The front of the new shuttle was an umbrella-like structure made from foamed alumina with a skin of zirconia tiles for protection from the heat of re-entry.

"If we're careful, we can move a lot of ore. With the North American economy growing, it'll be simple to slip significant amounts of platinum into the monetary system.

"We intend to take care of all dependents of casualties so their personal sacrifice doesn't become a financial problem," Ki said. "We want that to get around, so the new recruits for the Space Force won't worry about their families."

"I'd like to change some of my requisitions," Ed said.

"What d'you have in mind?"

"I think we ought to get more machine equipment, so we can set up our own manufacturing facilities—"

"Excellent idea. I'll let our people below know," Ki said.

"And recruit people who know how to use it, including machine designers, if we're going to do it right." Ed's eyes almost closed as he slowly nodded his head.

"Yes, good point." Ki's head moved in rhythm with Ed's.

Patrick Monahan smiled widely as Charlie Ramsey signed the document. "So, now it's official?" he said.

Ramsey looked up from his desk and nodded. "You're the new head of Security as well as Council leader. Kucinski now reports to you." He chuckled. "For how long is anyone's guess."

"Not long." Monahan moved toward Ramsey's desk. "Let me use your pen," he said. "I want to get these orders executed immediately." Outside, low clouds touched the top of the nearby skyscrapers in downtown Columbus.

Ramsey nodded as he gave his pen to Monahan. "We've got an indictment against MacPherson and Encirlik. Now we can seize their assets legally. Make sure whoever goes into the laboratory knows the importance of what they're looking for." He had already emphasized the secret process Meltem Encirlik used to cure Kucinski of being poisoned was to be kept secret; for their use only.

Monahan straightened up. "This one orders the Space Force to apprehend MacPherson and Encirlik, to use whatever means are necessary to remove them from the alien's ship."

Ramsey nodded. "I've already ordered two battle groups to mobilize and move to New Mexico to bottle up those aliens who set up housekeeping on our territory. They just might come in handy negotiating with the alien queen on that spaceship." He smiled. "Things are finally starting to go our way, right?"

"Yeah, well, maybe. I'll reserve judgment on that."

༕

A squad of brown-clad soldiers trotted in formation up the deserted tree-lined street to the main entrance of the three-story brick building that was the main laboratory of Ataturk Industries. Steel plates covered the windows on the lower level and a slab of steel on huge hinges was the front door. The soldiers halted and dressed ranks, their muzzle-loading rifles ready. They remained silent, waiting.

A clatter of hooves and the rattle of steel wheels on hard pavement announced the arrival of two artillery guns. "Halt," called the officer in charge.

He pointed to the main entrance, "Take out the door's hinges."

As the artillery crew unhitched the horses and wheeled the guns into position, the officer impatiently slapped his hand with a riding crop.

"Ah, sir," one of the artillerymen called. "We're ready."

The officer sniffed as he eyed the alignment of the guns. Satisfied, he waved his riding crop, his gesture indicating the soldiers to move further away. He waited until the soldiers, now broken into two groups, were at opposite ends of the laboratory. "One round each," the officer called.

Each gun fired directly at the hinges supporting the doors.

The explosive shells shattered the brickwork holding the hinges. As the smoke cleared, the doors, while still in place, sagged.

"Pull out the door," the officer said and waved his riding crop. "Use the horses."

A team of horses struggled, heaving on a rope attached to the door, their hooves sparking on the road. Eventually they stopped. After the addition of the second team, the horses pulled the door from its opening. It toppled flat on the ground with a tremendous thud, raising a large cloud of dust.

The dust cleared and revealed a dark and silent interior of the laboratory.

"Break out the lanterns," he said. "Platoon A," he called, "follow me." He advanced into the building with a soldier on either side, guns raised, the rest of the platoon close behind.

The officer consulted a piece of paper containing a diagram of the laboratory.

"Where is this Doctor Encirlik's office?" he muttered.

A light flicked on, lighting the hallway.

"What?" he said. "Who did that?"

"Er, I, er, brushed up agin' the wall, an' a light came on," said a ruddy complexioned young soldier. "I didn't mean no harm." He pointed at a switch on the wall.

"Hmm, let me see," the officer said. As he walked further down the main corridor and flicked another switch. More lights came on. "Lot better than the lanterns." He consulted the diagram. "We go left at the next corridor."

The officer stopped at a door that had a frosted glass panel. He rattled its knob. It did not turn. "Stand back," he said and hit the glass with his gun.

The glass shattered.

The officer picked several pieces of glass out of the window frame before reaching through to the inside lock. "Ah," he said, as the lock clicked and the door swung open. "We're in." He stepped inside and groped for the light switch alongside the door. He found it and flicked the switch.

He heard something click-snap, followed by the sound of glass breaking.

He sniffed.

Oil, he thought.

A ball of flame exploded from the center of the office, back-lighting a row of filing cabinets. It was the last thing he saw.

&

Klaus Loeser smiled. From the next room came the low rumble of thousands of pieces of metal thrashing together.

So, he thought. *This is the tenth batch.*

He was proud of his work. He knew he was a good master machinist, perhaps the best in Tacoma, and maybe even the best on the West Coast. He felt honored he'd been chosen for this task, which, while technically illegal, was for a noble purpose of funding the Space Force.

The ten-foot long ball mill rotated slowly as thirty thousand platinum coins tumbled against each other, acquiring a patina of use.

This batch of Maple Leaf counterfeit coins were perfect—each bore the Clan stamp of the Treasury authorizing its use as currency. Each coin was identical, each perfectly stamped. It was almost time to add a concoction of oil and soot to fill in the scratches and markings on the coins to make them look more like authentically used coins.

Each batch—thirty thousand coins—was worth three million new silver dollars. Since a laborer worked a week for one silver dollar, this was a lot of money. Soon, the tedious part would begin; packaging the coins in as many different types of bags, rolls, and tubes as he could imagine.

Neatness, tidiness, cleanliness, and consistency are so much more satisfying, thought Klaus, *rather than making these beautiful coins so nicked and grubby.* He understood well the reason, but his soul wanted perfection. So, with each batch, he always sent out a roll or two in perfect condition, rolled properly, just like they'd come from a mint.

Soon, the tight-faced, hard muscled men who dressed in drab civilian clothes and said very little would come to pick up the coins. They were the ones who also delivered sheets of shiny platinum made to the exact thickness Klaus specified for his stamping press. They paid him—and very well indeed—with silver coins that were truly authentic. Klaus knew better than to use his own product to pay his bills.

The next batch of coins will be different, he thought. *Since the dies for both the American Eagle and the Maple Leaf are showing signs of wear. I'll make a die for the Australia Koala. Now, that's a very pretty coin, more of a challenge.* He liked that; it was a chance to exercise his skill as a diemaker.

Suh-Joh stared at the humans. *So soft and vulnerable,* she thought. *Perhaps that is what makes them so dangerous. They need obscene weapons to compensate for their personal failings....*

"You say there a schism within the human species?" she asked. It was as her counselor predicted: Pretend to be an ally and they will fall apart in the absence of an external enemy.

The box made its low-pitched sounds and the humans talked between each other before their Mother spoke.

"A different faction is in control. This faction does not want friendship with Hoo-Lii. We are those who wish friendship with Hoo-Lii. We are no longer in control." The voice from the translation box was not easy to understand.

Suh-Joh turned to her counselor, Son-Nih. "Have the humans taken action against our hive on the Water-Gem?" she asked.

"None," Son-Nih said. "There appears to be movement of more humans near the hive, but no hostile action. Perhaps we should ask these humans if the new faction will be a danger."

"Yes," Suh-Joh said. *What is her name? Meltem?* "Human-

Mother, Meltem, what are the threats to the Hoo-Lii from the new human faction?"

The humans clustered together to talk in their deep-pitched voices for some time. "Honored Hive-Mother," Meltem said. "We believe the human faction will attack the hive on the Water-Gem to capture Hoo-Lii. The humans in craft above Water-Gem will not attack. I must talk to the humans in craft above Water-Gem."

Suh-Joh stared hard at the humans. "Soon, you may speak to the humans in the craft above the Water-Gem. Tell them not to use the obscenities."

"Obscenities? What are obscenities?" Meltem asked.

"Show them," Suh-Joh said. The holo-display flickered and an image of the fleet of the Council of Hive-Mothers appeared. The image expanded to just one ship. A bright point of light appeared, and for an instant, something flashed toward the ship.

"That is the weapon the craft above the Water-Gem used against those who attacked us."

The humans again huddled together before Meltem spoke. "We use that weapon when all else fails. I must speak to the craft above the Water-Gem, I tell them you wish them no harm."

Suh-Joh glanced at Son-Nih. His breathing flaps closed as though feeling relief at the human's words.

"Ul-Rik sent message the human faction wants me to send you back to them. I have not answered him. Why should I not send you back?" She opened her breathing orifices as to sense the flavor of the expected answer from Meltem.

"You gain no advantage to send us back," came the words of Meltem from the translation box. "We speak to craft above Water-Gem for you and your wish for no harm. They will listen to us. Those on the Water-Gem will harm your hive."

Suh-Joh rose off her resting mound and turned toward Son-Nih. "Start the evacuation of the hive on the Water-Gem. Retrieve as much food as possible."

Son-Nih flexed toward his Hive-Mother. "At once," he said and hurried away.

Suh-Joh paused before speaking. "Food, my ship needs food. Does the craft above the Water-Gem have food?"

Meltem spoke with the other human. "The craft above the Water-Gem may have food. Must speak to them."

Suh-Joh waved her mid-limb. "It will be arranged."

$$\curvearrowright$$

Ki Mapes stared at the monitor on the desk in his office. Josie Armstrong had hooked his office computer into the main monitor on the command deck and he'd found it saved him a lot of time. He was glad to have her back.

It looks like the Hoo-Lii have stepped up traffic between their Carlsbad operation and the mother ship, he thought. *I wonder what's going on?*

One of the two phones on his battered metal desk rang. "Hello?" Ki said into the handset. "Yeah, sure, put her on right away." He opened a drawer and took out a pad of paper.

"Yeah? Hello, Meltem, y'okay?" Ki listened for a few moments before he ceased frowning. "So, the Hoo-Lii don't like our nukes, eh?" He chuckled. "Well, don't tell them how much we don't like their laser, okay? So, did you know Ramsey ordered me to go get you from the Hoo-Lii mother ship? Fat chance of that. You must have really rubbed them the wrong way." Her following words made him frown.

"I see," Ki said. "I'd heard the pharmaceutical operation was a bone of contention, but apparently there's more to it than what's in the news ... Okay, when we get together, you can tell me about it ... What? Food?" Ki leaned back.

"I suppose it's possible. Lemme look into it. How much?" He wrote quickly on the pad of paper. "Okay, that's not an unreasonable amount. We should be able to run that past the long noses of Ramsey's agents ... Yeah, Pip Ryan has finished the heavy lifters Ramsey and Monahan know nothing about. Be a good shake-down run, bringing up a couple of loads."

Ki listened for a while. "Okay, but I think I should meet Suh-Joh and offer both my promise of non-aggression and the food at the same time. At the same time, pick you up." He paused.

"You don't want to come back to DS-2?" He nodded his head and pursed his lips while cradling the handset to his ear. "I suppose you're right. I can pretend to follow their orders better if I don't show my hand."

ૐ

Monahan entered Ramsey's office. The blinds were down and soft lighting gave the room a cozy appearance. "You know what that bitch did?" His voice was strained as though he'd been running hard.

"Which bitch?" Ramsey raised his eyebrows. "There're a lot of women in your life might deserve that label." He sat behind his desk with his shirtsleeves rolled up.

"I just heard that MacPherson's bitch, Encirlik, booby-trapped her damn office with a fucking firebomb. Killed Captain Podojil and six soldiers. Worse yet, destroyed all her files and notes. Now we don't have anything to go on for that longevity treatment. Goddam bitch." He sat down heavily.

"Maybe her technicians know how it works—" Ramsey began.

"I already thought of that, but according to our source, the two technicians who worked with her have disappeared, too." Monahan slammed his fist on the desk.

"You know who else has disappeared? Your favorite police-woman, Kucinski; she's gone, too."

"Where the hell are they going? Who's warning them?"

Ramsey took a deep breath. "You're supposed to be the security expert. Why don't you tell me?" He raised his eyebrows and steepled his fingers. "Let me see, you probably don't know that pain in the ass, Ki Mapes, is coming up with a steady stream of excuses why he can't execute our orders."

"Why don't you replace him?" Monahan snapped.

"With whom?" Ramsey said. "If it were a ground position, I've got lots of officers who know how to take orders, but that space thing, it's different. Most of the trained personnel are out west, and they seem to have a negative attitude toward our administration." He made a face as though sucking something sour. "It seems they're all fans of Mapes."

Monahan snorted disdainfully. "Gee, after we cut their budget in half, what a surprise."

"Well, your Chinese buddy, Guang Xhi, had the votes and it would've been stupid to go against that reality."

The phone rang. "Hello?" Ramsey said. He listened for several minutes "I see ... y'sure? Oh, you're not absolutely positive?" He silently mouthed a curse. "Well, why don't you find out? That's what you're paid to do." He slammed the handset back into the cradle. "They tracked Kucinski onto a plane that went out west. Then, supposedly, she took another plane that went to Groom Lake where she disappeared."

"If she's there," Monahan said. "She's out of circulation."

"He also got a report of a ship launching to orbit shortly thereafter from some place near Groom Lake, but no one knows whose or what ship it was. All other shuttles were accounted for. So, that was an unknown shuttle, maybe Hoo-Lii."

"What the hell is going on? Y'sure?"

"Ornsted's usually reliable."

"Where did it go?" Monahan asked, deep furrows between his eyes. "Those Groom Lake people keep good track of that stuff."

"They said it must have been high orbit, which means it went out of sight before they figured out its destination."

"Well, how many destinations could it have?"

Ramsey took a deep breath. "Either the alien mother ship, or Defense Station Two."

"Speaking of the aliens, when're your soldiers moving against the alien nest in Carlsbad?" Ramsey grimaced. "There's been a stream of alien shuttles in and out of there for the last two days. Heaviest traffic in months. Something is up. My people won't be ready for action until tomorrow. I want to send an ultimatum to those aliens after my soldiers move in."

He unrolled a map. "See here." He pointed. "They'll occupy the heights above the entrance with artillery and command their landing area. Once they do that, we'll have them by their nuts."

꒰

Suh-Joh rose off her resting mound and gestured to a servant, an unripened female who moved a holo-display unit before her. The brown curtains along the wall of the ersatz cave rippled and five humans entered, preceded and followed by several Chosen-Male warriors.

"You have kept your word," Suh-Joh said and the translation device uttered the guttural sounds of human speech. "You delivered food and a promise of no harm."

She gestured and the holo-display brightened to show an image of a spacecraft. It was rectangular in shape, with a dome-shaped end. At its other end were large, clamshell doors. Two pods on the side of the craft had openings, black and round—apparently engines. The craft rotated to reveal another side, which had the US flag and the logo "USASF" in bright red, white, and blue.

The holo-display expanded its image to include the front part of the Mother's Servant toward which the boxy spacecraft moved. Smaller Hoo-Lii craft, round and bug-like, appeared to close in on the human ship, and gently nudged it into close embrace with the Mother's Servant. The image faded.

"And now more," Suh-Joh said. "Ul-Rik sent new message. The human faction on the Water-Gem demand I send you back to them. They threaten to destroy my hive on the Water-Gem."

Her breathing flaps fluttered momentarily. "The hive is now empty, as is their threat. All my children are here and I have food."

The human-mother stepped forward and spoke. The translation device said, "We wish no harm to Hoo-Lii. We believe human and Hoo-Lii can help each other."

"Perhaps it is time to seek a new home," said Suh-Joh. "Maybe we will depart to Hool, then a new place. Do you wish to return to the Water-Gem? Or, to the human craft above the Water-Gem?" She extended her mid-limbs widely in a gesture of choice.

The humans moved close together and talked among themselves. The human-mother stepped forward. "We cannot return to Water-Gem or the craft above Water-Gem. We choose to stay with you."

Suh-Joh's breathing orifices flared momentarily and she turned to her counselor, Son-Nih. "Do they pose a threat to us should they stay among us?"

Son-Nih flexed toward the floor. "Honored Hive-Mother, they pose no direct threat to any Hoo-Lii and they may bring riches of knowledge to us. They are no match for our Chosen-Male warriors." He hesitated.

"Yet, their knowledge may infect us with ideas, alien ideas. If we are strong in our faith to the Way of the Mother, we should be able to withstand such things. But, as I know so well, these things are hard to predict." He flexed low. "If they prove to be a problem, we can always feed them to the insects...."

"Then let us depart."

"Sir, the big momma's moving," A voice said loudly from the handset. An image flashed onto the computer monitor.

"Direction? Velocity change?" Ki Mapes asked.

"Sir, it's on the same bearing as the previous Hoo-Lii ships, toward the anomaly." The voice paused. "They've just passed thirty-five klicks a second and increasing at a steady rate. It's my guess they're heading Pluto way."

"Thank you," Ki said. "Keep me informed of any changes." He put down the handset and plucked at his lower lip.

Not really a surprise, he thought. *They evacuated all of their people, or whatever they call themselves, from their Carlsbad settlement, and asked for food. Funny how they think corn and soybeans are the greatest gourmet foods ever invented.*

Ki picked up a handset. "Get me Minister Ramsey of the H-C, right away. Thanks." He waited a few minutes, thinking how Taylor, Meltem, Chris Kucinski, and the other two, he couldn't remember the names of the technicians who had accompanied them, had cheerfully gone onto the alien ship, plus the Qu'uda. *Different strokes*, he thought. The phone rang.

"Yes, Minister Ramsey, the alien mother ship appears to be heading for the anomaly, y'know, the transfer point...." He listened for a few moments. "Well, as far as we know, MacPherson and the others are still on board ... What, chase them? None of my Eagles are fully up to snuff ... Yes, sir," he said stiffly. He failed to tell him that two Eagles had the devices that let them enter the transfer points. "I understand, sir, right away sir." As he listened carefully, he pursed his lips and licked them.

"Yes, sir, I will ensure two Eagles will depart within forty-eight hours to chase and attempt to detain the alien mother ship. Yes, sir, I understand my orders completely." He gently lowered the handset to the cradle.

"Stupid, dumb sonnuvabitch." He sighed. "He'd send my boys to certain death if they attack the mother ship. I just hope they're smart enough not to obey my orders this time."

CHAPTER NINETEEN

FLIGHT

Gordon Felsbek frowned.

He'd been over the monetary data three times and the amount of money in circulation did not make sense. *There's too much*, he thought. *Perhaps the early records of the Clan are inaccurate and they put more money in circulation than these documents show.*

He had been chosen to head the Office of Budget Control because he had the skills of an accountant and the soul of a miser. He put his pen down and stared at the lending floor of the former Huntington bank. Two dozen neatly dressed people bent to their work.

My staff, he thought, *is the economic heart of the Re-established United States. This money in circulation problem,* he thought, *I'd better investigate it further and get to the bottom of it....*

ᘔ

The dark shapes in the large monitor flickered and faded, replaced by a series of points labeled with coordinates.

"These are the asteroids." Bud Inez's voice was tinny through the speaker mounted on the bulkhead above the monitor.

He was at L4 Earth-sun Lagrangian point, also known as the leading Trojan point at which asteroids collected. Bud had been drafted to lead the construction project and eventually run the new station. He'd grown tired of duty on the Eagles.

Ki Mapes stared at the monitor. "How many are there?" He went to get a cup of coffee since he had to wait eight minutes to get a reply due to the almost fifty million miles distance between L4 and DS-2. Half-a-dozen crew on duty in the command center craned their heads to see the images on the monitor. Around the perimeter of the room were electronic instruments, many with red and green lights flashing.

"We've counted seventy bodies ranging in size from two kilometers down to one-tenth kilometer diameter and smaller. They're spread out over about a thousand kilometers. There's hundreds of smaller bodies, but they're harder to see and count accurately on our instruments." Bud's voice rose and fell with the static.

"Have you identified a good candidate for the new defense station?" Ki picked up a file and began to read.

"Yeah." Bud's voice finally said. "We've found three metallic asteroids that are in the right size range, but we've gotta take a closer look to figure out which is the best of the bunch." There was a brief pause. "What's going on with the Deimos project?"

Ki picked up a clipboard. "Don't take too long," he said. "Kerr's already on the way with three tunnel borers and the metal caster will follow soon after." He referred to Ed Kerr who had constructed DS-3 from a metallic asteroid and would be in charge of this project.

"We don't know how much time we have. If those other Hoo-Lii return, we need to be ready for them. Our West Coast people will use the heavy lifter to bring you supplies." He paused. "Deimos, we're sending an old Eagle with a rack of soloships."

It was the project to establish a space station above Mars

near its outer Moon, Deimos. "We'll start by setting up extraction units to make it self-sufficient."

Under Deimos's dusty regolith was a clay-rock-metal matrix with almost twenty-percent water and an abundance of organic compounds. They would use this to make water and atmosphere.

"Then we start on infrastructure." He leaned back and closed his eyes.

The monitor flickered and a heavily pocked, dull gray, pear-shaped object appeared.

"This's a candidate asteroid for DS-4, maybe the best one." Bud's voice squawked. "It's iron-nickel, with a trace of platinum group metals." He paused. "Let's see, any problem getting recruits?"

"I hope it's not as rich as Trouble." Ki used the unofficial name of the small asteroid that was almost one-tenth percent platinum and had stirred up a political storm. He chuckled without mirth. "Recruits, no problem since we started providing death benefits." Smuggled asteroidal platinum was the source of the unofficial funding for the pensions paid to the relatives of those who died in the conflict with the Hoo-Lii.

Most of the new recruits came from the West Coast, same as the previous crews. "Do a thorough job of checking for internal faults or fractures before you start on the tunnels. We can't any afford wasted effort." Minutes ticked by.

"No." Bud finally responded. "Less than one-hundredth of one percent platinum metals. See its shape? It's almost circular at the fat part. Its diameter is about three hundred meters and it's four-fifty long—a perfect size. Also there's several CI-type asteroids nearby we can use for volatiles.

"Gotcha on checking stuff out. I'll get back to you in a day or so with more info. Count on us being ready when Kerr and his work crews arrive."

Monahan gritted his teeth. "Well, why haven't they caught up with them yet?" The office above downtown Columbus was stuffy, the result of being closed up tightly for winter and a sunny April day making it too warm.

Ramsey sat behind a cherry wood desk while Joyce sat on the sofa. "They've followed them for six months and haven't even tried to apprehend them. Now they're playing ring-a-round the rosie at Uranus."

"They think the Hoo-Lii mother ship is refueling," Ki Mapes said. "Which means they use helium-three and deuterium—"

"I don't care if they use matzo balls," Monahan said. "When are they going to do something about apprehending them?"

The sound of a sigh came from the speaker. "Well, our ships have to be very careful in their approach to the Hoo-Lii mother ship, what with its powerful laser—"

"What? Are your men cowards?" Monahan said.

Static grew loud in the speaker. "Mr. Monahan, I believe your remark is an undeserved slur upon the character and honor of the men and women of the United States Space Force. We suffered significant casualties defending Earth, placing ourselves willingly in harm's way to protect you."

"Sorry," Monahan said without conviction.

"Er, this is Ramsey." Ramsey's voice was low and soothing. "I believe that Mr. Monahan deeply regrets making that statement. We know how valiantly the men and women of the Space Force performed. We'd just like to catch the criminals who've taken refuge on that alien ship, who've fled justice. We're all a bit frustrated this hasn't happened yet."

"I advised you our ships weren't ready for duty when you ordered me to send them in pursuit of the Mother's Servant." Ki's voice grew louder, with a hard edge. "I had to send two poorly armed, barely repaired ships on a hazardous chase after the most powerful ship ever seen in the solar system. In addition, at the present level of funding, it'll take at least year to restore those ships of the Space Force damaged in the conflict back to their previous fighting condition."

"It's our view the alien danger is over," Ramsey said.

"Perhaps," said Ki. "And if it isn't? Who'll protect Earth? Are we going to get the funds to fix our ships?"

Ki already knew what their answer would be. However, with the secret flow of funds from the asteroid platinum, the damaged Eagles had already been restored to operating condition and—Ki suppressed a smile—eight additional Fast Eagles would soon be online and stationed at the new station being built at the L4 point.

"There are unnecessary items in your budget," Ramsey said. "You launched additional submarine hulls to orbit. What for, I don't know. And you haven't shut down the Tacoma operation—"

"Those launch operations came out of last year's budget. If they'd been canceled, we would have lost the money already spent. Tacoma cannot be shut down, it's our planet-side base—"

"When will your people apprehend the fugitives?" Monahan said. "Are you ignoring our directive?"

Ki cleared his throat. "If." He hesitated. "If those Eagles have the opportunity, the fugitives will be taken into custody."

"Then why haven't they stopped the alien ship and demanded they give up the fugitives?"

Ki took a deep breath. "In good conscience, I cannot order my people to sacrifice themselves to no purpose—"

"It's their job to bring the fugitives to justice." Monahan raised his voice. "That's their duty."

"Mr. Monahan." Ki's voice was loud and icy. "The alien ship has more firepower than all of my ships combined. It would be a suicide mission for two Eagle-class ships to attack the Hoo-Lii mother ship. If you direct me to issue the order they should attack, I and my entire officer corps will go before the Human Confederation Assembly and submit our resignations en masse, stating our reasons ..."

ᘓ

Taylor looked up as the brown drape swished open. It was Meltem entering the room. "Hi," he said. "Did you find anything out?" He rose from fabric pad on the floor and kissed her.

"Yes, lots." Meltem raised her eyebrows. "We're approaching Pluto, so we'll be close to the anomaly."

"Any chance of seeing it?"

Meltem shrugged. "I don't see why not. Everywhere I go in the ship, the Hoo-Lii seem to ignore me. Well." She hesitated. "Except when I get near Suh-Joh. Then those skinny, spine-covered Hoo-Lii start to get all twitchy. They won't let me near their food production center either, for some reason."

"What about the Eagles?" Taylor had found Meltem had a high status with Suh-Joh and that apparently rubbed off on the crew. As a result, when Meltem went on information gathering walks throughout the Mother's Servant and asked questions, they were answered. Taylor had found that his questions were usually ignored like he was a nobody.

"From what I can tell on the Hoo-Lii display, they're following behind us at, maybe, one thousand kilometers distance. They check on them regularly. I think that's because they know our fusion powered lasers don't have that much range."

"Anything else?"

"Yes, I found Ki Mapes gave them an old shuttle." Meltem chuckled and shook her head. "Ki gave it to them because the defectors brought him the Hoo-Lii craft. Apparently, Ki thought it was a fair trade."

Taylor's eyebrows rose. "Curious," he said. "What're they doing with it?"

Meltem took a deep breath. "Nothing with the shuttle, apparently. It's just sitting in one of their docking bays, doors all open and no one around it. I took a look inside. All of its instruments and computers are gone—"

"Gone? Are you sure?"

"Well, all of the slots and bays in the cockpit are now empty," Meltem said. "Wires hanging out with tags on them."

"I wonder." Taylor looked up, eyes blank. "They were very curious about our computers, especially when they learned we used solid-state devices, rather than bio-systems. Gee, from what I saw in their control center, our stuff must seem like it's from the Stone Age."

"We'll find out sooner or later," Meltem said. "Want to get something to eat?"

"Sure." Taylor laughed. "Another adventure." They'd found they never knew what food would be brought to them and learned by trial and error what items agreed with them. They still weren't sure from where or what the food came. It certainly didn't look like anything made of corn or soybeans.

ॐ

Walid Gharaguh wished he'd never been ambitious and worked hard to qualify as a commander of a Fast Eagle. But he had, and now was directing the chase of an alien ship that was stopping at the mysterious anomaly on the outer edge of the solar system.

All because there were "criminals" on board, who he knew were guilty of only being out of favor with the politicians in Columbus. Plus, he and Jim Hawley had the only two Eagles with the Hoo-Lii device that opened the space-time anomaly. He missed his wife, fresh tabouli, and the opportunity to pray in a mosque once in a while.

"Sir," said the navigation officer, who also functioned as the electronic lookout.

The voice broke Walid's quiet rapprochement. "Yes?"

"The alien ship has delta-vee change," the navigation officer said. "Its velocity is down to one point three klicks per second. Heading ..." He rattled off a string of numbers.

"Where's it going?" Walid said.

The navigation officer looked and sighed. "The anomaly, it's dead on for the anomaly."

"Time to arrival?"

The navigation officer tapped on the keyboard and stared at the monitor before him. A string of numbers scrolled down the bright blue screen. "Er, about seven hours, sir. I need to get distance ranging data to be more accurate than that."

"Close enough." Walid reached for the handset on his workstation. "Now hear this." His voice reverberated throughout the ship. "The alien craft is heading into the anomaly with significant velocity. Our orders are to follow. If the alien craft enters the anomaly, we shall follow."

However, Walid thought. *Not at one point three klicks per second, we're going to creep through.* He put the handset down and caught the navigation officer's eye. "Change our delta-vee to arrive with a velocity of point one klicks relative."

"Yes, sir," the navigation officer said.

It was six hours later when Walid received the call that made him hurry to the command center. "What is it?" he asked, winded from pulling himself through the ship under almost zero-gee conditions.

"We're getting a visual on something in front of the Hoo-Lii ship," said the technician who handled long-range data acquisition. "Something's happening out there."

"Put it on the main screen." Walid glanced at the large flat screen monitor mounted above his command station. "Maximum magnification."

A double-dot light source danced around in the middle of the screen and rapidly grew larger. One dot grew into the familiar doughnut shape of the Hoo-Lii ship. The other dot manifested itself as a giant transparent box-like grid of neon orange lines of glowing energy. The anomaly grew brighter as the Hoo-Lii ship drew closer. As the gigantic ring-shaped craft entered the glowing frame-like structure, its appearance changed from a solid to transparency and disappeared.

"Wow," somebody said.

Walid felt an icy hand grip his heart. His orders were to follow the Hoo-Lii ship, no matter where it went. He'd just seen a ship fifty times the size of his Eagle vanish before his eyes.

Merciful Allah, he thought. *I am in your beneficent hands.*

"Set course for the anomaly," Walid said. *At one-tenth klick per second, we'll enter that thing in about three hours.* "Batten down all loose items. Man the battle stations."

He picked up the handset. "Captain Hawley," he called to the second Eagle following close behind. "Follow our course into the anomaly. We'll continue to follow the Hoo-Lii ship." *That sounds brave*, he thought. *But my heart is full of fear.*

ૐ

"So," Suh-Joh said. "What do you think of this human technology?" She waved a mid-limb at the metal boxes taken from the human craft given by the humans which now were hooked into the Mother's Servant's navigation system. They filled the navigator's station to observe their transit through space-time.

"All tests show these primitive devices are immune to the disruptive effects of a relativistic transfer," said Son-Nih. "This, however, will be an operational test."

"Is it worth the risk?" Suh-Joh asked.

Son-Nih rippled his breathing orifices slowly. "If I were advising the Coven of Hive-Mothers, I'd insist armed ships be stationed at the transfer point into Hool's system." His spines briefly rose. "They are not fools, so, count on hostile forces waiting for us. Therefore, we must exit the transfer point at high velocity. We must depend on these primitive devices to keep our ship operational. I do not wish we should be like dazed dah-lii, slow and easy pickings."

"Son-Nih, my brave counselor, whom I hold in high esteem, by the Spirit of the Mother, lead me home."

Son-Nih turned to the navigator. "Maximum acceleration."

The long, luminous strings of the space-time anomaly began to collapse into the cubical structure found at the entrance to normal space. The nausea and never-where feeling swept through the ship as space-time collapsed around them. With a kaleido-scopic flash, the sky filled with stars as the cubical structure collapsed. They had arrived.

The Mother's Servant's engines continued to build thrust, even as the navigator babbled and struggled to regain control. The holo-display flashed into life, prompted into activity by the primitive human devices that were immune to relativistic shock. Yellow icons began to flash warnings, identifying craft nearby.

Son-Nih forced himself to concentrate on the holo-display. There were at least eight squared ships on course toward them, or the anomaly. It could be only one thing.

"Battle stations," he squeaked loudly.

"We have high relative closing velocity," the navigator said. "Perhaps we've surprised them."

"That was our intention," said Son-Nih. "Can we increase acceleration?"

The navigator's forelimbs flicked over the controls. "Only by one part in eight if we shut down all non-essential power uses."

"Do it."

A bright light flashed on one of the approaching craft.

An alarm bleated and stopped. "That was an energy beam," said the navigator. "It hit our forward shield."

"Prepare stern laser," Son-Nih said. At the rate of closure, it would only be moments before the Mother's Servant would pass through this fleet of ships.

"I'm picking up transmissions from the ships before us," a voice called. "It's the fleet of the Grand Coven of Hive-Mothers—"

"Commence firing as soon as we pass through," Son-Nih said. "They have already fired upon us. Let us return their greetings."

"Spirit of the Mother," cried the navigator. "It will be close."

She pointed to the holo-display where a ship rapidly grew large in the center of the screen.

"Collision?" Son-Nih asked.

"I don't know. Less than eight ship lengths clearance."

The image of a long, gray ship filled the screen and vanished. The Mother's Servant vibrated, as though a cord had been plucked, as the energy of the main engines flashed into a coherent infrared beam. The holo-display flickered and a small fleck in the center of the screen grew bright.

"One ship hit," a voice called.

The Mother's Servant vibrated again.

"Well?" asked Son-Nih.

"We're already out of range," a voice answered.

"Navigator, set course for the asteroid belt," said Son-Nih. "We'll hide there."

༂

Walid stared at the monitor where long, luminous strands seemed to extend forever before the Eagle. Even the stern view showed these neon tube-like lines and a ghostly view of the second Eagle, almost transparent against a garish beige backdrop.

Merciful Allah, he thought. *What have we got into?*

"Ah, captain, we're getting reports of a few crewmembers becoming sick, nauseous, upchucking," one of his officers said.

How long? Walid thought. *It seems like forever. Yet nothing changes except for those crazy luminous lines that continue to flicker, edges changing through a spectrum of colors.* He glanced around the command center. Half of the crew on duty had barf bags on hand. Something caught his eye and the long luminous lines in the monitor began to change, convolute into a cubical structure. At the far end of the box-like framing, a spot of dark grew, a darkness sprinkled with tiny points of light.

"We're coming through on the other side," Walid said.

The neon tube cubical structure collapsed with a flash of multi-colored light. All around was the velvet blackness of space, filled with the colored gems of strange star systems.

"Ah, bogies ahead," a voice called. "Range less than two hundred clicks."

"On screen," Walid called.

The radar screen's image appeared on the large flat screen monitor above Walid's command station. Dozens of lights winked across the screen. "Gimme optical," he called.

"Intense radiation," a voice cried, high-pitched with fear.

"What kind?"

"They're shooting at us. Energy weapons."

"That's a huge bunch of Hoo-Lii ships out there," came a voice. "They're showing flashes of beam weapon discharges."

Walid recognized the voice of the long-range data acquisition technician. The ship shuddered.

"Direct hit on front shield," someone shouted.

"Damage assessment?" Walid called. "Navigator, reverse ship's course and head back into the anomaly." He grabbed the handset. "Hawley? Are you there?"

"Hull integrity intact, all systems operational."

"Yeah," the voice of the captain of the second Eagle crackled from the speaker. "Looks like we've run into a hornets' nest."

"Reverse course and re-enter anomaly," Walid said. "We've got to get news back to Earth of this Hoo-Lii force."

"Gotcha," the voice crackled. "I see you're already executing a turn."

The Eagle shuddered again and a distant klaxon began to bray. *Hull breach*, Walid thought. *We're not going to get out of this alive.*

"Weapon systems. Open fire on closest available targets."

What he didn't know was that a cloud of vaporized metal washed over the two hulls of his Eagle, condensing on every surface, reducing the clarity of its communication laser.

"Ay-ay, sir."

Walid watched the navigation module. Another thirty seconds needed to complete the turn before the main engine could be brought up to full power.

Something made a loud crashing noise and the lights flickered momentarily.

"Shit," someone said. "They've wiped out our forward beam weapons. We can't shoot back."

The Eagle shuddered and the push that came from the drive being engaged made Walid sit quickly. "Navigator. Set course for the anomaly opening." He picked up the handset. "Hawley, I've completed my turn and under power back to the anomaly." He waited for a reply.

"This is Hawley, I dunno if we're gonna make it. We've been holed three times and have a lot of casualties. I've only got a fraction of my main drive's power." The static grew loud. "I'm gonna roll over and shoot my missiles at them—"

"What missiles?" Walid snapped.

"We have three left over from the last encounter. They were never taken out. They're small nukes. It's all I've got left. Look, Walid, I ain't gonna make it, so I might as well."

Walid took a deep breath. "Hawley, you are a very brave man, and you—"

"Shut up, Walid," Hawley said. "Missile one away, number two away. And three's off also. Missile ETA is sixty seconds, proximity fuzing and time limit ..." His voice faded out.

"Anomaly forming," a voice called.

"The Hoo-Lii have stopped shooting at us."

Walid glanced at the monitor above his command station. The strange cubical structure of light grew large. They were on direct course for its center.

"EMP one," a voice called, signifying a nuclear explosion.

"On screen," Walid said. In the mostly dark screen, a small blossom of light faded. Two more EMPs followed in quick succession. "Assessment?"

"Ah, I think one might have been on target. Two definitely were not close to anything when they detonated."

The world around them disappeared into the multi-colored gap in space-time, the place where time stood still and there was no place. They were alone, without even a star to guide them home.

Walid waited two days in orbit around Charon, Pluto's Moon, watching the anomaly to see if Hawley's Eagle survived. During this time, he prepared a full report on what they'd encountered and used the high-powered communication laser to send it to Earth, complete with images of the Hoo-Lii fleet. He was unaware of the laser's diminished output.

"Ships emerging from anomaly," a voice called. "Hoo-Lii ships."

"Time to depart for Earth," Walid said. "Maximum acceleration."

CHAPTER TWENTY

LIKE A DAA-LII IN A MANDIBLE

I, Kot-Nih, learned later the Others—the new servants—had used obscenities against the fleet of the Grand Coven of Hive-Mothers. True, the fleet attacked their ships that may have been pursuing Suh-Joh, but no one stopped to ask. However, the obscenities damaged only one ship—and not very badly at that—whereas the fleet destroyed a ship of the Others and chased the second ship back through the transfer point.

When our scientists examined the remains of the Other's ship, they confirmed it to be one from the Water-Gem world—a ship of the new servants. Its capabilities were few, and except for its obscenities, it was no match for the major ships of the fleet of the Grand Coven of Hive-Mothers.

I later learned Nah-Kih convened a Coven on the ships to agree upon a strategy. Eight major ships would remain behind and hunt down the heretic Suh-Joh. The rest of the fleet would use the transfer point to enter the system of the Water-Gem world.

ꙅ

"Without Suh-Joh's ship, the Mother's Servant, the new servants on the Water-Gem world will not be able to resist our forces. It will be a simple task, not unlike the taking of a daa-lii in the middle of crop season, a tasty morsel, indeed," Nah-Kih's voice twittered with an almost musical quality. She'd just proposed the fleet enter the transfer point without delay.

A rustle of voices swept the assemblage and the sweet aroma of agreement grew strong as the Hive-Mothers gave their assent.

"Then let us return to our ships and depart after the next sleep period to begin our conquest of this system, to garner even more riches for the empire of Hool."

The Hive-Mothers spoke as one in agreement.

ꙅ

I suppose at the time, this plan seemed logical and clear-cut. The Hive-Mothers would leave sufficient forces behind to apprehend Sub-Joh and the bulk of the fleet would overwhelm the primitives on the Water-Gem world....

ꙅ

The fleet of the Grand Coven of Hive-Mothers went through the transfer point in waves and waited until all ships arrived to assemble into formation before setting off for the inner planets.

"Nah-Kih," the pilot-navigator called. "There's a ship ahead of us, heading to the inner system." She pointed at the holo-display in the center of the instrument-filled room.

Nah-Kih looked at the tiny yellow icon on a projected course to the Water-Gem world. "Is it the ship that fled before us into the transfer point?"

The pilot-navigator's breathing orifices riffled with uncertainty. "It is too distant. Even at maximum amplification, I cannot resolve an image to clearly show the structure of the ship. Yet there are no other craft under power in the vicinity." She waved a mid-limb. "Logic says it must be them."

"Will it arrive at the Water-Gem before us?"

"Yes," said the pilot-navigator. "It has a head start and uses fuel at a profligate rate, as though certain of finding fuel at its destination."

"Which we cannot?"

"Our course plan will be slower, since we need to gather fuel at an outer planet before commencing our conquest of the Water-Gem." The pilot-navigator touched a control and pointed to the five outer planets. "Only these have atmospheres with enough light elements to fuel our ships. So, we must pause to refuel our ships before we proceed further—"

"Where?" Nah-Kih asked.

The pilot-navigator pointed to a smaller gas giant planet that was the seventh from the star. "Here. It requires the least deviation from our course."

"Do it." Nah-Kih departed the crowded room. She tuned into the general communication system and listened to the conversations flowing back and forth between the ships.

"It will be the home of many new hives," a voice said.

"With all that water, we can grow an abundance of crops and raise many progeny," said another. "I know I want land next to a body of water so large that I cannot see its far side."

"I want land surrounded by water."

Nah-Kih smiled. *They are almost like the young*, she thought. *Excited about our new world. Yet, we still have to catch a daa-lii before we savor it. Fortunately, this time, we are prepared, with more than enough power to do so, especially with the heretic, Sub-Joh, no longer available to help them.*

Charlie Ramsey stared out of the window of his office at downtown Columbus.

It was a corner office with a view and his knowledge of skeletons in closets ensured it had a good view. The tiny plaza below was bright green and splashed with colorful flowers.

He yawned as the monotone voice of Gordon Felsbek droned away on the speaker. "So?" Charlie Ramsey said. "What's the significance of this?"

"Well, someone is counterfeiting large amounts of platinum coins, which I can prove comes from an asteroid source." His voice rose slightly, as though announcing a triumph.

"Now wait a minute." Ramsey frowned. "Don't the Chinese handle all of the asteroid platinum?"

"Ah." Felsbek sighed. "They're supposed to; however, I've checked on how they handle it and I found they make it into their 'Panda' style coins which can be accounted for, well, most of it. Obviously some sticks to the fingers of their rulers."

He paused a moment. "This is different. The counterfeits are 'Eagle' and 'Maple leaf' coins, perfect copies except for the alloy composition. They have too much of the other platinum group metals, such as rhodium, present." He sniffed. "A dead giveaway when you know what to look for."

"Who's doing the counterfeiting?" Ramsey asked.

"I don't know," Felsbek said. "These coins are circulated primarily on the West Coast and ..." He hesitated.

"Go on."

"Well, there is one group of people that seem to have a lot of these counterfeit coins in their possession."

"All right, who are they, and who gives it to them?" Ramsey frowned. It was like pulling teeth to get information from this bureaucrat.

"Families of those who died in the space battle. They say it came from the government. Patently false."

"Oh."

The images of the hundreds of widows and orphans of the officers and crew of the Space Force who had been scorched and burned in the unprovoked Hoo-Lii attack ran through Ramsey's mind. Hundreds of men and women died violent, nasty deaths in the unforgiving cold of outer space, and now, their dependents received miniscule pensions from the under-funded military.

Hmm, Ramsey thought. *That might make a difference. Politically, it could be a problem.* "How much of the counterfeit money d'you reckon is in their hands?"

"That's the problem," Felsbek said. "I figure it's only about ten percent of the amount counterfeited which, all in all, is about one-third of total West Coast circulation."

Ramsey let out a whistle. "That means someone has made a shit-load of counterfeit money—"

"Exactly." Felsbek sounded satisfied. "More than we've raised in taxes on the West Coast."

"Where's the money being used?"

"I still don't know. It doesn't look like personal consumption, which puzzles me," said Felsbek. "So it doesn't fit the usual pattern of criminal activity. I only know it has had a very stimulative effect upon the economy of the West Coast. Industry activity levels are very high, particularly in Tacoma and other areas which support the Space Force." He paused.

"Space Force?" Ramsey frowned. "Don't they send all of the asteroid ore to China, right?"

"Perhaps that question should be addressed to the Space Force," Felsbek said. "I haven't been able to get a straight answer from them on that question."

The communications module chimed softly. Ki leaned forward and picked up the handset from his desk. His quarters also doubled as a private office with monitors that displayed the same data seen in the command center of DS-3. "Yeah?" he said. "Put it on the screen." He peered over the top of his glasses at the text that scrolled onto the screen:

HOO-LII SHIP—CAME THROUGH—MAXIMUM SPEED—EXPECT ARRIVAL WITHIN—GHARAGUH.

"What's with this message?" Ki frowned. "Is that all there is? Nothing from the other ship, either?"

"Ah, not sure," came the voice of the communications technician. "It was very weak. This was the best we could do, even when we washed it through the error-checking software."

"Direction?"

"Somewhere near Pluto, so we're pretty sure it's Gharaguh and Hawley on their way back." The technician hesitated. "Something must have happened to their laser com systems, mebbe micrometerorite damage or something."

"All right, thanks. Lemme know if you hear anything else," Ki said. *Oh, crap! Now an alien ship is coming with our boys in hot pursuit. Gotta get ready, no time to waste.*

Ki stared at a flimsy sheet of paper he'd received from Minister Ramsey's office. *So, they want to know if any asteroid metal was "diverted" to the West Coast?* He had an idea of what was going on, but he'd made a point not to know any of the details. *What's the term? Plausible deniability?*

He picked up the progress report on DS-4. *They've done wonders out there*, he thought. *I should inspect it sometime.* He glanced at the summary. *That sucker's gonna be bigger than an aircraft carrier*, he thought. *It already has twelve Eagles, and by next year, not only will it build Eagles or some future variation, it'll even have swimming pools and accommodations for over five thousand personnel —amazing.*

And, Ki thought. *The Deimos project, even with far less resources, is coming along well. The big mystery is what made all those tunnels within its interior*, he thought. *No one will say whether they're artificial or natural, just that they're millions of years old. Doesn't matter, we'll eventually get some archeologists up there. The important thing is we've now got a small station orbiting Deimos, which serves as a way station to Mars and serves as a refueling depot.*

The communications module chimed.

"Yeah?" said Ki. "Oh, hello, Butch. How're things on the

Moon?" He leaned back in his chair and put his feet up on his battered gray metal desk.

"Ah, Commander, we've picked up some signals coming from out Pluto way, Hoo-Lii signals." Butch's voice sounded tinny on the speaker. "We've had Ulrich translate them, and I've sent his transcript to you."

"Good work," Ki said. "I'll take a look at it."

"We, um, also got some faint opticals from the last location of Gharaguh's signal," said Butch. "It looks like there may be a bunch of ships heading in our direction—"

"A bunch?" Ki's feet hit the floor.

Oh, shit, he thought. *It wasn't just one alien ship being followed by two Eagles. That means it had to be a lot of Hoo-Lii coming back.*

"How many?"

"Hard to say at this distance. Can't get good resolution on objects that small in such faint light."

"Make an educated guess." Ki's heart began to pound.

"Well, er, it looks like there might be as many as eight faint, fuzzy objects," said Butch. "So, I'd hafta guess there could be eight ships, in a circular formation."

"You're not sure?"

"No. It could be something else, but." Butch paused. "Mebbe in two, three weeks I'll have better data."

"Okay," said Ki. "Thanks. Keep me informed." He tapped a control and stared at the monitor's screen. *What am I supposed to make of this gibberish?* he thought. *"It is our destiny," and "like a grub in a claw." I'd better warn the Human Confederation a Hoo-Lii fleet is coming. I tried to tell them, but they wouldn't listen. Well, we'd better get ready.* He opened the filing cabinet and pulled out a dog-eared document. It was his much-revised defense plan should the Hoo-Lii return.

Ki reached for the phone.

Charlie Ramsey leaned forward in his over-stuffed leather armchair and glared at the speakerphone on his desk, the corners of his mouth turned down. The window shades leaked in early afternoon sunlight, illuminating his desk and leaving much of his office in shadow.

"Commander Mapes." His face became even more florid. "You're not answering my question. What d'you know about asteroid metal being smuggled to Earth?"

"Minister Ramsey, you're not listening to me." Ki's voice warbled through the speaker. "There's a fleet of Hoo-Lii ships heading toward Earth. They'll be here within ninety days."

"I've heard nothing about this supposed alien fleet," Ramsey said. "I think that you're using this to avoid answering questions about theft, fraud, and mismanagement in the Space Force. If you don't answer me now, I shall be forced to issue a subpoena for you to appear, in person, before the Human Confederation Assembly."

"Minister Ramsey," Ki paused, "I don't know anything about this metal that's being smuggled down to Earth. We're using the metal from the asteroid to construct—"

"We have proof positive large amounts of counterfeit coins are made from asteroid platinum."

"Then perhaps you should direct your questions to the Chinese who handle the platinum concession," Ki said.

"Commander Mapes," Ramsey said. "I fail to see why you do not understand we've already exhausted that line of inquiry. These counterfeit coins appear mainly on the American West Coast. And most interestingly, in the hands of Space Force families who have lost relatives in the space battles."

"Why would you expect me to know anything about that? I don't have money in my budget for such activities. You've cut my budget requests for the last two years. It's not been enough to repair the stations and ships, or to ready them for battle—"

"Commander Mapes," Ramsey said. "I find your answers are

non-responsive. Be advised you will receive a subpoena to appear before the Human Confederation Assembly—"

"Minister Ramsey," Ki's voice rose. "Don't you understand I've got to prepare for the coming Hoo-Lii invasion?"

"Forget about these tales of alien invaders. I want some honest answers about this platinum." Ramsey banged his hand on the desk. "Your days commanding the Space Force are numbered."

The speaker clicked, then buzzed.

"Mapes? Mapes." Ramsey leaned forward. The buzz got louder even after he adjusted the controls. "Son of a bitch," he said. "He hung up on me."

༃

Ki swore silently. *A subpoena is a complication I don't need right now*, he thought. He took a deep breath and rubbed his head. He picked up the handset, "Get me Carver Washington, as soon as possible."

"Hello?" Carver Washington's gravelly voice rumbled from the speaker. "You there, Ki?"

"Carver, thanks for getting back to me in a hurry—"

"Well, ah heard you've got your titty in a wringer, an' when you called, I kinda figured you need help."

Ki sighed heavily. "That obvious?"

"Well, I don't know the details, but when that Ramsey an' his pack of wolves start howling about draggin' you in front of the HC Assembly and strippin' you of your office an' rank. Well, that's some serious shit."

Ki took a deep breath. "You know how we fund space defense and how it breaks the law. What you don't know is the scale of it. We've doubled the Space Force's funding by using platinum from the asteroid. More importantly, I've just learned there's a Hoo-Lii fleet heading in our direction and Ramsey wants to have a political show at the same time."

"This's fact, right?"

"You can confirm it with the Hendersons at the observatory."

"I'll take your word for it." Carver cleared his throat. "So, what d'you want me to do?"

"Stall Ramsey from issuing the subpoena for thirty days. By then, the observatory should have enough opticals to get a good estimate on the size of the fleet." Ki hesitated. "If it turns out I'm mistaken, that there's no Hoo-Lii fleet coming, I'll return to Earth and face the music."

Carver remained silent for a moment or two. "Man, if you're wrong, they'll eat you alive. You'll end up doing hard time."

"If I'm right, what I've done will be forgotten."

"Okay, I can bottle up the subpoena for thirty days."

"Thanks. I owe you for this."

~

"Commander Mapes," Butch Henderson's voice was high-pitched and static rose and fell.

"Yes?" Ki leaned back in his chair, away from his battered desk covered with sheets of paper that represented revisions and updates to the defense plan. He was satisfied the efforts to destroy evidence of their counterfeiting operation had gone well and Carver Washington had stalled the subpoena process.

"What is it?"

"I've lost track of the Hoo-Lii ships," Butch said. "They were crossing Uranus's orbit and they disappeared—"

"What?" Ki rose to his feet. "How can they disappear?"

"I'm not sure, it's not a good observation angle. They weren't on a direct course for Earth," Butch said. "I've reviewed the images leading up to their disappearance, and it just looks like each fuzzy blob winks out and never reappears—"

"Are you sure you saw something in the first place?"

"Why, yes, of course," Butch said. "It's almost as though they landed on Uranus, which, of course, is impossible."

Ki ran his hand over his forehead. "We have nothing close by," he said. "I recalled the tanker ship when I got your heads up on the Hoo-Lii," he said. "The tanker has been high tailing it back here with less than half a load of He3."

He paused. "Y'sure you saw them?"

"Absolutely."

Ki sat down slowly, as though in heavy gravity. "Maintain a watch on Uranus. It's the only thing we can do."

CHAPTER TWENTY-ONE

NOW WHERE?

Suh-Joh rose from the smoothly polished granite mound upon which she'd been resting.

Tiny naat-jii skittered across the floor of the ersatz quartzite cave that was her command center, seeking shelter at the base of the brown fabric covering the wall.

"Are you sure the Coven's fleet does not pursue us?" She arched her body toward her counselor, spines erecting.

"Most gracious Hive-Mother." Son-Nih flexed low. "There are ships following us. They are but a small fraction of the Coven's fleet. Even so, there are too many for us to stand and fight."

"So, what can we do?"

"We can hide among the asteroids for a while," Son-Nih said. "The new servants have requested they speak with us about the situation, they and their strange Others." He referred to the Qu'udas who accompanied the group of humans that fled Earth to the Mother's Servant. "They wish to help."

"Bring them."

Son-Nih turned and gestured to a Chosen-Male warrior who skittered through a brown curtain that hung over an entrance.

"They will be here soon. I think we should also include our scholar, Lil-Tih, for some of what they wish to speak about involves knowledge of the transfer points through space-time."

"The new servants know of such things?" Suh-Joh's breathing orifices flared as though confronting a strange prey.

"It was such knowledge of such things made me believe they should speak to you, most gracious Hive-Mother." Son-Nih flexed again.

The brown curtain rippled open. Taylor and Meltem entered, accompanied by two Chosen-Male warriors. They approached Suh-Joh and bowed in her direction.

Suh-Joh waved a mid-limb and emitted an aroma of welcome. "You have thoughts on what we should do." She pointed a mid-limb at Meltem. "Speak, Mother Meltem."

Meltem bowed again. "Most gracious Hive-Mother," she said. The device chittered out a translation. "My male partner, Taylor, a great warrior in his world, wishes to share his ideas on a proposed course of action." She waited.

Suh-Joh turned slowly to look at Taylor. "So," she said. "You are both counselor to Mother Meltem and a warrior. This I did not know."

Taylor bowed slightly and raised his translation device.

"Most gracious Hive-Mother, our world and ways are different than yours. In mine, I led a powerful faction until I fell from power." He paused as the machine twittered out his words.

"We cannot return to my system, for now there are many ships who wish ill to both you and me." Taylor wiped his brow. "As there, they hunt us."

"Yes," said Suh-Joh. "What think you?"

"The Coven's fleet is as dangerous to my people on Earth as it is to you, yet I cannot do anything about it." Taylor paused. "Neither can you. We are too weak."

"Why should I step in front of certain death for new servants?" Suh-Joh waved her mid-limb dismissively.

"There may be another way," Taylor said.

Suh-Joh's breathing orifices flared. "Speak."

"Your scholar, Lil-Tih, has discussed the existence of other transfer points with the Qu'uda scholar, YataBu—"

"Who are these Qu'uda?" Suh-Joh asked.

"They are the Others who come from another star system."

Suh-Joh's breathing flaps flared. "Others?" She turned to Son-Nih. "Do you know of this?"

"Yes, most gracious Hive-Mother. The scholar, Lil-Tih, has kept me informed of her conversations with the Qu'uda scholar."

Son-Nih hesitated. "Initially, there was great difficulty in communication." He spread both mid-limbs. "Once they established a common basis of science, they made much progress."

"So, what did she discover?"

"Perhaps it would be better if Lil-Tih and the Qu'uda scholar, YataBu, were to speak directly to us?" Son-Nih said.

Suh-Joh sank slowly onto her resting mound. The breathing orifices along her flanks emitted an aroma of agreement.

Son-Nih turned and gestured with his mid-limb.

The brown curtain swayed open and the tiny scholar, Lil-Tih, led by a Chosen-Male warrior entered, soon followed by a rotund and cloak-clad Qu'uda.

"Most gracious Hive-Mother," Lil-Tih twittered and prostrated herself in submission before Suh-Joh. It was the first time before her Hive-Mother since her apprentices had gone Disobedient.

"Rise, my little one, you have nothing to fear from your actions. You remained faithful, even as others deserted me," Suh-Joh said. "Who is this you bring before me?"

"It is a scholar from afar, DuKlaat YataBu," Lil-Tih said. "He possesses great knowledge of the workings of the universe, particularly in the mechanics of space-time."

Suh-Joh turned to look at the rotund figure before her. "Does your species possess the means to cross space-time?"

YataBu wobbled his headcrest. "No, our knowledge has been to delve deeply into the mathematics of space-time. We have not developed a practical means to open these strange points, which allow travel throughout the universe." He cleared his throat. It was the sign that he was about to speak at length.

"Most gracious Hive-Mother," Taylor said quickly. "I spoke of another way—"

"Yes, another way out of our dilemma of being forever hunted." Suh-Joh raised her head and her breathing orifices flared as though testing the air for prey. "Which is?"

"I have learned from conversations with your scholar you identified other openings in space-time with a large device at the outer edge of the Hool system," Taylor said.

"Yes, there are other transfer points, undoubtedly well-guarded by now." Suh-Joh turned to Son-Nih. "Find out if the Coven guards them, without revealing our position."

"At once, most gracious Hive-Mother." Son-Nih left.

"So, there may be other exits, but where do they lead?"

"I do not know," Taylor said. "Have you found all of them?"

"I, too, do not know," said Suh-Joh. "But again, where do they lead? Fertile worlds are far and few between, this we have learned over many generations."

"I wasn't thinking of looking for a refuge," said Taylor. "I thought we might seek allies to help defend my home world from the fleet of Coven of Hive-Mothers—"

"Allies? What allies? There are no other worlds of Hoo-Lii. Humans are too recent to space travel to have established colony worlds teeming with your kind." Suh-Joh rose from her resting mound to stare hard at Taylor.

"There is another world, filled with life, a technically advanced society," Taylor said softly. "The home world of the Qu'uda." He looked at YataBu.

Suh-Joh's eyes switched to YataBu. "Yours is a world of warriors?" she asked.

"Our world is crowded and yes, it has a warrior class," YataBu said. "For the secret of faster-than-light travel, they would pay a high price. They could even provide help in your time of need—"

"Why would they trust aliens who appear without warning in their system, seeking war materiel and warriors?"

"That is a good question, indeed," YataBu said. "We Qu'uda even built a deep-space observatory to guard against the surprise arrival of aliens." He paused as though he'd thought of something new. "Your appearance may cause concern."

"Have your species had contact with other aliens?"

"Yes," said YataBu. "We sought out the humans."

"Most gracious Hive-Mother," Son-Nih said.

"Yes, my trusted counselor?"

"We have detected signals at the two transfer points that makes me believe there are Coven ships guarding them," Son-Nih said. "As for the Ear to the Universe," He rippled his breathing flaps as though swatting an immature daa-lii fly. "It is both cold and without radiation. It appears unguarded."

It was expected the Coven of Hive-Mothers would have stripped personnel from the deep-space observatory for their fleet.

"Anything else?"

"Yes, the Coven ships have sent sensing probes into the asteroid belt. It is only a matter of time before one discovers our location." Son-Nih flexed low.

Suh-Joh turned toward Taylor. "It seems we are in a trap, with limited time left. So, how do we find the transfer point that leads to the world of ..." she hesitated as she looked at YataBu, "the Qu'uda?"

"Can we employ the Ear to the Universe to find other transfer points in this system?" Taylor asked.

"I cannot answer that question. Direct it to my scholar, Lil-Tih, and perhaps the pilot-navigator. They are skilled in such arts." Suh-Joh rose. "In the meantime, I must consult with my counselor and the pilot-navigator as to how we keep the prying eyes of the Coven ships from finding us." She turned and left the command center.

~

The pilot-navigator's center was warm and stuffy from too many bodies. It was redolent with the aromas of three species of life gathered around a jumble of electronic equipment assembled together with a tangle of wire.

"Look," Lil-Tih said. "It does accept the output from this sensor." She pointed to figures scrolling across a small instrument attached to a radio that had previously been in the space shuttle. "It amplifies the signal and converts it into a digital signal—"

"Why is this useful to find another transfer point?" YataBu asked. "Should we not concentrate on the radar device?"

The barely formed breathing flaps on the tiny Lil-Tih opened and relaxed. "The Ear to the Universe is much more sensitive than the radar device. What we could not do was amplify its signal beyond a given level, whereas, this technology," she gestured to the solid-state amplifier from the shuttle, "can take the very weak output signal and amplify it further; it converts it into a digital signal which your computer can process. That will allow us to see things previously missed."

"How d'you know this will work?" Taylor asked.

Lil-Tih rose upright and spread her mid-limbs. "I designed the Ear to the Universe," she said. "I know its capabilities."

"Oh, I see." Taylor nodded.

YataBu looked at Taylor. "Then the only thing left to do, is to test it...." He paused. "How do we know where each of these transfer points lead? Could it perhaps lead to the interior of a star?"

"That has never happened. However, we could send probes through first, which could bring back images and spectra of nearby stars," Lil-Tih said. "Our star catalog is extensive. That will let us find where the transfer point exits."

"How long will this take?" Taylor asked.

"Two, three, maybe four sleep periods," Lil-Tih said.

"Then it is time for us to tell Suh-Joh what we've found," Taylor said. "She fears the Coven ships may soon find us."

∿

Suh-Joh squirmed on her granite resting mound as though massaging her underside. "You are confident we can find other transfer points using the Ear to the Universe with this alien device, and quickly?"

"Yes, most gracious Hive-Mother," Lil-Tih said. "YataBu believes the energy discharges from the Coven ships' fusion drives will echo off the transfer points and make it easier for us to find them."

"Why does this sound too easy?"

Lil-Tih flexed into a position of absolute submission. Her tiny breathing flaps quivered with fear. "Oh, most gracious Hive-Mother, it is the result of combining Hoo-Lii technology with that of the aliens—"

"We have little time," Suh-Joh said. "Several probes draw near. We must leave the asteroid belt. In addition, we need to refuel before we embark on this voyage." She gestured to Son-Nih. "Explain what will happen."

"Once underway, the probes will detect our fusion drive," said Son-Nih. "So, we will set a maximum acceleration course for the closest gas giant planet. There, we will execute a course correction at the same time we collect fuel from its upper atmosphere." He paused. "The passage will be rough and fraught with danger. Yet, if we complete it successfully, we can coast, silent, cold, and invisible on our way to the Ear to the Universe.

"They will not expect us to go in that direction. We should have time to seek out new transfer points. Once we go to a transfer point, it is possible they will follow. May the Spirit of the Mother guide us and lead us on the path to safety."

"Perhaps we could deceive the Coven ships," Taylor said.

"What do you mean?" Suh-Joh asked.

"Send another vessel off in a direction different than taken by the Mother's Servant, a vessel that emits radiation similar to the Mother's Servant."

"Can this be done?" Suh-Joh asked.

"Perhaps," said Son-Nih. "I must consult with those who maintain our smaller vessels."

"Maybe we could help," Taylor said. "Use some of the equipment from our shuttle. Its engines are less advanced than yours and should yield a larger radiation signature."

"If it can be done, do it," Suh-Joh said.

ꝛ

Taylor gripped the strapping across the bed that held them tight and stared at the ceiling. The Mother's Servant began to vibrate, far differently and at a lower frequency than when its fusion engines operated at maximum power. It was a large amplitude vibration, one that shook the entire ship, rising in power and frequency until the ship began to sing like a low note on a bass viola, a song of power and violence.

Taylor grasped Meltem's hand and glanced at her. Between them lay Kemal, who had his arms wrapped about his mother's stomach. The lights flickered and a screech penetrated the bass harmonics.

Something clattered loudly.

That's got to be the decoy launch, Taylor thought. *I didn't realize how much strain this flyby would put on the Mother's Servant.*

The noise became constant, steady, and supplemented by the higher frequency vibration of the fusion drive increasing in output.

I hope that's a good sign, he thought. *I hope it means they've finished filling the fuel tanks.*

Almost abruptly, the deep bass vibration faded and stopped. The high-pitched vibration of the fusion drive eased into silence. Gravity shifted. Something popped and crackled.

The skin must've gotten hot, Taylor thought. *We must be back out in space.* He squeezed Meltem's hand and smiled. "Looks like we made it." He leaned over to kiss her quickly.

"Daddy," Kemal said. "I want a kiss, too."

Taylor chuckled. It felt good to be alive.

ॐ

Even though Hool was the brightest star in the sky, its light cast only dim shadows. Taylor watched silently as both Lil-Tih and YataBu installed the electronic module in the Ear to the Universe. Its dark, spidery framework orb was a gigantic antenna that listened for electromagnetic emissions from the gravity strings connecting the interstellar transfer points.

Thank goodness the old space shuttle worked as a decoy, Taylor thought.

They'd added another fuel tank to its payload bay and launched it at maximum thrust toward the transfer point leading to Earth's system. With the added fuel, the shuttle reached a velocity of almost three thousand klicks per second—one percent lightspeed—before running dry. Four Coven ships took the bait and set off in pursuit.

By the time they recognize they aren't going to catch it, Taylor thought, *they'll be on the other side of the Hool system. We bought some time.*

It took about ten sleep periods before Lil-Tih and YataBu were certain they'd located all the transfer points within the Hool system.

"It seems," said YataBu. "We can actually detect traces of other transfer points in other star systems. Well, perhaps," he said. "We detect other ripples that may be transfer points at great distance."

"Unfortunately," Lil-Tih said. "We found only one new transfer point beyond the three already known."

"Where is it?" Taylor asked.

"Further out and about quarter the way around the system," Lil-Tih said. "We do not know where it leads."

ↄ

"Will this transfer point lead to the Qu'uda world?" Suh-Joh pointed to the set of coordinates in the holo-display. The location was deep in the cometary belt, cold and far from Hool. The pilot-navigator's station was crowded.

"Most gracious Hive-Mother, it does not. It leads to a system of two suns whose planets show no signs of life," Lil-Tih said. "However, this transfer point is unknown to the Coven and therefore will lead to a region of space free from them." She flexed low in submission.

Suh-Joh's breathing flaps flared slightly. "That is one good reason for us proceeding there."

"Perhaps," Taylor said. "We should bring the Ear to the Universe with us. This place is distant from the Qu'uda system, so we will need to seek additional transfer points."

"Can we bring it?" Suh-Joh asked.

Son-Nih's breathing flaps rippled. "We shall have to fabricate a cradle to carry it, but that is not a difficult problem for our engineers—"

"Then do it and quickly." Suh-Joh turned to leave. "I fear the return of the Coven ships, for I am sure they have already realized their mistake."

CHAPTER TWENTY-TWO

HOME SWEET HOME

Taylor watched the now-familiar cubical framework of glowing energy form with the growing black spot in the center. It was the end of the gravity string, which meant they'd soon be in normal space.

Two jumps, he thought. *We're finally getting the hang of it. Even able to figure out which direction we'll go prior to making the jump. It's funny, how we humans are less nauseated by the jump than the Hoo-Lii, and the Qu'uda not at all. Meltem had no answer for it, but, as she said, she wasn't a specialist in alien medicine. Hah.*

The cubical framework that marked the terminus of the gravity string collapsed with its usual colorful flash. Distantly, a star dominated the sky, glowing with an orange brilliance. Taylor touched the control and columns of characters scrolled through the holo-display, finally stopping. The astrogation computer identified the spectral signatures of the stars in the sky and located where they were in space. He glanced at the set of characters scribbled on a piece of paper and compared it to the one in the holo-display. His heart began to beat faster; it was the same set of characters. They'd arrived in the Qu'uda system.

Someone—Hoo-Lii—chittered something.

Taylor's translation device spoke, "Is this the system?" It was the scholar, Lil-Tih.

"Yes, I believe so," Taylor said.

"I must inform our Hive-Mother immediately."

꩜

The holo-display and a communications module in Suh-Joh's command center glowed brightly. Billy spoke to Taylor. "I am ready." He glanced at Suh-Joh on her resting mound.

Suh-Joh rose, breathing flaps flaring. "Proceed."

Billy took a deep breath. "This is Bilik Pudjata," he said in his native Qu'uda language, using his original name. "I wish to speak to Pi'Rup, the prime communicator." He repeated his message twice. He stepped away from the module and squatted on a brown cushion that matched the floor covering. "It will take time." He referred to the time lag for the message to travel from the outer limits of the system to the planet Qu'uda, located close to its sun.

"Are you sure they will receive this message?" Suh-Joh asked, breathing flaps flaring as though sniffing out something dangerous. She moved restlessly.

Billy wobbled his head. "The communicator is set properly. At the power levels used, they will hear it." He paused. "They may not answer immediately, especially if they feel the need to quoon over their response."

"I do not understand what you mean," Suh-Joh said.

"Ah," Billy said. "In my society, where all have an equal voice, decisions are made by consensus, by a communal process of 'quooning.' The decision-making process takes time."

Suh-Joh's breathing orifices ceased moving, as though listening for a distant sound, not sure whether it was predator or prey. She said nothing and draped herself over her resting mound and closed her eyes. The communications module remained silent. No craft appeared in the holo-display. Time passed slowly.

A deep grunting voice, speaking the language of Qu'uda, broke the silence and continued for some time.

"What did he say?" Taylor asked.

"He wants to know if I am the same Bilik Pudjata that departed for Earth on the Egg-that-Flies. If so, where am I, because he cannot understand how I can have returned since they've detected no sign of that ship."

Taylor looked at Suh-Joh as the translation device converted Billy's words into the Hoo-Lii language.

Suh-Joh's breathing orifices flared as she stared at Billy. "Explain everything, but reveal nothing of our capabilities."

Billy bowed slightly toward Suh-Joh. "As you wish." He turned to the communicator and began to speak rapidly in the deep, grunting sound of the Qu'uda language. He continued for some time.

"What did you tell them?" Suh-Joh asked.

"I told them what happened on Earth and the difficulties experienced there. Also, the Qu'uda ship, the Egg-that-Flies, returns with DalChik and carries many wrigglers—our young—that were rescued by humans, as well as much technology. In addition, I told them of our problems and our need for aid."

"Did you tell them about our use of the transfer points through space-time?" Suh-Joh asked.

"No, I did not."

"Then let us wait to hear their response."

༄

"I do not like this." Billy pointed to the small group of icons in the holo-display. The icons indicated ships at high speed on course toward the Mother's Servant from Qu'uda. "Pi'Rup said nothing about sending ships. I fear the Defenders have taken the initiative."

After the translation device rendered his words into Hoo-Lii, Suh-Joh asked, "Defenders? What are Defenders?"

"They are the military, those who defend Qu'uda."

"Ah, Chosen-Male warriors," Suh-Joh said. "Son-Nih, prepare our defense, immediately."

"No," Taylor said. "We must not fight with the Qu'uda. We need them as allies."

"Then you must persuade them not to attack us," Suh-Joh said. "I am sure if I sent emissaries, they would not be understood."

"True," Taylor said. "Look, let me and someone who speaks their language take a ship and meet them while the Mother's Servant hides in the outer limits of the system."

Suh-Joh spread her mid-limbs. "So be it."

~

"This doesn't look good." Taylor pointed at the small holo-display. The Defenders' ships had taken up a circular formation around their ship, the "Young Offspring," a Hoo-Lii shuttlecraft during their approach to Qu'uda for the past seven days.

As they drew closer to the planet, the ring of Qu'uda ships tightened.

Taylor and Cha KinLaat donned vacuum survival suits, complete except for the helmets.

"No clear consensus has emerged," Cha KinLaat said. "That means our fate may hang under the claws of the Defenders."

"What do you expect?"

"Perhaps, a Defender seeking glory will try for a kill." Cha KinLaat flexed his claws. "And I am without the means to defend myself." He touched the controls. "We are now close enough to prepare a course to go into orbit." A series of characters flickered across the holo-display.

Taylor sighed. "Okay, let's do it."

A vibration, almost a rumble, rippled through the Young

Offspring as its ion drive came to life and fed thrust to the attitude control jets. They began to rotate into the vector that would orient them for the final braking burn to match their velocity to the orbital requirement.

An alarm squawked.

Cha KinLaat looked sharply at the display on the wall. "Great Egg," he said. "They're attacking."

In the center of the holo-display, a slabby, box shaped craft grew large. Flashes appeared at the extremities of its rectangular shape. The Young Offspring shuddered and rang hollowly. Alarms bleated into life. Air howled and doors clanged shut. With a sigh, the breeze stopped. The ion engine shut down. Somewhere, air continued to whistle softly. Yellow icons flashed vigorously in the holo-display while columns of figures scrolled. Alarms, though subdued, continued to bleat.

"Cha KinLaat. Put your helmet on, now." Taylor yelled as he struggled with the helmet for his vacuum suit, rotating it until it locked into position. He looked up and saw Cha KinLaat still did not have his helmet locked on tightly.

"Let me help." Taylor released his safety harness, stepped forward, grasped the helmet, and twisted. It clicked into place.

A brilliant light lit up the cabin, along with a tremendous crash. Lights failed, leaving absolute darkness.

Excruciating pain radiated from his legs. "Help!" Taylor screamed. "My legs."

A dim, soft yellow light flickered into existence and slowly brightened. The floor had buckled upward, smashing an equipment module into his legs, trapping them against the seat. He opened the emergency medical pouch in the suit's pouch and stabbed himself with a syrette of painkiller.

Cha KinLaat spoke rapidly in the Qu'uda language for several minutes.

Taylor heard another Qu'uda voice, slow and measured, reply. It was as though it was at great distance. He felt dizzy, almost disconnected. *It's the painkillers*, he thought.

Cha KinLaat and this Qu'uda voice spoke back and forth for some time.

"Taylor," Cha KinLaat said. "That was Pi'Rup, the prime communicator. He ordered the attack on us stopped." He rose and dust sparkled in the golden light.

"Thank God," Taylor said. "What else did he say?"

"They want proof that I am who I say I am and that the Egg-that-Flies is not held hostage—"

"How're you going to do that?" Taylor said.

Cha KinLaat reached into a pocket in his suit and held up a silvery wafer. "This holds images of our wrigglers and the Egg-that-Flies. I made it to keep their memory fresh. Pi'Rup has agreed to let me show this to all of Qu'uda, for the quooning."

"What quooning?"

"The quooning on whether we live or die."

Taylor sighed. "I hurt," he said. "My legs, something bad has happened to my legs." His world faded away.

$\backsim$

The voices sounded all wrong.

In fact, Taylor thought. *It sounds like someone's belching. How can anyone have that much gas?* He moved and sharp pains coursed through his legs. Memory came surging back. *Something's wrong. The gravity seemed too strong and the light's too yellow. Damn, where am I?*

"Taylor?" a voice asked.

Taylor opened his eyes. Long vines hung down the walls of a pale yellow room. Water dripped somewhere. There was an unfamiliar fragrance, a mixture of ammonia and fruit; apricot? And a spice; cloves? He turned his eyes toward the voice.

"Ah, you are awake. Good." It was Cha KinLaat. "You have been unconscious for almost two sleep periods. You lost a lot of body fluids. We gave you water mixed with the electrolyte salts of your body, as your mating partner, Meltem, advised."

"Where am I?" Taylor realized he wasn't on a bed, but on some kind of fibrous platform with a thin, brown fabric sheet.

"We are on Qu'uda," Cha KinLaat said. "Many things have happened in the last two days. The Defenders who attacked us have been pushed to the outer fringe of our society. Their act was against that of the quooning."

"Which means?" Taylor had this fear, a feeling that things weren't going to turn out the way they wanted them.

Cha KinLaat wagged his head. "Once Qu'uda saw how the humans and the wrigglers interacted, the quooning became one of support, even to send ships back to Earth."

"There's got to be a price," Taylor said.

"Yes, the Hoo-Lii will give the Qu'uda the devices that open the transfer points into space-time—"

"How did you manage that?" Taylor asked.

"It was YataBu who talked to the community of scientists. He convinced Qu'uda in the quooning this was a prize so valuable it was worth anything we asked."

"Gee, I never thought the old guy was very persuasive," Taylor said. "I always thought he was kind of a crotchety old fart."

"I do not understand what you mean. YataBu is very close to the center, a scientist of the highest stature. His words are believed and valued."

Taylor tried to move. A sharp pain lanced up his leg to his groin. "Ah," he said. "That hurt."

"We have used all the pain medication in your suit and mine," Cha KinLaat said. "We have no more. Our medical people are afraid to use our drugs on you." He wobbled his head-crest. "You will be on a shuttle soon, a fast shuttle. It will take six sleep periods for it to meet a ship from the Mother's Servant, one with your mating partner, Meltem, on board. She insists she meet you as soon as possible."

"Is this going to be a constant acceleration course?"

"Yes," Cha KinLaat said. "The fastest possible course."

"You're sure the Qu'uda will help us?"

"Yes, that is part of the agreement for them to get the devices that open the transfer points."

"Yes, but when?" Taylor groaned as another part of his body made its presence felt. "When will they go to the solar system?"

"Half the Defender ships that followed us to Qu'uda will come with us to the Mother's Servant. We leave immediately."

"How many ships?" Taylor asked.

"Thirty-two ships, a full pod of armored battle craft. The crew will no longer be solely Defenders, but includes those who volunteered to leave Qu'uda," said Cha KinLaat. "Already the Hoo-Lii have started to make the devices for the Qu'uda ships. Suh-Joh said she will lead them through the transfer points and show the way."

"Good." Taylor couldn't resist a trace of a smile.

Right, he thought. *She wants them to follow behind the Mother's Servant, right under her main laser weapon.* "Sounds fine. What about supplies?" Something made him want to take control and plan the mission, a habit from the past.

"Every ship in the pod will bring extra water and other supplies, as specified by Bilik Pudjata," Cha KinLaat said. "Enough to get us back to Earth's system."

"Seems you've thought of everything," Taylor said. "Now, if there were only some way to make these legs comfortable."

It was six days Taylor did not want to remember. He slept only fitfully, conscious of a pain throbbing with ever-increasing intensity, dominating his whole being. Fortunately, there was no infection due to the alien nature of the environment and the bio-incompatibility of human and Qu'uda life forms.

When he saw Meltem, it was like the vision of an angel, a stern and business-like angel. It was only minutes after she arrived, he recalled, when she lifted the syringe and said, "I need to operate. This will make you sleep."

Taylor awoke and realized he no longer felt the jackhammer of pain working on his leg. His mouth was dry and the room seemed to keep moving. He closed his eyes and could hear voices.

"Ah, you're awake. Good."

Taylor opened his eyes to see Meltem, hair stringy and unkempt, dark shadows under her eyes.

"Gee, Meltem, you look, well, not so good." He wondered why he said that. "How're you? How's Kemal?"

The room had the bare metal walls with brown curtains that made him think of Suh-Joh's command center. It still moved. A ventilation system sighed, bringing the complex odors that confirmed he was in the Hoo-Lii ship.

"We're both fine." Meltem chuckled. "I can see my patient is feeling better. You've become discriminating about the appearance of your nurse." She grasped his wrist and glanced at a stick-on monitor. "Well, your vital signs are good."

"Where am I and what's going on?"

"You're on the Mother's Servant. We've just made a jump through the first transfer point." Meltem switched monitors and took another reading. "Billy and Cha KinLaat are busy teaching their Qu'uda buddies what they must do. They didn't come through the transfer point in very good order. As for you, sweetheart, you had a compound fracture in your left tibia that'd begun to knit. So, I had to break your leg again to set it and reinforce it with a strip of titanium. Fortunately, there're no complications. However, you're going to be on crutches for at least six weeks, plus rehab afterwards."

"Meltem, thank you." Taylor reached for her hand. "I'm so glad you're here, with me. For a while, I thought I'd never see you and Kemal again. That's what I feared the most."

Meltem sighed. "I was worried about you, too, stuck out there among those aliens, without any kind of care."

"When can I get up?"

"You'll have to stay off your feet for a few days."

Taylor groaned. "How am I going to know what's going on?"

"Talk to your buddies," Meltem said. "They said something about getting a holo-display for you. My priorities are a little different," she said. "I want to get a bigger bed moved in here, big enough for both of us."

CHAPTER TWENTY-THREE

IT IS OUR DESTINY ...

Nah-Kih looked at the astrogation data in the holo-display. The pilot-navigator stood quietly behind Nah-Kih in the small, austere station.

On every wall were displays monitoring the condition of the ship and its location in space. A thin yellow line in the holo-display depicted the course of the Coven's fleet from the gas giant where they had gathered fuel. Their course took them wide of the Water-Gem—over one-third of a planetary orbit. In two sleep periods they would use the system's star's mighty gravity to change course and shed velocity. Once past the star, they would set course for the Water-Gem and attack the new servants, coming out of the glare of the system's star to ensure their surprise.

"So," Nah-Kih said. "We have our course around the star and deceleration flight plan all the way to the Water-Gem?"

"Yes, most gracious Hive-Mother," the pilot-navigator said. "I do not believe they will be able to distinguish the energies of our fusion drives from the glare of this star. It is much brighter than that of Hool."

Nah-Kih's breathing flaps rippled and she emitted the aroma of approval. "Keep me informed of any changes or any unusual events." She made her way out of the room.

2

The cavernous rotunda, ornate with tall columns and polished marble, the home of the Assembly of the Human Confederation, was silent.

Ki straightened up and held his head higher. A trickle of sweat ran down his back. A motion to dismiss him from the Space Force and remand him to trial had been made by Minister for Security Ramsey.

After four hours of testimony, his stomach was in an uproar. "Sir," he said, "I did not steal property from the Human Confederation for personal gain or enrichment—"

"Your counterfeiter confessed," Ramsey said, stabbing his finger in Ki's direction. "He made millions for you from the platinum you stole from all humanity." He looked down at his notes. "We caught one Klaus Loeser, a machinist in Tacoma, with a workshop full of equipment contaminated with platinum, asteroid platinum, with dies to make coins identical to those legally issued. He confessed to counterfeiting millions for you."

"Sir, the money went only to pay for goods and services used by the United Space Force, which belong to the Re-established United States—"

"Was the money authorized by the United States? No. Did the Human Confederation give it to you? No," Ramsey said. "Comptroller of the Currency, Mr. Felsbek, testified none of the money was appropriated, issued, or even authorized for issuance. Therefore, Commander Mapes, you stole the platinum, counterfeited it into coin of the land and spent it as you saw fit, on your pet projects for your personal aggrandizement and, in the process, lining your pockets and those of your cronies. You did this, knowing full well most of the world lives in abject poverty,

227

eking out the barest of living, while you bought anything that caught your fancy."

Angry voices filled the Assembly hall.

"That money was spent on space defenses for Earth," Ki said. "Defenses that'll be needed in a matter of weeks—"

"Yes," Ramsey said. "We've heard this before from you, a massive fleet of alien Hoo-Lii are about to descend upon our defenseless planet, to rape, pillage, and plunder. Sure. And you're the only superhero who stands between them and us. Really." The corners of Ramsey's mouth turned downward. "A fleet no one else sees." He pointed his finger. "Something even your friends at the Moon observatory can't see."

The trickle of sweat down Ki's back increased. *Why can't they find them? They're there. As for Gharaguh and Hawley, I haven't heard another peep from them. I'm not crazy*, he thought. *I know they're coming.* He straightened up. "Space is large, Mr. Ramsey; there's lots of places a fleet of ships can hide, especially if we can't see the flare of their drives—"

"Right, keep spouting your techno-mumbo-jumbo; that'll make everything all right." Ramsey laughed. His smile faded and he pointed his index finger. "You've demonstrated you'll say anything to hide the fact you're a common thief."

A collective gasp swept the Assembly hall. Few knew the true details of the fierce fight and the terrible casualties of the Space Force's earlier battle with the Hoo-Lii. It was shocking for a hero to have fallen so far and to have become a common thief.

Ki hesitated. "I only did what I believed was necessary to protect Earth. I did it, and I'd do it again. I took an oath to protect the Earth against attack from space—"

"From an enemy no one can see, one you created to justify your thievery, so you could build your palatial empire in the sky. You pretended to send out ships to chase an alien ship that fled from Earth and disappeared."

Ramsey sipped water from a glass and cleared his throat. "I call the question. Is there a second?" It was the motion to strip

Ki Mapes of his commission. He smiled and glanced toward the Sino-Asian block.

Guang Xhi rose to his feet. "I second the motion."

Ramsey pointed to the clock. "There will be a thirty-minute recess before the roll call vote begins."

Carver Washington slouched back in an over-stuffed leather chair in a small conference room, elegant with walnut furniture and flowered silk wallpaper. The voices in the corridor outside were faint and muffled.

"Ki, you ain't got the votes," Washington said. "I've tried to cut some deals, but they've got a case against you that resonates with the third world—"

"Don't you understand why I did it?" Ki Mapes perched on the edge of soft leather couch, leaning forward.

Carver sighed. "It don't matter to me why you did it. All they see is you making all that money, a ton of money, and spending it without them having any say so." He sighed again. "By doing that, in their eyes, you were saying you were above them, their authority, you were more powerful than them. Ain't nothing that's gonna piss off a power-grabbin' politician more than that." He rubbed his face. "Ki, you're a good man, I know it, but they're gonna shit on you, big time."

"You still don't get it, do you?" Ki rose and walked back and forth. "Sometime soon we're gonna get hit by the Hoo-Lii, and this time, they'll be more of them."

"Well," Carver said in a carefully neutral tone. "I just wish the Hendersons had confirmed that."

Ki stopped pacing to stare at Carver, his dark face gray and drawn. "Don't you believe me, either?"

Ki studied the giant screen at the rear of the rotunda that showed the vote had gone against him. He sighed. Only twelve representatives had yet to vote. The outcome was inevitable. The giant screen flickered. The columns of names and votes disappeared into blackness. Points of light materialized. Within the points of light, a circle of dots glowed brightly. Numbers scrolled across the screen's bottom.

Murmurs rose in the Assembly hall.

"Omigod," Ki said in a whisper as he recognized the image. *Someone's put up a real-time picture, probably from the Moon observatory.* He looked around and realized that few, if any present, understood what was on the screen.

"This is Butch Henderson," a voice echoed from the giant screen's speakers. "From the Moon observatory ..."

Well, I guessed that part right, Ki thought.

"A large fleet, maybe sixty craft, is coming from the direction of the sun on a direct course for Earth. Our estimate is that they'll go into orbit in twenty-four to thirty-six hours. We've confirmed these images with radar data from our orbital defense stations. We believe this is the Hoo-Lii fleet we spotted three months ago in the outer part of the system."

As one, delegates in the Assembly hall rose to their feet, yelling and screaming, drowning out Henderson's words.

"Ki," Carver shouted. "C'mon. It's time to get out of here. You've got more important things to do than listen to this bunch of idiots. We've gotta get you back in command."

"I thought you didn't believe me?"

"Well, the Hendersons came through for you." Carver shrugged. "Maybe, I'll just wish they hadn't. This looks like real trouble."

༄

Al Belasario found command of DS-2 difficult after Commander Mapes left. Things had turned to shit in a hurry. A rain of missiles came without warning. The huge cylinder that was DS-2, the former Qu'uda ship, rang with metallic booms from the onslaught of high-velocity impacts. The external sensors on the sunward side, the direction from where the attack came, went offline almost immediately.

Al swore as images showed flashes of light in the dock area, flashes that came from volatilized metal, as streams of molten iron and fast-moving fragments ripped the two Eagles parked there into useless pieces of junk.

"Damn," Al said. "I can't launch anything." He wanted to fight back but had nothing available.

He'd never expected kinetic weapons of such magnitude, projectiles that cut through the one foot of stainless steel that was the outer wall of the docking area. He checked the monitors for damage in the habitable section that had been carved out of the original asteroid. No penetrations were reported in that area in spite of numerous impacts.

"DS-3, report in," Al called.

Time ticked by slowly. A high-pitched voice came from the speaker amid the noisy spits of static. "We're under attack by Hoo-Lii forces. They hit us with kinetic weapons and followed up with energy beam weapons. Our external infrastructure is pretty well trashed. There's no damage to the Eagle within the docking area. We're preparing it for launch—"

"Don't send it out yet, not until the attack lifts." Al said. "Make sure it's got a full load of X-ray lasers."

"Read you loud and clear. We're working on getting our external sensors back online."

"Keep me informed," Al said. "I'll let Earth know our status." He knew they'd taken a severe pounding.

The Hoo-Lii, he realized, *had surprised us with their return, and they'd brought more powerful weapons than before. They'd learned their lesson.*

ᘰ

Ki felt the gee-forces increase and it reminded him how much he disliked space travel. The first two hundred and fifty kilometers to escape Earth's gravity well were crushing. Then came a brief period of zero gravity, which his body never accepted well. This trip would be different; it would be under a constant acceleration of one-gee—all the way.

He looked to the front and saw the pilot and navigator bent over their tasks, not raising their heads.

No windows in a heavy lifter, he realized. *That's how spacecraft have evolved, they don't need windows, particularly at the front.*

The heavy lifter wasn't a particularly agile or fast ship; it was a huge box with two large fusion drives powering it to orbit, along with a thousand tons of cargo and fourteen passengers.

The monitor before Ki brightened to show a schematic of their course. A large red square appeared, one-third the way around Earth from them. A vector arrow pointed in their direction. The gee-forces pressing him into the seat eased back to normal gravity.

"Ah, just want to let y'know where the bad guys are," came a voice from an overhead speaker. "It looks like they're in a high orbit around the Earth. We're in a different flight path and shouldn't have any problems with them."

So, Ki thought. *A constant acceleration trip to the halfway point, then constant deceleration. It won't take us long to get to DS-4. I'd better find out what's going on out there.* He picked up the handset. "Get me DS-4 on a tight-beam link."

Ki waited patiently.

"This is Bud Inez, DS-4," a tinny voice said. "We saw the Hoo-Lii fleet attack DS-2 and 3. We're preparing six Eagles to return to Earth to repel the Hoo-Lii fleet. They'll be carrying dumb missiles as well as fusion pumped X-ray lasers for a fast run attack. My plan is to have the Eagles round Earth in the opposite direction of travel of the Hoo-Lii to minimize contact time and maximize relative velocity difference for the kinetic missiles...."

Good, thought Ki. *No sense wasting our Eagles in a slugfest.*

"... They'll drop the X-ray lasers as they pass through the Hoo-Lii fleet," Bud said. "They'll orient themselves to fire across the width of the Hoo-Lii fleet...."

Ah, thought Ki, *good. Maybe they can get more than one ship with each laser.*

"... And the Eagles will return to DS-4." Bud paused for a moment. "One other thing. Fast Eagle Four, under Captain Walid Gharaguh, arrived at DS-4 sixteen hours ago. Fast Eagle Four has sustained significant damage and will be out of action for some time. Captain Gharaguh reports Captain Hawley and the crew of Fast Eagle Six made a heroic sacrifice to allow Fast Eagle Four to return with their information about the Hoo-Lii fleet. Over and out."

Ki hesitated a moment before speaking. "Commander Inez, this is Commander Mapes. I'm on my way to DS-4. DS-2 and 3 are effectively out of commission. Your plans to attack the Hoo-Lii fleet are approved. Do not take excessive risks with your Eagles. Keep in mind, we need to pressure them to prevent them from taking direct action against Earth. They're all we have left." He hesitated. "Provide me with your thoughts on how to do this within twenty-four hours. My ETA at DS-4 is about eighty-six hours from now. Over and out."

$$\rlap{\rotatebox{90}{\supset}}$$

"... Reduce velocity by point six klicks per second to lower orbit to match that of the enemy," a high-pitched voice said over the speaker. It was the strike force navigator who was coordinating their attack.

Bud Inez could feel his heart begin to pound. *Our six tiny ships are attacking fifty enormously large Hoo-Lii vessels—we must be effing crazy. The only thing going for us is surprise and speed. The relative velocities would approach thirty klicks per second.*

Bud toggled up the front visible view on his screen. *Nothing, the Hoo-Lii were still below the horizon. Thank God for the Hendersons on the Moon*, he thought. *They've been our eyes.*

"Prepare to deploy kinetics and chaff," a voice with a soft Texas accent drawled. Bud recognized Berkowitz's voice.

He'd explained they would release the "dumb missiles" in spread patterns to rip through the Hoo-Lii fleet and also confuse their sensors as to the Eagles' locations. Canisters of metal debris would lead the way and scatter radar-reflecting material along their flight paths to blind the enemy.

"Releasing kinetics and chaff." Something clanked and rattled.

Berkowitz had been in charge of the missiles in the first battle against the renegade Qu'uda and had volunteered for this mission. Berkowitz was a cool customer under fire.

Light glinted off something on the horizon. Bud increased amplification. A doughnut shape grew in the screen. "The Hoo-Lii." He took a deep breath.

"Removing locks on fusion pumped X-ray lasers," Berkowitz's voice said. All the missiles were under the control of the battle management computer, with every missile having an individual target. At this velocity, human reflexes were just too slow. "Launch sequence initiated. Lasers away."

Bud felt nothing. The missiles carrying the lasers were too small to affect the inertia of the Eagle.

Now, he realized. *It was time to get the hell out of here.* "All Eagles, maximum thrust."

According to plan, the Eagles would increase speed, rising to a higher orbit and away from Earth. That should get them into the safety of outer space and out of range of the Hoo-Lii fleet.

Right, thought Bud. *We'll give them kinetic missiles and a cloud of metal fragments as a gift.* He hoped that the chaff would buy protection as they passed above the Hoo-Lii.

The cluster of doughnut shaped ships rapidly drew closer. Sparkles of light danced over the ships from the beam weapons.

Bud watched carefully as the Hoo-Lii ships began to sink

beneath them. Then he saw there were other craft with the Hoo-Lii, hundreds of small craft. As the Hoo-Lii ships disappeared beneath them, Bud shifted to rear sensors.

Soon, he thought. *The kinetics will strike. Those that miss their targets will chase the Hoo-Lii out of this orbit level when they come around again.* He saw two Hoo-Lii ships puff out small clouds of debris and vapor. A sparkle of bright flashes came from the smaller craft clustered close to the larger ships, like a bundle of firecrackers.

Yes, he thought. *Now, the fireworks.*

Several dozen points of light grew—like flashes from electronic cameras, only they lingered longer and brighter, and were within the Hoo-Lii fleet. The ships appeared unchanged.

I wish we could tell which ones we hit with the X-ray lasers, Bud thought.

"Ah, this is Krishnamurthy on Eagle Four dash Two." The voice carried a trace of the singsong of the Indian subcontinent. "We sustained a direct hit on our main hull. We've lost most of our air and suffered significant casualties. Having a great deal of difficulty in maintaining control."

Bud picked up the handset. "All ships, this is Inez. Cut drives. Match course and stay with Eagle Four dash Two. Prepare for evacuation."

He changed setting on the handset and announced, "Mobilize mini-shuttle. Eagle Four dash Two is crippled. They need help." It would take twenty minutes to get the rescue craft ready to take off, he realized. "Navigator, bring us to point five klicks from Eagle Four dash Two."

"Eagle Four dash Two, this is Inez. We're matching courses and sending our mini-shuttle. Is your docking lock still functional?"

"I don't know," said Krishnamurthy. "That was the general vicinity of where we took the hit."

Oh, shit, thought Bud. "Get everyone into vacuum suits. If necessary, you can evacuate through the missile tubes."

It took six long hours to evacuate the survivors from Eagle Four dash Two, four hours longer than Bud had imagined. There were areas of the Eagle that were impossible to enter due to the damage.

What did this? he wondered. *It must have been an energy beam. Never saw it*, he thought. *But then why would I?*

"Sir, the Hendersons report that we've got a group of Hoo-Lii ships heading our way," came a voice.

"How long before they get here?"

"They've just about completed another orbit heading our direction. They are still well below our velocity. I don't know their acceleration and ETA—"

"How long? An hour? A minute? A day? Just gimme a ballpark number." Bud felt his blood pressure rise.

"Two hours or less." The voice was hesitant.

"Break off rescue operations," Bud said. "We're gonna have company if we don't get out of here soon."

"Commander Inez," Krishnamurthy said. "There are still six of my crew trapped in the damaged area—"

"We can't stay here." Bud looked at him, face drawn. "Those ships can do worse to us than what got you. I don't like it, but I'm responsible for all the ships." He turned away and picked up the handset. "How long before the mini-shuttle is stowed?"

"Ah, we'll be back in about ten minutes. We'll need twenty more to get battened down—"

"Step on it," Bud said. "Navigator, figure a course vector for DS-4 and transmit data to all ships. We depart together and we'll stay together."

౨

"Unknown ships approaching."

Nah-Kih rose off her resting mound. "From whence do they come?"

The invasion would start after the next sleep period and this news had startled her from her rest.

"Six ships, same orbit in retrograde direction, approaching fast." The pilot-navigator's voice chittered with fear.

"Transfer image data to my quarters." Nah-Kih turned and looked at the holo-display against the wall that glowed into life. Six yellow icons, in a circular pattern, occupied the center of the display, with numbers below to indicate their flight parameters.

"Warn of approaching predator," she said.

The six icons momentarily became fuzzy and the holo-display flickered and refreshed. The new image contained many more yellow icons. The number of icons began to proliferate, filling the display with a yellow haze.

"They employ countermeasures," the pilot-navigator said. "It must be an attack, activate defenses." She operated desktop controls and the image on the screen changed to the velvet black of deep space. Within the dark hung six points of light, accompanied by many much smaller specks of light. The range indicator dropped rapidly. "They're almost upon us."

The points of light expanded and disappeared.

"They have passed us," as the pilot-navigator spoke, something struck the ship with a bang.

Alarms began to squeak. The holo-display flashed orange and then showed a representation of the Hoo-Lii fleet. Six of eight squared ships flashed warning orange. Another column of figures appeared of which more than half flashed orange.

"What happened?" Nah-Kih asked.

"We have been attacked," the pilot-navigator said. "Remote sensors report that many obscenities were exploded in our midst. Initial reports show six capital ships no longer respond." She paused. "Many of the invasion shuttlecraft have been damaged."

"How many?" Nah-Kih asked.

The pilot-navigator remained silent.

"Well?"

"I fear, most gracious Hive-Mother, that more than half have been destroyed or damaged beyond repair." The pilot-navigator's voice rose to a shrill chitter of fear. "And those not damaged, do not respond to our queries."

"What else?" Nah-Kih said.

"Forgive me, but it appears that most of those craft held the best of our Chosen-Male warriors for the occupation of the Water-Gem," the pilot-navigator said. "And several of the Hive-Mothers who had chosen to be in the vanguard."

"We must not let these new servants flee," Nah-Kih said. "Dispatch eight capital ships after them. Follow them and destroy them. We shall take the Water-Gem, it is our destiny."

⌇

Bud Inez stared at the diagram on the monitor. At one side were the L-4 asteroids and the opposite side showed a red square depicting the pursuing Hoo-Lii craft. In the center, a yellow triangle crept closer to a small, flashing green dot. It was almost turnover time, when the Eagles would shut down their drives and reverse direction to begin deceleration.

"Prepare for zero gravity conditions in three minutes," a voice announced. Preparations for turnover had started several hours earlier. They had stood down from battle stations since they'd increased their lead on the Hoo-Lii ships.

Bud latched his seat belt and switched the view on the monitor to a radar display showing the Eagles were in a roughly circular formation, all within two kilometers of each other.

It should be soon, he thought and glanced at the clock.

"Drive shutdown in ten seconds," the voice announced over the ship's address system.

The vibration and hum of the main drive faded to silence. Gravity from its thrust vanished. "Rotation commencing."

Bud changed to the visible display of the ships outside.

It was like watching a ballet as all the Eagles turned in unison. Their rusted double hulls were cluttered with tacked-on equipment and scarred with multiple weld lines. Each was capped with a giant tent made of stainless steel slabs and foamed rock insulation. They moved with a precision that made him think of dancing hippopotamuses.

"Rotation complete," the voice announced. "Main drive restart in sixty seconds and counting."

They'll all start exactly together, Bud realized. *No one's hand would be on the throttle, just a stream of electrons doing their thing. Now*, he wondered. *How long will it be before the Hoo-Lii start to decelerate?*

Simultaneously, the brilliant cones of energy of the Eagles' fusion drives flickered into existence and grew brighter as engines came up to full power. The ships decelerated at one Earth gravity, falling toward the small cluster of asteroids that held Earth's last remaining defense station.

~

In the hours since Ed Kerr had learned of the Hoo-Lii fleet's presence, he hadn't slept much. Neither had the crew of DS-4.

He mentally reviewed what he'd accomplished: activated remote radar systems on outlying asteroids, installed the weapon systems, and linked them with DS-4 via tight-beam laser links. Lastly, he'd sent workers in solosuits to move masses of metallic debris on top of the station's vulnerable exterior installations.

I think we've got enough supplies to last, Ed thought. *If not, we'll just have to make do. Thank goodness Commander Mapes arranged for extra deliveries in the last three months. We've still got containers of stuff that we haven't opened and have no idea what they hold. Fortunately, we diverted the tanker ship of Helium-3 to DS-4 rather than going to Earth, meaning we've got plenty of fuel.*

"Captain Kerr," a voice squawked. "Incoming message."

Ed picked up the handset and listened.

"This is Commander Mapes on Heavy Lifter Four. Expect our arrival within two hours. We're coming in with a full load. Mapes out."

CHAPTER TWENTY-FOUR

THE BEST DEFENSE ...

"Let me give you a quick tour of DS-4," Ed Kerr said.

"Y'know, you told me what you were doing here, I just never grasped all the implications."

Ki found DS-4's long corridors and spacious rooms made him feel it was more of a place to live than a battle station.

The corridors' walls had a shiny, rippled surface, with insulating panels that had streaks of purple and brown from the natural color of the asteroid's rock.

"Is there anything beyond those walls?" He pointed to a side corridor littered with equipment and stacks of cardboard cartons ending in a welded metal bulkhead.

"That's another section that's still being tunneled," Ed said. "Or was until a couple of days ago when we heard the Hoo-Lii were coming. It'll double the capacity of DS-4."

"More yet?"

"That section will have a simulated outdoor park and recreation area, as well as more manufacturing facilities. There's a gym planned, along with two theaters, several restaurants, and more residences."

"I see," Ki said. "You've done a lot so far." This part of the station looks finished. *It's the floor*, he realized. It was as smooth as ceramic tile and reflected the light from the overhead fixtures. "What's the floor made of?"

"It's the rock-like material left over from the volatiles extraction operation," Ed said. "It's been foamed and fused."

At first the swimming pool, which also doubled as a water reservoir, seem odd to Ki, for its surface curved slightly.

Ah, he thought. *It's following the radius of the asteroid rotation.* He also noticed the same curvature in the corridors, although it wasn't as apparent due to the airlock doors.

In a corridor with many side rooms, a section of raised floor panels revealed piping, conduits, and wiring. Many of the rooms in this area had wiring hanging from the ceiling, debris piled in the center, or was occupied with busy workers.

"We haven't finished all the living quarters in this section." Kerr's voice was almost apologetic.

The size of the medical center both comforted and worried Ki. "I hope we never need its capacity," he said. "It looks like a combination hospital and emergency trauma unit."

"It also meets the needs of families on the station," Ed said. "Besides, preventive medicine makes sense."

Ki followed Ed through a large open square that reminded him of a shopping mall where half the stores were empty. In the center were planters filled with untilled mounds of dirt. "How come so many?" He waved at a bar and a small restaurant that had tables sitting outside under parasols, as well as a furniture store and small supermarket with a stack of empty cardboard boxes in front. The stores had few customers.

"We've probably overdone the stores, but since tunnel boring is very messy in the presence of oxygen, we decided to make the community areas large on first pass rather than come back later."

"How many people are here now?"

"Oh, we're about twelve hundred now." Ed continued on

down a long corridor, which ended at a set of massive doors. "This is the command center," he said.

Inside was a large, high-ceilinged room with banks of monitors along two sides. Each wall was covered with large flat screen monitors. A dozen men and women clad in tan jumpsuits sat on chairs before metal desks below the monitors. Voices rose and fell, muffled by the soft polymer flooring and acoustic tile on the ceiling. Each desk had multiple data entry controls as well as specialized remote sensing readouts. A section of one wall had open bays with wires hanging out. "We've got the sensors on the outer asteroids hooked into the system," Ed said.

This is the plushest command center I've seen, Ki thought. "How long d'you think those sensors will last?" he asked.

"Most of them are well protected, buried," Ed said. "We use laser line-of-sight data links. Our receivers will be the weakest point in the system if we come under attack—"

"When we come under attack," Ki said. "What else?"

"There's six remote missile launchers, plus four soloships depots." Ed pointed to a monitor. "The motion of the asteroids means we periodically lose line of sight. We have alternate path backup. Even so, we're out of touch from time to time." He sighed. "Best we could do in the time available."

"Speaking of weak points, how will this station stand up under attack, missile bombardment, for example?"

Ed shrugged. "Well, there's about thirty-five feet of metal at the thinnest point to the surface. Should be thick enough." He frowned briefly. "If they hit us with something really big at very high velocity, we'd be in a world of hurt. But then, they've got to hit us. There's a lot of asteroids around us and we're well hidden."

"What're our vulnerabilities?"

"Well, we generate a lot of heat, so we've got a significant IR signature." Ed smiled thinly. "We made sure a half-dozen other asteroids have similar IR signatures. Then there's traffic. If they spot a ship coming in, that'll confirm our position. We also plan to buzz some soloships around when the Eagles dock."

"Speaking of Eagles, what's their situation?"

Ed glanced at the monitors. "Joey, what's happening?"

"Eagles are maintaining flight plan. They completed turnover twelve hours ago and began a deceleration flight path," a technician at the radar console said. "Hoo-Lii ships continue to increase velocity and are closing in on the Eagles. They'll be in range of the Eagles in six hours. ETA is twenty-two hours."

Ki picked up a handset. "Get me Inez." He turned toward the crew of the command center. "What kind of long-range weapons are available?"

A stocky, dark-skinned man spoke, "We've got twenty-four Tridents set up and ready for launch." He shrugged. "Range, well, that doesn't mean anything out here. Their full burnout velocity is in the fourteen to fifteen klicks per second range. They carry ten MIRV'd warheads, each rated at one-fifty kilotons. They're the biggest and baddest bang we've got."

"Ah, they're closing on us," Bud Inez said. "At this rate, they'll be in range before we get to DS-4."

"Hit 'em with your nukes," Ki said. "That'll make them quit chasing you, or at least slow 'em down."

"We only have two left on my Eagle," Bud said. "We're saving them as a last resort."

"Use them, we brought more," Ki said. "Once you get here, you can out-maneuver them. From what Kerr tells me, they won't find it a friendly place."

"Yeah, that's right," Bud said. "I'll get back to you later, as long as they don't get us first."

Ki nodded and spoke into the handset. "One last thing, Bud, we're gonna launch a MIRV'd Trident directly at you. This is what I want you to do...."

The pilot-navigator of the ship, the Vale of the Mother, stared at the data in the holo-display. "Why are the craft of the new servants reducing velocity?" She tapped a control panel. More data scrolled through the display. Her breathing orifices flared as though catching a hint of dangerous predator.

Five icons within the holo-display designating the ships of the new servants blinked yellow. Beyond, a faint yellow haze indicated the signals had bounced off something else, further out, something that shouldn't exist in this part of empty space— it was a small cluster of asteroids.

"Most gracious Hive-Mother." The pilot-navigator used a priority code in the communication system. "The new servant's destination is ahead, it is a group of asteroids to which they decelerate—"

"Is it a trap?" Buk-Tih, the ship's Hive-Mother asked.

The new servants had already launched missiles at them, which they'd destroyed with beam weapons before they got close. The memory of what happened while in orbit around the Water-Gem was still fresh. The new servants' use of obscenities destroyed six of their major ships. That made every Hive-Mother cautious.

"Why are asteroids in this location?"

"It is an orbital resonance point," the pilot-navigator said. "A trap? I do not know. The images are poorly resolved at such a distance." She hesitated. "Though we close upon the ships of the new servants, if we maintain our course, we shall arrive and pass the asteroids with significant velocity—"

"Advise all ships to commence maximum deceleration as soon as practical," said Buk-Tih. "In formation."

"At once, most gracious Hive-Mother."

"Inform them we have found the final nest of the new servants. After we destroy this one, nothing shall be in our way to take possession of the Water-Gem. It is our destiny."

ᘰ

Ki stared at the transcript of the encoded tight-beam transmission.

So, he thought. *Al Belasario is alive and well on DS-3. He wants to kick some ass with Eagle Three-Two; one of the original "fast" Eagles that's armed and ready to go.* He felt a tremendous sense of relief at learning that his wife, LaTasha, was unharmed and safe on the station.

Ki found most of the message's contents gave him little encouragement. DS-2 had only two operational spacecraft—the second was a heavy lifter that could be used for evacuation in an emergency.

If this isn't an emergency, Ki thought, *nothing is. I don't want any suicide missions. I want them to keep the Hoo-Lii off-balance until we can figure a way to land a decisive blow. I never imagined the Hoo-Lii would return in such force, fifty plus spaceships, big mothers, too. Right now, I've got nine Eagles, assuming the five being chased get back intact, plus the one Al has, Gharaguh's wreck, and two more at Deimos, plus a hundred or so soloships.* He rubbed his head.

Leaning back in his chair, Ki looked around his new office and found its minimal furniture emphasized its spaciousness. He still wasn't used to it, but the two monitors on the wall with the sound turned down low kept him abreast of events taking place in the command center. There was even a private bathroom— quite unlike his earlier command posts—he found he liked it.

"Okay, send this message to DS-3," Ki spoke into a handset. "To Al Belasario." He paused. "Do not confront any Hoo-Lii ships directly. Use Moon-derived data to place kinetic debris in counter orbits used by Hoo-Lii ships. I'll let you know when it's safe to evacuate personnel to DS-4." He looked at a picture of LaTasha. "Be especially careful about putting non-combatant personnel in harm's way. End of message."

"Sir," a voice called from the intercom. "The Hoo-Lii ships have started decelerating."

"Damn," Ki said. "Can we reset the release point on the

Trident's warheads?" He looked at the stocky, dark-skinned man in charge of the missiles.

"No, sir. Not at this range."

♎

Buk-Tih glanced at the calculations.

So, he thought. *We should still have excess velocity when we reach the new servants' nest. Perhaps that is not a bad thing.* He remembered the first encounter with the new servants on the first expedition and how they used passive weapons. *Yes, it may be to our advantage to pass by quickly, the first time, and gather information on what the new servants have on these asteroids. Especially at a range where we can clearly see anything in our path.*

"Plot a course that will allow us to pass the asteroids while in an englobing formation," Buk-Tih said. "I want our ships to examine these asteroids from all directions and seek out the precise location of the nest of the new servants."

"At once, most gracious Hive-Mother."

The holo-display's image expanded to include all of the asteroids at the orbital resonance point. A faint green line extended from the tiny cluster of yellow points into the heart of the asteroids that indicated the course of the five craft of the new servants. The pilot-navigator calculated the course for their eight ships. A new set of orange traces extended like a cone around the asteroids.

"Most gracious Hive-Mother, the new course is now on display." She stared hard at a tiny flashing icon. She tapped a control and faint lines extended from the flashing icon. "Another craft or missile approaching," she said. "It originates from the asteroid and is on direct course to us."

"Will it intercept us once we assume the new course?"

The pilot-navigator brought up the course projection and expanded the display. A red line extended toward the point of the cone of yellow lines. By the time the red line reached the yellow cone, it passed clearly between individual courses of the Hoo-Lii ships. "Most gracious Hive-Mother, it will not intercept our course."

"Watch it carefully," Buk-Tih said. "It could be a trap."

"Yes, most gracious Hive-Mother." The pilot-navigator distributed the new navigation parameters and coordinated the course change without ceasing deceleration. She changed the display to look at the object coming from the asteroids. This time she could see the yellow icon had separated into three objects. As she watched, the three yellow icons disappeared, replaced by a hazy, yellow circle.

"Missiles from asteroids have separated into multiple objects," the pilot-navigator announced. She measured the rate of expansion against their closing speed. It would be close. "Recommend expanding course divergence." She preferred caution to close calls.

Buk-Tih's voice chittered loudly. "Are we in danger?"

"Yes, most gracious Hive-Mother, I believe the missiles from the asteroids have become many and are on a diverging course, seeking to destroy us—"

"Expand course divergence," Buk-Tih said. "Quickly."

It took the pilot-navigator a few moments to calculate and transmit the new course to the fleet. She watched the data develop in the holo-display, as columns of numbers scrolled through the screen.

We are out of danger, she noted. *The five craft of the new servants that we pursue had already passed the circle of missiles. Now*, she thought. *They have slipped beyond our range. They will reach the asteroids.*

ॐ

"Do not approach DS-4 directly," Ki said. "Each Eagle should seek shelter behind a different asteroid." He realized the circular formation of the Hoo-Lii would give them an opportunity to gather data on all the asteroids as they passed. "Plot trajectories at Hoo-Lii craft."

The missile technician bent to his task, fingers flying over the control panel. He glanced up at a monitor and waited. A column of amber figures scrolled down the black screen. "Course trajectory plotted on enemy craft," he said. "Weapons armed and ready. On your order, sir."

$$\backsim$$

"Spirit of the Mother." The pilot-navigator stared at multiple green dots representing the asteroids floating in the holo-display. Five of them carried a yellow flashing icon representing significant heat sources and six more carried orange icons that indicated minor heat sources. "Most gracious Hive-Mother," she called. "The new servants have spread throughout these asteroids, they occupy at least five of them."

"Is it a trick?" Buk-Tih asked.

"At this distance, the heat sources appear quite similar."

"Continue observation."

The pilot-navigator switched sensors to look for metallic objects. The five craft of the new servants they pursued immediately appeared in the center of the display. One after another, more glowed into being with many metallic objects. She sighed and began the discrimination process, first sorting by size, then by movement and rotation, lastly by heat generation.

When she combined the data, she emitted a tiny whiff of pleasure. "Most gracious Hive-Mother," she called. "I think I've found the new servants' nest...." She went on to explain what she had done.

"Yes," Buk-Tih said. "Your logic is reasonable." She hesitated. "Provide coordinates to the Chosen-Male warriors in the missile section. Prepare to strike their nest as we pass."

The pilot-navigator set up a simulation of their position when they would pass the asteroids and plotted the course of the missiles from their eight ships. Asteroids would shield the nest from three of their ships' missiles unless they were released early or late, somewhere other than the passing position.

It took little time to compute the next optimum position for the three ships whose missiles were blanked. An early shot appeared to be the best alternative for them. The pilot-navigator advised the Hive-Mother who approved the change in plans.

"First set of kinetic missiles launched," the pilot-navigator said. The holo-display showed three sets of faint red lines converging on the asteroid indicated by a green icon. She switched the holo-display to visual to watch their impact. A cascade of brilliant white flashes on a smaller asteroid marked the accuracy of the missiles. "Prepare for the second set of kinetic missiles." She waited for the Chosen-Male warriors to execute the launch at passing.

Again, they peppered the surface of the same asteroid with heavy metal missiles that flashed into incandescence from impact.

"Commencing maximum deceleration now," the pilot-navigator announced. She knew the plan was to return to the asteroids and seek out what was left of the new servants' nest, to eliminate any that might have survived.

She glanced at the holo-display and her breathing orifices flared wide. She recognized the strange chemically powered missiles of the new servants rising from six separate asteroids, all on course for their ships.

"Incoming missiles," the pilot-navigator screamed. "Activate defensive weapons." She knew the range was close, almost impossibly close. "Shut down engines." Instead of slowing further, the ships would maintain speed. The missiles drew closer and closer, accelerating constantly, leaving the strange white cloud-like trail behind.

Several impossibly bright flashes filled the holo-display before it went dark. The pilot-navigator lowered herself to the deck in a position of absolute submission. "Spirit of the Mother, save us."

∿

Dust filled the air. Lights flickered on the control panels as a series of thudding shocks rattled the control center. The large flat screen displays on the walls sparkled with intermittent flashes of light.

"Tridents launched," came a voice from a speaker on the wall. A second series of hammering shocks produced another shower of dust. A ceiling panel popped loose and fell.

"Life support status?" Ki Mapes asked. Dust on his mahogany brown face seemed almost like pale makeup.

The technicians bent over their controls, most speaking rapidly into their handsets. One looked up. "Sir, the central corridors are still maintaining pressure. Outer door to dock number one is gone. No damage estimate yet on the Eagle."

"Tridents on course and running hot."

"Enemy has shut down their main drives."

Ki glanced at Joey, the missile technician. "Release warheads whenever you can."

"Aye-aye, sir." Joey hunched over his controls. "Now released."

"Somebody get these damn sensors back online," Ki said. It sounded almost like a wish rather than an order.

Slowly, heads rose from the control consoles and looked around, almost expectantly, as if waiting for another impact. "Is it over?" someone asked.

The flat screen display above Ki glowed into life to show a field of stars on a velvet black background. The field dissolved and reformed on a doughnut shaped object that could only be a Hoo-Lii ship. Something glared, illuminating it brightly.

"I need an overall view," Ki called. "I need to know what's happening in the big picture."

"Radar will be back shortly," a technician said. "I hope," he added softly as he bent closer to his control module.

"This is Captain Inez," a voice crackled from a speaker. "It appears that none of the Eagles were targeted, so, we're okay. How about you folks, in DS-4? It looks like you got spanked hard by several dozen missiles."

"This is Commander Mapes. What happened to the Hoo-Lii ships? Did we get any with the Tridents?"

"From here, it looks like you might have winged one, but then I can't see all of them—"

"This is Captain Stolz," a voice called. "I believe we might have winged two of them. We didn't record any direct hits from here, however, two showed signs of secondary heating, sufficient to cause course deviation." He hesitated. "I'd guess they got pretty shook from that, not to mention radiation damage."

"Where are they now?" Ki demanded.

"Ah, looks like they're continuing on, drives still off."

The second large wall monitor glowed into life.

"We've patched a temporary link through," a voice announced from the speaker. "We'll keep it open until we get a new line installed. The entrance to Dock Number One got trashed and we lost the main conduit coming in. Won't take long."

"Ah, this is what DS-4 looks like ..." Stolz's voice trailed off. The pear-shaped asteroid that was DS-4 rotated slowly in the center of the screen, its dull gray exterior marked by tiny acne-like splotches. The image zoomed closer. The splotches resolved into shiny, bright frozen splashes. A linear scale appeared and moved to a splotch that now filled the screen. A kinetic missile had made a crater fifteen feet across and seven feet deep in the asteroid's iron-nickel surface.

Ki looked around and raised the handset. "Inez, Stolz, advise us immediately of any changes by the Hoo-Lii."

"Yes, sir." Both voices spoke almost in unison.

"Commander Mapes," a voice called. It was a mousy blonde

woman who wore the emblem of the Space Observatory on her tan jump suit. She was on temporary duty from the Moon station.

"Yes?" Ki could not recall her name.

"The missile impacts have imparted motion to DS-4," she said. "It isn't much, but it could cause us to drift into another asteroid in time—"

"Figure it out and let me know."

"Yes, sir," she said.

"The Hoo-Lii have resumed deceleration," a male voice called. "Wait," he said. "Five of them have lit their drives ... three are continuing to coast onwards."

"Plot courses on those decelerating," Ki said. "Launch MIRV'd missiles at them."

"Sir. The outer blast door on Dock Number One has a large hole and the inner airlock door has several holes." The technician hesitated. "The front of the Eagle got hit hard and the dock facilities were trashed, too."

"Missiles away."

Ki looked up at the monitor. Five billowy white plumes marked the trails of the Trident missiles, becoming the merest trace as they reached out toward their destination. The image zoomed in to reveal the doughnut shapes of the Hoo-Lii ships. Tiny sparkles of light pulsed at irregular intervals from them.

"Uh-oh," Joey said. "We just lost one of the Tridents, and another." He bent to his control panel and typed rapidly. "I released the warheads early," he said. "Lower probability of target acquisition, higher survivability quotient." He frowned as though he'd eaten something bitter. "Time to contact, three, two, one, zero."

A tiny point of light grew to fill the screen of the monitor, then faded almost as fast to complete blackness.

"Er, I think we lost a charge-coupled amplifier," a woman's voice said. "Give me a moment. Okay, that should do it."

Prickles of light grew in the monitor, to resolve into four doughnut shaped objects.

"Something's different," Ki said.

"Hoo-Lii ships changing course while under power," a voice called. "Now they've powered down."

"No, they're reversing course." The technician's voice had risen an octave.

"Plotting course for missiles," Joey said.

"Launch when ready," Ki said.

ౌ

The pilot-navigator on the Vale of the Mother was frightened. *In less than one sleep period,* she thought, *the new servants had used more than eight squared fusion obscenities upon them. They had killed or wrecked four of our eight ships sent in pursuit of the new servants' tiny craft. It wasn't right. And now, they continued to launch more missiles at them.*

"Most gracious Hive-Mother," the pilot-navigator said. "These missiles do not readily change course. We can avoid them by changing our velocity—"

"Then do it." Buk-Tih's breathing orifices flared. She emitted aromas of anger and fear. She had already given the orders to leave this nest of new servants and return to the main fleet above the Water-Gem planet.

The pilot-navigator flexed in submission and bent to her task. She hoped if they had to return to this nest of new servants, it would be with overwhelming force. "New course plotted. This will take us around the new servants' nest."

CHAPTER TWENTY-FIVE

SERVANTS MUST BE DISCIPLINED

"Eagles Two-Six and Eight approaching DS-3," Captain Stolz's voice crackled from the speaker.

"Good luck on your mission." Ki Mapes glanced around the command center. It had taken two weeks for DS-4 to recover from the Hoo-Lii attack.

Finally, he thought. *Maintenance has fixed the fallen ceiling and buckled floor tiles. The airlock and outer doors to dock number one now functioned, but the Eagle inside was beyond repair, fit only as a source of parts.*

He'd decided Stolz would lead a two-ship flight back to DS-3 and carry the battle to the Hoo-Lii. "I hope this isn't an exercise in futility," he said.

"Belasario had some success with just one Eagle," Bud Inez said. "And he did it without nukes."

Ki rubbed his hand over his non-existent hair. "Well, he's taking all our nuke missiles." He would only deploy two Eagles since they lacked the missiles for all five craft. He hoped the nukes would keep the Hoo-Lii off-balance to prevent their invasion of Earth.

"Commander, any word from Pynchon?" Bud asked.

Ki took a deep breath. "He's on his way back from Deimos with both Eagles. He's bringing twenty soloships, too."

"Any nukes?" Bud sounded almost hopeful.

"None."

"Well, we're now down to just two outposts," Bud said.

Ki sniffed and sighed. "Right." He didn't need reminding they'd abandoned their station above Mars, just days after he'd ordered Defense Station Two to evacuate.

DS-2, based upon the old Qu'uda ship, the Little-Egg-that-Flies, had taken a beating in three assaults by the Hoo-Lii and was now out of munitions. In the last attack, the Hoo-Lii warriors had penetrated as far as the main corridor that led from the badly damaged docking areas to the living quarters.

Belasario's crew had flooded the main corridor with a mixture of hydrogen and oxygen. On ignition, the detonation had split the main corridor and ruptured the main docking bay. The explosion had killed hundreds of Hoo-Lii boarders.

The remaining crew and families had fled to DS-3 on the only remaining craft, a heavy lifter. Some of those in the heavy lifter's uninsulated cargo hold had suffered frostbite.

Why, Ki thought. *Haven't the Hoo-Lii landed on Earth?*

He was sure they would have by now.

Nah-Kih spread her mid-limbs. "We must take possession of the planet below, and soon," she said.

"If they use their obscenities upon our ships while we are on the Water-Gem, we could be trapped here," said Buk-Tih.

Unlike the Hive-Mothers who had remained with their ships above the planet, she had seen fusion explosions up close while chasing the new servants to their asteroid nest.

"Our food supplies will not last forever," Nah-Kih said.

"We have lost many of our Chosen-Male warriors." Buk-Tih

referred to the initial encounter as they had orbited the planet where a barrage of kinetic missiles had caught the shuttlecraft carrying their invasion force.

"Many are so contaminated by radiation," she said, "we cannot feed their corpses to the food insects."

"They fought without regard for their own ship," said Nah-Kih. "Damaging it beyond use and then abandoning it."

"And killing many of our warriors." Buk-Tih emitted a sour odor of displeasure. "We cannot take any more of these losses."

"These new servants must be disciplined for the tactics they use. One on one, they are no match for our warriors."

"There are many new servants below, perhaps too many for us," Nah-Kih said. "The loss of so many landing shuttles is a problem. We can only land eight, which is too few to establish a limbhold against a determined foe, especially one who uses obscenities freely and is so willing to die."

"These new servants are soft and easy to kill. We are more powerful than they are, but they use forbidden weapons. If only we had weapons of such power that did not violate the Way of the Mother. There must be a way to make them submit—"

"Ah!" Nah-Kih's breathing orifices flared as though about to seize a prey. "There is a way to discipline the new servants. Consider ..." She explained her idea, even identifying where they would strike. "And so, I say we dispatch eight ships on this mission."

"That is a daring act."

"Once underway, our entire fleet will join the mission, to see it succeeds."

Buk-Tih clasped her mid-limbs and emitted the sweet odor of agreement. "I like this plan. So it shall be."

～

As soon as Taylor started getting around on crutches, his condition became a source of curiosity to the Hoo-Lii. Suh-Joh invited him to her command center for a discussion. Her counselor, Son-Nih, sat silent a short distance from her.

"We do not save warriors who have serious injuries such as yours." The translation device converted Suh-Joh's high-pitched chittering into a flat Midwestern voice.

"What happens to your badly injured warriors?" Taylor asked.

"We feed them to the food insects," she said.

"What food insects?" Taylor asked.

"They are what you eat. We have many varieties, some reserved only for me," she said. "As Hive-Mother, I choose to eat only the most flavorful of foods."

Taylor paused. After living among the Hoo-Lii for several months, he knew Suh-Joh ruled the three main social levels with an iron hand—warriors, priests, and servants. It had been a surprise to find she was the mother of all of the servants and about half the warriors. That interested him more than knowing his food came from carrion-eating insects. "How did you become the Hive-Mother?" he asked.

Suh-Joh rose from her resting mound. Her breathing orifices flared and air whistled in. "Ah, you do not know my history," she said. "Let me tell you of it...." She settled comfortably onto her resting mound and began to speak.

Taylor listened intently to the narration of what he soon realized was a story of epic proportions. Her rise was from a lowly servant, elevated by a powerful Hive-Mother who chose her to restore genetic diversity to their bloodlines. He was surprised to learn she had been exiled for bestowing longevity upon her counselors, and she'd built this ship solely as a means of bringing her hive with her.

"It was your gift of water, to my servants, that made us believe you chose to become our servants, also."

Taylor smiled without warmth. "That was only an attempt to communicate with you. When we give water, it means nothing," he said. "Our species would never submit to become servants without a fight."

"Yes," she said. "It has become apparent yours is a warlike species." She hesitated. "Yet, you do not have a servant class, why is this?"

Taylor stroked his chin before answering. "In the past, there were servant classes. As we evolved, heredity had less and less to do with power. Those with skills and knowledge rose, and our society mixed thoroughly, producing a desire to be equal."

He paused, realizing Suh-Joh had emphasized birth and reproduction as being key to understanding their society.

"I believe it may also be due to our means of reproduction, which is different than yours," Taylor continued. "Half are male. Half are female who have the capacity to be a mother. So, each offspring is raised by a mother, learning as an individual, not needing to be chosen, not needing any special ripening, except for the coupling with a male. That makes us very individual."

"Such chaos, such a difficult society to control."

"True, but we've learned how to live together," Taylor said. "Our leaders are chosen by all the people in our society, those who meet the needs of society."

"Excuse me, most gracious Hive-Mother," a small unripened female said, a servant who prostrated herself against the floor. "The pilot-navigator asked me to advise you we are ready to jump into the Hool system upon your command—"

"Tell him to proceed according to plan." Suh-Joh waved a mid-limb.

The tiny servant rose and scurried away.

"Tell me about your beliefs, those which guide your behavior and establish the rules for right and wrong," Suh-Joh said. "Do you follow the Way of the Mother?"

Taylor's leg had started to itch. He tried to reach inside the cast on his leg for some relief. It also gave him time to gather his thoughts. "That is not an easy question to answer, for we have formal rules, which we call laws. Then we have customs and traditions based upon our religious beliefs that come from far in our past."

"Ah," said Suh-Joh. "Then you do have something that is similar to the Way of the Mother, something that is strong and based upon principles, to live and die for. Principles that are age-old and time-tested, administered by those who are the keepers of the truth...."

As Taylor listened, he realized their religious beliefs shaped their laws, and the keepers of the religious beliefs were responsible for Suh-Joh's expulsion.

"In our society, the rules made by society are stronger than those from out of our ancient past. Laws are made by men, for men, and administered by men—"

"This cannot be." Suh-Joh rose up from her resting mound. Her breathing orifices flared and she lowered her head to stare at Taylor. Her spines slowly erected. "Surely the ancient principles are the most honored and the strongest?"

Taylor felt somewhat intimidated. "Most honored Hive-Mother," he said. "We are a different species, different in appearance, with a different reproductive process, so it is only logical we are different in the way we structure our society and the way we manage it."

Suh-Joh exhaled noisily and her breathing orifices shut tight. As her spines began to quiver, a warning bleat announced an imminent jump through space-time. "We must continue this discussion later," she said. "I had not realized it was possible for a society to exist on such principles, one similar to the ways of our 'Disobedient' ones—" The alarm bleated louder.

"Go," she said. "Go to your quarters."

ᘓ

The pilot-navigator of the Mother's Servant brought the ship's engines to maximum power.

This, she thought. *Is one step from madness. To rely upon the primitive technology of the new servants of Earth to guide us through the space-time opening is an act of faith greater than believing in the Way of the Mother. Then again*, she thought, *it got us through the previous opening without any problems. But at maximum power?*

Behind, in close formation, the massed Qu'uda ships followed. The pilot-navigator had warned there were hostile Hoo-Lii forces in the system they were about to enter. The strategy was to enter fast and set a course for the opening in space-time leading to the Earth system.

"Be sure we execute the course change together," said Son-Nih, the grizzled and scarred old warrior, counselor to the Hive-Mother. "We do not wish to give the Coven's ships that guard these entrances time to gather their forces."

"Yes, honorable Son-Nih," the pilot-navigator said. "Between our speed and our allies, they will not choose to fight. I expect they will flee before us."

"Let us pray your expectations prove true." Son-Nih's experience in battle made him cautious at every step of the way. "I prefer to fight battles I know I shall win, not to enter ambushes that require divine intervention by the Spirit of the Mother as the sole means to survive."

"Preparing to enter the Hool system," the pilot-navigator called.

She crouched and waited for the nausea and disorientation that always came as the tunnel through space-time collapsed. She hated the sensation and took minor comfort the human electronics would keep the ship fully operational during the period when she was incapacitated.

"Spirit of the Mother," she cried, not wanting to but unable to withstand the need to seek solace. Odors of fear and revulsion filled the air. Twitters of confusion and calls for help echoed through the ship.

Four yellow icons appeared in the holo-display. An alarm bleated loudly as an "enemy" designation flashed brightly. A column of figures scrolled through the holo-display indicating the new course parameters. The drive engine faded as vector engines turned the ship onto its new course. Echelons of small yellow icons marched into the holo-display, all turning to their new course. They were the Qu'uda ships following the Mother's Servant, spreading into a defensive alignment behind.

"What is happening?" Son-Nih asked.

"The Coven's ships have not engaged their engines," said the pilot-navigator. "They make no attempt to follow."

"Let us wait and see what they do," said Son-Nih. "Before we reach that conclusion."

The main engine came back to life, filling the Mother's Servant with the high frequency vibration as its fusion drive increased output. Within the holo-display, a faint green line extended from the icon that depicted the Mother's Servant. The images shrank until the whole system of Hool became visible. The faint green line traversed across almost one-third of the system to a tiny red dot that blinked slowly.

"It is a long way to go," said Son-Nih.

"They do not pursue us," said the pilot-navigator.

"It is a tactical error. They should join forces with the Coven ships at the next entrance to space-time."

The pilot-navigator looked at Son-Nih and realized why Hive-Mother Suh-Joh held this old priest-warrior in high regard. "Then you do not expect trouble when we enter the next opening?"

"Always expect trouble."

∾

"Most gracious Hive-Mother," said Son-Nih, flexing himself before Suh-Joh. "What is your wish?"

Suh-Joh beckoned to her counselor. "Come," she said. "Sit next to me. I need your insight."

Son-Nih rose up from the quartzite floor with its brown floor covering embossed with the crossed quill representing Suh-Joh's hive and sat before his Hive-Mother. "You honor me."

"Please forego the platitudes, I need your insight on these ..."

Suh-Joh hesitated, "humans. I choose to use their name for themselves, because I do not believe they will ever be our servants. You listened to the discussion between the crippled warrior, Taylor, and myself?"

"Yes, it was most enlightening."

"Do we take them as allies, or do we feed them to the insects?" Suh-Joh asked. "They do not follow the Way of the Mother and profess many of the same things as the Disobedient."

"This is true, most gracious Hive-Mother," said Son-Nih. "However, they have been true to their word and did provide food in our time of need. They have sought out allies to aid us against the forces of the Coven—"

"Does that not also aid the humans in their fight with those who wish to bend them to their will and make them new servants?"

"This is true." Son-Nih hesitated. "However, they have a courage that seems unlikely in a species who seem so unsuited for combat, and a lively intelligence that lets them seize our technology quickly." He stared into the distance. "It is their willingness to fight, even against the greatest odds, and their grasp of tactics that persuades me it is better they be our allies than our enemies." He flexed low. "Excuse me, I am but an old warrior, prone to ramble—"

"Son-Nih, please, I value your counsel—"

An alarm bleated.

"Yes?" Suh-Joh asked.

"Forgive me, most gracious Hive-Mother," came the voice of the pilot-navigator. "There are ships clustered before the entrance to the opening in space-time, so tightly clustered as to prevent our entrance."

"Son-Nih, join the pilot-navigator and decide upon our course of action."

"Yes, most gracious Hive-Mother."

𝄢

Son-Nih stared at the cluster of yellow icons in the center of the holo-display. "You're sure they are directly over the entrance to the opening?"

"Yes, honorable Son-Nih," the pilot-navigator said. Softly spoken voices muttered in the background of the navigation station, both human and Hoo-Lii.

Son-Nih turned to Taylor. "So, what would you do?"

Taylor raised his eyebrows. "We really have no choice for we cannot remain in this system, so, we must go through. Therefore, we should prepare to battle with the ships guarding the entrance. We have the larger force and should prevail."

"Your logic is correct," Son-Nih said. "How?"

Taylor took a deep breath. "If it were me, I'd attack with the Mother's Servant, directly upon the Coven's ships, deploying the main laser. The Qu'uda ships should decelerate and attack from one side, in a half-circle formation."

"Half-circle formation?"

"Yes, do not let them think they are trapped and must fight to death. Give them an opportunity to flee."

"Why?" asked Son-Nih.

"If they flee, we will suffer less damage and fewer casualties. Remember, a cornered foe will fight with desperation," Taylor said. "We need to save our strength. A larger foe lies ahead."

Son-Nih turned to the pilot-navigator. "Did you understand what the human meant?"

"Yes, honorable Son-Nih."

"Plot courses for our allies and coordinate our attack."

CHAPTER TWENTY-SIX

A CHANGE IN TACTICS

A voice called. Ki rolled over and stared at the ceiling. It was higher than what he'd been used to on his previous vessels. His eyes moved to the walls. They were beige, tinted with tiny patches of colors. He could feel LaTasha's warmth next to him. Her quiet snores were both familiar and comforting. He pulled the covers up and closed his eyes.

"Commander Mapes." The voice was insistent, urgent.

He opened his eyes again. "Yes?"

"Long distance radar shows a group of ships heading away from Earth, roughly in our direction. The Moon observatory reports eight Hoo-Lii ships—the big ones—left orbit about three days ago. It may be another attack underway—"

"Coming." Ki rose from his bed, careful not to disturb his sleeping wife and padded into his dressing room, quietly closing the door behind him. He still wasn't used to the generous space on Defense Station Four. But, as Ed Kerr said, "might as well make this outpost as comfortable as possible. Trips home will be far and few between." Ki found as time passed, he tended to agree more and more with that comment.

He dressed quickly and headed to the command center. "What do we have?" He looked around for the coffeepot.

A tactics officer, Levin, said: "It's coming up on your display, now." A circle of dots on the green background of the radar display glowed anew each time they were swept by the baton of light that represented the probing radiation.

"At current velocity, they'll be here in less than five days. If they slow down, then it'll be about twelve days."

Ki got a cup of coffee and saw Bud Inez coming into the room. "Well, what d'you think we should do?"

Bud rubbed his eyes. "Depends on whether they make a fast pass or come to visit." He covered a yawn. "A fast pass, well, we could send a bunch of soloships under remote control into their flight path. Y'know, load 'em with canisters of metal pieces and strafe 'em good."

"If they decide to stay a while?"

"That gets to be more interesting." Bud sat down at a monitor and tapped on its keyboard. "We've put together some low velocity guns, gas powered, that we can maneuver with the soloships. We've also got three Eagles that should be more maneuverable than those hulking Hoo-Lii ships." He spread his palms and shrugged. "We don't have any more nukes."

Ki pursed his lips. "Mebbe we can make them think that we do." A trace of a smile crossed his lips. "We could launch a bunch of soloships in a cluster at them, and then spread them, just like the MIRV'd warheads." He frowned briefly. "We need something that'll generate an EMP."

"How about overloading a klystron? Y'know, a directional radar transmitter, focused on their ships?" Levin said. "Yeah, I know it's a pale imitation of the real thing, but it might fool them since they've already been hit by our nukes."

Ki nodded. "How about adding a flash?"

"Easy," Bud said. "Tinker with a laser and we can get a high intensity flash, bright enough to fake out a sensor, especially if it's tightly focused."

"If they do get close?" Ki asked. "Are we gonna be able to hold out?" He remembered the pounding DS-4 took previously.

"Kerr's people have filled all the missile impact craters with metal, properly welded in," Bud said. "The new outer door to Dock Number One is twice as thick as the previous door."

"I sure wish we had some nukes," Ki said.

ౚ

"What're they doing?" Ki asked. He couldn't understand why the Hoo-Lii ships had stopped short of their position. Sure, they'd scattered into far looser formation when the fake nuke went off when they'd finally halted. DS-4's crew had detected numerous radar scans directed at them but there had been no missile bombardment. The lack of action made Ki nervous.

"Sir," Levin called. "They've sent out four shuttles." He pointed to the large monitor mounted against the wall above Ki. Tiny flecks of light crept away from the eight larger illuminated dots. "It looks like the smaller ships are heading toward an asteroid."

"Are they within range?" Ki asked.

"Not really. If we took a shot at them, they'd see it coming with lots of time to move," Levin said. "Doesn't look like they're coming any closer. They're doing something with a small asteroid."

"What kind of asteroid is it?" Ki took a sip of coffee.

"I dunno. It's one of those asteroids that crosses Earth's orbit. There're a lot of those out here." Levin shrugged. "Maybe the folk at the Moon observatory know."

ౚ

Taylor watched the images in the holo-display transmitted from a Qu'uda craft specially equipped with sensors. The Mother's

266

Servant continued to decelerate tail first, fusion drive at maximum thrust toward the opening in space-time.

"Activate laser conversion sequence," Son-Nih called.

The ship shivered and thrust faded as all the energy in the fusion drive became light energy. Gravity lessened. One of the Coven's ships at the space-time entrance sparkled briefly. The line of Qu'uda ships coasting toward enemy ships flickered with pinpoints of light. Thrust returned to the Mother's Servant as the laser shut down.

"Vector adjustment starting," the pilot-navigator said.

A wave of vibration swept the ship as it turned to aim its laser at another target. Another burst of vibration arrived as the vector engines brought the induced rotation to an end.

"Under attack," a voice squealed out.

"Damage?"

"Minor, so far. Hull breach in outer ring," one of the pilot-navigator's assistants said. "A previously vacated section."

Taylor listened carefully to the words coming from the translation device. He wished he could understand what they said directly, but realized that was a physical impossibility.

"Coven ships rotating," the pilot-navigator said.

Taylor stared at the holo-display. Symbols scrolled through the display from each icon representing an enemy ship. *I wish I could read their script, too*, he thought. *Maybe one day that'll be possible.*

"Coven ships starting to move away from entrance to space-time anomaly," the pilot-navigator said.

Vector arrows appeared on the icons representing the enemy ships in the holo-display, growing longer as their engines built power. The vector arrows pointed away from the approaching line of Qu'uda ships.

"Resuming course for entry to space-time anomaly," the pilot-navigator called. The vibration from the main drive ceased as the Mother's Servant began its rotation. "Navigation data transmitted to Qu'uda ships."

Taylor watched the holo-display show the Coven ships continuing on their course and build velocity. They were retreating away from the opening to space-time. None appeared to be damaged.

Perhaps our ships did hit them, he thought. *But they hadn't damaged their drive systems.* He felt the vibration underfoot as the ship's main engine started up.

"Prepare to enter space-time anomaly," the pilot-navigator called. "Qu'uda ships resuming formation."

Soon we'll be home, Taylor thought as he hobbled on his crutches back to his quarters. *Then the real battle will begin.*

෬

"What're they doing?" Ki asked.

The radar display showed a cluster of Hoo-Lii craft around the small asteroid. The specks of light on the bright green field in the monitor showed only their location. "Gimme an optical."

The monitor faded into blackness. A fuzzy point of light appeared in the center of the screen and wobbled as the magnification increased. A dark gray blob in the center had four slivers of white surrounding it. Tiny violet tongues protruded from the ends of the four Hoo-Lii craft. "Looks like they've just turned on their drives and they're about to vamoose." The technician's voice faded. "That can't be."

"What's going on?" Ki asked.

"They're under full power but they ain't moving."

"Why not?"

For a moment, no one spoke.

"Er, I think they're moving the asteroid," Bud Inez said. "It's the only reasonable explanation."

"Why?" Ki asked.

"I dunno," Bud said. He turned to the technician operating the optical scanner. "Gimme the spectroscopic data on the asteroid."

"Just a minute," a voice muttered. "I need to check the data the Moon observatory sent us." The technician tapped away at the keyboard for a few moments. "Ah, that should do it...." A table of figures scrolled down the monitor that showed the major components were silicates, organic compounds, and water. "They have it classified as probably an Ivuna or CI class asteroid."

"Hmm," Bud said. "Mebbe it's to replenish their consumables."

"Asteroid is acquiring delta-vee," a voice said.

"What's its direction?" Ki asked.

"Er, its direction is ..." The voice hesitated for a moment. "It's away from us. Yes, it's away from us."

"Keep an eye on it. Lemme know if there's any change," Ki said. "Tell the crew to stand down from battle stations. This doesn't look like a threat to us anymore."

Buk-Tih stared at the holo-display. She feared the new servants would attack during the delicate maneuver of attaching towlines to the asteroid. So far, all they had done was shine radiation at very low intensities at them, causing no harm.

"All tow lines attached," the pilot-navigator called. "Shuttles returning to ships."

Now, Buk-Tih thought. *We can get under way. What was it the pilot-navigator said; We must compute a course to a point in space where the Water-Gem planet will be during the time it takes to change the asteroid's course.* Buk-Tih didn't understand celestial navigation; that was the pilot-navigator's responsibility.

"Executing departure routine," the pilot-navigator said. "Prepare for main engine ignition." She stepped back and watched the holo-display as the computer program controlling all eight ship's drive systems slowly increased power and began to drag the asteroid away from its present course. The holo-display showed the countdown for the asteroid to reach the right place would take eight squared sleep periods.

$$\mathcal{\sim}$$

Madeline Henderson stared at the data displayed on the computer monitor. She glanced back at the image gathered by the interferometer that used almost the full width of the Moon as its base width. "Butch," she said. "This bothers me."

Butch looked up and scooted his chair over to his wife's workstation.

The rock-walled room held racks of electronic instruments and multiple monitors. A large table sat in the center, strewn with papers and books. A small table in the corner held tea and coffee making supplies. The Hendersons practically lived in the operations center of the Moon observatory since the Hoo-Lii reappeared, to supply data to the Space Force.

"What is it, m'dear?" he said.

"I don't like the course of these Hoo-Lii ships," Madeline said. "They didn't start to decelerate at the halfway point."

Butch peered over his wife's shoulder. "Isn't this the group who picked up a carbonaceous asteroid? For supplies or something?"

Madeline turned and stared at him for a moment. She turned back to the computer and tapped out a series of commands. She sat back and waited for the response. Due to the distance, it would take several minutes for the signal to reach the asteroid.

"Why did you request a Doppler radar scan?"

"I want to see if there's separation between the asteroid and the Hoo-Lii ships towing it toward an Earth orbit," Madeline said. "Their approach angle makes it hard to tell that from the optical interferometer data."

"Can I get you a cup of tea while you're waiting?" asked Butch. "I'd like a cuppa myself."

"Thanks, Butch, that'd be nice."

Butch busied making tea as Madeline set up a computer program to massage the incoming Doppler radar data.

As the Doppler radar data popped onto the computer screen, Madeline sipped at her favorite orange-flavored tea. She watched the computer program capture the data and the screen refreshed its new output. Slowly she put her cup down, her hand to her mouth, and stared wide-eyed at the screen.

"What is it, m'dear?"

"They've separated and the Hoo-Lii ships are slowing down." She hesitated and pointed to the image on the monitor. "You see where this is going?"

"We'd better double check these data," Butch said.

Tea forgotten, Madeline's fingers flew over the keyboard. She set up a series of tests to validate her discovery. After an hour, both she and Butch were sure of their facts. "We must let the Earth know." Madeline glanced at the calendar on the wall. "We won't have line-of-sight until next week. We can't wait until then to send them a message."

Butch took a deep breath. They'd avoided detection by the Hoo-Lii so far by using only shielded line-of-sight laser communications. "That only leaves radio."

"We'll have to take a chance, this is too important. We must use the radio to warn them the asteroid's going to collide with Earth." Madeline's face was pale. "Especially since it looks like its impact point might be in North America."

CHAPTER TWENTY-SEVEN

TO THE RESCUE

Ki stared at the message that just scrolled across the monitor. His stomach tightened and he caught his breath. "The Hoo-Lii have put an asteroid on a collision course with Earth. The Hendersons estimate this asteroid will arrive in twenty-six days. Its impact point is somewhere in the middle of the North American continent." Ki felt a cold chill grip him.

"Omigod," he said. "They plan to kill every man, woman, and child on Earth."

He picked up his handset and pressed the public address button. "All officers will meet in theater A at eleven hundred hours." He repeated the message, again emphasizing the word "all." He had ninety minutes to get ready.

"Get me Belasario." Ki spoke into the handset. "Yes, I'll wait." He activated the phone's speaker and sat down behind his desk. He began jotting notes on a yellow legal pad.

"Commander Mapes." Al Belasario's voice warbled slightly. "I heard the news from the Hendersons. I've been expecting your call. First, let me give you an update on the situation here...." Al talked for about five minutes, spelling out the shortage of munitions, the condition of both Eagles after three encounters with the Hoo-Lii. He finished by saying, "... and we have twelve nuke missiles left."

"Okay, Al, listen up." Ki glanced at the legal pad. "First, hold off on any more missions. We're coming to DS-3 with all of the Eagles. Second, contact Earth and get them to ship up every damn nuke they can get their hands on. You might wanna get a hold of ..." He checked his pad. "Tim Van Minh, he's the guy who builds the fusion X-ray lasers. He's also reconditioning old nukes. Yeah, I know you're gonna say there aren't any nuke missiles left, you're probably right. I need nukes, as many as possible. Getting them up to DS-3 might be tough, however this is what I've got in mind...."

$$\approx$$

The pilot-navigator of the Mother's Servant glanced at the holo-display. Nothing nearby. The tiny planet near the entrance to the opening in space-time steadily fell further away. Behind, the Qu'uda ships followed in tight formation. This part of the humans' system, distant from its star, was quite empty.

A tiny green icon appeared in a corner of the holo-display and began to flash, indicating a radiation intercept, probably a signal. The pilot-navigator instructed the computer to acquire it and display it.

"This is the Moon observatory calling DS-4, please come in DS-4." The message repeated.

The pilot-navigator recognized the sounds made by humans when they spoke. However, she did not understand it. She realized it was unusual to detect such a signal at this distance. *Perhaps it is some kind of odd alignment*, she thought, *or an accident.* Soon, a long string of human speech followed, still at the same strength. She recorded the signal and decided she would play it the next time a human showed up in her navigation station.

$$\approx$$

"Most gracious Hive-Mother." Taylor bowed. "Now we are in my home system, I wish to contact my fellow humans on Earth, to find out what has happened since we left."

Suh-Joh waved a mid-limb toward Son-Nih, her counselor. "What say you? Is this a wise course of action?"

"It may not be prudent," Son-Nih said. "For that could reveal our position to the Coven's fleet. If we can arrive without them knowing, we could have a significant advantage."

"We could send a tight-beam message, one which only humans can understand," Taylor said. "That way, even if the message is overheard, they will think that it is only a human craft—"

"We do not need to be ambushed," Son-Nih said. "We must be silent in our approach, to maintain our advantage."

"So be it," Suh-Joh said.

Taylor gave a slight bow toward Suh-Joh. "As you wish, most gracious Hive-Mother." He'd come to realize she expected this type of respect from all who met her. He turned and walked back to his quarters. Any further argument was futile.

The pilot-navigator flexed toward Son-Nih, "Honorable counselor," she said. "I have detected a transmission, from humans. However, I do not understand it."

"Play the transmission."

"Immediately, honorable counselor." Again, the pilot-navigator replayed the message. There were many words the translation device did not know.

Son-Nih listened carefully. "This is most difficult to understand. We need a human." He gestured to a Chosen-Male warrior. "Bring the human Taylor."

"You sent for me?" Taylor asked as he entered the tight quarters of the navigation station.

"Yes," Son-Nih said. "We received a transmission, in human language, but its words are not clear. What does it mean?"

Taylor listened to the message twice. It was weak and garbled. As he began to understand the import of the Henderson's message, his stomach lurched.

"My world is threatened," Taylor said. He sketched a diagram to explain. "The Coven ships are moving an asteroid toward Earth. If it drops on Earth, it will sterilize all life on the planet. Please," he said. "Please help us. We must stop them."

Son-Nih stared at Taylor; his breathing orifices flared wide, as though sniffing out the truth of his words. "Come," he said. "We must bring this to the attention of my Hive-Mother."

Taylor found it difficult to keep up with Son-Nih, who moved more rapidly than usual. The unripened ones stepped clear of their passage, flexing as they passed. Somehow, even before they arrived, the servants knew they were in a hurry.

"Most gracious Hive-Mother." Son-Nih flexed more deeply than usual. "I have learned the Coven undertakes a most extreme sanction against the humans ..." he began and told of what they had learned. "And so, the human Taylor wishes our assistance to save his species."

Suh-Joh swiveled her head toward Taylor. "Is this so?"

"Yes, most gracious Hive-Mother," he said.

Suh-Joh slumped lower over her resting mound. "Perhaps after we arrive, we might be able to do something."

"On our current course, we shall arrive too late."

"I understand your concern." Suh-Joh rose, her breathing flaps flaring. "We cannot go any faster."

Taylor feared, no, knew they would be too late and would arrive at a devastated world.

Humanity had survived too much to have it end like this. Chills ran down his spine and his heart began to race.

He prostrated himself before her. "Most gracious Hive-

Mother, I beg of you to help my people. Please help my people in our fight against the Coven. The very survival of my species is at stake, please, I beg of you—"

"Taylor," Suh-Joh said. "Come, sit next to me. Let us think of a way to help your species...."

ॐ

Taylor felt both hope and fear as he watched ten Qu'uda battle craft reverse course. He still wasn't sure of the wisdom of sending one-third of their forces back to the entrance to the space-time anomaly. Son-Nih had made persuasive arguments for the need to block the escape route should the Coven's fleet flee.

Yes, he thought. *If only the combined forces of humans, Qu'uda, and the hive of Suh-Joh could get them on the run. The Qu'uda craft would wait, hidden behind Pluto, to surprise the Coven fleet.*

Taylor learned the Mother's Servant's engineers had expressed great concern about running the engines in an over-powered state for an extended period. In addition, by the time they reached Earth, the Mother's Servant's fuel supplies would be so low that it would not be able to return to the gas giant planets to refuel. So, the Mother's Servant would continue toward Earth at its current rate.

The vibration from the Qu'uda battle craft's drive engines was constant and almost audible as it maintained acceleration at one and one-half Qu'uda gravity. Taylor was pleased he was in the Qu'uda battle craft that would arrive first. He knew the Qu'uda, being from a higher gravity planet than Earth, would have no problem keeping up a higher rate of acceleration.

Now, the question was; will we arrive in time? If only I could contact Ki Mapes, he thought, *and find a way to coordinate our action. I have no idea how to make the most of our forces. Son-Nih was adamant about radio silence. I hope he's right.*

In the holo-display, Taylor could see the second third of the Qu'uda battle craft maintaining formation with the Mother's

Servant. They would follow but at a slower pace, to choose the time and place of their attack depending upon what happened to the vanguard.

As Son-Nih had stated, "...We may be needed to save you." This, too, bothered Taylor, but Son-Nih had insisted a second wave attack might be needed to break the spirit of the warriors of the Coven's fleet.

I sure hope this works, he thought. *If it doesn't ...*

Under full acceleration, the Eagle's vector engines cut in abruptly to produce a turn. Something creaked and a high-pitched whistle of an air leak began.

"Beam weapons deployed," a voice called. The technicians in the command center bent tensely over their equipment.

Ki stared at the radar. At least a dozen missiles now headed toward them, launched right after they'd dropped a batch of kinetic missiles directed at the Hoo-Lii ships towing the asteroid toward Earth. "Gimme optical," he said.

The monitor changed from the radar's bright green to black sprinkled with points of light. A bright dot swam into the center and expanded to reveal the doughnut shape of a Hoo-Lii capital ship. Three fireflies of light flashed brilliantly.

"Three incoming destroyed," a voice called.

"We'd better get the rest," Ki said softly to no one in particular. His grip on the chair's armrest grew tighter.

"This is Eagle-Seven, we've just taken a hit. Heavy casualties and losing air. Request permission to withdraw." The voice was high-pitched, almost falsetto.

Ki hesitated a moment. *That was O'Neil*, he thought. *A good officer, not prone to exaggerate.* He picked up the handset and keyed the ship-to-ship communications channel. "This is Commander Mapes, Eagle-Seven permission to withdraw granted. Good luck."

"Two more missiles destroyed." The voice, once almost triumphant, now wavered with uncertainty.

"Reverse engine vectors—maximum power," Ki called.

The momentary shift in gravity was followed by a wrenching sensation as an invisible hand grabbed them from the opposite direction. Something popped and creaked. Air started to whistle again and a warning buzzer sounded. A babble of voices erupted.

This boat was never designed to be pushed around like this, Ki thought. *Plus it's taken a helluva beating lately.* The whistle of leaking air subsided. *Gonna need more than patchwork when this mission's over—if we survive.*

"Missile avoidance maneuver successful," came a voice. It was breathy as though its speaker was exhausted.

"Second team, deploy the Big Boys," Ki called.

"Three Big Boys under way, running hot and true."

"Let's get the hell out of here," Ki said. He could see four Hoo-Lii ships turning toward them. It was only a matter of time before more missiles came their way. Their attack on the convoy moving the asteroid toward Earth gave three Eagles approaching from the head on direction a chance to launch the Big Boys. If they were on target, the three mega-bombs' staggered explosions should break up the asteroid and deflect its remains away from the Earth.

The past few weeks contained very little good news. Out of the three heavy lifters sent up from Earth, only one reached DS-3 with its cargo of nukes. Ki knew only too well they'd had no successes in their battles with Hoo-Lii, only losses. Five Eagles remained spaceworthy enough for this mission and now, another was probably out of commission.

A tremendous bang shook the Eagle. Dust filled the air, and as air screamed, a draft touched Ki's clothing. Klaxons began to hoot. Red lights flashed brightly. The dust began to drift away.

"What the ..." Ki said. He shut his mouth. His crew knew what to do. The scream of leaking air subsided. As the klaxons fell silent, he could hear distant voices, high-pitched and urgent. Some of the flashing red lights went out.

"Hoo-Lii ships now dead astern, we're under kinetic missile attack. Reversing beam weapons," the voice, calm and unemotional, chanted out the information.

"Took a hit in aft living quarters. Specifically, ship's head and shower compartment." The voice hesitated. "Holding tank ruptured. Whew, it's kinda messy in here."

"Big Boys still on track," said a different voice.

"More incoming missiles."

Ki braced himself. *Dear Lord*, he thought. *Save us.*

"Beam weapons have acquisition on incoming missiles. All clear for the moment." The voice was high-pitched and uncertain. "Beam weapons lit."

"Two Big Boys destroyed, last one tracking hot and true."

"Burned off the last of the incoming."

Ki glanced at the monitor overhead. In the center of the screen was a dark gray, almost circular mass. The scale showed the asteroid was about four hundred feet in diameter. He knew that it weighed well over sixty million tons.

They'd calculated that its relative velocity to Earth at time of impact would be about thirty kilometers per second. He shuddered when he thought about the amount of kinetic energy it possessed—too much. The clock ticking in his head told him it was time for the last Big Boy to do its thing.

A brilliant point of light filled the screen. The monitor went blank. "Out of Service" floated across the screen.

"I'll get a new charge-coupled collector online."

Ki recognized the voice of Josie, the optics technician who'd been loaned by the Moon observatory, but never got a chance to return to her original post. *Good kid, she's got some real cojones ... well, guts*, he thought.

The message on the monitor vanished. Fuzzy spots of light shivered and shrank to points. The scene moved, streaking trails of light across the screen before jerking to a halt. Six jagged objects performed a languid dance as they slowly drifted apart, surrounded by an expanding halo of smaller fragments, tumbling, reflecting light with faint flashes. A scale popped into view.

"Plot the course of the larger pieces," Ki called. The scale showed the largest was almost four hundred feet long by one hundred and fifty—a giant spearhead. It was still deadly.

"Ah, most still look like they're on course to Earth," a voice said. "Several probable misses due to divergence. Need more data to refine course projections."

Ki picked up the handset. "All ships, return to DS-3." He turned and glanced at the command center. Many of the technicians showed sweat stains on their tan jump suits. He keyed his tactics officer's private line. "Okay, Levin, gimme the score on the enemy."

Levin's voice was calm and methodical. "We got three probable hits with our kinetics. At least they show no interest in following us. There're five capital ships changing course. Ah, I believe they plan to follow us."

"Good," Ki said. "When they do, deploy XRLs."

"Yes, sir," Levin said.

The fusion pumped X-ray lasers—XRLs—had been mounted on soloships fitted with TV controlled guidance systems. Ki hoped the XRLs would work as designed. The solosuits would carry the XRLs into the oncoming path of the pursuing ships. They also had a radiation detector that would sense when fired upon by a beam weapon. That would be the trigger to detonate the bomb powering the laser. It was the first time they'd had this combination in their arsenal.

That oughta discourage 'em from following too close, he thought. *At least, I hope it does*. There was the danger of backflash hitting the Eagles, but that was a risk they had to take.

Scrolling to damage assessment, Ki realized every Eagle had damage, even though they'd reinforced their front and rear shields prior to this mission. *We don't have much time left before we*

make our final stand. We have to deflect the incoming asteroid fragments
away from their impact with Earth.

რ

The harsh deceleration of the Qu'uda battle craft made it impossible for Taylor to find a comfortable position. He hoped it
wasn't affecting the setting bone in his leg. Meltem had begged
him not to go, but he knew that he must. "How much longer?"
he asked. In the high gravity, his leg ached constantly around the
area of the surgical incisions, but he refused to take any pain
medication that might slow down his thinking.

Cha KinLaat bobbled his head crest. "Two sleep periods," he
said. "Then we coast for one more."

They had discussed the tactics several times and knew they
needed more information prior to any action. Under high deceleration, their passive sensors could not see through the plume of
the drive engines. To Taylor, it seemed like they were flying
blind. He also worried the flare of their fusion drive engines
might be detected, even though calculations showed that their
small craft would appear as tiny pinpricks of light against the
backdrop of the Milky Way. "So, we'll have one day to see what's
happening and decide upon tactics?"

"Yes," Cha KinLaat said. "And make any course corrections
needed for our pass." They'd already decided the Qu'uda battle
craft would pass through the Hoo-Lii fleet at high speed,
deploying kinetic missiles. After that, they would decide the
next step.

რ

Ki stared at the command center crew. All looked exhausted
after two days of continuous running battle with the Hoo-Lii
fleet. Red lights flashed continuously on the damage assessment
panel and showed the crew quarters and galley were open to

space. He knew many of his crew hadn't survived the last attack. All of the soloship XRLs had got only one Hoo-Lii ship, plus given them a dose of radiation, too.

We've got three nukes left, and we've got to make them count, he thought. *We're still faster in the turns than the enemy, thank God. But three chunks of the asteroid are still on course for Earth*. The Henderson's had confirmed that using radar data. He reached for the handset.

"Attention, all hands." Ki spoke slowly and carefully. "We will resume our attack. The objective remains the same, to place the nukes where they will deflect the asteroids away from Earth." He paused. He could see crewmembers glancing at each other. They'd tried three times to get close enough and had taken a beating each time.

"This time, we'll approach head on, deploy at speed. We will not change course," Ki said.

Several crewmembers bowed their head and with lips moving silently, finished by making the sign of the cross.

"We shall fly straight through the enemy fleet." Ki knew at that range, the enemy's beam weapons would find them. *Dear Lord*, he thought. *Let us succeed, for all mankind.*

Ki felt rather than heard the impact. Lights failed. Klaxons wailed. Gravity vanished. Weak incandescent emergency lights glowed, revealing sprawled bodies among a cloud of dust and sheets of paper. "Status?" Ki called.

"Direct hit on main drive engine. We've lost primary power." Levin cleared his throat. "I'm powering up the auxiliary generator and bringing the vector engines to full power. We're gonna need them."

"How long?" Ki asked. He'd known the answer before Levin spoke. *Didn't even get to turn back to the asteroid. We're sitting ducks without power and blind to what's approaching.* "Radar," he said. "What's the status?"

"It's coming." The voice was high-pitched.

The overhead monitor began to glow green. As white spots

developed, Ki recognized the formation of the four Hoo-Lii ships. They're getting closer, he realized. "Prepare to engage vector engines for a jinking sequence." He noticed the other Eagles continued on their way back to DS-3.

Good, he thought. *At least we still have a chance to stop the asteroid.* The overhead lighting in the control center flickered back to life.

The tiny flechettes of light departing from the Hoo-Lii ships told Ki another round of missiles was on its way.

Wait, he told himself. *Wait until they're real close before we start dodging. Let 'em think we're dead in the water.*

"Optical back online," Josie called.

"New unknowns approaching on orthogonal course," Levin called from the radar station. "Relative velocity about two klicks per second, course vector will take them ..." He hesitate, "between us and the Hoo-Lii ships."

Ki stared at the monitor. The image changed to show greater volume. Ten tiny points of light moved toward the spots that designated the Hoo-Lii ship. *They'll pass by us in seconds*, he thought.

"Any make on the unknowns?" He glanced at the ranging data on the missiles. "Begin jinking sequence, now."

"Ah, no," Levin said. "Computer doesn't recognize any of them. Configuration different than Eagles, but have about the same reflectance, so they're ... wow."

His voice went up an octave. "What the hell? The unknowns just opened fire on the Hoo-Lii. Whoever they are, they're just in time."

CHAPTER TWENTY-EIGHT

ICE STORM

Ki sniffed.

The reek of aged urine and fermenting feces was stronger, over-powering the smell of unwashed bodies and burnt wiring. The status board lights flickered, many red, indicating out-of-condition parameters. Emergency lighting, faded and yellow, made shadows everywhere. Somewhere, people moaned in pain, voices rising and falling in panic.

A voice crackled from the speaker, "Commander Mapes, this is Taylor MacPherson with the Qu'uda squadron, Vanguard of Bu."

Ki grabbed the handset. "Taylor? Is that really you? Are you with the guys who rode to the rescue?" He kept his eye on the monitor, watching the radar display. The Hoo-Lii ships had changed course and ceased pursuit. It looked like they were returning to escort the asteroid fragments.

"Yeah, that's us. The Mother's Servant is also on her way, along with more Qu'uda battle craft." Taylor spoke rapidly. "What's the situation here? We picked up a message from the

Hendersons about an asteroid heading for Earth. Is that why you're out here?"

"That's right. I'll tell you about it later." Ki paused. "I've got more immediate problems. My main engine is dead. I need a tow. Can your guys help out?"

"We've got to shed some velocity before we can get back to you. Let me check."

As Ki waited, he noted one of the Hoo-Lii ships lagged behind the other three. *Hmm, another damaged, good*, he thought.

"Ki?" Taylor said.

"Yes?"

"It'll take about six hours before we get there. Can you hang on for that long?" Taylor asked.

"I think so now the Hoo-Lii ain't bothering us anymore." Ki glanced at the status board. Their power was down to fifteen percent, they had no water, and almost seventy-five percent of their air was gone. "We're pretty beat up. I think we can last six hours."

I hope, he thought. He looked around and the first time in a long time, saw a smile or two among the crew.

～

The holo-display in the First of the Vanguard of Bu showed a model of the solar system as Taylor worked to coordinate their forces. At the Mother's Servant's current rate, she would arrive too late. There must be a way to get them here more quickly. He noticed Venus was approaching opposition with Earth and wondered if their relative positions could be used to change both velocity and direction of the Mother's Servant.

"Er, Cha KinLaat, how do I ..." He explained his idea.

Cha KinLaat spoke rapidly and the holo-display brought up the image of Venus and Earth. A pale curving green line came from the border of the holo-display and wrapped a tight retrograde turn about Venus before curving back toward Earth. A table of symbols appeared.

"Yes, Taylor, it is possible. Do you wish to transmit this to our spiny friends?"

"Our Hoo-Lii friends." Taylor didn't approve of the name Cha KinLaat used for the Hoo-Lii, but he definitely needed the Mother's Servant to push the asteroid fragments off their course to Earth. "Yes, please. Use my translation device to send the message. Tell, no, ask Suh-Joh to consider this as a means to help us. Tell her the message is from me."

ల

"Where did those ships come from, like a swarm of stinging naad-lu?" Buk-Tih asked. The holo-display in the navigation station showed the craft decelerating at rates far higher than any Hoo-Lii craft could attain. "Are they returning?"

The pilot-navigator flexed low. "Most gracious Hive-Mother, I cannot say." She touched a control and the image changed. Several yellow vector lines emanated from the group of craft. She pointed. "This suggests they may go to aid the stricken craft of the new servants," she paused. "Or to finish it off."

"Who are they?"

"I do not know," the pilot-navigator said. "Perhaps they are the Others—"

"Others? Impossible, how would they know we are here?" Buk-Tih asked. She knew that space was immense, empty and an easy place to hide unless someone knew where to look.

"Most gracious Hive-Mother," the pilot-navigator said. "There are sources of radiation from a place on the Water-Gem's Moon. Some of this radiation is similar to the new servants' communications. Other radiation is like that used for direction and ranging pulses—"

"So, there is another nest of new servants?" Buk-Tih said.

"Yes, most gracious Hive-Mother, I believe so—"

"Why did you not tell me sooner?"

The pilot-navigator prostrated herself in the position of maximum submission. "Oh, most gracious Hive-Mother, I caught but a small whiff just recently, while bringing the Instrument of Discipline to the new servants' home I saw almost continuous radiation, like that is used for ranging and direction—"

"If you do not wish to become insect food, you must bring such things to my attention sooner." Buk-Tih raised her spines and flared her breathing flaps, emitting an aroma of anger. "Send a barrage of kinetic missiles onto that nest. It must be silenced immediately."

෪

"Madeline, Madeline," Butch called. "There's something here I don't like." He leaned back in his chair and pointed at one of a half-dozen glowing monitors displaying electronically gathered data.

The rock walls had racks of electronic equipment with tiny diode lights that blinked and glowed. Something beeped softly in the background. The heart of the Moon's observatory was deep underground.

Madeline looked over Butch's shoulder at the monitor. "You're right. It looks like it's heading directly at us and it's moving quite fast."

Butch glanced up at his wife. "You thinking what I'm thinking?" Furrows creased his brow.

"It looks like the Hoo-Lii have found us and intend to shut us down." Madeline rubbed her hands together while frowning. "All we can do is seal everything up tight," she said. "We'll probably lose our surface facilities."

Butch's frown deepened. "We should be safe in here, shouldn't we?"

"We can only pray," she said.

↶

The Water-Gem grew large in the holo-display. Buk-Tih examined the image carefully. "You are sure that the Instrument of Discipline shall strike the most populous areas?" she said, pointing at the planet's image.

The pilot-navigator flexed. "Yes, most gracious Hive-Mother, this area is where most of the signals originate, and this area," she pointed to a place on the opposite side of the planet, "is the most heavily populated area. The new servants did us a favor by splitting the Instrument of Discipline into several pieces. Now we can target individual locations."

"Be sure you transmit course vectors to those manipulating the pieces." Buk-Tih rippled her breathing flaps.

"Yes, most gracious Hive-Mother."

The expedition had grown tiresome to Buk-Tih and prior to every sleep period, she heard complaints from Hive-Mothers whose ships had been damaged by the new servants.

Those with damaged ships and those who had lost their Chosen-Male warriors in the assault on the new servants' satellite expressed the desire to leave and return to Hool. Only the authority of the edict issued by the priests of the Spirit of the Mother kept the fleet together.

Buk-Tih knew they had to conquer the Water-Gem, and soon. Food was in short supply. Even after all the dead had been fed to the food insects, she realized culling would be required. The aged and infirm servants soon would be fed to the insects to ensure the rest did not starve.

Only seven more sleep periods and the Instrument of Discipline would strike, Buk-Tih thought. Only seven more sleep periods until the new servants surrendered. It was comforting. She turned to leave the navigation station, a small and miserable place she had to visit all too often. It was time to return to the comfort of her resting mound and time for a generous meal.

An alarm bleated.

Buk-Tih looked back at the holo-display from the exit-way. A bright yellow icon flashed at the outer edge of the displayed image. A column of figures scrolled downwards.

"Spirit of the Mother, save us," the pilot-navigator said. "It is them again, the Others, except this time, there are twice as many." She pointed to a second icon flashing on the opposite side of the image. The original group of Others were once again heading toward them, as well as the new group.

"Are you sure?"

"Look." The pilot-navigator pointed to the figures that appeared alongside each yellow icon. "They will arrive at the same time, from opposite directions."

"When will they arrive?" Buk-Tih asked.

"Less than one-half of a sleep period."

"Warn the other Hive-Mothers and activate the battle alarm."

ᘔ

"May the Spirit of the Mother bless this decision." Buk-Tih spread both her fore- and mid-limbs in a gesture of supplication.

Out of the original fleet to depart Hool, less than half of the ships were capable of deep space operations. Only a few shuttles remained after their first encounter with the new servants. The Hive-Mothers on the surviving ships no longer wanted to stay and fight the Others. It was time to go home.

"Pilot-navigator, provide the coordinates for the entrance to the space-time anomaly, so we may leave this Mother-cursed place."

The pilot-navigator flexed. "It is done, most gracious Hive-Mother. The data are entered into the course computers."

"Then let us depart."

The holo-display showed the ships of the fleet turned as one.

The pilot-navigator's breathing orifices flared briefly and emitted an aroma of approval. The warning icons of the Others' ship continued to close. She watched as velocity vectors emerged from the ships of the fleet and felt the thrust underfoot.

Perhaps, she thought. *We can escape the jaws of this trap.* She feared these strange craft that accelerated so strongly. On the last pass, they'd damaged many ships of the fleet.

The pilot-navigator noted it would take one-fourth of a sleep period to cancel out their velocity toward the Water-Gem planet, even under maximum cruise acceleration. By that time, the remnants of the Instrument of Discipline would be far away, and, she hoped, so would the Others' ships. She altered the holo-display to focus tightly on the new group of Others.

Odd, the pilot-navigator thought. *One of the ships is much larger than the rest.* She sought out sensors that would reveal more of the characteristics of the larger ship.

"Spirit of the Mother," she said in a whisper. "It's the Mother's Servant. She's made an unholy alliance with the Others." At the same time, she realized the smaller ships were on a different course. The Mother's Servant continued onward toward the path of the Instrument of Discipline, whereas the smaller ships had increased acceleration on an intercept course with the fleet.

"Most gracious Hive-Mother," the pilot-navigator called. "The Others, they've changed course to pursue us."

"What?" Buk-Tih asked. "When will they arrive?"

The pilot-navigator hesitated. "I will get the information," she said, as she gathered the data for the computer. Since the Others had much higher initial velocity, and could accelerate at a higher rate, it wasn't a simple calculation. Instead of an orthogonal course intercept, this was a trailing angle calculation. Velocity vectors traced curved yellow paths through the holo-display and a column of figures scrolled down alongside. "At our current rate of acceleration, they will arrive in about one and one-half sleep periods."

"How much can we increase our acceleration?"

"Not all ships can withstand greater acceleration," the pilot-navigator said. "Their damage makes that dangerous for them."

"What about our ship?"

"It is capable of increasing acceleration by one-fourth." The pilot-navigator did not like the direction of this conversation.

"Prepare a spread of missiles to lay down against the Others that follow. In the meantime, calculate a new course for us should it be necessary to increase to maximum acceleration," Buk-Tih said. "I do not wish to die in the mandibles of the Others."

$$\tilde{\sim}$$

Bilik Pudjata watched the fleet of Hoo-Lii ships turn and accelerate in unison in the holo-display. "They must be under control of one ship," he said.

The center station of the Bird-of-War was cramped, with dark green biocomputer pods lining its walls. The squadron of the second Vanguard of Bu had just executed a turn to pursue the Hoo-Lii fleet. Instead of an approach at right angles to their course, they would be almost on the same course by the time they caught them.

"I do not like to attack from this direction," ZahGeb DuBu said. He was the most central Defender of the second Vanguard of Bu. "It is fraught with the danger from weapons dropped by the pursued." As he spoke, a small cluster of tiny points departed from the Hoo-Lii fleet. "Hah, as I feared."

"What is it?" Bilik asked.

"They send missiles down the path we must take to pursue them," ZahGeb said. "To avoid them, we must either destroy the missiles, or go out of our way."

A tiny yellow star appeared in the holo-display and expanded to reveal the crested head of Cha KinLaat DoMar. "Greetings, Defender ZahGeb, it is obvious the enemy prefers to flee rather than face your renowned ferocity."

ZahGeb silently bobbled his head in acknowledgment.

"It is with respect we ask you to join us and pursue the

asteroid fragments and divert them from their course to the planet Earth," Cha KinLaat said. "With the enemy fleeing, this is a more immediate danger."

ZahGeb again bobbled his head. "I understand and agree."

"I support this proposed tactic," Bilik said. Even though he knew that ZahGeb reported to Cha KinLaat, the form of quooning had to be preserved, to reduce the urge of the Defenders to try to dominate in matters military. "Taylor MacPherson has requested transfer back to the Hoo-Lii ship, the Mother's Servant. He wishes to be present when they divert the larger of the pieces of the asteroid from their course."

∿

The elongated, tetrahedral mass of jagged, gray rock slowly rotated. Shadows and sunlight chased over its sharply broken surface. An outer section—the former surface—rolled into view, smoother, darker and, heavily pock marked.

Taylor MacPherson had just arrived by soloship onto the Mother's Servant. It had been his first time in a soloship and he hadn't enjoyed being in such a small craft for such a long distance. However, being reunited with Meltem and Kemal made up for the experience.

The Mother's Servant had matched velocity with the largest asteroid fragment and now prepared to push it off course. "How're we going to move the asteroid?" Taylor asked.

The pilot-navigator barely looked up. "It is all a matter of timing," she said. "Calculate when the desired push point will come around and place the ship there."

Taylor had learned the pilot-navigators came from the finest breeding stock, and if not chosen for this profession, they were potential candidates for ripening into Hive-Mothers. Their extensive training made them masters of their art. "I see," he said. "Just like that?"

"Even though it is well within her capabilities, I think it wise not to distract her," Son-Nih said.

"Yes, honorable counselor." Taylor had learned many forms of address were expected within the Hoo-Lii society and so he used them whenever possible.

The surface of the asteroid filled the holo-image. The image dissolved, replaced by one from afar. Taylor knew there were small craft providing additional views of the closing procedure. The plan was to place the armored nose of the ship at the surface point of the center of mass of the asteroid and apply thrust. The Mother's Servant had to be at the right place on the asteroid at the right time. The image showed the distance between ship and asteroid closing. Darkness descended as shadows crept over the contact point.

Taylor felt a shudder run through the ship. Vibration from the main engines rose.

Damn, he thought, *not a moment of hesitation.*

He watched the image in the holo-display, now shrinking the size of the asteroid and ship. A column of figures scrolled down through the image. "What's happening?" he asked.

"The Mother's Servant is giving the asteroid a new course vector. It will not take long—"

A crack followed by a bang interrupted Son-Nih's words.

In the distance, a high-pitched alarm began to bleat.

The pilot-navigator danced around her station, both fore- and mid-limbs in action.

The image on the holo-display zoomed in. Bright lights bathed the point where ship and asteroid made contact. A section of the asteroid had carved off and slowly cartwheeled away from its parent.

The vibration from the main engines died. A higher pitched vibration of the maneuvering engines rose. Doors began to slam shut. Alarms bleated louder.

Taylor watched, horrified, as an asteroid fragment slowly collided with the outer ring of the Mother's Servant. He felt the ship shudder as though in pain, and then came a crashing roar. The air pressure dropped. Alarms increased in intensity.

"Spirit of the Mother, save us," the pilot-navigator cried.

"Stay here," Son-Nih said. "Set a course for the human satellite above the planet. I must see to the fate of the warriors in the quarters that were just crushed." He skittered out, escorted by a Chosen-Male warrior.

"Pilot-Navigator, open a communication channel to the Qu'uda ships," Taylor asked.

The pilot-navigator paused in her task to touch different controls. "Speak," she said.

"Billy, Cha KinLaat, the Mother's Servant sustained damage while pushing the largest of the asteroid fragments. Apparently, this asteroid material is very fragile. Please calculate the flight path of this piece." He hesitated. "I think the only option left is to use the nukes to generate heat induced thrust."

He didn't have to explain how this worked, for both Billy and Cha KinLaat had seen this done to the Little-Egg-that-Flies. "DS-3 has nukes. Go get them, and get some Space Force personnel to deploy them. Hurry, we only have three days left."

ෆ

"Taylor MacPherson." The voice was weak and the signal filled with static. "This is Charlie Ramsey. I order you to return to Earth to face the charges against you. If you refuse, the Space Force has orders to detain you."

Taylor chuckled. "So, Ramsey, you're still more concerned about an ancient warrant for my arrest than the fate of the Earth? Don't bother to answer the question. I'll return when this problem's solved, not before." He leaned back and raised his leg while he waited for the response. It itched inside the cast. *Only another week*, he thought.

"Even in wartime, the rule of law prevails," Ramsey said. "I'm ordering the Space Force to detain you and return you immediately to our custody to face the charges against you at the Superior court in Columbus, Ohio."

"This is bullshit," Taylor muttered. "Look," he said loudly. "Earth is still in danger. There's several asteroid fragments heading toward Earth, possibly even North America. Taking care of that problem comes first." He slammed at the controls and cut the connection.

Taylor saw the pilot-navigator watching him. "What is going on out there?" He found it odd the translation device would change the pilot-navigator's high-pitched chittering into a male speaking with the flat twang of the Pacific Northwest.

The pilot-navigator flexed slightly in Taylor's direction. "The ships of the Others, the Qu'uda, return from the human satellite above the planet. Their acceleration is very high."

"Show me." Taylor waved a hand at the holo-display.

The pilot-navigator ran her forelimbs over the controls. The image of DS-3—their destination—disappeared to be replaced by six points of light. A small cluster of yellow icons appeared in the center of the display. "The asteroid fragments," she said and then gestured at the six points of light. "The Qu'uda ships."

Taylor realized the Qu'uda ships were decelerating at maximum rate as they approached the asteroid fragments. He also knew the Qu'uda could not be relied upon to deploy nuclear weapons for they considered those who used them to be insane.

Well, he thought. *Sometimes it doesn't hurt to be thought of as being a little bit crazy. That's why they have Space Force personnel on board with them. There won't be any doubts in their minds.*

"Switch to optical view," he said.

"Very far away, not a good image."

"Please, the optical view."

The holo-display became black with tiny points of light in the center. They grew larger, until the largest of the asteroid fragments was barely visible as a fuzzy spearhead shaped object. Nothing seemed to be happening.

Taylor waited patiently.

Six points of light blossomed and grew to fill the holo-display with a brilliant glare. Almost as fast as the light appeared, it faded.

"Give me the flight paths of the asteroid fragments now," said Taylor. He listened carefully.

"Spirit of the Mother, preserve us against those who would use such obscenities, may the spine of your righteous justice strike down and poison those who—"

"Pilot-navigator," Taylor said loudly. "Analyze the course of the remaining asteroid pieces. It is my world that is in danger. Perhaps you could pray for its survival, also?"

The pilot-navigator prostrated herself against the floor. "Forgive me, but the Way of the Mother—"

"Plot the course."

The image in the holo-display flashed and became filled with points of light, yellow vector lines and a blue globe that represented Earth. Point by point, lights faded along with extraneous lines. One point remained with a bright green vector line extending toward Earth. Impact time was two hours.

"Where will it hit?" Taylor asked.

The pilot-navigator spread her mid-limbs. "Within here," she said. The blue globe expanded and rotated to show an image of North America. A circle expanded; somewhere in the Midwest.

ᘓ

It was an evil fascination, watching the asteroid fragment, over ten million tons of rock and ice, slowly cartwheeling its way toward the bright, blue planet.

Even now, Taylor could see its impact point was hard to estimate. The Qu'uda Birds of War made a final effort to move it, but it was not enough. They had no more weapons.

"Advise everyone to seek shelter underground or in hardened structures. Do not remain in combustible buildings, due to thermal radiation." Taylor listened to the offered warnings and updated estimates of impact time and place.

It's futile, he thought. *Much like the Human Confederation Assembly taking so much time to realize the enormity of the danger. Just like Ramsey, more concerned about seeking political advantage.*

Sure, he thought. *They can't see the battles going on out here, the heroism of the Space Force personnel, willing to die for those who treat them as a disposable piece on a political chessboard.*

"Impact, ninety seconds. Atmosphere contact, eighty-five seconds."

Five seconds to traverse one hundred kilometers of atmosphere, Taylor thought. *The real heating will begin in the last ten kilometers.* He watched, as the tiny dark mass against the blue and white seemed to float downwards. A faint red glow outlining the dark mass quickly brightened until it formed a brilliant point of light, casting moving shadows on the surface of the planet.

"... three ... two ... one ... impact."

The brilliant point of light expanded enormously. Concentric circles expanded rapidly as shock waves ripped the atmosphere. A darkly glowing fungous shape rose high above the cloud deck, expanding, to fade into an evil, black stain reaching even into space.

"Impact point is, omigod, it's Columbus, Ohio!"

"Recheck data and get ground verification," Taylor said.

Columbus? Oh, no, he thought. *That's where Joyce lives, and the Human Confederation Assembly, and Carver Washington ...*

"Impact point location confirmed," a voice said. "Columbus, Ohio."

CHAPTER TWENTY-NINE

A GIFT OF WATER

Suh-Joh rose from her resting mound and extended her mid-limbs. "They destroyed your principal hive and did great harm to your species. May the Spirit of the Mother reach out to you and bring you comfort in your time of loss." She paused. "They must be punished."

The ersatz cave that was Suh-Joh's command center was still and quiet. No longer did Chosen-Male warriors stand on guard against the brown curtain-lined walls.

"Go," she said. "Go with the Others and pursue them. If the Mother's Servant were capable, I would go also. Take my counselor, Son-Nih, with you. Use his wisdom in the way of all things Hoo-Lii. He will guide you on ways to punish them."

"Thank you." Taylor nodded. "There are too many of them for the first Vanguard of Bu to handle alone." He referred to the squadron of Qu'uda ships stationed near the space-time anomaly near Pluto. "We must get there before they enter the portal. Most gracious Hive-Mother, may I use your pilot-navigator to communicate this?"

"Yes." Suh-Joh again spread her mid-limbs. "May the Spirit of the Mother nurture you and bring you comfort."

Taylor bowed to Suh-Joh, turned, and left through a curtain-covered portal. He now walked without a crutch since Meltem had replaced his cast with a lighter support framework. *I need to get more weapons before we leave.*

The pilot-navigator flexed. "Honorable Taylor," she said. "I have opened a communication link with the Others."

"Thank you," Taylor said. "Hello?"

"Ah, Taylor, your spiny friend hailed us, but we could not understand her squeaky voice."

Taylor recognized Cha KinLaat's deep sonorous tones. "Please advise ZahGeb DuBu the second vanguard should prepare to pursue the enemy at high acceleration—"

"Of course. The course coordinates shall be given to each ship," Cha KinLaat said. "We await your arrival."

"First, we need more weapons," Taylor said. "If we must fight, I intend to win."

"The destruction on your world has made you insane—"

"No, not insane," Taylor said. "When we fight, we fight with whatever weapons we have." He hesitated. "The asteroid was more powerful than any of the nukes we used."

He'd learned the explosion of the asteroid impact on Columbus was equivalent to one megaton, wreaking destruction over an area thirty miles in diameter and killing a half million persons. There was no radioactive fallout since it was a kinetic explosion.

"I am justified in using them."

"So be it," Cha KinLaat said. "As long as it is not our doing, then we can close our eyes and take no responsibility for your insanity—"

"Thank you," Taylor said. "I'll join you as soon as I can. In the meantime, there are other things I must do. 'Bye." He turned to the pilot-navigator. "Please get a connection to the technical center at Hopkins Airport." The center was the former

Cleveland airport adjacent to Rocky River where Tim Van Minh and Ashley O'Neil produced reactors and weapons.

"Yes, honorable, Taylor." The pilot-navigator worked with the controls and waited.

"Hello?"

Taylor recognized Tim's voice. "Tim, this is Taylor. Listen, this is what I need, and I need it in a hurry...." He went on to explain what he wanted and how to deliver it to the Qu'uda ships at DS-3.

"I'll get right on it," Tim said. "Should have it there in about three days—"

"Make it two days, we've got to catch the Hoo-Lii fleet before it reaches the portal."

~

Two hectic days later, Taylor and Son-Nih boarded the Qu'uda Bird-of-War to join Cha KinLaat. They rode up in the same heavy lifter that carried the cargo of weapons Tim had gathered, plus supplies for both squadrons. "How long before we can depart?" he asked.

The pilot station was small. Its front bulkhead filled with a large viewscreen and dark green biocomputer containers lined its other walls. It smelled like a greenhouse with overtones of rotting vegetation.

Cha KinLaat talked with ZahGeb DuBu for a few moments. "He said once we get the supplies stored, we can leave. The current schedule is by the end of this ship's day."

Taylor glanced at the clock on the wall and then to his watch. He did the calculations in his head—about twelve more hours.

"Good. Have you contacted the first Vanguard of Bu and let them know what is coming and our plans?"

Cha KinLaat talked with ZahGeb, who bobbled his head crest. "Yes, they have been informed. In addition, we received a message the remote sensing station on the Aten-asteroid has spotted the Hoo-Lii fleet. From its data, we have an accurate estimate on their arrival time. It seems they travel slower than their normal speed. Perhaps their ships are damaged and cannot operate normally—"

"Good," Taylor said. "That'll make our job easier. Are there Space Force personnel stationed on each ship?"

"Each Bird-of-War has a Space Force officer in charge of your weapons," Cha KinLaat said. "They have the responsibility to use them." The stiffness of his headcrest indicated the degree of his distaste.

"Send a message to the first Vanguard," Taylor said. "Advise them to conceal their presence as long as possible." He paused. "Also tell them the second Vanguard has human weapons officers and the humans will use nuclear bombs if needed to ensure our victory."

$$\text{~}$$

Every joint in Taylor's body ached. High gravity acceleration punished his body, especially after becoming accustomed to the lower gravity regime of the Hoo-Lii ship. He found it odd that Son-Nih never mentioned it.

On the pilot station's viewscreen, Pluto appeared as a pale green-blue orb with its companion, Charon, faintly visible as a small, dark gray Moon. The first Vanguard of Bu had used Charon's mass and magnetic field to conceal their presence.

Forty-two Hoo-Lii ships decelerated in single file on a direct course toward the entrance to the space-time anomaly. Being faster, the Birds of War steadily closed the distance behind them. Taylor knew they would arrive before the first Hoo-Lii ship entered the anomaly.

ZahGeb talked rapidly back and forth with the most central Defender on each Qu'uda ship, coordinating their actions. "It is time," he said. "The first Vanguard of Bu begins their move."

A cluster of tiny points of light emerged from Charon's

shadow. The bulkhead screen shifted from optical view to the battle management mode, showing size, velocity, and distance. The first Vanguard assumed a circular formation as it moved before the entrance to the anomaly.

"It is time to do the insane thing." ZahGeb touched Taylor's arm. "Advise your people."

"Attention," Taylor said. "Launch first tranche."

The screen showed ten tiny slivers emerging from the ships of the second Vanguard in a circular pattern, which converged onto the Hoo-Lii fleet in a parallel course. The missiles flew faster and faster, until they formed a perfect circle around the Hoo-Lii ships. The ten points of light flared with an awful brilliance, forming a circle of fire around the drawn-out Hoo-Lii fleet.

"Son-Nih," Taylor said. "Say your piece." He listened to the translation device as the aged counselor twittered away.

Birds chattering, he thought. *Very advanced birds.*

"The Others are here, Others who are enraged at the destruction on their world, who demand you pay for your acts with your freedom. If you do not wish to be incinerated in the unholy fire of obscenity, you must prepare the gift of water."

It's almost incomprehensible, Taylor thought. *It's a different culture and a different language through a mechanical translator. Even if I wanted to learn their language, much of it is beyond my hearing range and vocal cords.*

"Do not enter the space-time anomaly, for the Others will use the unholy fire within its cavity."

Not likely, Taylor thought. *We haven't got a clue what would happen should we drop nukes in there. Could be the end of the universe, could be nothing.*

"You have but one chance, give water." Son-Nih's breathing orifices flared and remained open. He stopped speaking.

"We cannot offer water to the Others ... They do not follow the Way of the Mother ..."

The translation device could not keep up with the rapid pace of twittering from the speaker. Taylor wondered what those few brief phrases meant.

"Ah," said Son-Nih. "That did not stop you from believing when the Others offered water, you took them to be your new servants. This then, too, applies to you."

On the battle management screen, Taylor could see the first Vanguard of Bu had stopped directly in front of the opening to the anomaly and tightened its formation.

The Hoo-Lii fleet decelerated, still in its linear formation. The second Vanguard of Bu formed a circle behind the Hoo-Lii fleet. For several moments, there was silence, a long silence punctuated by nervous glances and sudden body movements.

"The Others are preparing to launch their obscenities," Son-Nih said to the Coven's fleet.

"To whom shall we bring the gift of water?"

Son-Nih drew himself up to his full height. His breathing flaps flared fully open. His spines slowly erected. "As representative of the Others and the Hive-Mother Suh-Joh, I hold the appointment as the receiver of the gifts of water."

Appointment? Taylor thought. *Who appointed him, whatever?* "Er, Son-Nih, please explain what's going on?"

With a wave of his mid-limbs that looked like he was flicking away a fly, Son-Nih continued: "The giver of water must be the Mother of the Hive, and the giving shall be here, on the ship of the Others. The Hive-Mother shall come only with her counselor."

That wasn't an answer to my question, Taylor thought. "Son-Nih, what's going on?"

Son-Nih's breathing orifices waved multiple times. "Honorable Taylor, do you want to destroy all the Hive-Mothers of Hool? So many that the species of Hoo-Lii may not survive? I think not. I will not allow it. So, what do you wish with them?" His mid-limbs spread wide. "They surrender their authority to me, in the name of Hive-Mother Suh-Joh, then they may return to Hool."

"You mean you want to let them go home? What's to stop them from returning in the future, mebbe even stronger than before?" Taylor began to feel irritated Son-Nih had taken over negotiations and hadn't revealed his negotiating tactics.

"Once they give water to Suh-Joh, they will become servants of Suh-Joh and will do as she bids. She has no desire to wage war upon your species, only to restore our world to its former glory, a world rich in resources and diversity."

"Lemme get this straight," Taylor said. "You're telling me you've arranged the terms of their surrender?"

"Did you wish to fight a battle here? If you do, I advise against it. Though dispirited and damaged, there are far more Hoo-Lii ships than yours. Even with your obscenities, you would not escape unharmed. Facing certain death from unholy obscenities, they would fight hard and try to take as many of you with them as possible. Many, if not all, of your ships would suffer damage."

"Well, okay, you've got a good point," Taylor said. "If we can avoid a battle, fine. We want to end the danger of the Hoo-Lii ever invading again. If we have to fight, we will."

"My Hive-Mother, Suh-Joh, has seen your willingness to do battle and die, yet she also recognizes you do not understand the ways of the Hoo-Lii."

"Well, yes, you're right," Taylor said. "So, what happens when these Hoo-Lii give you water?"

"My Hive-Mother will order they destroy all their weapons and then return to Hool. Later, she will ripen new Hive-Mothers and command them to work hard and restore vitality to our world." Son-Nih rose up. "It is difficult to explain. It is enough to say Suh-Joh wishes peace between our species and our worlds. Though I am but a humble servant, a mere tool to bring this about, I see clearly the wisdom of her wishes."

Taylor turned to Cha KinLaat. "What do you think?"

"If the Hoo-Lii believed they were about to be slaughtered, do you think they would stay in one place, without fighting back?" Cha KinLaat wobbled his headcrest. "It is a strange way to select the most central person of their society, but the ways of humans and Hoo-Lii are alien to us Qu'uda."

"Gee, that sounds like a 'do it' to me." Taylor scratched his chin. "Okay, Son-Nih, start the water ceremony, or whatever it is." He fought the urge to yawn.

I'm tired, he thought.

Son-Nih flexed. "My Hive-Mother believes you are a brave and wise counselor to Meltem. She counseled me you would understand and make the right decision." He turned and began to chitter at a high pace. "... the honorable Son-Nih requests the presence of the Hive-Mother, Bok-Tah and one companion to visit the principal ship of the Others."

Son-Nih glanced at Taylor. "This will take some time, for we can receive only one Hive-Mother at a time. We shall record this ceremony and broadcast it to the Hoo-Lii fleet, so all the Chosen-Male warriors and unripened ones may see it. Then they will know their Hive-Mother is no longer supreme in their lives."

"Diplomacy," Taylor said. "A long-winded way to avoid a war. Well, anything to avoid a bloodbath."

The crater was visible from orbit—now a round lake—which now occupied the place that was formerly Columbus. Water flowing down the Scioto and Olentangy Rivers had filled the crater in the time it took for Taylor and the Qu'uda Birds of War to travel to Pluto and deal with the remnant of the Hoo-Lii fleet.

Taylor still had misgivings about releasing the Hoo-Lii of the Coven, to disappear into the opening in space-time. However, both Son-Nih and Suh-Joh stated their certainty they would not return. When they got back to Hool, they would deal with them.

The heavy lifter shook and the roar of re-entry became louder. The heavy lifter carried no cargo, only passengers, and as such was less stable on descent. Taylor knew this, yet he found he grasped the arms of his seat more tightly than usual.

It's only a few more minutes, he thought.

The fierce hand of deceleration tried to tear him from the seat as the shuttle began to shudder and vibrate. The buffeting and roar of tortured atmosphere eased as the ship's velocity slowed.

Taylor felt the attitude of the heavy lifter change as its nose came up.

Final approach, he thought.

A loud thump shook the cabin and deceleration again tried to pull him from his seat.

Fifteen seconds more, he thought.

The deceleration eased. Somewhere below, tires thumped on an ancient runway, its uneven surface reflecting the unceasing efforts of many winters trying to force the huge slabs of concrete out of the ground. The heavy lifter became still.

"Welcome to Rocky River Space Center."

Several moments later, a door clanged open and sunlight flooded in.

"Hey, Taylor," a voice called. "You got people waiting for you out here. C'mon, hurry up."

Now what? Taylor unsnapped his restraint harness. He grabbed his bag and marched unsteadily to the door.

"Taylor, oh, Taylor."

Even though the sunlight dazzled him, the sound of Meltem's voice guided him unerringly into her arms. He looked at her. "Meltem, sweetheart, it's so good to be home."

"Shut up and kiss me."

"Daddy, Daddy."

Still holding Meltem, Taylor bent and picked up his son, Kemal, and held him tightly.

"Oof," he said. "You've grown."

It was only after the memorial services did the hastily summoned delegates from around the world get down to dealing with loss of the Human Confederation Assembly. With many of the leaders of the Re-established United States and most of the representatives to the HC Assembly dead, Taylor used the military to establish a provisional government.

"Look," Taylor said. "We must replace Columbus with a government that is representative and effective. This is a stop-gap until we do so."

The old hall on the campus of Baldwin-Wallace University, the site of the original organizational meeting for the Re-established United States, still had its stained and broken windows. Its maple floor was gray and scuffed, covered with battered and chipped folding chairs. From the stage, behind a row of scarred and scratched metal tables, sat the cadre of military officers.

"First, we reaffirm we shall enforce all existing laws, respect all existing property rights, and preserve the civil liberties of our citizens." He looked up and down the row of the military officers. "Do we have agreement on that?"

The military officers nodded their assent.

So, Taylor thought. *We start all over again.* He sorely missed Carver Washington's presence and his political skills.

And Ki Mapes, I hope he's all right.

Ki and his crew had caught a backblast of radiation from an X-ray laser and Meltem was treating them.

"Next item on the agenda ..." Taylor continued with the restoration of the governmental functions lost during Columbus's destruction. He knew these steps were essential prior to moving onto the issue of the space-time opening into their system.

Until we know how to defend against surprises emerging from it, he thought, *we're vulnerable.*

Through the day, Taylor and the military established provisional authorities to deal with the gaps in the government and the recovery effort in the devastated areas around Columbus.

There are a lot of injured and homeless people, and fortunately, he realized, *there's no radiation to compound the problems.*

By day's end, Taylor realized they could not delegate all of the responsibilities. *I'm going to have my hands full for some time,* he thought. *We're all going to have our hands full.*

CHAPTER THIRTY

THE WAY OUT

"Daddy, Daddy, Mommy says it's time to eat."

Taylor looked up from his paper-strewn desk.

It was in his old office in Marting Hall on the campus of Baldwin-Wallace University. Mitch Doaks, the head Administrator of the College, had converted a whole floor into an apartment to accommodate Taylor and his family. He found he liked the arrangement; so did Meltem.

"Okay, Kemmy, I'll be there in one minute."

"We have a visitor."

"Oh," Taylor said. "Who is it?" He knew no one got by Mitch Doaks's security without a good reason.

"It's Mr. Mapes—"

"Ki?" Taylor said. "He's here?" He rose quickly. "Can't keep Commander Mapes waiting, can we?" He hurried to the door and into the corridor.

Ki Mapes, even thinner than before, had lost all of his hair, even his eyebrows. His bright brown eyes sparkled brightly, and his wide smile revealed even teeth.

"Taylor." His voice, deep and resonant, boomed the length of the hall outside the office. "Good to see you. How've you been?"

"Fine. The question is how are you?" *He's changed*, Taylor thought.

"Well, that little lady of yours worked a miracle." Ki ran his hand over his bald head. "That SC-DNA treatment got rid of all the radiation damage." He paused and glanced back as though worried about being overheard. "She tells me it will add significantly to my life span."

Taylor smiled. "Right, and LaTasha will get the same treatment." His smile faded. "It also means you're a candidate for the task force."

"I see." Ki's lips tightened. "I guess I can be part of the Treaty Force."

He referred to the agreement worked out over the past year since the surrender of the Hoo-Lii Fleet at Pluto. An alliance between humans, the Qu'uda, and Suh-Joh had concluded that to prevent further tragedies, they must control the transfer points through space-time. It was obvious if the portals were guarded; no force could enter another's system.

Currently, five Qu'uda Birds of War and three Eagles were on rotation at Pluto to guard against anything that came through the opening into space-time. Each species wished to preserve its own culture and way of life, which again, made the transfer points the key to preservation. "So that means time at Pluto?"

"Yes," Taylor said. "Initially, we need to get a permanent station on location staffed with our new allies."

He referred to the three species agreeing to respect each other as equals based on the principle each and every system would remain separate and free, with each system contributing forces to the transfer points.

"That should take place soon. By the way, I've submitted my resignation. I won't run for another office."

"I see," Ki said. "Well, there's plenty to do elsewhere."

Taylor slipped his arm around Ki's shoulder. "Kemmy said it's time to eat. That means you're joining us, right?"

༄

As the shuttle drew closer, Taylor saw DS-3 expand within the view screen. The long, cylindrical shape that was originally the Qu'uda ship the "Little-Egg-that-Flies" had changed. It now had three long, spindly slips made of metal frameworks extending from openings leading to the interior docks. The seven Hoo-Lii capital ships that hung from first slip were the derelict craft left over from the battle. They now had become the source of parts to build other ships.

A large double-ring craft, on which workers swarmed with flickering weilding torches, hung close to DS-3 on the second slip. Taylor barely recognized the Mother's Servant due to the changes and expansion to its capabilities. *Soon*, he knew, *it would depart and return to Hool.*

A second Hoo-Lii ship, with a single living quarters ring, was also on the second slip. That must be the ship of Lil-Tih, who he'd heard had been ripened to Hive-Mother status by Suh-Joh.

Which one, he thought, *will be the Pluto station?* The only other ship that looked near completion was on the third slip, on the opposite side of DS-3. That was an armored version of a Hoo-Lii capital ship.

"D'you see it?" Ki asked.

"The one on the other side of the station?"

"Right." Once Ki agreed to lead the human component of the crew of the "Portal Guardian," as this ship was known, he'd become involved in its design and specifications. Based upon his experience from the recent battles, he'd insisted the Portal Guardian be heavily armored with a large inventory of weapons.

It also had a second habitable ring, which provided separate space and quarters for each of the three species. Additional fuel and storage containers filled the volume between the two rings.

Hangars for shuttle and battle craft lined up along the central shaft of the station. Three fusion drive units replaced its original single engine. Beam weapons protruded from the outer edge of the living quarter rings. It would not be a pushover, Ki had declared. Rumors of stockpiles of fusion bombs on board the Portal Guardian had never been confirmed or denied.

"We'll take a look as soon as we get our personal effects transferred," Ki said.

"Can we take a run out to see the developments at DS-4?" Taylor asked. He knew that a second metallic asteroid—much larger than DS-4—was under development to build the International Space Force Academy.

"The Portal Guardian needs a shake-down cruise and that'd be a good destination." Ki maneuvered a bag onto his shoulder and began floating down a cable and conduit lined corridor that led to the airlock entrance of DS-3. "Time to go. Be glad to get back to gravity," he said. "I like being in space, but I've never gotten used to this zero-gravity crap."

～

Taylor found the mixture of alien and human technologies in the Portal Guardian a little disturbing at first, but the technicians had been excited about the potentialities of blending them.

So far, he found they'd been right. The former Hive-Mother's quarters, a large ersatz cave, was now the command center of the Portal Guardian. Wiring and electronic modules hung on its formerly bare walls. In the center was a large holo-display.

"It is not much to look at." Cha KinLaat gestured to the image within the holo-display, referring to the new academy. A lumpy, gray asteroid rotated slowly. At one end, were the flickering lights of fusion welding torches. It was the only location on its surface that revealed any activity. "Everything but the docks is inside."

"How big is it?" Taylor asked.

Cha KinLaat touched a control and a scale scrolled across the screen indicating that the asteroid was a little less than two kilometers long, with a diameter of about one kilometer.

"Big sucker, isn't it?"

"That and its rotational velocity means Earth-normal gravity for those within," Cha KinLaat said.

Cha KinLaat had spent time with the construction team to learn the use of tunneling and construction equipment that would be sent to Charon where the permanent station guarding the entrance to the space-time anomaly would eventually be constructed. It would be a large, permanent station, built to have separate, comfortable facilities for all three species.

Taylor also knew this facility, much larger than DS-4, would also have weapons manufacturing shops, large sections for growing food and metals refining capability. The stated objective was to make it completely self-sufficient when finished.

He doubted that would ever happen. *Too difficult*, he thought. *Too many specialized items that can only come from Earth, and some items too expensive to be made or raised.*

"How's recruiting coming along?" He referred to volunteers to attend the Space Force Academy who would eventually see service guarding the entrance to the space-time anomaly.

"Ah," Cha KinLaat said. "Your people seem eager to join, even when they do not know they will get life extension treatment." He paused. "I am glad there will be humans who live longer. I would not want to know those who die so quickly, that they will not be with me throughout my life."

"I suspect there may be rumors about that," Taylor said. Since the treatment of the crew on Ki's Eagle and their resulting life extension, interest in joining the Space Force had grown. "Fortunately, that allows us to pick only the best."

"Suh-Joh has agreed to treat more of her people with the synthetic hormones that add to the life of the Hoo-Lii. She did not seem to think it should be done to many."

Taylor chuckled. "She believes she can give birth anytime she needs more servant or warriors."

"Such profligate birthrate," Cha KinLaat said. "On my world, we must strive for the right to become with egg, even just one egg. To do so, we must move closer to the center and prove our value." He changed the image in the holo-display to a tiny asteroid orbiting around the future academy. "This is a battle station, with capabilities to drive off anything we have seen so far."

Taylor doubted anyone could foresee all future threats. "Any word on Billy?"

"Ah, Bilik Pudjata," Cha KinLaat said, "I look forward to his return. It should be within thirty of your sleep periods."

"So, you expect him to join us on the Portal Guardian?"

"Yes," said Cha KinLaat. "I do believe he wants to serve as a representative of Qu'uda to Earth. He is very close to the center here. Whereas, on Qu'uda, many would challenge his right to be at the center. It would be very stressful."

"So, who will be on the ambassador's staff?"

Cha KinLaat wobbled his headcrest. "It will be some of the young who were born here, along with their mothers. That would solve the language problem and ability to understand your strange ways."

Taylor chuckled. "Strange ways? Yeah, I guess we all have our strange ways." He pointed to the holo-display where a shuttle-craft drifted slowly closer. "Looks like our ride has arrived. Time for our inspection tour."

ટ

Pluto hung brightly in the center of the holo-display, looking like a greenish-blue grapefruit.

Taylor watched the five Qu'uda Birds of War, slabby delta-shaped craft, drift closer. More distant were three double tube-shaped Eagles. It was time to replace them. The deep, sonorous tones of a Qu'uda Defender filled the room.

Cha KinLaat leaned forward, attentive, listening closely. "He says he is glad we have arrived. He wishes to return to Qu'uda, to its warmth, its water, and its many people," Cha KinLaat said. "He also wishes to come aboard to visit with us after he gets rid of those terrible weapons the Space Force officers brought with them."

"Can't blame him," Taylor said. "Being cooped up in those tin cans all this time." The Birds of War had never been designed for extended patrol duty. "Sure, tell him we'd be happy to see him before he departs." *Probably also wants to replenish his supplies*, he thought. "Let him know we have quarters for the Space Force personnel."

A tiny point of light expanded into a cubical gridwork of neon orange lines of energy that became brighter and larger. Deep within its infinite depths, a tiny spot increased in size as it drew closer to the outer framework. The ship had a double-doughnut around a central shaft configuration, which confirmed it was Suh-Joh's ship, the Mother's Servant.

Taylor recognized it and relaxed.

Perhaps we worry too much, Taylor thought. *Perhaps there is no danger at all from the two other systems.* He'd come to realize the portals to the openings in space-time led to other systems not yet investigated. And, he knew, the day they would be explored was drawing close, for the Space Academy had graduated its first class of officers who would rotate through duty rosters on the space stations within the inner planets. The opening into space-time still baffled the researchers. Even YataBu KuKlaat had no answer for what natural process caused their existence. He had begun to speculate they might be artifacts.

If so, Taylor thought, *the science behind their construction is far beyond what we know.*

Deimos, he thought, *still puzzled the archeologists, for there were traces of tunnel excavation that seemed artificial. However, not one artifact had been found, and no date could be set for the excavation.*

Mars, with its buried aquifers, had water in abundance, which the surface research teams used for their basic needs and fuel. He felt a sense of pride, realizing the economy of Earth had changed radically for the better by the introduction of Qu'uda fusion technology. Regular shipments of helium-three and deuterium from Uranus provided almost free, clean energy.

"Hoo-Lii, Tay-Lor." The synthesized voice of Suh-Joh warbled from her speech translation device. "I bring greetings from Hool to you and mother Meltem. My world is at peace, and its hives once again thrive."

"Most gracious Hive-Mother, Suh-Joh," Taylor said. "Welcome to the portal to our system. We, too, are at peace, and my people prosper."

"I opened the archives under the Vale of the Mother," Suh-Joh said. "Within, I found an ancient account of a visitor, which we called the 'Others,' however, this visitor is unlike your species, or those of the Qu'uda."

"You mean there is another species of intelligent life elsewhere?" Taylor's heart quickened.

"It was a long time ago and this is the only record, one that refers to ancient verbal history of our pre-literate society." Suh-Joh paused. "The archive is the only storehouse of history to survive our Great War. The record was emphatic there were visitors. I wish to find out if this is so."

"How will you do that?"

"I wish to travel through the unentered portals."

Taylor took a deep breath.

Garrison duty at the portal had grown wearisome. Sure, there was research; however, something was missing from his life. He recognized most of his life had been filled with uncertainty, and even though he had known great fear many times, that was a time he felt truly alive.

He also knew the construction project on Charon would soon be advanced far enough to eliminate the need for the Portal Guardian to remain on station around Pluto.

"Sure," Taylor said without hesitation. "Sounds like a great idea. When do we leave?"

CHAPTER THIRTY-ONE

WHERE ARE THEY?

"Do you see the pattern?" DuKlaat YataBu said in a deep, sonorous voice typical of someone from Qu'uda.

It was warm in the sensory detection center with its racks of electronic modules on the walls. Three holo-displays filled the center of the former command center. Qu'uda, Hoo-Lii, and humans crowded around the large holo-display that held a constellation of multi-colored points of light.

The ship, the Mother's Servant, was on the fifth year of its exploratory voyage through space-time.

Suh-Joh twittered something. "Explain," came the voice from the translation device.

DuKlaat made a yellow line trace through the display, connecting points of light twinkling with bright green halos. "These are the portals through which we have traveled." He touched another control. The yellow trace shrank rapidly as the display filled with ever-increasing numbers of points of light. "This is the spiral arm of our galaxy."

The yellow line curved within the scattering of points of

light showing the star systems within the outer portion of the spiral band that was the Milky Way.

"It follows the spiral arm...." Taylor said.

"Exactly," DuKlaat's voice boomed. "Only those stars which are far enough out to avoid the deadly radiation of the galaxy's core."

"Are you sure there are no portals that go toward the center?" Taylor was almost sure he knew the answer.

"Absolutely." DuKlaat wobbled his headcrest. "Remember when we tried every portal in every system for two years?" He pointed to a section of the yellow trace, which expanded into a network of tiny yellow lines interconnecting a band of stars. "We stopped when we found we just continued to move in paths parallel to the spiral arm."

"Yes." Taylor recalled out of the three hundred systems they visited they had discovered a total of six planets of the right size within habitable zones. Each planet's atmosphere contained oxygen, a sure sign of life. They had chosen not to approach any closely in case they held intelligent life.

Only one radiated electromagnetic signals, confirming it possessed a technological civilization. They had left a carefully concealed recording device, which they would retrieve later. Most planets had conditions inhospitable for life to evolve. Even so, each system was different; some with strange variations in astronomical possibilities that the researchers had begged time and time again to stay in one system to investigate further. But they always went on.

Suh-Joh twittered again. "I understand. The lack of randomness to the direction which we can travel through the galaxy confirms these portals are artifacts."

"Exactly," DuKlaat's voice rumbled. "True, but it is odd every planet with the right conditions for life to evolve has oxygen in its atmosphere."

"Yes," Taylor said. "Even stranger we all share the same

genetic building blocks of DNA, which means we all come from a common evolutionary mechanism."

"So, do you think the creator of the portals is also responsible for the spread of life within this galaxy?" Suh-Joh moved her paat-kli to the area near her breathing flaps. "The mother of all life?"

"Or father," Taylor said with a chuckle. His smile faded. "But who are they?" he asked. "Where are they?"

"We have traveled over but a miniscule fraction of this stellar highway," DuKlaat said. "I would need a thousand, no, ten thousand of my lives to go through every portal. Perhaps we have not encountered their creator because we haven't gone far enough."

"Or, we passed them and never recognized them." Suh-Joh rippled her breathing flaps in a way others had learned showed she was amused. "As perhaps, they never saw us."

"Or chose not to be seen, as we do," Taylor said. "Whomever they are, they did not create the portals to dominate the galaxy, nor did they choose to expand and fill the universe with their own kind." He hesitated a moment. "Or did they?"

PERSONAE

CLAN MEMBERS

Taylor MacPherson: First leader of the Clan and first President of Re-established United States.

Billy Potato: Also known as Bilik Pudjata to the Qu'uda. Highly modified and augmented. The former leader of the Fed, now the principal instructor in the University of High Technology.

Joyce Vargas: Administrator of the Central Electric Power Authority. Ex-wife of Taylor MacPherson.

Ashley O'Neil: An engineer chosen to handle difficult construction projects.

Dr. Meltem Encirlik: A medical doctor trained in a pre-Collapse medical school who uses Qu'uda technology to develop a life extension treatment and a wide range of pharmaceuticals. Wife of Taylor MacPherson.

Joe Del Corso: Minister for Education.

Mitch Doaks: Head administrator for the university.

Tim Van Minh: Engineer specializing in electronics and communications; war injuries have left him crippled.

Charlie Ramsey: Minister of Defense.

Sean Monahan: Deposed leader of opposition due to suspicions about his involvement in the assassination of Ned Biehl.

Patrick Monahan: Cousin to S. Monahan; elected to House of Representatives; leader of opposition. Later becomes General in State Security forces and other political offices.

"Carver" Washington: Minister of State/Speaker at the Human Confederation Assembly.

Chris Kucinski: Leader of Joint Chiefs of Staff for State Security.

Elroy Stanek: Military aide to Chris Kucinski.

Butch & Madeline Henderson: Astronomers extraordinares.

Ed Kerr: Commander of DS-3 and ally of Taylor MacPherson.

Hans Stolz: A Horse Soldier who makes the transition to Space Force officer.

Don Ulrich: Linguist—develops system to communicate with the Hoo-Lii.

Guang Xhi: Chinese representative at Human Confederation Assembly.

FORMER US MILITARY OFFICERS

Malachi "Ki" Mapes: Former submarine commander & hero of first space battle. Commander-in-chief of the Space Force.

Pip Ryan: Commander in space engineering corps.

Al Belasario: Executive Officer to Ki Mapes, also Space Force Defense Station commander.

Bud Inez

Space Force battleship commanders:
Hermann Stolz
Les Pynchon
Walid Gharaguh
James Hawley

Josie Armstrong: Astronomy student assigned to the space station.

HOO-LII AND THEIR EQUIPMENT

Kot-Nih: The priest-Narrator.

Suh-Joh: The Hive-Mother that sponsors the expedition to investigate the radio anomalies, daughter of Lok-Nih.

Son-Nih: Chosen-Male warrior, ripened by Lok-Nih and favored by Suh-Joh. First the strong-arm of Suh-Joh, then her counselor.

Lil-Tih: Scholar recruited by Suh-Joh.

PERSONAE

Nah-Kih: Young Hive-Mother with political aspirations.

Buk-Tih: Hive-Mother on the "Vale of the Mother" ship.

Disobedient: The sect of Hoo-Lii who rejected the traditional way and ripen all members to sexual maturity.

Mother's Servant: Suh-Joh's immense transport ship. Has extremely powerful ion engine pumped laser defense. Carries several thousand passengers. (Also "Vale of the Mother")

"Good Child": A deep-space craft having faster-than-light (FTL) capabilities; carries a standard crew of eight squared (64) Hoo-Lii.

QU'UDA AND THEIR EQUIPMENT

Mata ChaLik BuMaru: Former leader of Defenders of Qu'uda on the Egg-that-Flies. Now serving prison sentence on Andros Island for crimes against his own people.

DalChik DuJuga: Leader of the "Home-Seeker" faction and de facto commander of the Egg-that-Flies.

DuKlaat YataBu: Principal analyst for the Keepers-of-the-Egg.

Cha KinLaat DoMar: Close friend of Billy and works closely with humans on defense projects.

ZahGeb DuBu: Defender in squadron of Vanguard of Bu.

Egg-that-Flies: The massive fusion powered spacecraft made from an asteroid with interstellar range, belonging to the Qu'uda.

Bird-that-Soars: Fusion powered atmospheric space shuttle; interplanetary range, belongs to the Qu'uda.

Little-Egg-that-Flies: The ship made from a small asteroid and fitted with a fusion drive; used by the Qu'uda for their return to Earth. Captured by the humans and re-named Defense Station 2.

Bird-of-War: Fusion powered battle craft; heavily armored and possesses powerful particle beam weapons, also carries a squad of armed Qu'uda.

A SOCIETAL GLOSSARY

HOO-LII

An ancient and acrimonious post-high technology civilization that evolved on the planet Hool in the "Mother" (also known as Alpha Mensae) star system. Their society is continually roiled by struggle for living space and resources; earlier in their history, they bred to the brink of a population collapse, fought a series of vicious wars that wasted much of the planet's surface. Peace came after a matriarchal religion evolved, bringing strict prohibitions on the use of weapons of mass destruction. The society has a rigid caste system, highly restricted breeding rights with autonomous family units of "hives." Low-level warfare between the hives is constant in the struggle to gain scarce resources.

The Hoo-Lii have colonized two other star systems; one a settlement on the planet Kamah in the "Sisters" (also known as Zeta Reticuli) binary star system; and a prison planet—Chud-Loo—in the "Daughter" (also known as 82 Eridani) star system. The Hoo-Lii possess interstellar spacecraft which have faster-than-light drive and use digital signals to communicate with each other.

The Grand Council of Hive-Mothers—those Hive-Mothers

allied against Suh-Joh, united in opposition to her use of synthetic age-extending hormones on unripened ones (servants).

THE QU'UDA

A hermaphroditic egg-laying race inhabiting the Qu'uda planet and star system (also known as Epsilon Eridani). The planet, with vast oceans, orbits close to their cool, red-orange star. The Qu'uda are an ancient civilization that has had space travel capabilities for many millennia. The race is very homogeneous and strongly oriented to conformity; the preservation of the ideals of the community are a very strong driving force within their civilization. Their government is by consensus; personal biocomputers link with the center of the community for real-time feedback. Have long had fusion power and mine deuterium and hydrogen from the atmosphere of the gas giant planet in their system as a source of fuel for their spacecraft.

EARTH CIVILIZATIONS

The post-Collapse civilizations have recovered and developed into a military-based government, with consolidation underway. A loose collection of communities around the world grow powerful from technology acquired from the Qu'uda, an alien species. The human society is re-arming, for they know there are space-based civilizations that are aware of Earth's existence.

Clan—the original extended family which expanded to first conquer Ohio, then through treaties, re-establish the United States of America.

Human Confederation—those nations of Earth that get alien technology and restore civilization, forming a loose alliance for defense against possible alien invasions.

ABOUT THE AUTHOR

Malcolm Wood, born in England, came to the USA at age 14 and graduated from Aurora, Ohio High School and Kent State University with a degree in chemistry while working full-time. Three years later, he fulfilled a self-made promise and spent two years traveling around the world. After resuming a career in chemistry, he obtained a MA in economics. About thirty years ago, he became a registered professional engineer in two disciplines (petroleum and environmental engineering), leading to a career in finance, and later, environmental consulting.

It was about this time he resumed writing fiction while working for a company that prepared economic analyzes on specific industry sectors. Since these publications contained a significant element of fiction, it motivated him to start writing fiction. He attended numerous writing workshops and joined the Cleveland Science Fiction Critiquing group (also known as the

Cajun Sushi Hamsters from Hell), which had such writers as Geoff Landis, S. Andrew Swann, Charles Oberndorf, and Maureen McHugh. Their critiques and comments pushed Malcolm hard to improve his craft. Almost twenty years ago, he formed the West Side Writers Fiction critiquing group, dedicated to writing at a professional level. During this time, he finished twelve novels and a biography of his travels.

His activities include obtaining a private pilot's license and a competition driver's license. In addition to writing, he has found time to ski, hunt, taste wine, and enjoy gourmet food.

IF YOU LIKED ...

If you liked Dawn, you might also enjoy:

Stranger
by M.B. Wood

Ignition
by Kevin J Anderson & Doug Beason

Alternitech
by Kevin J Anderson

OTHER WORDFIRE PRESS TITLES BY M.B. WOOD

Collapse
Stranger
The Blue Gem
Like a New Star

Our list of other WordFire Press authors and titles is always growing. To find out more and to see our selection of titles, visit us at:
wordfirepress.com